THE PLAYER NEXT DOOR

A NOVEL

K.A. TUCKER

ALSO BY K.A. TUCKER

Ten Tiny Breaths

One Tiny Lie

Four Seconds to Lose

Five Ways to Fall

In Her Wake

Burying Water

Becoming Rain

Chasing River

Surviving Ice

He Will Be My Ruin

Until It Fades

Keep Her Safe

The Simple Wild

Be the Girl

Say You Still Love Me

Wild at Heart

THE PLAYER NEXT DOOR

K.A. TUCKER

Edited by Jennifer Sommersby

Published by K.A.Tucker

Manufactured in the United States of America

For all those who need a fun and flirty escape.
I promise,
there are no masks or threats of quarantine within these pages.
There is definitely close contact.

ONE

September 2007

I survived Day One without puking or crying.

Do they make T-shirts with that slogan? They must. I can't be the only person to head back to school after summer vacation with a broken heart. Though, I'd be lying if I wore that T-shirt. I *did* cry today; I just didn't do it in public. I ducked into a restroom stall as the first fat tear rolled down my cheek and then spent my entire lunch period with my butt planted on a toilet seat, struggling to muffle my sobs as giggling girls streamed in and out, oblivious.

And all it took was one look from Shane Beckett to cause that reaction. Or rather, the lack of a look. A passing glance as we crossed paths in the hallway between third and fourth period, when his beautiful whiskey-colored eyes touched mine before flickering away, as if the momentary connection was accidental.

As if the seventeen-year-old, six-foot star quarterback for the Polson Falls Panthers and I hadn't spent the summer in a semi-permanent lip-lock.

As if last night, sitting in his father's car outside my apartment building, he didn't tell me that we were getting too serious, too fast, and he couldn't handle a relationship right now, that he needed to focus on football, and I was too much of a distraction.

That one vacant, meaningless look from Shane Beckett in the hall today was worse than anything else he could have done, and it sent me stumbling away, dragging my obliterated spirit behind me.

The rest of the day has been a painful blur, with me cowering in the same restroom stall after the last bell rang to avoid the crowd. I foresee myself spending a lot of time in there. Maybe I should hang an occupied sign and declare it mine for the school year.

"Hey, Scarlet." Becca Thompson, her stride buoyant, flashes a sympathetic smile as she passes me on the steps outside the front doors of Polson Falls High.

"Hey," I manage, but the bubbly blond is already gone, trotting down the sidewalk, no glance backward, almost as if she hadn't greeted me at all. She's nice enough, but I shouldn't be surprised by the lukewarm friendliness. We've never traveled in the same circles, her being the popular cheerleader and me being the reticent mathlete who slogs away at the local drive-in movie theater every weekend in summer. We'd exchanged nothing more than polite greetings before Shane and I started dating, despite our mothers working together at the hair salon for years.

Couple that with the fact that Becca is best friends with Penelope Rhodes—a.k.a. the Red Devil, otherwise known as the worst human to walk these dank halls—who was away in Italy all summer, and I'm not surprised that I'm persona non grata once again.

Becca obviously knows Shane and I broke up. They *all* must know. But at least she acknowledged me, so I guess there's that.

She's heading toward the parking lot now. That's where the jocks and cheerleaders and otherwise popular crowd hang out, congregated around the cars their parents bought for them, talking and laughing and ignoring the peasants.

I check my watch. It's been twenty minutes since the last bell. Most of them *should* have left by now. With a heavy sigh, I tuck a wayward strand of my mouse-brown bob behind my ear, hike my backpack over my shoulder, and amble down the path, ready to avoid eye contact and walk the eight blocks home where I can hide in my bedroom for the rest of my life—or at least for the night.

Rounding the bend, I spot Steve Dip heading this way with two other guys from the football team. My stomach clenches. There's a reason the wide receiver and Shane's best friend is nicknamed Dipshit. He's an obnoxious ass with a cruel sense of humor.

I hold my breath, hoping he'll ignore me, like everyone else seems to be.

Our eyes meet and he winks. *No such luck.* "Hey, BB. You cost me fifty bucks!"

I frown. *What?* I have no idea why he's calling me that, but it can't mean anything flattering, especially not with the raucous laughter that follows.

He brushes a hand through his cropped hair. "Tell Dottie I'm gonna come in for a *quickie* later, will ya?"

"Bite me," I throw back, my cheeks burning as we pass. How long has he been sitting on that stupid joke? It's far from the first time I've heard something along those lines. When your mother's the town bicycle, everyone feels the need to share their punch line with you. He never dared say a word about her when Shane and I were together, but I guess it's no holds barred now.

"Is that an offer?" Steve grins. "'Cause it sounds like that'd be more action than Bex got this summer."

I lift my middle finger in the air and speed up, wanting to put as much distance as possible before this knot in my throat explodes into tears. I told Shane I wanted to take it slow and he said that was fine. He never pushed me.

Did he tell his friends? Was he laughing about it with them? Mocking me?

The parking lot has emptied out with only a few students lingering. Aside from Dean Fanshaw, no one left is associated with Shane and that crowd. Thank God.

Dean is Shane's very best friend and, unlike Steve, isn't known for being a jerk. What he *is* known for—and for good reason, based on what I witnessed—is boning every girl who's willing. Currently, he's too busy mauling Virginia Grafton's neck against the hood of his truck to notice me.

I keep my eyes forward as I rush past them and his red pickup, trying my best not to think about warm summer nights stretched out in the back of it, cradled between Shane's long, muscular thighs, my back resting against his chest, struggling to focus on the movie playing on the drive-in screen ahead.

I'm so focused on *not* catching Dean's attention that I almost miss the two sets of legs dangling over the open tailgate, tangled in each other.

Almost.

One set, long and male, I recognize instantly. It's the shoes I recognize, actually—white Vans. Shane's favorite.

The other legs are shapely and lead into a short, powder-pink skirt that I distinctly remember from second period English.

I'm frozen in place as I watch Shane and Penelope Rhodes lost in a kiss, Shane's fingers woven through her fiery-red hair, while his other hand slips beneath that tiny skirt.

I was *so* wrong.

Ignoring me earlier was *not* the worst thing Shane Beckett could have done today.

TWO

August 2020

I inhale the stale air in the living room, rife with the smell of old wood steeped in summer's humidity. The widow Iris Rutshack left the house spotless, at least. Or rather, her children must have, because I can't imagine the ninety-year-old woman on her hands and knees, scrubbing grime off the thick pine baseboards.

I smile with giddiness.

This place is *mine*.

I used to walk past this charming clapboard house every day on my way home from school. I'd admire the pale blue exterior and the covered porch running along the front, adorned by a matching set of rocking chairs that Mr. and Mrs. Rutshack—old even back then—filled every afternoon, watching the kids go by. On the odd day that their watchful gazes were distracted by a singing bird at their feeder, I'd stick my hand between the fence pickets and steal a bloom from the wild English-style garden that bordered the sidewalk.

Then I'd keep going all the way home to our low-rent apartment complex, my feet growing heavier with each step closer. When I closed my eyes at night, I'd imagine I was drifting off to the rhythmic sound of creaking chairs and cricket chirps, and not to the barfly screwing my mom on the other side of a too-thin wall.

"Thanks, Gramps. Whoever you are." My voice echoes through the hollow space as I wander. Technically, my father's father bought the house for me. He was never a part of my life, but he knew who I was—the product of a fling between his twenty-eight-year-old, truck-driver son with a criminal record and my then-fifteen-year-old mother—and was kind enough to name me in his will.

The house needs some TLC, more evident now that the furniture is gone. Nothing fresh paint, new lights, and a belt sander to the worn golden oak floors can't fix. I knew that when I put an offer in, and ever since I signed the sale papers, my butt's been glued to the shabby couch of my Newark apartment while I've binge-watched home-reno shows for inspiration. Of course, most of it I can't afford. Slowly but surely, though, I'll turn this place into the charming seaside retreat—minus the sea—that I've always envisioned.

Checking the time, I fire off a quick "Where are you?" text to my best friend, Justine, and then head to the porch to wait for the U-Haul. They were supposed to be here an hour ago. I'm annoyed, but I can't be too annoyed, seeing as Joe and Bill—Justine's brother and boyfriend—are driving two hours each way to move me in exchange for beer and burgers and a night on air mattresses.

Well, I'm sure Justine will repay Bill in some sordid way that I'd rather not think about.

Leaning against the post, I smile at the hum of a lawn mower churning through grass in the neighborhood. I'll have to pay a neighborhood boy to cut my front yard until I can afford my own mower. The gardens, I'll tend on my own. Iris and her husband doted on this property for sixty years, and I promised her I'd keep them thriving. Maybe that's a tall order, seeing as I have yet to keep even a cactus alive. First stop tomorrow is to replace my long-lost library card so I can borrow some gardening books.

The low picket fence—more decorative than purposeful—that lines the front yard has seen better days, the layers of white paint peeling away, many of the boards needing new nails to secure them upright. The wooden rocking chairs will need attention too. They rest where they always have. Iris left them, saying they belong on this porch. I can't bring myself to sit in one just yet, so I settle on the slanted porch steps instead.

Two children coast along the quiet, oak-lined street on their bicycles, throwing a curious glance my way. I'm sure they saw the For Sale sign out on the curb weeks ago. In a town this small, everyone is interested to know more about the woman moving into the neighborhood.

They don't have to worry about me, though. I'm a native of Polson Falls, Pennsylvania, merely displaced for twelve years when I dashed away to college in New York, allured by the idea of starting over in a big city where people hadn't heard the names Scarlet or Dottie Reed. It was fun for a time, but I've since learned big cities aren't all they're cracked up to be, and the luxury of anonymity has its own set of challenges. Like, how hard it is to catch a break in a school board where you have no connections. Seven years of substitute teaching while waitressing in the evenings to make ends meet dulled the luster for that life.

It seemed like providence then, when I made the obligatory trip home to visit Mom for her birthday and ran into my elementary school principal at the 7-Eleven. Wendy Redwood always loved me as a student. We got to talking about my teaching career. Thirty minutes of chatter and what felt like an impromptu interview later, she asked me if I'd ever consider working for her. Lo and behold, she's *still* the principal at Polson Falls Elementary and was looking for a sixth grade teacher for the fall. Sure, there were hiring considerations and board rules and all that, but she could navigate around them. Wink, wink. Nudge, nudge.

I smiled and thanked her and told her I'd think about it. At the time, I couldn't imagine entertaining the thought, but then I drove down Hickory Street for shits and giggles, only to see the open-house sign in front of my childhood dream home.

Within fifteen minutes of stepping inside, I was dialing Wendy Redwood for the job and considering what I should offer on the property. It all seemed like kismet. I mean, the house was at a price almost too good to be true, and the school was two blocks away!

I sigh as I sip the last of my cold, burnt gas station coffee. This is a fresh start, even in an old world full of familiar faces. Besides, it's been more than a decade since I last roamed the halls of any school here. Those painful years and cruel people are far behind me.

The peaceful midday calm is disrupted by the chug of a garage door crawling open, followed by the deep rumble of a car engine starting. A long, red vintage muscle car backs out of the garage next door and eases into the open space beside a blue Ford pickup. I can't tell what kind of car it is, but it's old and in pristine shape, the bright coat of paint glistening in the August sun.

I never asked Iris about the neighbors. The two times I've been here—once during the open house and once after I'd signed the paperwork for the offer—nobody was home on either side. Both properties look well maintained, though. The bungalow with the muscle car has new windows and a freshly built porch off the front. There isn't much in the way of gardens—some shrubs and trees—but the lawn is manicured.

I watch curiously as the driver's side door pops open and a tall man with wavy, chestnut-brown hair steps out, his back to me as he fusses with his windshield wiper. Coffee pools in my mouth as I stall on my swallow, too busy appreciating the way his black T-shirt clings to his body, showing off broad, sculpted shoulders, muscular arms, and a tapered waist. He's wearing his dark-wash jeans perfectly—not so baggy that they hang unflatteringly off his ass, but not so tight that cowboy boots and a wide-brimmed hat come to mind.

Damn.

I hold my breath in anticipation, hoping my neighbor will show me a beautiful face to match that fitness-model body. What a stroke of luck that would be, to live next to a gorgeous man. A *single,* gorgeous man, I pray.

Finally, my silent pleading is answered as he turns and his gaze drifts my way.

I struggle not to spew coffee from my mouth as my keen interest turns to horror.

Oh my God.

Someone, please tell me this is a mistake.

Please tell me I'm not living next door to Shane Fucking Beckett.

THREE

What is Shane even *doing* back in Polson Falls?

The last I heard, he was flying high on a full-ride football scholarship, somewhere in California. Mind you, I heard that way back in senior year, when people were strolling through the halls, bragging about the college offers they'd opened after school the day before. Back when all I could think about was getting out of this town and all the assholes in it—him being the king of them.

Shane Beckett can*not* be back in Polson Falls and living next to me.

He just can't.

But, oh my God, he *is* heading this way, stalking smoothly across his lawn to mine, his long legs easily maneuvering over my picket fence. He strolls along my driveway toward me, eyeing my dented Honda Civic on his way past.

He must not realize who I am. There's no way he'd be so casual in approaching if he did. I look a lot different from the girl he slummed it with for a summer, back before our senior year. The boring, mousy-brown bob I used to sport in high school is gone, replaced by sleek, tawny hair that stretches halfway down my back. My once-average figure has been honed by years of running and yoga. And while I still sometimes shop at thrift stores for my clothing, I've acquired a discernible palate for higher-end consignment purchases. Even now, on "moving day," my worn Guns N' Roses T-shirt looks trendy paired with black leggings and jeweled sandals.

Shane has changed too, but not by much. Being the star quarterback, he was always lean, but fit. He's much bigger now, his neck thicker, his shoulders broader, his top clinging to a solid, curvy chest, his jaw more sculpted and angular. And the hair he always kept cropped is longer, gelled in a tousled, messy style.

He's *still* gorgeous. In fact, he's *more* gorgeous than he ever was. I'd recognize him from a mile away, even all these years later.

I'd recognize him as the guy with the deceptively sweet dimples who smashed my seventeen-year-old heart into a thousand pieces.

I sit up straighter and pull my shoulders back to meet him head-on, readying myself mentally as my gut churns with nerves and my pulse races. Thank God I slipped on my sunglasses when I sat down. At least I can hide the panic from my eyes as he comes to a stop three feet from me.

Those full, soft lips that I remember kissing for hours—so long that my own were left chapped and sore some nights—stretch with a wide smile. "Scarlet Reed."

His voice is deeper and sexier than I remember, and my stupid, traitorous heart jumps at the sound of my name on his quicksilver tongue. The first time he said my name, the night he asked me out, it took me forever to pick my jaw up off the drive-in concession counter. I was so shocked he knew who I was.

Obviously, he knows who has moved in here.

I clear my throat, trying to maintain calm. "Shane Beckett." *Shane Fucking Beckett.*

Sliding his hands into his pockets, he climbs the first step and leans against the railing. It creaks under his weight. "Your dream came true." His warm eyes drift over the face of the house. They're as stunning as I remember them, speckled with gold flakes and rimmed with dark brown. "You bought the old Rutshack house."

"You ... you remembered?" I sputter, unable to mask my surprise. I mentioned my secret wish to own this place on our first official date—a balmy night in early July, the humidity making my hair frizz and my skin slick. I was so nervous, I babbled the entire time. I was sure he regretted asking me out.

Shane's gaze drops from its inspection of the porch ceiling to settle on me. His eyelashes are still impossibly thick and long, his nose still slender and perfect. "I remember a lot about that summer."

My chest tightens, and pain I'd long since thought faded flares with renewed vigor. "So do I." The sweet words, the longing looks, the gentlest touches. He told me I was one of the coolest girls he'd ever met, and it didn't matter that my few misfit friends would never gel with his many popular friends, or that I wasn't a cheerleader or an athlete.

He said he didn't care that my mom and I lived in an apartment on the shady side of town, or that she was caught in a compromising position with our *married* town mayor the night of our school's Christmas pageant when I was twelve.

He swore he wasn't the player everyone said he was, and he was okay with taking things slow, that he wouldn't push me to give him my virginity.

He told me that he thought he might be falling in love with me.

I remember it all because it was in stark contrast with the personality one-eighty he pulled in the last week before school, when he started avoiding my calls and breaking plans. He dumped me the night before classes began, claiming he wasn't looking for a serious relationship through senior year.

What he meant was, he wasn't looking for a serious relationship with *me.*

Worse, he wanted it with Penelope Rhodes, the daughter of the scandalized mayor having the affair with my mother. She'd made my life hell since seventh grade, and he knew it.

Shane flinches ever so slightly, the only sign that he's aware of what a thoroughbred douchebag he was in high school. "You look different."

"I'm surprised you recognize me."

"Iris told me who she sold to." He chews his bottom lip, hesitating. "I probably wouldn't have known it was you at first. Not with those giant sunglasses covering half your face."

"They're Prada." Five seasons ago, but still. And I feel stupid for announcing that.

His eyes bore into the lenses as if trying to see beyond them. "Take them off."

I hate Shane Beckett with every fiber of my body, I remind myself. Even the fibers between my legs that are stirring right now, as I imagine him asking me in that deep, sexy voice to take something else off. *Everything* else off.

A medley of short horn blasts sounds and a moment later, the U-Haul pulls in.

I release a shaky sigh of relief, saved from the risk of bending to his will. I need to regain my composure before I come across as the love-struck teenager I used to be. I'll *never* allow myself to be that around him ever again.

"My friends are here."

"Do you need any help with—"

"Nope," I cut him off curtly, hauling my body up to charge down the steps, inhaling the intoxicating hint of bergamot and mint on my way past. My annoyance flares. He even *smells* sexy.

I march across the lawn, needing to get away from Shane and fast. "Finally!" I holler as Bill slides out of the passenger seat, followed by Justine.

Her sharp, hazel eyes immediately land on Shane. "Who is *that*?" she asks in her thick Bostonian accent.

"Can you wait until I'm out of earshot before you drool over another guy?" Bill shakes his head as he wanders to the back of the truck.

"Nobody. Can you stack the orange- and blue-stickered boxes in the dining room? That way we can get to the bedroom furniture as fast as possible. Pink-stickered boxes go upstairs. The ones with the green stickers are for the kitchen." I spent three days researching how best to organize my belongings for efficient unpacking.

Justine studies me warily. We've lived together since freshman year of college, and she can tell when I'm pretending to be indifferent while there's a four-alarm panic fire burning inside me. But because she's my very best friend, she also knows when not to push.

"Come on, guys, you heard the boss!" She claps her hands. She's barely five feet tall and diminutive in every regard except the range of her voice and her larger-than-life personality.

Her brother, Joe, jumps out from the driver's side. "Gotta take a piss first," he announces, heading for the porch.

"Put the seat down when you're done!" I holler after him. I don't know how many times I've fallen into the toilet in the middle of the night because Joe was crashing on our couch and had forgotten the common courtesy.

Shoes crunch against the gravel driveway behind me, setting off a fresh wave of tension.

Just keep on walking back to your side.

Justine thrusts out her hand. "I'm Scarlet's best friend, Justine. And you are …"

Despite my greatest effort not to, I steal a glance in time to see the deep dimples form with Shane's sexy smirk. Those dimples fed a lot of girls' fantasies, including mine. Back before we dated,

I used to spend all of chem class waiting to catch a glimpse of them.

"Shane. I live next door." He accepts her hand.

"*Shane*. From *next door*." God, I'm going to get an earful of lewd suggestions later. "Well, it's nice to meet you, Shane. Have you lived in this thriving metropolis long?"

"All my life, except for a few years while I was away at college." He nods toward me. "Scarlet and I go way back. We were friends in high school."

A loud, unattractive snort escapes me, earning raised brows from them both.

"Where'd you say you want these?" Bill rounds the corner, his arms laden with a cumbersome box, the top marked with a blue sticker.

"Dining room. Far wall."

He juts his chin at Shane on his way past.

Shane looks from him to the truck, and back again. "Are you sure you don't want my—"

"I don't want anything from you," I blurt, and my cheeks immediately burn. But I'm not going to let myself feel bad for being rude. Shane deserves it and far worse.

He holds up his hands in a sign of surrender and backs away slowly. "All right, Scar ..."

Ugh. I always hated that nickname.

"But, just so you know, I'm around if you ever need help." He juts his thumb in the direction of his house.

"Thanks. I'm good." I spot Joe storming down the steps and add on impulse, "Because I have him!"

"Huh? You have me for what?" Joe's face fills with confusion.

"For *everything*." I rush over to loop my arm around his waist and sidle close to his tall, lanky body, giving off the impression that we're a couple. *Just play along*, I silently will him, staring up into his baby-blue eyes.

If there's one thing I know about Joe, it's that he's had a not-so-secret crush on me ever since I went with Justine to Boston for Thanksgiving, back in sophomore year of college. He knows I'm not interested, but that hasn't stopped his shameless flirting. Pretending we're together isn't an issue for him.

He throws an arm around my shoulder and pulls me close until my face is mashed up against his chest and my sunglasses are sitting crooked. "That's right, babe. You don't need nobody else."

Shane's gaze flips between the two of us before shifting to my house, an unreadable look touching his face. "I hope you're a handy guy." With that, he heads back over the white picket fence.

"Does this mean I get to sleep in your room tonight?" Joe whispers.

I give him a hard shove in the ribs, earning his grunt.

FOUR

"Can't believe you actually did it, Reed." Justine settles into a rocking chair and hands me a Corona, the cap already twisted off. Her smile is wistful. "Is it weird to be back here?"

"*So* weird. Never thought I'd see the day." I suck back a mouthful of cold beer, parched after hours of hauling furniture, scrubbing cupboards, and unpacking boxes. A quick glance in the hallway mirror earlier proved that I shouldn't look in a mirror again until after I've showered. "I still can't believe this house is mine. *And* that I have a full-time teaching job."

It's a far cry from where I was at the stroke of midnight into a new decade this past New Year's—living off ramen noodles and afraid of what my uninspiring future held. A few months later, a lawyer appeared on my doorstep to tell me that a grandfather I'd once met briefly had died, leaving me—not his son, who'd fallen out of favor years before—everything he owned.

Turns out it was enough to buy this place outright, and not battle with the bank for a mortgage they'd never agree to anyway.

"Cheers to that. You deserve this. I'm so happy for you." We clink the necks of our bottles and watch in comfortable silence as a middle-aged couple coasts along the street on their bicycles. It's after eight and nearly nightfall. The guys are inside, listening to the ball game on the radio while they put my futon frame together.

"When are you going to see Dottie?"

"This week, I guess," I say reluctantly. "I kind of have to, right?"

"She *is* your mom," Justine agrees with equal enthusiasm, her free hand toying with her messy topknot of black hair.

Dottie's also a narcissist with loose morals, and a functioning alcoholic—styling hair by day, downing glasses of chardonnay by night. She doesn't touch a drop of it while on the clock, but once her shift is over, look out. There's been more than one embarrassing story about her being escorted out of the local watering hole for being too drunk.

I sigh. Justine has a good idea how deep and dark the rabbit hole goes with my mother.

"I'll deal with her when I have to. Tonight, it's all good times."

"It's going to be strange, not seeing you every day," she pouts.

"You'll just have to come visit me. A lot." I clink my beer bottle against hers again. We've lived together since we were eighteen years old. It was a random roommate match that turned out to be a godsend. Justine is family to me. She's the one and only person I've ever been able to count on over the years. "Besides, I'm sure Bill will be a great roommate."

"Yeah, *after* he's housebroken. Why are boys so gross?" She cringes. "Thirty-three years old and he still leaves his socks everywhere. Dirty, smelly socks rolled up in balls, *all over* my bedroom floor!"

I laugh, even as my attention wanders to my neighbor's property. The red muscle car is gone. I heard the engine rumbling hours ago, and I found myself wondering where Shane was going and when he'd be back. I'm sure he has a girlfriend. No one looks like that and doesn't have a girlfriend, at least not for long.

"So, are you going to make me ask?"

"Huh?"

Justine points a finger a Shane's house, her eyes wide. "What the hell was that about earlier, with Mr. Hot As Fuck who you iced out?"

We've been so busy with the move, I've been able to avoid that conversation all day. I sigh. "I dated him for, like, two minutes back in high school."

"And?"

"And we broke up. End of story."

"No." She shakes her head vigorously. "You've dated plenty since I've known you, and you have never given enough of a shit about the guy to be harsh after the fact."

"Yeah, well, Shane deserves it." For all that I've told Justine, Shane Beckett is one painful, humiliating story I've kept buried, convincing myself he was the part of a past I'd never have to face again.

"Spill it, Reed."

She's clearly on a mission to ferret information, and I'm too tired to fend her off. I give her the rundown.

By the time I'm done, her face is twisted with disgust. "Why tell you he thinks he's falling in love with you and then dump you to hook up with someone else?"

"Because he's a total player *and* a douchebag." And I was too stupid and enamored to see it. "He was just trying to get laid before the summer was over."

"But you didn't sleep with him, right?"

"No." I almost did. The night we broke up, I tried to sway him with my virginity, desperate to make him change his mind. Things went further than they ever had between us but stopped before it went too far. *He* stopped it. I walked away telling myself he obviously wasn't attracted to me anymore, which was a crippling hit to my ego. In hindsight, I figured it was likely because he'd already started something with Penelope and was struck by a millisecond of decency, warped as that may be. When I look back on that entire disaster, my willingness to so freely give him what he'd clearly been chasing all summer is my biggest regret.

"His friends had bets going about how long it'd take for me to put out. They nicknamed me BB." I give her a knowing look. "Blue Balls." I'm not sure if I prefer that nickname over Scar, Scarface, and the tad cleverer, Pacino.

She rolls her eyes. "*So* original. Man, I would have punched him right in *his* blue balls."

"Yeah, well ..." I shrug through another sip. "It was my own fault. I knew better." I'd had a crush on Shane since the Beckett family moved to town in fifth grade. I'd heard the rumors, I'd seen him cycle through the pretty girls, and yet the night he flirted with me during my shift at the drive-in concession stand, I was a giggling fool. All I could think was, "Shane Beckett is interested in me?" I should have turned and run the other way.

But he was the sexy high school football star, and I was *nobody*. And when he asked me to grab a burger at the Patty Shack, a greasy spoon in town, I was too stunned to use my brain.

Of course, I said yes. I spent the entire next day pinching myself and trying on everything in my closet, and even a few more modest things from my mother's closet.

He pulled up to our shabby building in his dad's green Buick with a smile and two cans of Coke. He opened the door for me. In fact, he was the perfect gentleman the entire night, no devious intentions in sight. When he dropped me off, he laid the sweetest kiss on my lips and asked if he could see me again. It was like a dream that I kept waiting to wake up from.

Unfortunately, when I eventually did wake, it was to a nightmare.

I sigh. "Whatever. Once a player, always a player. I don't want anything to do with Shane Beckett ever again." It doesn't matter how attractive he is, and he is up there with the most beautiful men I've ever laid eyes on. Despite my anger and attempts to forget him, I still secretly use him as a physical benchmark against the guys I've dated since.

They always come up short.

Justine's lips twist in thought. "So, you *really* wouldn't put out at seventeen?"

The incredulity in her voice has me reaching across to smack her arm. "Shut up!"

"What! It's just ... you've come a *long* way since then, Padawan." She gives me a pointed look.

"Whatever. I had a reputation to uphold." Or rather, a reputation *not* to uphold. I'd heard the rumors abound, wondering if I was my mother's daughter. It's probably why Shane targeted me in the first place. The last person I wanted to be compared to was Dottie Reed, so it wasn't hard to keep guys out of my pants throughout high school. The hell if I would provide fodder for any more rumors about the Reed women by even entertaining the idea of a blow job.

College was another story. It was like a "don't give a shit" switch got flicked somewhere between unpacking my suitcase in my dorm room and downing the nth red SOLO cup of draft beer. I lost my virginity that very first night, to a guy named Chris who was a lot cuter at the party than he was in his bed the next morning. I had regrets—namely, why didn't I just lose it with Shane? Someone who actually meant something to me? But I quickly washed them away with more parties, more alcohol, and more guys.

By the time my final exams came around that year, I'd mastered the art of giving head, pulling declarations of undying love from the guy I was pseudo dating—and he wasn't the type to throw around those words casually, even in the heat of the moment.

I didn't love him, though. I've never loved any of them.

"And how long has it been since anyone's dusted down there,

by the way?" Justine asks, looking pointedly at my crotch. She's never been shy about sex talk.

"I don't need anyone. Have you seen the latest additions to my collection? I labeled the box 'Me, Myself, and I.'"

Justine cackles.

Meanwhile, I silently admit that it's been too long since toys weren't my source of pleasure. Nine months, to be exact. Five, if I consider the disastrous blind date Bill set me up on with one of his stock trader friends. He was cute, though not my type, but it'd been awhile and I was desperate to feel something besides a pink vibrating object inside me. The guy got slobbering drunk on red wine, so much that his entire mouth—teeth included—was stained purple. And when he went down on me later in his apartment, I couldn't help but liken it to a drooling golden retriever working away at a bowl of Dog Chow. I faked the orgasm and when he stumbled to the bathroom, I yanked my dress down and called it a night.

Justine sighs and then a devilish smile takes over her pretty face. "You should mess with him."

I frown. "What do you mean?"

"Your neighbor. You know … a little game of cat and mouse." She waves her hand in front of her as if she's a feline batting at a toy. "Make him think you've forgiven him. Tease him. Then, when he's begging you for it, send him home with his dick in his hand."

I snort. She can be so crass sometimes. "Have you *seen* him? That sounds like as much torture for me as it does him."

"Right." She pauses. "So then play him like he played you. Play the player. Bang him and then treat him like trash."

"Tempting." Thoughts of a naked Shane swirl in my head. I've felt his erection before and remember it being impressive, but we never got far enough for me to take measurements. "I'm too old for stupid games. Besides, he stopped being interested in me years ago."

Justine smirks. "I haven't met a guy who *isn't* interested in you."

"Sure, you have. Bill isn't interested in me."

"You're right. He's interested in you and me. *Together.*"

"A guy can dream!" comes Bill's holler through the open window.

We break into a fit of laughter as my cheeks redden, and I wonder how long those two idiots have been listening.

A loud crack sounds and suddenly I'm falling into Justine, spilling beer over myself. "What the ..." Peering down, I find a piece of the rocking chair lying on the porch floor, the wood snapped in half.

"Shit," Justine mumbles. "That can't be good."

Dammit. "I guess these relics were bound to go at some point." Still, it sucks that it had to happen on my first night here.

"It's just an old wooden chair. It's not like the house is falling apart."

"Right." My gaze drifts over the place, noting how the front steps lean to the right, and the eave separates from the roof over in the far corner.

And just how many fence pickets need a fresh nail.

But it's nothing I can't fix, I tell myself with a smile. This house is the start of my new life, and it's 100 percent mine. That's all that matters.

FIVE

I do a slow turn in the center of my attic bedroom, taking in the countless corners and moss-green walls. The room eats up most of the second floor, leaving only enough space for a cramped three-piece bathroom and a walk-in closet on the other side of the staircase opening. There isn't even a door to close off my bedroom from the main level. The Rutshacks hadn't used this bedroom in years, the stairs too steep and narrow for them in their old age. Instead, they settled into a tiny room off the kitchen that I've earmarked for an office slash spare bedroom.

Between dormer windows and the steeply pitched roof, there must be a million edges in here. It's going to take me days and a boatload of patience to paint this room, neither of which I have, not when it's stifling hot up here, not when I have an entire main floor to freshen up first.

With a yawn, I flick the wobbly light switch, throwing my room into darkness. I amble for my bed, intent on passing out face-first, covers off, after a long, hot two days of settling in.

A room in the back corner of Shane's house glows, stalling my march to unconsciousness. I have an unobstructed view through a large window into Shane's bedroom, I'm guessing, by the king-size bed adorned in navy-blue bedding.

Shane steps into view and my stomach flips.

I haven't seen him since our run-in yesterday morning, though I did hear the low rumble of his car's engine as he pulled into his driveway late last night. A date, maybe? A booty call? Thankfully, I was distracted with my friends and the house to think too much on it.

I watch as Shane kicks his shoes to the side, and then his hands are moving, grasping the hem of his black T-shirt and lifting it up ... up ... and over his head, revealing a smooth, taut chest, his muscles prominent and shapely.

I groan. He was built in high school when he was seventeen. He's thirty now, and that is *all man*.

I shouldn't be spying on him. But he shouldn't be undressing in front of a window. It's his fault, really. Though he's probably used to having his privacy. He likely knew the Rutshacks slept downstairs. He hasn't considered the possibility that a pervert moved in.

And that's what I am right now.

I fully accept this as I take a safe step back into darkness and watch Shane casually toss his shirt into a corner, my fingertips tingling. What would those powerful shoulders feel like beneath my nails? What would they look like, tensing above me as I lie on my back beneath him, my thighs splayed?

He fumbles with his belt buckle and zipper. His jeans fall to the floor, taking my jaw with them as I get a good look at that delicious V-cut of his pelvis, leading down to dark gray boxer briefs. His legs are powerful, his thighs down to his ankles perfectly proportioned.

"Why do you have to be *so* perfect?" I mutter with bitter envy, staring in unabashed admiration as he steps out of his jeans, leaving them in a heap.

His thumbs hook around the elastic waistband of his boxer briefs.

I should not watch this ... I should not watch this ... I need to turn away now ...

Shane's hands pause, his position shifting to give me his side, his attention riveted on the corner of the room. The TV, I realize.

"Come on ..." I hold my breath like the scoundrel I am, desperate to catch a glimpse of what I fought so hard to resist for an entire summer.

Suddenly, as if only remembering his uncovered window then, he turns and peers out of it.

I yelp and stumble backward, though there's no way he can see me. Right? I frantically glance around, confirming there isn't a beam of light in here that would give me away.

After a few beats, he strolls into his adjoining bathroom, his sculpted, round ass in cotton shifting deliciously with each step. He still hasn't drawn curtains or blinds. He's either unconvinced that I'd be lurking in the dark at midnight on a Sunday, watching him undress, or he's unconcerned by the idea.

My guess—because Shane Beckett is an arrogant ass—is the latter.

What would it feel like to be with him after all these years? He used to be able to make me hot with a simple touch against my neck, a fingertip trailing along my skin. But maybe he's a terrible lay. Maybe his talents end with those sensual, all-consuming kisses and magic hands.

Who am I kidding? Penelope was more than willing to tell everyone within earshot about Shane's ability to find a girl's G-spot when I doubt Neanderthals like Steve Dip had any clue that females could orgasm.

Shane is gone from view just long enough that I can calm my breathing and evaluate whether I want to be *this person* who spies on her neighbor from the shadows. Then he reappears.

This time, without his boxer briefs.

"Oh my God." My mouth goes dry as I take in *all* of Shane Beckett for the first time. The sight of him naked has heat flooding my body. It's only for a few seconds, and then he taps a switch and the room falls into darkness, save for the flashing glimmer from the TV. There's a mirror on the wall to the right of his headboard, and it reflects the sportscaster on his screen. Sports highlights. Still a jock.

Punching the pillow a few times to fluff it, he slips into bed, hiding half his beautiful body from view, hooking one arm beneath his head, his free hand resting on his bare stomach. It's like his bed was positioned for prime viewing from my room.

His gaze seems to settle on my window.

And his free hand disappears beneath his sheet.

I hold my breath, waiting to see a rhythmic rustling around his groin, evidence that he's jerking off, but he simply lies there, a naked Adonis catching up on stats.

What is Shane like when he comes? Does he grit his teeth? Does he yell and moan? Or is it a series of guttural noises? Does he hide his face or is he unabashed, letting you see the intense pleasure seize him? Does he come fast and hard or after a lengthy grind? It's funny—these weren't things I thought about as a seventeen-year-old girl but as a thirty-year-old woman, just imagining the sound of him orgasming turns my breath ragged. I can't remember the last time I was this turned on. Certainly not with Red Wine Golden Retriever Man, and I was drunk and desperate that night.

My free hand ventures to the thin, silk strap on my camisole, my pinky finger curling under, gliding down around the deep scoop neckline, teasing my flesh. I let out a hysterical giggle. This is insane. Why am I watching this? And worse, I'm practically drooling. What happened to my bitter resolve? One look at naked Shane and I've forgotten all the pain he caused me? And then what happens the next time I have to look him in the eye?

Nothing good can come of this. I'll just be piling on regrets.

"That's enough for one night." I peel myself away from the peep show, whispering a sour "Good night, asshole" as I crawl into bed.

Accepting it's going to be a long while before my pulse settles.

SIX

Mom yanks the black smock off the man and sweeps the round, horsehair brush over the back of his neck to remove any last clippings, all the while chomping on her gum. Based on the clumps of salt-and-pepper hair pooled around the chair, the man came in with at least four inches more hair than he's leaving with, his new style cropped short. "See, Clive? This is *way* more distinguished-looking than that comb-over."

The man's soft blue eyes study his reflection in the mirror ahead with intense interest, the look in them one of happy surprise. "You were right, Dottie."

"I'm always right." Her mulberry-painted lips stretch wide in a smile and her manicured hands smooth over his shoulders in an affectionate way that probably isn't appropriate but is standard practice for my mom. "Cindy's gonna love it. I'm tellin' ya. She'd have to be blind not to."

He grins, sliding from his chair and pulling out his wallet. "So, I'll see you at McTavish's on Friday night?" My mom's favorite watering hole.

"You know it. Come and say hi." She winks at him.

How my mother hasn't been run out of town by jealous wives

and scorned girlfriends is beyond me. There've been more than a few tense face-offs over the years, some of them—slaps, tear-filled accusations, screaming matches in the grocery aisle—I've witnessed firsthand.

Dottie Reed has always maintained that she can't help attracting the opposite sex. It must be that alluring pinup girl vibe she says she gives off. That she spreads her legs for any interested man has nothing to do with it, *oh no*.

Mom winks and waves bye to Clive. When he's out the door, she acknowledges me. "What are you doing here, hon? I thought we were meeting at my place at six?" She glances at her wrist to confirm that it's only five.

I haven't seen my mom since her birthday two months ago, but I'm not surprised it doesn't spark a maternal instinct to wrap her arms around me in a welcoming hug. She only finds that motherly bone three drinks in.

"Yeah, I know, but I'm starving, and I figured you're here anyway, so we can walk over and grab dinner early." And this eliminates the chance for her to rush home to down a bunch of happy-hour cocktails beforehand.

She shrugs in a "fine, I guess" way, her indigo-blue eyes drifting over my locks. "Do you want a cut while you're here?"

"No. I'm good, thanks." She offers to cut my hair every time I step inside Elite Cuts, a no-frills hair salon that's catered to Polson Falls for decades. I haven't taken her up on it in years, since I realized not all hair stylists are equal, and there are plenty who are a hell of a lot more competent and creative than my mom. Plus, she's liable to lop it all off, insisting a bob suits my face shape best.

She leans closer to the mirror, her red-clawed fingertips combing through her hair as she inspects her roots. She's religious about hiding all evidence of gray, and she's been doing it with platinum blond as long as I can remember. I've suggested maybe a change to a soft golden or a subtle chestnut would be nice, but Dottie abhors change when it comes to her appearance. She's been trying to hold fast at twenty-five for the past two decades, in looks and lifestyle. Ironically, it's her lifestyle that's starting to age her beyond her forty-six years.

She's still attractive, her makeup impeccable, her hair always styled, her clothes on the more risqué side but flattering for her curvy figure. But under these lights, I can see the lines that her latest round of Botox injections couldn't hide, creasing her forehead and curving around her lips, and there's a touch of sag at her jowls that nothing short of surgery will erase.

"So? What's new?" she asks.

"Nothing much. Just settling into the house. I'm going to start painting tomorrow—"

"I'm heading out now! Scarlet's treating me to dinner," she hollers to her boss. She likely wasn't paying attention to begin with.

I roll my eyes at her lack of interest and at the assumption I'm now made of money. When she caught wind of the inheritance, she insisted she deserved at least half of it for all the sacrifices she'd made while raising me alone.

What I remember of her raising me is nights alone with Alphagetti when I wasn't old enough to use the stove unattended, her sneaking out of the apartment after tucking me in to head to the bar, holes in my boots because she spent the money on collagen injections and ephedrine pills or whatever other diet craze was in fashion.

When she demanded half the inheritance, I almost caved, but Justine talked me off that ledge. Mom and I came to verbal blows —her, airing all the ways she could've had a better life had she not been burdened with a child; me, venting about all the ways my life could've been better had I not been saddled with *her* as a mother. I didn't hear from her for almost three months after that. I assumed the label of orphan.

But then she called. She apologized. She said she had been

wrong. I'd never heard her use those words before, and I assumed it was the end of the world. I peeked out the window for hailing fire and brimstone.

In the end, I accepted her apology because, well, she's all I have, and she wasn't *all* bad. She certainly never scolded me like most children's parents did. There were times when we'd curl up on the couch with a bowl of homemade popcorn and a movie I was far too young to watch, she'd let me play with her makeup whenever I wanted, and once in a rare while she would surprise me with a shopping spree to the mall for new clothes. I never had a curfew, or really any rules at all. Most kids might say I had it made. But I would rather have had a mother who didn't have a reputation as the town harlot.

Since her apology, things have been marginally better between us.

"No problem, Dot. Have fun!" Ann Margaret Thompson, a kind, tolerant lady in her late fifties with silver hair and disproportionately wide hips, pauses mid snip on a teenage boy to grin at me. "Good to see you back, Scarlet."

I smile. "Good to be back." I'm guessing she was the driving force behind my mother's apology. The woman is basically a saint. After the scandal with the mayor, when Dottie Reed lost her job at the upscale salon in town—she was bad for business, according to the owner—Ann Margaret offered her a job here. I'll never understand why, but I'll be forever thankful.

"I hear you're gonna be teaching at the elementary school!"

"I am! It was all rather unexpected."

"The best things happen when you least expect them." She casts me a wink as her foot pumps the pedal on the chair to raise it. She wordlessly puts her hand on the back of the boy's head, tilting it forward so she can shave his nape with clippers.

"Ready, Mom?"

"I just need a minute to powder my nose." Mom opens a deep drawer at her station and pulls out an enormous apple-green bag and heads for the back, her heels clicking against the mocha tile floor. She might be the only woman in the state who is willing to cut hair in stilettos all day just to make sure her legs look good.

I sigh, knowing "a minute" will be more like ten.

I study the small hair salon while I wait. Elite Cuts hasn't changed at all since Mom started working here eighteen years ago. The same boring beige paint coats the walls, the same palm-tree-shaped coatrack sits in the corner, the same hair-model portraits line the walls—of hairstyles from the eighties.

Even the community bulletin board still hangs on the wall, cluttered with flyers and handwritten ads for babysitters and special events.

Annual Own a Hunky Hero for a Night.

"You're kidding me. They still do this?" I cringe at the fluorescent-orange page as I scan the details about the auction in December. It's for a children's charity, to buy them presents for Christmas. Women can bid for a night out with one of the county's emergency workers.

I remember seeing the flyers around town when I was younger and thinking how cheesy and inappropriate it was, even back then. Plus, it's *so* not PC. It specifically says a woman can bid on a man. What if a man wants to bid on a man? Is that against the rules? Has anyone ever tried it? And what if there's a female firefighter or police officer or paramedic?

Though, knowing how behind the times Polson Falls is, there likely aren't any.

In a smaller headline, there's also mention that next year's firefighter calendars will be available for purchase. I cringe. A Polson Hills firefighter calendar? Are you kidding me?

I hear my name being called, but my mind is too busy picturing the round-bellied men I saw lingering around the front of the station when I drove by yesterday on my way to get groceries. I mean, I get it's for charity, but *still.*

"So, what do you think? I'll let her know?" Ann Margaret asks.

"Huh? I'm sorry, what were you—"

"Okay, are we *finally* ready?" Mom strolls out, her face freshly powdered and glossed, her boobs extra perky from being plumped and adjusted. She says it like she's been waiting on me all this time.

Her smoky eyes dart to the Hunky Hero flyer I was gaping at and a gleeful laugh escapes her. "We should go together! That'd be a fun mother-daughter night, don't you think? And you can bid on a man."

My face twists with disgust. "Ew. No."

"What?" She frowns, as if confused by my reaction. "It's the best night of the year around town."

"*You've* gone to this?"

"I haven't just gone. I've won." She winks conspiratorially. "Fire Chief Cassidy last year."

I have no idea who Fire Chief Cassidy is, but I'm surprised to hear Mom gave money to charity. Then again, if the reward involves an even semi-attractive man, I guess she'd be all about doing a good deed.

For the children, of course.

"And what does owning a *hunky hero* entail exactly?" I air-quote those words. "Bragging rights? Or do you actually go out to, like, dinner and a movie?"

"I'm sure that's all the dowdy women around town get out of it." She studies her nail lacquer, a devious smile touching her lips. "But what a night that was."

I bite my tongue. Seriously, is there no man my mother *won't* screw? And she basically paid for this one.

"So? Are we going to dinner or what?" Her heels click against the tile as she marches for the door. "I could really use a drink."

SEVEN

Who the hell cuts grass at *eight* in the morning? Isn't there a law against that?

I struggle to tamp down my annoyance at the grating sound of the lawn mower in a neighboring yard as it carries through my open windows, knowing that my foul mood is thanks to an emotionally draining evening, followed by a restless night.

Dinner with my mother was exhausting, as usual—listening to her gossip and judge until her speech slurred, about who's going through a divorce and which woman needs to take better care of herself before she drives her man way. Looks and money, that's all that seems to matter to Dottie Reed. There isn't much in the way of substance to her personality, a grim reality I clued into long ago. There also isn't any point in calling her out for it. It'll just put her in a snit, and I have no interest in fighting again.

Thankfully, she has never required my attention on the regular and I suspect that won't change, even with me being back in town. I've bought myself at least a month before I have to make a phone call, two months for another stab-me-in-the-eye dinner.

I couldn't get home fast enough last night, but when I finally did, it was to a sweltering house. I woke up in a pool of sweat at 6:00 a.m., thanks to this never-ending heat wave and lack of air conditioning, a fact I was aware of but didn't seem to grasp until now.

Iris Rutshack ran a portable air conditioner from her ground floor bedroom window, one that she took with her. If these temperatures don't let up soon, I'll be forking over cash for a unit. Another thing to add to the long list of must-haves.

I suck back a mouthful of coffee as I assess my charming but dated kitchen—the butter-yellow cupboards adorned by hinges that sit on the outside, the green, yellow, and white mosaic tile backsplash that gives the space a festive look. I've scrubbed everything down, and yet the thirty-year-old, avocado-green appliances still look grimy. Especially the stove, which Iris warned in a note sometimes "acts up." I'm not sure exactly what that means yet, but it needs to go, as soon as my paychecks start rolling in.

But for now, it's all about cleaning up the front yard and painting the main floor walls before I have to switch my focus to getting my classroom ready for my sixth graders.

I smile into my giant coffee mug.

My walls. *My* class. I'm not sure what makes me more excited.

And I have little time to waste.

Grabbing my bucket of cleaning supplies, I shove it under the sink, out of the way, and then crank the sink tap, intent on washing the pile of dirty dishes. A strange metal clank and pop sounds, followed by a distinct hiss. A moment later, cool water touches my bare feet, pooling on the worn beige linoleum floor.

Panicked, I crouch and open the cupboard doors.

And get hit in the face with a burst of cold water.

I let out a shriek as I'm doused. Turning my face to avoid the brunt of the blast, I fumble blindly beneath the old cabinet, frantic to find the shut off valve before my entire kitchen floods. Ten seconds later, I finally locate it.

"Shit!" I curse, spotting the culprit—a rusty, rotted pipe. It must have snapped when I shoved in the bucket. Now I don't have a functioning kitchen sink. I can't live without a kitchen sink.

I'll have to phone a plumber today, I accept with bitter resignation.

Grabbing my new set of tea towels—a housewarming gift from Justine—I sop up as much water as I can and then, loading my arms with the soaked, dripping rags, I carry them out back. I throw them at the ground by the clothesline, my frustration swelling.

This is *not* how I was supposed to start today.

"Is everything all right?" a deep male voice calls out, startling me.

Shane is perched on a picnic table in his backyard, his long, jean-clad legs splayed in front of him, intently focused on something round and metal in his hand. Several other pieces sit on the table beside him, set on oily rags.

Great. Just who I don't want to deal with right now, even if my heart is suddenly hammering in my chest. A visual of Shane, completely naked, sears my memory, and my face flushes. This is *exactly* why I should not have spied.

I struggle for composure, and when I can't manage that, I shift my focus back to the dish towels, strangling out the sink water before stretching them on the clothesline.

Twenty seconds later, footfalls approach on the soft grass. "Scar? Is everything okay?"

"Why wouldn't it be?" I answer in a forced bored tone.

"Well ... because I heard you scream, and you look like you took a shower in your clothes." There's humor in his voice.

"A pipe under my sink broke," I finally admit. *Crap.* My gaze drops to the white tank top that I slept in, noting how the cotton clings in a very sleazy wet-T-shirt-contest way, highlighting the fact that I'm not wearing a bra. My cheeks flame with embarrassment as I struggle to hide my assets from his view, all while continuing with my task. He touched my breasts that summer, countless times. Slid his hand up my shirt and pushed aside the lace, teasing my flesh with the deft skill of a boy who had done it many times before. I let his mouth on them a few times before I stopped him, afraid it'd go too far if I didn't. Does he remember?

"Can I take a look?"

"What?" I croak.

"At your kitchen pipe," he says slowly, frowning. "Can I look at what happened?"

Oh. Right. "Are you a plumber?"

"No, but—"

"Do you know *anything* about plumbing?"

He smirks. "More than you do, I'm guessing."

I grit my teeth and count to ten in my head, checking my temper. The bitch tone I use when I'm shutting down flirtatious guys at bars is emerging. While Shane deserves whatever attitude he gets from me, I don't want to be the scorned woman flashing her bitterness thirteen years after a high school summer fling. That's pathetic. "I think I should have an actual plumber fix this."

He pauses. "Okay. I can give you the name of a good one in town."

"That … would be helpful." Shane always was a nice guy. Until he wasn't.

From the corner of my eye, I catch him folding those cut arms over his chest. "It'll cost you a hundred bucks just to get him through your door and then another few hundred—at least—to replace what I'm guessing are corroded pipes. Plus parts. So, I'm thinking it'll end up being anywhere from five hundred to a thousand, by the time he walks out your door."

"You can't be serious." I groan in dismay, forgetting about wet rags and revealing shirts for the moment as my palms push through my damp hair. I can't afford that right now. I also can't afford to go without a kitchen sink until my first paycheck.

"For an *actual* plumber, yeah, I am." Shane shrugs. "*Or* you could ask your neighbor who's done a bunch of reno jobs to see if he can fix it. No charge."

Scorned heart or not, I'd be an idiot to deny letting Shane try.

"Fine," I mutter begrudgingly, stealing a glance at his handsome face. He hasn't shaved yet today and his chiseled jaw is coated in a sexy stubble. His hair is also in disarray, like he just rolled out of bed, threw on some clothes, and came outside. It's annoyingly adorable, and I feel the urge to comb my fingers through it.

His golden gaze drifts over my features. There's a long, uncomfortable pause and then he says, "I've got time now."

"Right." I clear my throat, struggling to push aside thoughts of Shane Beckett rolling out of bed. Naked. Because I have a vivid idea of what that might look like. I orgasmed to that mental image the other night before I could fall asleep.

His dimples appear with a curious smile, as if he can read my mind. "Lead the way, I guess?"

I toss the last of the towels to the grass to deal with later and let him trail me through the side door off the kitchen, sensing his eyes on my back the entire way. I wish I'd had the foresight to change out of my pajamas before I went traipsing around my backyard.

Then again, my ass *does* look incredible in these cotton shorts.

Justine's suggestion to play cat and mouse with him rings in my ear, but even the idea of it has my stomach jumping with nerves. Where do you begin with a guy like Shane? I'd likely embarrass myself. At least I wouldn't make the mistake of falling in love with him. Once was enough.

But what would it be like, after all these years? To feel those lips and hands on me again, to show him all that I've learned, that I'm not the same girl I used to be …

Fuck him and then pretend he doesn't matter.

Except he's my freaking neighbor. I'd have to deal with

running into him every time I step out of my house. And, with my luck, that would end up being every goddamn morning for the rest of my life, until one of us moves. Or dies.

I reach for the door handle but somehow Shane comes from behind to grab it before I have a chance, pulling the door open for me. Yup, and he was always a gentleman too. Another part of his deceptive charm. Another reason I was utterly in shock by the way he broke me.

I step into my kitchen. "Shouldn't you be at work?"

"I have today off." A pause. "Shouldn't *you* be at work?"

"I start when the school year starts." I hesitate, not sure how much I want Shane to know about me. "I'm going to be teaching at Polson Falls Elementary. Sixth grade." It's one of the few in the area that go from kindergarten to eighth grade.

"*Sixth* grade." His brow furrows. "That should be interesting."

"Yeah. Hopefully they won't be too hormonal yet."

He nods slowly. "You really did everything you set out to do, didn't you?"

Except get over you, apparently. I bite my tongue before that slips out. I point to the sink. "I shut off the valve."

Shane edges around me in my cramped kitchen, his chest brushing against my shoulder on his way past—stealing a breath—and crouches in front of the open cupboard. "You got a flashlight?" he asks, squinting.

"Yeah, I think so. Hold on." I weave around the last of the boxes to get to the living room and rifle through my toolbox—a practical and sweet housewarming gift from Joe.

"Did you do a home inspection first?" Shane calls out. A metal clank sounds.

"No." What was an inspector going to tell me that I didn't already know? Besides the fact that a kitchen pipe would explode within forty-eight hours of me living here. The truth is, I'm pretty sure I would have bought the house no matter what an inspection report revealed. The toilets flush, the fridge keeps things cold, and both the furnace and roof were replaced within the last five years. I figured any other problems, I could deal with as they came up.

"It was between me and a couple, and they wanted the inspection as a condition. I didn't. That's why I won." Plus, I made sure the agent relayed my personal history with this little house. I wasn't just anyone, looking to buy a cheap property near the school that I could then demolish to build a bigger, newer house. I wanted to preserve this place.

"I'm not sure 'won' is the right word," Shane mutters under his breath.

Flashlight retrieved, I head back into the kitchen to find him flicking the cupboard handle, now dangling loosely. "That *wasn't* broken a minute ago," I say with an accusing tone.

"It just needs a new screw." He peers over his shoulder at me and his gaze drops to my chest again—I really need to go change—before drifting farther down, taking in the full length of my bare legs. The look sends a small, unwanted thrill through my body.

"Here." I thrust the flashlight into his hand and then make a point of stepping away and folding my arms over my chest. Shane Beckett, freshly out of bed, on his knees ogling me is a sight I *don't* want to enjoy.

Resting a sculpted forearm on the counter above him, he leans forward, shining a beam of light into the dark, cramped space as he inspects the maze of pipes. "Damn, this is all original," he muses. "It all needs to be replaced."

"Big surprise." I figured that already.

With another moment of study, he sighs and shuts off the flashlight, then climbs to his feet. "All right, I'll be back in about an hour."

"Where are you going?"

"The hardware store. I'll grab what I need to fix this up for you."

"You know how to do that?" I ask skeptically.

He smirks. "I've done it a few times, yeah. And if I run into problems, I've got friends I can call." He turns to face me, reminding me that he has a good eight inches on me. He always had to stoop when we kissed. Or I'd rise on tiptoes and press myself against his broad chest for support as I reached for his lips.

I swallow hard, the memories of how much I loved his full, soft mouth against mine—of how hot I was for him, of how hard it became to keep our relationship PG-13—flooding back to me with surprising clarity. It seems a betrayal to my seventeen-year-old wounded self to accept his help now. But what other choice do I have?

"Okay," I finally say, though with no small amount of reluctance.

"See ya in an hour." His soft chuckle trails him out the door.

EIGHT

Of all the things I imagined would happen when I moved into my new house, having Shane Beckett sprawled out on my floor was not one of them. But here he is, his broad, muscular body taking up half my kitchen, his head resting in my musty old kitchen cupboard as he bangs and clamps and solders away.

My seat at my two-person table affords me the ideal vantage point over the spectacle and, try as I might to focus on the paint chips laid out in front of me, I can't keep my attention from veering over to where his black T-shirt has ridden up, exposing the thick pad of muscle across his abdomen and the dark trail of hair that disappears beneath his belt. And, hell, as if that doesn't force my gaze farther to the sizable bulge inside his jeans, pressing against his zipper. There's nothing sexy about my sink or my corroded pipes. Shane *can't* possibly be hard while doing this, and if that's not an erection, then ... *Damn.*

I may have gotten the full-frontal, R-rated version of his body last night, but it was at a safe distance. *This* is not a safe distance. I could almost straddle him from here, my kitchen is so small. What would he do if I climbed on top of him right now?

"Hand me that wrench?" Shane's deep voice suddenly cuts into my depraved admiration.

I duck my head but it's too late, he's caught me ogling his crotch.

I clear my throat as my cheeks burn. "This thing?" I hold up a shiny, long tool.

He reaches out his free hand, smirking. "Yeah, that thing."

He watches me intently as I lean forward to close the distance, his eyes darting downward. I realize that, yet again, I'm flashing him, thanks to the loose T-shirt I changed into. My hand flies up to press the material to my chest. At least I'm wearing a bra this time.

He refocuses on his task, his Adam's apple bobbing with a hard swallow. "I have to say, I was surprised to hear you were moving back."

"Why?"

"I don't know. You just always seemed so intent on getting away. You know, because of your mom."

Most people in town have heard at least one story about Dottie Reed. The infamous Christmas pageant tale is the most prevalent—it resulted in Mayor Peter Rhodes's expulsion from office and a lot of judgment for Melissa Rhodes, who chose to stay married to him despite his infidelity. That's the story Mom's best known for.

But to Shane, back in the day, I divulged my darkest tales about being her daughter. Things I didn't disclose to anyone else, mainly about how embarrassed and ashamed I was of her behavior. He knew why I always stayed his hand before it could venture past the buckle of my jeans. He said he understood. He said he didn't see me as a replica of her, but that he respected my wishes.

"What she does is her business. It has nothing to do with me or who I am as a person."

"Glad you see it that way." He offers me a gentle smile. "Do you still talk to anyone from high school?"

"Not really. Jeremy Beagly occasionally. Mainly on Facebook." Jeremy and his parents lived in the apartment below us. We'd walk to school together sometimes.

"Emo Man? Has he learned to smile yet?"

I roll my eyes at the stupid nickname that stuck. "He's going to film school in LA now, doing really well." He stopped dying his hair black and traded in his tight jeans for board shorts. And yes, he does know how to smile, based on the pictures he's posted. It probably has a lot to do with being away from the assholes who mocked him in high school.

"What about Becca?"

"Thompson?" I let out a derisive snort. "No." We may have become close that summer that Shane and I were together, but that friendship ended when Shane and I did. The last time I had any interaction with her was the day I muddled through the mortifying topic of premarital sex during our senior debate class—I had to argue "pro," against her. Afterward, I walked in on her and Penelope laughing hysterically in the girls' restroom and got the distinct neck-hair-spiking impression that I was the center of the joke.

The scandal between Penelope's father and my mother sparked a feud between Penelope and me that lasted until I left town. It was Penelope who initiated it. I was content to lay all blame at my mother's stilettos. But I guess she needed to exact revenge on her family's humiliation the only way she knew how.

She was at the root of dozens of ugly rumors floating around about me through high school—everything from my lack of hygiene to weird sexual fetishes. I know she heard about my little summer fling with Shane, because she made a point of practically mounting him in the hallway any time I happened to walk by. To my face, however, she pretended I didn't exist, and I was more than fine with that.

But that day in the bathroom, with Becca by her side, Penelope made a point of turning to me with a sweet, vindictive smile. *I just thought you should know*, she started, and then went on to detail how embarrassed Shane was about slumming it with me for, like, a second, and how relieved he was that he hadn't been stupid enough to sleep with the Polson Falls High whore—I was still a virgin, mind you—but that he'd gotten himself tested twice anyway just to be sure he hadn't caught *something* from touching me.

I gritted my teeth and ducked into the stall to hide my tears as Becca stood by and Penelope cackled, wondering if any part of what she said about Shane's regrets were true.

"I thought you and Becca might have ended up being friends. Don't your moms work together?" Shane asks.

"Yeah, they do. But I'm pretty sure the Red Devil wouldn't have approved of that."

"The *Red Devil*?" Shane pauses in his work to flash an amused look my way.

"Don't tell me I have to elaborate for you?"

"Nah. Just never heard that one before." He chews his bottom lip in thought.

Is he offended? Does he think I'm being petty?

Do I care?

Nope. She was an awful person in *every* way.

"What about you?" I ask, because despite telling myself I don't care, my curiosity has been sparked. "Still friends with Dean Fanshaw and Dipshit?"

Shane smirks. "Yeah, we keep in touch. Fanshaw's still in town. Steve's living in Philly now. He got married in June. I was a groomsman."

"There's a *Mrs*. Dipshit now?" What must she be like?

He chuckles. "There is."

"Poor, foolish woman," I say with mock concern. What kind of person would marry that moron?

"Can't argue with you there, though he's not so bad anymore. He's working for an insurance company. I think they're trying for a baby."

I *hope* he's changed, because the asshole I knew in high school shouldn't be allowed to procreate. I hesitate. "What about Penelope? Still talk with her?" After the welcome back from Italy make-out session I witnessed that stabbed me through the chest, she and Shane ended up together for the entire senior year, earning prom king and queen crowns before riding off into the college scholarship sunset together.

But it's been twelve years since high school ended and I don't see a ring on his finger. I sure as hell didn't see a redhead in his bed. So, when did the fairy tale end?

"She's in Dover. We're ... civil. So, your boyfriend lives in Boston?"

I frown. "Who?"

"The guy who helped you move. Jim, was it?"

"*Oh.* Joe." I study the various shades of blue that I'm considering for my bedroom. *Right. That lie*. "Yeah, Boston."

"How long have you guys been together?"

"Three years?" That shouldn't have come out sounding like a question.

Shane makes an odd sound.

"What?"

"Nothing. Just ... three years together and you bought a house how many hours away from him? Is he planning on moving here?"

"We'll see." Can Shane tell I'm lying? I've always been a terrible liar. And what of his relationship status? A guy like him must be seeing a clueless sucker or three. But if I ask, it'll sound like I'm interested in him and there's no way in hell I'm ever going down that road again. "How's that new pipe coming?" I had a whole day of errands I was planning on, and yet I can't seem to peel myself away from the kitchen. Because I don't trust Shane

Beckett alone in my house, I tell myself.

His triceps strain as he uses the wrench on something, before testing something else with his fingers. His abs flex beautifully as he pulls himself up to a sitting position and then gets to his feet. "I think we're almost good to go. I'm gonna turn the main water back on. Scream if something bad happens."

"That inspires confidence," I say as he disappears down the narrow set of stairs into the dark and dingy basement. This house is old—like, dirt floor and stone walls in the basement old. I've only been down there once and have no plans on going back ever again, the visuals of a Blair Witch-like bogeyman in the corner too vivid to ignore.

Moments later, heavy footfalls pound back up. "I didn't hear screaming." Shane heads for the sink.

"The day is young."

He chuckles as he kneels. "Okay, let's try out my handiwork." He glances over his shoulder at me, and I try not to admire his face too much. "Ready?"

I give an exaggerated thumbs-up and hold my breath as the valve squeaks open with a twist of his wrist.

No hissing, no spraying water.

"So far, so good." He reaches up to open the faucet. After a short sputter to force out the air bubbles, water streams out.

"You actually did it!" I exclaim, sounding dumbfounded.

He leans back on his haunches, grinning. "Told you. Good as new."

I sigh with relief. Shane Beckett, of all people, saved me from spending a ton of money I don't have.

Wiping his dirty hands on a rag, he tosses his tools into a black, rectangular toolbox. "Hopefully the rest of the pipes will hold until you can afford to have them replaced."

"Yeah. Hopefully." I muster as much sincerity as I can. "Thanks, Shane." He's still a douchebag, but he's a douchebag who's knowledgeable and willing to fix my house. "What do I owe you?"

"Nah. Nothing." He waves dismissively.

"No, seriously. I need to repay you."

"Well, then how about dinner with me? The Patty Shack's still around."

Are you fucking kidding me? I spear him with an "Are you on drugs?" glare. We had our first date there.

He holds his hands up in surrender. "As friends."

"Well, yeah. *Of course,* it would be as friends," I scoff. As far as he knows, I'm dating Joe. I'm not about to cheat on my fake boyfriend with him. But uneasiness gnaws at my insides. Shane may have helped me today, but we're a far cry from reminiscing about the good ol' days over hamburgers and milkshakes. Getting friendly is a bad idea. "Where are the receipts from the stuff you picked up at the hardware store?"

"In there, I think." He juts his chin to the plastic bag sitting on the counter.

"I have to go out so I'll grab cash for you and bring it by as soon as I can."

"No rush." He leans over to grab the handle on his toolbox, his forearm straining with the weight. "And let me know about dinner."

That's a hard pass. I press my lips together to flash him a tight smile that hopefully says as much.

He saunters toward me, his leg brushing against my thigh ever so lightly. I can't decide if it was an accidental or intentional move. "You should go with this one." He taps the periwinkle paint chip. "It matches your eyes."

Shane always did say he loved the way my irises looked more purple than blue in certain light. He'd spend long moments studying them during lazy afternoons at Pike's Park beneath the gnarly oak trees. *I keep getting lost in them,* he'd whisper, and I'd swoon like the lovesick idiot I was.

I shift my body away and keep my focus on the table, desperately trying to ignore the electric current coursing through me at his proximity. "You don't even know which room it's for."

"Which room is it for?"

I hesitate. "My bedroom." Why does divulging that to him sound like a dirty suggestion?

"Well, then it's definitely perfect." His voice has dropped an octave. "Anyone you bring up there won't *ever* want to leave."

My blood pounds in my ears. What the hell does that mean? Is Shane Becket flirting with me? After what he did all those years ago?

I will not look up at him.

I will keep my eyes forward.

On his belt buckle, apparently. And the sexy V-shape I know is hiding beneath his clothes, his body chiseled with muscle as if hand-carved.

"Scar ..."

I sigh heavily and then force my head back to meet that beautiful whiskey-colored gaze. "What?" My disloyal heart stutters, despite the bitterness I grip tightly. Dear God, how did I *ever* hold fast at second base with this guy? Even now, my thighs are growing warm with a need to feel his hips between them, my palm twitches as I imagine his hard length within it. Men should not be built to look like him. It's not natural.

That sexy, sharp jut in his throat bobs with a swallow. "I didn't mean for things to go the way they went."

"Which part didn't you mean, exactly? The part where you told me you were falling in love with me? Or when you dumped me because you weren't ready for a serious relationship, only to hook up with Penelope the next day and then completely ignore me for the rest of the year? Which part *exactly*, Shane?" *Way to get it all out in the open, Scarlet.*

He winces. "Look, I was an idiot back then. A lot has changed and I'm not the same guy. Can't we please be friends again?"

"Is *that* what we were?" Because what I remember is going from virtual strangers to falling into a teenaged summer romance, the likes of which Nicholas Sparks has surely written about. Then, crushing reality followed, delivered in heart-shaped lies.

And soon enough we were back to being strangers, passing each other in the hall without a single word exchanged, his arm roped around Penelope's tiny waist.

His gaze drifts to my mouth, lingering for a long moment, his lips parting ever so slightly before lifting to meet my eyes again. "No. We were more," he admits.

"No, we weren't. You played me. You were hoping for an easy lay. Sorry, you went after the wrong Reed." I hate that my voice cracks, revealing the pain that has remained dormant for all these years.

His jaw clenches and I swallow against the tension-riddled air in my stuffy kitchen, acutely aware of the tremble coursing through my core. What did Shane think would happen when he heard I was moving back? That we'd just pick up where we left off, as if all the crap since we last talked never happened? That I wouldn't be able to resist him, because no other female ever has?

As if I'd ever trust him again. No, I'm not tumbling into this trap. My heart still wears the jagged scars from the last time I fell for his charm.

I steel my nerve. "We're neighbors. How about we leave it at that."

He bites his bottom lip. "Let me know if you need help around here. And seriously, you should go with this color." Damn, again with that low, gravelly tone.

"Hmm … I don't know," I feign nonchalance. Meanwhile, his voice skitters along my spine and up my inner thighs. "I'm thinking more along the lines of a harsher shade. It's called Blue Balls. BB for short. Ever heard of that one?" I smile sweetly.

Recognition fills his face. He pauses, as if weighing the right response. In the end, he merely nods, turns, and strolls toward the door.

"And Shane?"

He pauses, his eyebrows raised in question.

Put some curtains up on your window. It's on the tip of my tongue but I can't bring myself to say it. That would mean confessing to spying on him. It would also cut off my view into his bedroom, and that's not something I'm willing to give up just yet. Though, watching Shane in his bedroom is one thing. If he brings a woman home and I have to witness *that,* I'll be miserable.

I clear my throat. "Thanks again, for fixing this."

He flashes a small, crooked smile. "Any time." He ducks to fit through the side door and then he's gone.

And I'm left fumbling with paint chips as I try to shake off the shock from having Shane Beckett back in my life.

Periwinkle was my top color choice anyway. That I'm choosing it has *nothing* to do with Shane.

Nothing at all.

I groan. Dear God, how am I supposed to live next to that man?

NINE

I knock on the solid gunmetal-gray door a second time and fidget while I wait.

But there's no need to be nervous because Shane's truck is gone. It's 9:00 p.m. and he's obviously out.

I look down at the envelope of cash in my hand, repayment for the plumbing materials he bought this morning. Should I come back tomorrow, or push it through the mail slot in his front door and be done with him?

Holding onto it would give me an excuse to see him in person, though.

An excuse that I *shouldn't* be looking for, I remind myself as I stand here in my favorite flirty sundress and wedge heel sandals, my long hair flat-ironed sleek, my skin buffed and moisturized, my lips shimmering with cherry-flavored lip gloss. All entirely unnecessary to deliver cash to my neighbor, except I felt a spiteful urge to look far better than I did this morning, soaked by an exploding pipe.

The truth is, Shane has been in my thoughts *all* day—at the library, the paint store, wandering down the aisles of the grocery store. I can't shake him. His face, his body, his words, his throaty "Let me know if you need any help."

What if thirteen years *is* too long to hold on to a grudge? We all did stupid, cruel things in high school. I had Jeremy dump a guy for me during my sophomore year because I didn't have the guts to do it. I've said mean things and spread rumors that were likely false. I've gossiped. I, like every other person in the world, am not perfect. I certainly wasn't as a teenager.

But that was high school, and we've all grown and changed since then, I accept, my focus drifting over the small porch, to the baseball bat and two gloves propped in the corner, the potted plant on the step, and the wooden "welcome" sign.

Was I too cold to Shane earlier, given he's only been nice to me since the day I moved in?

Is it time to forgive and forget?

What on earth are you trying to convince yourself to do, Scarlet?

Before Shane pulls into his driveway and catches me waffling by his door, I shove the envelope through the mail slot and hurry back to the safety of my home.

It'll all be worth it in the end.

I set the can of exterior white paint and my toolbox down on the porch and size up my first big home improvement task for the week, sleep still lingering in my body. The weather forecast says no rain for the next three days, so it seems like a good time to make my little house's curb appeal a priority. At 7:00 a.m., it's too early to go banging on loose boards, though, unless I want to make enemies in my new neighborhood. Thankfully, there are enough weeds sprouting in the beds to keep me busy for another hour or two, until hammering nails is reasonable.

With that in mind, I head for the old garden shed on the side of the house, noting Shane's truck in the driveway. The deep rumble of the engine sounded a little after eleven last night. Despite the overwhelming urge to shut off my lights and catch another unintentional strip tease, I stayed in my bed, gripping my book tightly.

I yank on the metal shed door and it opens with a screech. Iris was kind enough to leave her tools for me. I find the basics—a shovel, spade, pitchfork, a few trowels, and other hand tools. They're simple but well-kept, not a speck of rust on them. And old. So old, I'm surprised her family didn't try to pawn them off as antiques.

I'm sizing up the shovel and the spade, deciding which I should be using for my task, when Shane's front door creaks open. My heart instantly races, despite my best attempt to not care. I busy myself, pretending to be enthralled by the hoe as I listen to his keys jangle with his steps.

If Shane notices me, he doesn't look my way. A moment later, I hear a door slam and an engine roar to life. His pickup truck eases down the driveway, Shane behind the wheel, his forearm resting out the open window, his skin looking golden against a cerulean T-shirt. He must be heading off to work. Curiosity overwhelms me. What does Shane do with his days? What happened to his promising football career?

I guess I could find out if I would just talk to him.

If I cared enough to ask.

Which I most certainly do not.

With a resolute sigh, I grab the shovel and set to work.

I keep my attention on my brushstrokes, pretending not to notice Shane's truck pulling into the driveway at half past eight the next morning. He didn't come home at all yesterday, and he's wearing the same T-shirt he left in.

I ignore the way my pulse races, instead dipping my paintbrush into the can of white paint as I warn my idiotic hormones. *You remember what happened the last time you got mixed up with that. It didn't end well then either.* My gaze remains locked on my work as his truck door slams shut, but from the corner of my eye, I see the lone figure strolling across the lawn, toward me.

"Morning!"

I stifle my sigh. I decided over the last twenty-four hours that polite indifference is the best way to handle Shane going forward, seeing as I *do* have to live next to him. "Good morning."

"You've been busy." He studies the length of the fence. "It's looking good."

"Thanks. I'm taking a break from scraping paint and hammering nails. And a few fingers." I hold up my injured hand that I spent last night icing. I'm probably going to lose my thumbnail.

He cringes. "Give me ten and I'll come help you."

"I'm fine, thanks."

He shakes his head. "Don't be stubborn. We'll get it done twice as fast together."

Finally, I dare meet his eyes. They're as rich and golden as always, though touched by dark circles and weariness. "You sure you're up for it? Seems like you had an *eventful* night." *Screwing someone.*

"Nah, work was pretty slow."

"You were *at work*? Since *yesterday morning*?" My voice is laced with sarcasm. His eyebrows arch and I feel compelled to add, "Your truck is loud. I heard you leave."

"Oh." He nods slowly. "Well, yeah, shifts at the fire station are twenty-four hours long."

Fire station. I frown. "Wait. You're a *firefighter*?"

He smirks. "Why do you say it like that?"

That *did* sound snarky. "No reason. It's just … for *Polson Falls*?"

He laughs, as if my surprise is amusing. "For the whole county. Yeah."

"Huh." Star quarterback with a football scholarship and a shiny future ends up back in this tiny town, working for the local fire department? When was the last time there was a real emergency around here? I don't know what to say, so I settle on, "I can't see it being too busy for you guys, like, *ever*."

"I'll have you know, I've saved more than a few distressed kittens in my day." He winks. "It's a real crowd-pleaser."

"Not as much as the calendar, I'll bet," I mutter before I can bite my tongue. Apparently, the models aren't *all* old and portly.

"Yeah, that's earned me a few dates too." That grin of his turns downright devilish. "How about I bring you a signed copy later?"

"I prefer the one I have, thanks." As a gag, Justine gave me an eighteen-month calendar with pictures of various insects mating because I hate bugs and she's an asshole. Ironically, I've found the skillfully taken pictures of spiders and centipedes getting busy helpful in dealing with my phobia.

Plus, the last thing I need to do is feed Shane's ego by accepting that offer. I'll just privately google the images later. They *must* be online somewhere. "So, whatever happened to football, anyway? You were good." I thought the NFL was a given. The guy was throwing sixty yards with acute precision at seventeen years old.

His playful grin wavers a touch. "I blew out my knee sophomore year. Surgery, physical therapy, the whole bit. That was basically a career-ender for me."

Shit. "I'm sorry."

"Yeah, well ..." He shrugs. "That's life, right?"

"But you're okay now?"

He bends his knee, as if on instinct to test it. "Enough to haul bodies out of burning buildings, yeah."

Has he ever had to do that? A question for another time, perhaps. Especially when I have so many others to ask. "Why back to Polson Falls, though?" Of all the places he could have landed, why back *here*?

He pulls his bottom lip between his teeth in a pensive look. "You *really* didn't keep in touch with anyone, did you?"

I shake my head mutely.

"Because of Cody." He lets a beat pass. "My son."

My mouth drops open.

"I share custody with his mom. The Red Devil." He starts backing away, heading for his house. "Let me grab a quick shower and then I'll be out to help you with that other side, so you don't lose any more fingers. I think you'll need those to write on the chalkboard, Ms. Reed."

I stare after his sleek body as he disappears inside without a backward glance, as if he's avoiding the aftermath of the bomb he just dropped.

Shane has a *son*?

With *Penelope Rhodes*?

My stomach clenches as if it's taken a hard punch.

TEN

"A *kid?*"

"I know." An hour later and I'm still trying to come to terms with the knowledge that Shane had a baby. The fact that it was with Penelope—that they share something so special together—makes me want to hurl. She was a vicious bitch back then, and I'm having a hard time believing she's gone through a complete metamorphosis since.

"When? How old is he? Did they get married?" Justine fires off question after question.

I shake my head in answer, though she can't see it through the phone. "I don't know. He came over and went straight to work on the other side of the fence. I'm not going to yell across the lawn, drilling him for details."

"But they're over?"

"He said they're 'civil,' whatever that means." Maybe civil after a divorce? Ugh. Just imagining him marrying *her*—him, down on one knee, professing his undying love—and them having *a baby* together makes my chest ache.

"So ..." There's a long pause on the other side of the call. "Is he *nailing* your *fence* nice and hard?"

"*And* she's back." I chuckle, glancing over my shoulder to make sure Shane's not within earshot. Thankfully he's far on the other side of my front yard, his concentration on a wobbly fence post, brushing the sweat from his forehead with his biceps. It's half past ten and already sweltering hot. "Remind me why I called you again?"

"Because I'm your best friend and this was too good to keep to yourself," Justine retorts. "Plus you want my advice."

"I do?"

"Yeah. On what it's like to bang a dad."

"Please tell me, oh wise one," I mock wryly, playing into whichever dirty direction Justine decides to take this. No matter how somber the mood, I can always count on her to lighten it up with appalling jokes and sexual innuendo, delivered in that Bostonian accent that somehow adds to the punch line.

"Well, I am the expert, after all."

"What's Bill's kid's name again?" I tease. Bill has a five-year-old daughter from his first marriage who lives in a Boston suburb. He sees her one weekend a month and over holidays, a painful trade-off he had to accept when he moved to New York for his job. Justine could count on one hand the number of nights she's spent with the two of them.

"That doesn't matter. What matters is that you need to make sure you call him Daddy while you're riding him. Repeatedly. Extra points if you scream it while you're coming."

"Ew! No!"

"I do it to Bill all the time."

"And he likes that?" I cringe.

"Oh, no. He hates it. Once, he couldn't even finish."

I snort. "You are *evil*."

"I know," she hisses conspiratorially.

"Scarlet?"

I jump at the sound of Shane's voice right behind me. I didn't hear him approaching. "Yeah?"

"Sorry. I didn't realize you were on the phone."

"No, it's okay. It's only Justine. What's up?"

He gestures behind him with a thumb. "That last post by the house is rotten. It's soft all around the base. I should replace it before it takes the whole section down."

"I'll bet Shane's *base* isn't soft right now," Justine purrs seductively in my ear.

I purse my lips, struggling not to burst out laughing as heat crawls up my neck. "Is that hard to do?"

"*So* hard, big daddy," Justine answers.

"Shut up!" I hiss into the phone, a giggle escaping before I stifle it.

Shane's brow pinches curiously. "Nah, not the way this fence was put together. I'll have to take down the section first, but it'll be fine."

"That'd be … thanks." Is he this helpful with everyone? Why didn't he do all this for Iris when she was here? *Maybe because he wasn't hoping to screw her,* that cynical voice in my head warns.

He pushes a hand through his wavy hair, sending it into disarray. "No problem. I'm going to grab a water and then head over to the mill. You want one?"

"Yes! Oh yes! Give it to me, Daddy! Yes!" Justine moans into my ear, and by the surprised look that flashes across Shane's face, loud enough that it carried to him.

"Still have mine." I wave my half-empty bottle in the air, my cheeks flushing.

He flashes a deep-dimpled smile and strides past.

"What is *wrong* with you?" I ask as soon as Shane is out of earshot.

"Where shall I begin?"

My eyes trail after Shane, admiring his body, his walk, his *everything.* "Oh God …" I mutter, more to myself. I'm in deep trouble.

"So, what are you going to do?"

"I don't know. This is horrible. I'm like a hormonal teenager again." Except one who wouldn't have any control over her sexual urges around this guy. We're not teenagers anymore, though. We're two adults living next door to each other. He's a hot single dad who rescues kittens and is handy with home repairs.

Shane suddenly turns to look back at me.

"Shit." I drop my gaze, pretending to focus on my picket fence. "I just got caught staring."

"Good."

I scowl. "What do you mean, good? How is that *good*?"

"What's he doing now?"

I hazard a glance back. "He's almost at his porch stairs. And I think he's … yeah." I watch slack-jawed as he reaches over his head and pulls his T-shirt up and over his head, revealing that golden tan and corded muscle. He must spend his days at the fire station working out to have a body like that. "He just took off his shirt." He wipes the cotton over the back of his neck and then tosses it over the railing. "And now he's gone inside."

"So, Daddy's made the first game move. Your turn."

"What? No, he's just hot and sweaty. And stop calling him that. It's creepy."

Justine cackles. "Bullshit. He knows you want him."

"I do *not* want him."

"Really? How's that fence coming?"

I look down to see that I've been brushing the same spot since I got on the phone with Justine ten minutes ago. "You've been distracting me."

"Please, a newborn baby could see through your lies."

"Fine. He's hot as hell," I admit. "But I don't want anything to happen between us."

"Why not?"

"You mean *besides* our past?"

"From *a hundred years* ago? Yeah. Besides that." She sounds irritated with me.

It throws me off. "Well … because of my fake relationship with Joe, for one thing."

Her loud bark fills my ear.

"What? It's safe!"

"How long do you think you can keep that going before you just look pathetic?"

"I was aiming for Christmas?"

"Scarlet, stop being stupid!"

"*No,* getting involved with Shane would be stupid. Russian roulette-level stupid." He imploded my life once and that was enough, thanks.

"Okay, well, when you're ready to stop being a shrew and have some fun, let me know. I'll give you some tips. Not that you need any, you little minx."

With an exasperated sigh, I end the call and turn my attention back to my task, shifting over to the next picket just as Shane's door creaks open and he strolls out.

I keep my head down while my eyes strain so I can stare inconspicuously at the ridges of his hard torso. He pauses on the top porch step to suck back half his water, giving me ample time to admire the way his throat pulses over his swallows.

At some point, I stop pretending not to watch. At some point, I start gaping openly.

"Come with me to the mill!" he hollers, pulling on a fresh T-shirt. He takes his time pushing his arms through the sleeves before sliding it over his head and sauntering to his truck. His beautiful, chiseled body disappears behind a veil of white cotton, much to my dismay.

I finally break free from my embarrassing gawk fest. "I should stay. I want to get this side done today." And get my tongue firmly back in my mouth.

"Suit yourself. Be back in a bit." He climbs into his truck. "Hey, do you have a fire extinguisher in your house?"

"No? Why?" Is he about to suggest I go put myself out? Am I *that* obvious?

"Everyone should have one. Just in case."

Oh, right. He's a firefighter. "'Kay, Safety Sam. I'll get right on it." I mock salute, earning his head shake as he cranks his engine.

I watch as he coasts down the driveway, his tanned arm resting on the open window.

Deep dimples pierce his cheeks as he grins at me.

Maybe Justine is right. Maybe we have started playing a game. If so, I'm pretty sure Shane's several points ahead.

ELEVEN

"Done?"

I drop the brush in the empty can and pull myself off the grassy ground with a heavy sigh. "For today." I'll need to buy another can of paint to finish the last side.

Shane stands next to me, his arms folded across his broad chest as he surveys my yard. "It's a big improvement."

"Yeah, it is." I still don't know what those fuchsia and mauve flowers are, but the petals are popping against the crisp white paint and the freshly churned and weeded soil. "Now I just need to find someone to cut my grass until I can afford a mower."

"Borrow mine whenever you want. I'll leave it out for you."

I hesitate. "Thanks. I might take you up on that."

Shane secured every loose picket, something that would have taken me another two days—and likely many more injuries—to do, and I wouldn't have done it half as well. He also replaced the post, which required a lot of digging in ninety-five-degree heat, which resulted in him taking his shirt off *again* and me painting half my hand while my tongue lolled out *again*.

All this, after having worked a twenty-four-hour shift.

A giant check mark added to the "Just give him another chance, you bitter shrew" box.

"Tired?" I ask, though all I have to do is look in his eyes and see the answer.

"I never sleep well at the station. Too many snorers." He smiles sheepishly and checks his phone. "I'm gonna grab an hour or two before dinner." He starts moving toward his house, and I admire the way his damp T-shirt clings to his shoulders as he walks away, wishing he hadn't put it back on.

I'm not ready to part with that view yet.

"I'm throwing in a lasagna for dinner. It's nothing great but you should come over and help me eat it," he hollers, as if reading my mind.

Dinner with Shane would be nice. Why shouldn't I say yes? It'd be rude to not accept. And we seem to be getting along. We'd talk, we'd laugh. He'd tell me all about his son. He'd acknowledge what an idiot he was for leaving me for Penelope all those years ago and then strip off his clothes, fall to his knees, and beg me to forgive him. And I'd get to feel the thread count of his sheets against my bare skin.

Shit. Look how easily I let that train of thought go down an indecent path.

"I can't. I have plans tonight," I lie.

He nods, and I might be wrong, but I think his furrowed forehead hints at disappointment. "You going out somewhere in town?"

"Not sure yet," I answer vaguely. "Any recommendations?"

"Try Route Sixty-Six—the old Luigi's by the river. They opened a few years ago."

"Luigi's closed down?" That restaurant was there forever.

"Yeah. Luigi had a heart attack in the middle of a busy Saturday night shift. Dropped dead in the dining room. We were the first ones there." A somber look fills his face. "I hate those shifts."

"I guess so." How many people has Shane saved? How many has he lost? Is he happy in his life?

"Anyway, you should check it out. We go there a lot. Friday nights are popular. They've been doing really well."

"Maybe I'll try it."

"So, rain check on that lasagna, then?" He watches me, a hopeful glint in his eye that looks adorable.

"We'll see," I say noncommittally, nodding toward his house. "Get some sleep. The kittens of Polson Falls are counting on you."

He laughs, showing off perfectly straight white teeth. Ugh. He's even hotter when he laughs. "Listen, I'll leave the mower in my shed for you. I picked up an extra shift for tomorrow and then I'm away for the rest of the week."

"Okay. Thanks."

He smiles. "Don't miss me too much."

"Only if a pipe bursts." And yet I note a distinct twinge of discontent over his impending absence, an urge to ask him where he's going, when he'll be back, and most importantly, who he'll be with. Collecting my paint supplies, I turn toward my porch, noticing the red fire extinguisher that sits at the top of the steps. A housewarming gift, Shane announced, when he returned from his supply run.

"You know, I missed you," he calls out after me.

"Good." My chest tightens. What I would have done to hear that, all those years ago. As far as I could tell, I no longer existed to him. But why is he telling me this now?

"Didn't you miss me? Even a little bit?"

Every minute of every day for weeks, even as I sobbed into my pillow, wondering how he could be so cruel, replaying all the visuals of him and Penelope together, until my heart felt like it had shrunk by three sizes and hardened into an impenetrable cast.

Steeling my nerve, I plaster on an indifferent mask and turn back to find him watching me. "You had your chance with me,

Shane Beckett, and you blew it." With that, I disappear into my house.

TWELVE

It's almost 7:00 a.m. when I make my way out to my front yard, still sleepy.

A flash of silver catches the corner of my eye. A sporty Acura is parked beside Shane's truck that wasn't there last night when I went to bed. It looks like he had an overnight guest.

My gut tightens with the thought of Shane at home screwing someone after flirting so shamelessly and inviting me for dinner. But I guess flirting with me doesn't mean he isn't also seeing someone else.

"Oh, you've changed, have you?" I trudge to the garden shed, intent on lashing out at the last of the garden weeds as a way of quashing this unwelcome wave of disappointment, with the proof that Shane is still and always will be a douchebag player.

The sound of his front door creaking open has me diving behind the overgrown lilac bush between our houses.

"Call me tonight?" I catch Shane say in a deep, throaty voice.

"Of course," a female voice answers sweetly. "Thanks again. I really needed this."

"As if I'd ever withhold it from you."

I stifle my snort, as my insides burn with jealousy.

"Drive safe, okay? And call me when you get there."

I cower behind the bush as heels click on the stone walkway, moving away from the house. It serves as the perfect shield, allowing me to spy like a lunatic, waiting for the owner of those shoes and sweet words to appear on her walk of shame to her car.

Long, flame-red hair that stretches halfway down the woman's back sways as she marches, her emerald-green dress swirling around toned legs. It's the way she walks that makes my skin prickle with recognition. It's that same prissy gait of a certain head cheerleader when she was stalking onto the field, pom-poms by her sides.

Penelope Rhodes.

The car engine starts with a low purr and, in seconds, she takes off down the driveway, seemingly in a rush.

They're civil, huh? Civil enough for Mommy and Daddy to still have the occasional sleepover. I can't believe it. Shane is *still* screwing Penelope Rhodes. "You lying sack of shit." I was right to erect a Shane-proof wall. He's the same whiskey-eyed phony he was in high school.

Knuckles rap against my front door.

"Finally!" I exclaim with equal parts irritation and relief. I'm in a pissy mood. Todd the service technician was supposed to be here between nine and noon, and it's now after one. I'm heading to school tomorrow to start setting up my classroom. I can't sit here all day, waiting for him, and if I don't get my internet and cable hooked up stat, I'm going to kill someone.

Likely Todd.

I wipe my palm—smeared with Benjamin Moore CC30—on my sweat-soaked T-shirt and open the door.

And frown. "Becca?" A much older version of Becca Thompson, anyway.

"Hey, Scarlet!" she exclaims with a fluttering wave of her hand. Her bright green eyes scan my clothes, my paint-speckled skin, and then my messy topknot before settling on my face. "Long time, no talk, huh?"

"What are you doing here?" I blurt.

"Uh …" A nervous laugh escapes her lips. "My mom mentioned me coming by, didn't she?"

I struggle to recall what Ann Margaret was prattling on about the other day while I was engrossed with the Hunky Hero auction flyer. What the hell did I agree to?

"I brought your favorite!" She holds up a plastic Subway sandwich bag. "Turkey club, extra mustard."

"That's my mother's favorite, not mine," I say, more to myself. My mother *would* assume her favorite sandwich is by default *my* favorite. I don't even like subs; there's too much bread.

"Oh." Becca's arm falls to her side, her high spirits deflated.

Becca did go to the effort, though. But *why* is the question.

I force a polite smile. "Did you want to come in?"

She nods vigorously.

I lead her into the kitchen, watching her take in every square inch of my humble abode with acute interest. When she catches me staring at her, she smiles brightly. "It's so cute!"

"Thanks." I'd like to think she's being genuine. She was never evil like Penelope, but she was an enabler all the same, sitting back, saying nothing. "Have a seat."

I feel her gaze on me as I pour us each a glass of ice water.

"You look *amazing*."

I snort, peering down at my ensemble—a baggy blue-and-white charity run T-shirt and a ratty old pair of sweatpants that I turned into shorts by cutting off the legs.

"You're super pretty now. I mean, you *always* were, but you look good with long hair. And you're crazy fit. Not like me." She laughs in a self-mocking way, shifting in her chair at my kitchen table. "I *wish* I could still eat five thousand calories and not gain weight, like back in high school."

I can't help but do another fleeting scan of Becca. She's still cute, her hair that same warm honey-blond shade but cut to her shoulders and layered; her broad smile is still her best feature. But she has filled out some, her once-skinny cheerleader form morphing into something more akin to her mother's pear-shaped figure—smaller on top and heavier on the bottom.

"My mom said you're going to be teaching at Polson. I'm a teacher there too!" She tries for another round of excessive enthusiasm that reminds me of her younger version, bouncing around on the football field. "It's my second year. I had fifth grade last year but I'm taking seventh grade this year. Anyway, we're going to be coworkers, so I thought it'd be a great idea to come by and say hello. I know when I started last year, it was scary. I didn't know anyone or anything, and a lot of the teachers there have one foot in retirement. They don't put any more effort in than they have to, so you won't get much help from them." She's rambling. She's nervous, I realize.

"That's nice of you." I set the glass of water in front of her.

Becca sighs heavily. "I was a jerk to you in high school. I'm sorry. I don't have an excuse for it—you never did anything to me."

"I never did anything to Penelope either." It slips out before I can stop myself.

"Except be Dottie's daughter. *And* date Shane for that summer." She raises her hands in a sign of surrender when she sees my scowl. "Penelope has *always* been crazy jealous when it comes to him. She went psychotic on *me* once when Shane gave me a hug!"

"Really? But you guys are best friends." As much as I don't care what happened, I find myself desperate to mine any valuable Shane-related information that I can.

"We *were*. Until our first year of college, when everyone was back in town for Thanksgiving. She accused me of trying to steal Shane from her, even though he'd already broken up with her by that point." Becca shrugs. "What can I say, she showed her true colors. Of course, she blamed her pregnancy hormones, but she hasn't been pregnant for a long time and she's *still* a giant bitch."

It takes a moment for her words to register. "Wait, Shane dumped his *pregnant* girlfriend?" My faces screw up. What kind of asshole does that, even if it is Penelope?

"He didn't know she was pregnant when they broke up," Becca defends. "And she was cheating on him *big* time."

My jaw drops. Penelope *cheated* on Shane? She had him all to herself and she threw that away for another guy?

Becca looks at me curiously. "Wait, you didn't know about all this already?"

"I left this place behind when college started and didn't look back." The only person who could have relayed anything was my mother, and if the story doesn't involve her as the main character, she tunes out instantly.

Becca gives me a sympathetic smile. She must have an idea what I was running from, what I've gone through with my mother. Everyone knows who Dottie Reed is, but no one knows better than Margaret Ann. "There are still rumors floating around that Cody's not Shane's biological son." She waggles her eyebrows suggestively. "Anyway, I cut ties with Penelope after that fiasco. I'll say hi to be polite if I see her around, but I have no time for mean girls in my life. Especially now that I'm dealing with the pint-sized versions of them. That's draining enough. It was a bit awkward, though, having Cody in my class."

"You taught their son?" I ask absently, my mind working to create a visual of Penelope and Shane's son. *If* it's even Shane's son.

"Yeah. Polson Falls is *way* better than the elementary school in Dover, so they send him here. I had him last year. He's a good kid, overall, and one of the popular ones, of course. You'll like teaching him."

I choke on my water. "Wait, what do you mean? *I'm* teaching their *son*?" Does Shane realize this? I think back to our conversation the other day, about me teaching sixth grade. What did he say again? It was going to be "interesting." Is that what he meant? Interesting that *I*'d be teaching Satan's spawn?

"Thank God he's an easy kid, too, because Penelope's one of *those* parents. You know, the kind who thinks their kid poops rainbows and should get special treatment." Becca prattles on, seemingly unaware of my mortified reaction. "And then there was all the drama between her and Shane. She tried to get him back for years. I heard things were *really* ugly between them for a while. She even used Cody as leverage, threatening to take Shane to court for full custody. Stupid way to say, 'I love you, please take me back,' right? At one point, I heard Shane refused to be in the same room as her. I don't blame him. But, she's finally over him. Thank God, for Cody's sake, more than anyone." She tsks. "Poor kid."

"Are you sure she's over him?" I ask warily.

"Oh, yeah." Becca's head bobs furtively. "She's pretty serious about Travis. That's the guy she's living with now."

Does Shane know this? Of course, he must. They share a son. Does he care that she's screwing them both? Or, a small hopeful voice preens in the back of my mind, is it possible that I've totally misinterpreted that exchange between them on the porch this morning?

"It's what I heard from Josie Hilton, anyway, and she always knows the good gossip." Becca starts listing names of people I might remember—with much younger kids than Cody—but I'm still stuck on this flood of new information. Will I have to sit across from my desk at parent-teacher conferences and act like the three of us don't have any history? Do Shane and Penelope come together or does Penelope handle the school stuff?

Will she remember me?

Will she still be an enormous bitch?

"Crazy, huh?" Becca asks, pulling me out of my thoughts.

"Yeah. Crazy," I mumble in agreement. This entire situation is getting more complicated by the day. "I had no idea Shane was going to be my neighbor until the day I moved in." And now I can't seem to escape him.

"Bet that was a nice surprise." Becca's eyes light up with amusement.

"It was definitely a surprise. I wouldn't call it a nice one."

She grimaces. "Has he said *anything* at all about what a jerk he was to you back then?"

"He apologized." I shrug, playing it off as no big deal. Because it shouldn't be. And yet hearing Becca acknowledge his appalling behavior makes me feel oddly better. Maybe I wasn't entirely invisible to *everyone* my senior year.

"I think losing his NFL dreams and becoming a dad knocked his ego down a few pegs. He's actually turned into a nice guy. Helps out a lot around the community. He's always part of any charity events."

"Being a nice guy was never Shane's problem." He was always nice, especially to the female population. Even when he was crushing their hearts.

"Right." Her lips twist. "He's still a *huge flirt*. It doesn't look like he's in a rush to settle down."

What does that mean? Is he fucking every eligible woman in a hundred-mile radius of Polson Falls? Offering a side of dick with every smoke alarm test? I'm beginning to sound like Justine.

Becca drops her voice conspiratorially. "He's the big ticket at the charity auction every year. Raises *a ton* of money."

"Oh my God." I shake my head as the pieces click. I can't believe I hadn't put them together already. Shane's a firefighter, and hot as hell. *Of course* he'd prostitute himself for the children. Does it stop at dinner and a movie with his prize winner, though?

At least my mother can't afford him.

"They can fall over him all they want. *No*, thanks. I'm over that."

"I don't blame you." Again, with that sympathetic wince. "But, hey, we all did stupid stuff back then. You wouldn't believe *half* the things the kids are doing these days, and they're not even teenagers yet. There are a couple you need to be ready for." She waves the turkey sub she brought, as if trying to tempt me.

Pushing aside my wariness at this new connection—or rather reconnection—I settle into the chair across from Becca. It'll be nice to start my new job with an ally.

THIRTEEN

Shane's truck rolls into his driveway at seven on Monday, the night before school starts, as I'm deadheading the last of my late-blooming Shasta daisies—thank you, Polson Falls Public Library, gardening section, for helping me identify what's on my property and what the hell to do with them.

Ever since my lunch with Becca, I've been replaying what I saw and heard that morning on Shane's porch in hopes that I misinterpreted it, and telling myself that I don't care either way.

The truth is, I *must* care, because I'm still thinking about it.

And despite every intelligent fiber in my body telling me I don't care that Shane is home, I can't ignore this hum of excitement that ignites inside me, seeing him again.

He hops out and stretches his arms over his head, as if cramped from a long drive.

"Holy shit …" Wherever he took off to, it didn't involve basic grooming. His jaw is covered in a thick layer of stubble, only adding to the wild mane of unkempt wavy hair atop his head.

He spots me in my yard and tosses a casual wave before heading over with a confident, relaxed swagger.

"Where on earth have you been?" I eye his loose tank top,

trying my best to focus on the dirt streaks on his arm and not on the muscle that's peeking out along the sides.

"Camping. Upstate New York." He loops his thumbs in the low arm holes of his top, pulling the cotton far enough away to flash me a glimpse of his impressive chest.

I swallow against the sudden dryness in my mouth and avert my gaze farther south to his powerful legs. Nothing hints of his devastating knee injury except for the surgical scar obscured beneath dark hair. "Like, *camping* camping?"

He grins. "Like sleeping bag under the stars, catching our dinner in the lake, sitting by the fire. Just me and a bunch of the guys."

So, no women, I note, with far too much relief.

I sniff. A waft of smoke, bug spray, and sweat touch my nostrils. "Yeah, smells like it." Oddly enough, on Shane, it's far from unpleasant.

He bursts out in laughter, his eyes twinkling mischievously as they roam over my yard. "You finished painting."

"Yeah." Not just the fence, but my living room, and front hall too. It's amazing what a fresh coat of a neutral gray can do.

"Looks *really* good, Scar. Hasn't looked this good in years."

I smile. "Thanks." This exchange is ... nice. Civil.

And yet is it just me or is the air between us electric?

"So, you ready for your first day tomorrow?"

"I think so." Becca has turned out to be a godsend. She helped me navigate around the school, introducing me to staff and procedures so I could swiftly set up my room. Then, this past Saturday night, she arrived on my porch with a bottle of wine and her class picture, to walk me through my students, highlighting the brown-nosers and the troublemakers, the ones with challenges at home, the best friends and worst enemies, the frenemies.

Cody was in the class picture too. He looks like Penelope, save for his brown hair.

I hesitate. "I'm teaching Cody this year." Wendy Redwood handed me my class list and there it was—Cody Rhodes.

I'm not sure what reaction I was expecting from Shane with this news—perhaps a cringe, at how awkward this might be? But he smiles secretively. "Good."

"*Good?*"

"Yeah. Maybe having a hot teacher will finally make that kid want to go to school."

My stomach flips. There he goes, flirting again. Does he realize what it does to me?

Of course, he does.

"Good luck tomorrow." With a wink, he turns to head back toward his house, his track shorts clinging to his ass.

I can't help myself; I need to know. It's been driving me insane. "So, you and the Red Devil are still a thing?"

His feet stall. "What?"

I instantly regret saying anything. "Nothing."

He turns, his face filled with confusion. "No, seriously. What are you talking about?"

I sigh. "I saw Penelope at your house before you left. *Early*."

Realization dawns over his face and he laughs. "No, we're not together. She's living with another guy. Has been for almost two years."

"So, what was that about?" If it was a booty call, he wouldn't admit it to me, would he? I watch him closely.

"She stopped by on her way to work to get me to sign some paperwork."

"*Paperwork*," I repeat doubtfully. "At 7:00 a.m."

"Yeah. So she could take Cody to Montreal to visit her friend. I had to sign an authorization letter that said I was aware she was taking him across the border."

My mouth drops open as whatever skeptical retort I was going to throw out dies on my tongue.

I really needed this.

As if I'd ever withhold it from you.

They were talking about a stupid form for their son.

I struggle to squash my sigh of relief, but I suddenly feel a hundred pounds lighter. Maybe he isn't still the douchebag player, after all.

Shane saunters back over to the fence, his palm sliding along the post as if testing the smoothness of my paint job. "I'm not with Penelope. I'll *never* be with Penelope again," he says slowly, clearly, as if to make sure I can't possibly misinterpret that. "I'd rather saw my own dick off then let it anywhere near that woman."

I wince. "That's a tad drastic." And it would be tragic, if what I saw while spying from my window is any indication.

"That's how serious I am." His hard expression amplifies his words. "The only thing I don't regret about her is Cody. I'll never regret him."

Even if he's not really yours? Does Shane question it? Does he know one way or the other?

So not a question I can ask at this stage in our neighborly relationship.

He sighs heavily. "Do you think you can try to forgive me for the stupid, regrettable shit I did when I was seventeen, and give me a chance to *at least* be your friend?" He emphasizes the "at least," as if he's gunning for more. Or maybe that's what I want to hear.

I swallow. The last few days have been enlightening for me, especially now that Becca and I are on the path to camaraderie once again. If I can't forgive this man for something he did when we were still kids, maybe I deserve to be labeled a shrew. "When you say it like that ..."

The smile that takes over his face is devastating. "You know, you seemed bothered a minute ago. Like you care who I'm with. Or care that I'm with anyone."

"I don't." I adjust my tone so it doesn't sound so clipped—so false. "You can do whatever you want. Or *whoever* you want," I add, on impulse. "If you don't mind, though, can you close your bedroom curtains on those nights?" Because I'd hate to catch a glimpse of it, no matter what lies I tell myself about Shane being with another woman not bothering me.

His eyes narrow as recognition sets in.

I've just outed myself.

Yes, you've undressed in front of your uncovered window.

Yes, your neighbor knows you sleep naked.

Yes, she's a peeping Jane.

"*Only* on those nights?" he finally asks. He doesn't seem the least bit embarrassed.

I, on the other hand, feel the back of my neck burning. "I'm broke. I need free entertainment." I make a point of ogling him. "You'll do, I guess." What am I doing? Am *I flirting* with Shane? Have I gone mad?

He crouches opposite me, meeting me at eye level across my picket fence, his powerful, shapely shoulders within reach of my fingertips.

"What?" I ask warily.

He hesitates. "What if I said I wanted *you*?"

My traitorous heart hammers inside my chest, the possibility that Shane is pursuing me again far too thrilling given our past. I wasn't expecting that. It's bold. Then again, Shane never lacked confidence.

I try to play it off with a derisive snort. "You're kidding, right?"

He peers intently at me. "What if I said I wasn't?"

There are too many what-ifs in this conversation. Yet, the way he's acting right now—his heated gaze darting to my mouth, his lips parted, his breathing audible—I'd say his intentions are far from wishy-washy. None of it matters, though.

I steel my spine. "I told you, you can't have me again."

"Is it because you have a boyfriend?"

"I don't have—" *Oh, fuck. Joe.* I keep forgetting about him. "No. Not because of him. We broke up anyway." Why did I just say that? Joe was a solid alibi.

"You don't seem too upset about that."

I shrug. "It was inevitable. Long distance and all."

He seems to weigh that for a moment. "So, you're single again?"

I'm struggling to suppress my smile. Shane so blatantly pursuing me isn't as easy to shrug off as I expected. "More like happily unattached."

"Is it because you're not attracted to me anymore?" He manages a straight face for all of two seconds before it splits into a smug grin.

I can't help my laugh, even as my cheeks flush. We both know damn well that I *am*; he's caught me gawking too many times to argue otherwise. "Someone came back from his brush with nature loving himself a bit too much." I'm sure it serves him well when he's posing for calendars and selling his wares on stage for charity come December.

"Nah." He reaches out to snap a spent Shasta daisy off its stem. "I just had a lot of time to think about things while I was away. About things I want in life."

My pulse races. What does that mean? What things? Shane was thinking about *us* while away? About *me*? Becca said he didn't seem to be in any rush to settle down, but has that changed?

He rests his arms over the top of the fence and stares at me, and there is a knowing glint in his eye. A challenge. He's waiting for me to say more. Or maybe he's expecting me to melt into a puddle at the slightest sign of his interest.

Been there, done that. I won't allow myself to be *that* girl again. But I'm also realizing that I don't want to be at odds with Shane anymore.

"I'd be willing to *try* to make friends work," I offer. "But just know that I don't trust you. I probably never will."

"*Never?* Seriously?" He winces. "But it was so long ago."

"It doesn't matter how long ago it was." I hesitate. "You hurt me." It's terrifying to declare that to him, as if I'm making myself vulnerable.

He licks his lips. "There's not much I can say except that I'm sorry. If I could go back in time, I'd do a lot of things differently." He adds that last part quietly, more to himself.

It's comforting to hear him apologize—again—but he's right. We can't change the past. "Let's just keep things as they are, okay? Simple." And brimming with sexual tension.

His piercing eyes are locked on mine. "If that's what you want."

What I want at this moment is to trail him into his shower and help scrub every inch of sweat and grime off his tanned, hard body. With my tongue. "We're neighbors. And you have a kid with Penelope." I can't hide the appalling tone from my voice when I say her name. "*And* I'm Cody's teacher." Is there something in the rule book about screwing your student's father?

"So, let's not complicate things. I get it." He sighs with reluctance, the sound boosting my confidence. "I guess I can do just friends."

Let's hope *I* can.

I take in his features, focusing on the scruff along his jawline. I'm not sure if I prefer him this way, or clean-shaven. "You're not keeping this thing, are you?" Impulse possesses me, and I reach up to drag tentative fingertips through the bristle, testing its prickliness. What would it feel like to have that scraping along the insides of my thighs?

Shane leans into my touch, his lips parting.

I pull my hand back as if I've stroked an open flame. Touching Shane is just as dangerous.

"What are you thinking about?" Goddammit, his voice has turned husky.

I'm thinking that remembering why I shouldn't get tangled up with Shane Beckett again is getting harder with each passing moment. "That you really should grab that shower." I sniff and curl my nose for effect, though he doesn't smell that bad for a guy who spent days sleeping in a campground.

A low, deep chuckle reverberates in his chest. With a heavy sigh, he climbs to his feet. "Do I need to draw my curtains tonight or can you control yourself?"

"Depends what you're doing in there." I'm flirting again. While I should be appalled by myself, instead a thrill courses through me.

He flashes a mischievous grin—and those dimples—as he backs away. "I'll be thinking about a certain elementary school teacher. Should be a good one-man show."

Oh my god. He actually went there. "Friends don't masturbate about friends!" I holler after him, his sordid promise warming my thighs.

A gasp sounds. I turn to catch the dirty look from a couple as they walk past, their beagle pausing long enough to lift his leg against my freshly painted fence. *Son of a ...*

I duck my head and focus intently on the last of the Shasta daisies until the people have rounded the corner, all while the reality that I've just smashed open Pandora's box with a sledgehammer looms.

This is Shane Beckett I'm dealing with, I remind myself. My first love, my first heartbreak. Still the most beautiful man I've ever laid eyes on. Rationally, I can't stop myself from being attracted to him.

What I can—*must*—stop myself from doing is acting on it.

FOURTEEN

I don't know who else Penelope was screwing at the time, but Cody Rhodes is, without a doubt, Shane's son. I couldn't see it in the tiny class picture but he has the same shade of hair and beautiful, whiskey-colored eyes as his father.

Unfortunately for Cody, the rest of his features firmly resemble his mother. It's like having a young male version of Penelope Rhodes staring back at me in my classroom, his T-shirt two sizes too big for his skinny frame. For his sake, I pray the boy inherits his father's physique when he hits his growth spurt.

I peel my gaze away from him and calmly take in the entire group of eleven-year-olds settling into their seats—nine boys, sixteen girls—twenty-five kids who look like they'd rather be anywhere in the world but here. They know that's not an option, though, so they've at least made a solid effort. Most of them are wearing squeaky new shoes and prudently selected first-day-of-school outfits. Of course, there are the few whose families can't afford new things. Their shoulders are slouched as they silently evaluate their classmates, hoping no one will notice that their generic sneakers are the same ones they wore last spring, only with fresh laces. I recognize those kids. I was one of them, once.

I take a deep breath and plaster on a brave smile, though inside I'm a nervous mess. "Good morning, everyone. I hope you all enjoyed your summer vacation and are excited to be back."

Groans carry through the room, but I ignore them, letting my smile grow wider. This is *my* classroom. These are *my* young minds, ready to be molded and impressed upon. I've dreamed of this moment for years. "I'm Ms. Reed, and I'm excited to be teaching you."

"So?" Becca sidles up beside me to rinse her coffee mug at the staff-room sink. Her pink, button-down blouse is a shock of color against the drab beige walls, and it complements her blond locks nicely. "How was your morning?"

"Good! I think? Hot, though." The school isn't equipped with central air, and the fans I've strategically positioned in the corners have done little to help, especially with twenty-five prepubescent bodies packed into the room. By the end of math, my navy dress was clinging to my damp skin and students were staring vacantly at me from their desks, like sweaty little red-faced zombies, uninterested in anything I had to say.

"Tell me about it. Some of my male students haven't embraced the value of regular showering and deodorant yet and they *really* should, especially in this heat." Becca scrunches her nose. "I don't understand it. My mother never had to remind me to bathe when *I* was twelve."

"My best friend still has to remind her boyfriend to shower sometimes, and he's *thirty-three*. She has *a lot* to say about gross, smelly boys, though."

Becca laughs. "Is she a teacher too?"

"Justine?" I snort. She doesn't even like children. "No, she's a recruiter for a skilled trades agency." She deals with construction workers, electricians, plumbers, and the like all day long, the majority of whom are men.

"That's ..." Becca's nose scrunches. "I wouldn't have the first clue how to do that job."

"Yeah, neither did she, and she hates it, but she's really good at it. She fell into it after college." Her uncle needed an assistant and she needed a job, so she stepped in. The next thing I knew, she had her own office and box of business cards, she was interviewing machinery operators about their background, working trade fairs, strolling around our kitchen in her underwear while discussing copper fittings over the phone, and a thousand other things that bore me to tears when she tries to explain them.

But I'll forever be amused when I watch her—a dainty, dark-haired nymph—open her mouth and make a three-hundred-pound male welder blush with her brash words.

Becca smiles. "She sounds really interesting."

"She is. I miss her a lot. She's coming to visit this weekend, actually."

"Oh, that sounds like fun." I can't help but note the waver in Becca's smile. Along with the rundown of my students, Becca updated me on her life over the past decade. The latest change was her moving back to Polson Falls after breaking up with her boyfriend of two years—the older brother of a girl she says we went to school with who I don't remember. She's been single ever since and, though she didn't come right out and say it, I think she's lonely.

I hesitate, but only for a second. "Hey, you should come out with us, if you don't have any plans. We're just going somewhere local."

"Maybe I will. Thanks for the invite." She smiles softly. "I'm glad you moved back to town, Scarlet."

"Yeah, no worries. It'll be fun." Though Becca's liable to lose her jaw on the floor after ten minutes with Justine.

I busy myself with filling my water bottle at the cooler before the staff room gets crowded.

"How was Cody?"

"Fine. He's quiet, but he seems like a good kid. Despite his mother being Satan."

A snort escapes Becca before her expression smooths over. She glances around, as if checking to make sure no one else heard me. Maybe it's uncouth to label your student's mother the Antichrist on the first day of class, but it *is* Penelope Rhodes we're talking about. She had half the school believing I was working as a cam girl at fourteen years old. "I guess he got *some* of his traits from his father, at least."

"Who *is* Shane, by the way."

Becca frowns curiously. "How do you know? Did you ask Shane?"

I snort. "Are you kidding me? No. But look at Cody's eyes, with those gold flecks around the irises?" He stopped at my desk before heading for recess and I got tangled in them for a moment. "And he has his dad's dimples. And when he smiles, the corner of his mouth, right here"—I tap the edge of my mouth —"buckles like Shane's does."

"Oh, *wow*."

"What?" I ask warily.

Becca grins, as if she's just discovered something exciting. "You still have it bad for him."

"No, I don't!" I shake my head to emphasize my words. "He's an arrogant ass."

"Who you still have a crush on," she says matter-of-factly.

"Do you not remember what happened between us? Besides, I'm a thirty-year-old woman. And a teacher. I don't have a silly crush on my neighbor," I scoff.

"Thirty-year-old single teachers can have a silly crush on their smoking-hot neighbor." She raises her hands in surrender at my warning glare. "Okay! You're right. I believe you." She hides her amusement behind a sip of water. She does not believe me.

Playing my words back in my head now, I'm not sure I believe me either. "Besides, it's not like anything could happen between us. I'm teaching his son."

Her lips purse. "I don't think there's an official rule against it."

"Maybe not, but it would be frowned upon."

"Yeah, I guess," she agrees with reluctance. "Unless you kept it under wraps for this year. I mean, you're old school friends and next-door neighbors, so it's not shocking if you're seen together. No one *needs* to know what *else* you're doing together." She waggles her eyebrows.

"Secret relationships with my student's father is not how I want to start my teaching career here." Lies and scandal. That sounds right up my mother's alley, not mine.

Becca sighs heavily. She must sense she has no chance to persuade me otherwise. "But, still … wouldn't that be romantic? You two getting back together after all these years?"

Several more teachers filter into the staff room for lunch-hour recess, thankfully halting that conversation from going any further.

Becca wasn't exaggerating when she said half the staff here have one foot in retirement. The early-morning conversations I've heard so far all revolve around grandkids and countdowns to winters in Florida. Becca and I are two of the youngest staffers, part of what Wendy has referred to as "the new wave." She claims that within five years, Polson Falls Elementary will be run by entirely new faces. Wendy herself must be thinking about retirement soon.

We exchange smiles with Karen Faro and Heidi Mueller—two primary grade teachers—and then shift into a corner to allow them space to use the sink.

"So, will our first paycheck deposit by close of business Thursday night or Friday morning …" My question drifts as a woman sweeps into the room and glides to the refrigerator, the wooly material of her faded black dress—far too heavy for this heat wave—swirling around her Birkenstock-clad feet.

"Holy shit. Madame Bott *still* teaches here?" She always insisted on being called *madame*, though I doubt she has a French bone in her body. Tension curls through my limbs as childhood memories flood back. I didn't see Madame Bott here last week while I was setting up. I would have remembered. I'll *never* forget the woman who cornered me in our classroom at recess, holding a picture of her husband in her white-knuckled grip, demanding to know if I'd seen him with my mother recently.

I *had* seen him—from my bedroom window as he was dropping off my mother late the night before—but I'd played dumb. Even at nine years old, I knew those adults were doing something wrong.

"It's Mademoiselle Parish now," Becca whispers. "Her husband left her for one of the mothers on their daughter's soccer team."

Didn't see that one coming.

I watch the woman, who must be in her early fifties, while absorbed by a strange sense of déjà vu. Age has added softness to her waistline and weight to her jowls. Jet-black hair that once reached her tailbone is now threaded with gray and sits at her chin in a frizzy bob.

As a child, she intimidated me with her dark, calculating eyes and her thin smiles, and the way she was often caught muttering to herself. We were convinced she was a witch. She could still pass for one.

"Does she still wear that talisman necklace with the bird feathers and the—"

"Yup." We share a look. "Last spring, one of her students broke his leg and insisted she put a hex on him for not finishing his assignment."

"I guess some things haven't changed." One thing that *has*

changed is me. I'm an adult. An equal. I won't be intimidated by this woman ever again.

Flinty, dark eyes suddenly swing in our direction, landing on me as if homing in on a target. "Scarlet Reed."

My back stiffens. I don't remember her voice being so shrill.

Her lips stretch in a thin smile as she saunters over. "Wendy said she hired you."

I force a polite smile. "Hello ... Mademoiselle Parish, is it?" I wait for her to wave off the formality and suggest her first name. We *are* both teachers now.

"You came back. I heard you'd left, but you're back." She says it in an airy way, as if she's learning this just now, through some unseen source.

"Yes, I did. Mrs.—I mean, Wendy—made me an offer I couldn't refuse."

Her shrewd gaze roams my facial features, as if sizing them up, as if sizing *me* up.

Yes, I remember what you did all those years ago, I want to say.

Yes, I could have gotten you into hot water had I reported it. I probably still could.

Does she feel guilty?

I steal a glance at her necklace and the beaded eye staring back at me. She used to stand in front of the class and claim she was "all-seeing" as she toyed with that thing between her lengthy fingernails. Students called it her witch eye.

Did it see Mr. Bott banging the soccer mom?

She makes an odd hissing sound between her teeth. "You look like your mother." I note a distinct edge in her tone, one fortified with distaste. "Time will tell," she mutters under her breath, so low that I barely catch it. She turns on her sandaled heel and strolls out of the staff room, her lunch bag dangling from her fingers, her lips moving unintelligibly.

"Okay, that was weird. Even for her." Becca grimaces. "What did she say, at the end?"

I never uttered a word to anyone about that exchange with Madame Bott all those years ago, and there's no point doing it now. "Nothing new." It's just another line item on the long list of shit I've dealt with for being Dottie Reed's offspring. What's jarring is that I forgot what this felt like—being judged for my mother's sins, and by people who should focus more on their own mistakes. I forgot what it felt like to have someone look at you and ponder if the clichéd apple-and-tree metaphor was accurate.

I sigh, hoping the act will shed the uncomfortable cloak that comes with that old identity. If I let it get to me, I'll start regretting moving back to Polson Falls.

No, some things haven't changed at all.

Shane's front door creaks open as I'm hauling cans of paint from my trunk. My attention veers to his porch before I can stop myself, and my stomach flips with a nervous flutter at the prospect of seeing him.

But it's Cody who trots down the steps, a football tucked under his spindly arm. When he spots me by my car, his brow furrows first with recognition, and then surprise. It's still surreal to me that Shane has an eleven-year-old son.

My arms are weighed down by paint supplies, so I offer Cody a smile and nod.

He responds with a half wave.

Shane emerges a moment later, and my stomach does a second nervous flip. He hasn't shaved yet, his face still scruffy. I intentionally avoided peeping into his bedroom window last night, but I assume he showered.

"That's my new teacher," I hear Cody say in his boyish voice.

"Oh yeah?" Shane's gaze touches mine for a moment before it

drops to scan the paint cans in my hands. "What's her name again?"

I stifle a snort. He's playing dumb. How cute.

"Ms. Reed."

"Don't you think we should go over and help Ms. Reed?"

"But you said we'd play—"

Shane snatches the football from his son's impatient grasp and trudges toward me. "Hey, there!"

Cody lingers behind, kicking a loose stone with his sneaker, reluctant to follow.

"Go long!" Shane hollers over his shoulder.

That seems to perk the boy's spirits. He takes off, his skinny legs pumping fast as he tears across the sizable front lawn. That's the great thing about our houses—deep lots. He reaches the other side of their yard just as Shane stops next to me, balancing the pigskin between the tips of his fingers. I forgot how big his hands are.

"Heard you had a good first day." His deep voice is melodic and soothing.

I inhale the delicious scent of bergamot—yes, he showered. "Cody said that?"

"Maybe not in so many words." He smirks. "But his grunts were definitely happy grunts."

I chuckle as I consider my day. Yes, the teaching part went off without a hitch, despite the stale air and oppressive heat in the classroom. "Did you know Bott is still teaching there?"

"Yeah, Cody asked to move schools before eighth grade." Shane shudders. "That woman freaked me out when I was a kid."

"She *still* freaks me out."

He crooks his neck to check the label, and I admire the hard lines of his jaw. "What are you painting now?"

"The kitchen."

"White?"

"Yeah. I figured that'll give it a fresh look, and maybe I'll resist burning it down before I can afford to renovate."

He winces.

"Oh, sorry. Should I not joke about things like that with a firefighter?"

"Not if you're being serious."

I laugh. "I'm not. I love my house. Old, rotted pipes, creepy basement, and all."

"Good. Because I've seen people do some crazy shit for insurance claims."

"Even in Polson?"

"*Especially* in Polson. What about those?" He juts a chin toward the three other gallon cans in my trunk.

I sigh, dreading the upcoming task. "Those are for the bedroom." And the sooner I finish, the sooner I can hang my curtains and artwork. There's something about waking in chaos every day that leaves me feeling … well, chaotic.

"I'm working this weekend, but I should have some time next week, if you want help."

Why does Shane's casual suggestion stir such excitement? "No, I'm good, thanks."

He gives me a doubtful look. "I've been up there before. It's a pretty big room. With a lot of edges. Are you sure?"

"That inviting you into my bedroom for *any* reason is a terrible idea? Yeah, I'm sure."

"I'd be on my best behavior. Scout's honor." The devilish smile he flashes and the way he studies my mouth suggest otherwise.

And here we are, flirting again.

"*Dad*!" Cody calls out, impatient.

"Yeah, yeah." Shane winds back and launches the football into the air with the same effortless grace he had at seventeen. The ball smoothly lands in the cradle of Cody's arms. "Yup. Still got it." Shane caps it off with a playful grin.

I can't tell if he's referring to football or his looks. Yes to both, but he doesn't need his ego stroked. "Eh." I shrug, feigning indifference.

His jaw drops. "What do you mean, 'eh'? You saw me play in high school."

"A few times."

He snorts. "Yeah, right. You went to *all* the games. You'd sit up on the right side, near the announcer booth. It was like it was *your* spot. For *years*."

I frown. "You saw me there?" He never told me that. I assumed I didn't exist to him before that summer we dated.

"Of course, I did. You wore this long, red-and-black sweater that you'd hug around your body like you were cold, even when it was seventy degrees out. I always felt like I should run up there and give you a hug."

I *did* always wear that sweater. It was old and ratty, and I loved it. And my fifteen- and sixteen-year-old self would have died from happiness had Shane Beckett run into the stands to even acknowledge me.

"You stopped coming senior year," he murmurs, more to himself, his brow puckering.

How could I go? I couldn't be in the stands after that summer, couldn't handle *not* existing to him again, couldn't bear watching Penelope maul him between quarters.

Shane's staring at me with an odd expression now. Has he finally figured out how far back my wild crush on him went? That the *only* reason I ever went to the games in the first place was to watch him? I didn't care if the team won. I wanted *him* to win.

I offer another nonchalant shrug. "What else was there to do on a Friday night around here?" *Besides pine over Shane Beckett.* Desperate to change the subject, I nod toward Cody, who is shifting the football from one hand to the other, waiting for his father to stop gabbing with his teacher so they can toss the ball. "How often do you have him?"

Shane follows my gaze. "This week? Tonight and Thursday. Penelope has him for the whole weekend. We try to alternate. It all depends on my schedule, but she usually works with me on that."

"That's nice of her," I offer begrudgingly. If I'm giving Becca and Shane another shot, maybe it's time I consider wiping the slate clean with her too. Or at least ease up on the satanic name-calling.

"Dad!" Cody whines.

"Just give me another minute, bud! Here, let me carry those up for you." Shane reaches for the handles, his hands sliding over mine and settling there. The simple move has brought him well within my personal space. I'm acutely aware of the heat radiating off his body as he looms over me, waiting for me to let go—or maybe he's enjoying the contact as much as I am.

This feels as good as it did when I was seventeen, when he'd weave his fingers through mine.

Scratch that. It feels *better*.

I make the mistake of looking up, and I get caught in the gold flecks of his irises and fringe of long, dark lashes. It brings me back to so many years ago, to warm summer nights when we'd stand like this and I'd stretch on tiptoes and revel in the softness and skill of his lips. He always was an incredible kisser.

He exhales and his breath skates across my cheek. The urge to find out if his lips feels better now than they did at seventeen overwhelms me. Suddenly, it's impossible to remember why I won't allow this—us—to happen again.

"Hey, Dad! You ready?"

Cody.

I snap out of the spell and shake my paint can-laden hands free of Shane's touch—and free my sensibilities from his magnetic charm. I take a pointed step back. "Seriously, Shane, I can handle this. I don't need help."

"Were you *always* this stubborn?"

"Were you *always* this desperate for my attention?" I throw back but soften the cutting words with a smile. "Go and play with your son. I can handle carrying a few cans of paint on my own. I'm not one of your damsels in distress."

He watches me intently, as if he wants to say something more.

"What?"

He gives his head an almost indiscernible shake. "Nothing. We're having lasagna tonight. Plenty for three."

"You eat a lot of lasagna."

"It's all I'm good at making," he confesses with a chuckle. "And that kid is picky as hell. So? What do you say?"

Eat dinner with Shane and his son? He throws that invite out so casually. Wouldn't it be weird for Cody to have his teacher over for dinner? Would it make him question what's going on between his father and me? Or maybe I'm reading way too much into the invite.

Either way, it's probably not a smart idea. "I have dinner made, but thanks anyway."

He nods to himself, as if he expected that answer. "Another time, then?"

"Maybe." I march toward my front porch, silently enjoying his continued efforts. When I reach my steps, I steal a glance over my shoulder to find Shane sauntering backward, still watching me, an unreadable smile on his lips.

Has he figured out that he's wearing away at my defenses? That one of these days, I just might bend, then break?

It's tempting.

He doesn't notice the football flying toward him until it slams into his backside. He jumps—more from surprise than anything, I think—and curses, but follows it up with a chuckle, as Cody's childish giggles sound.

My own laughter follows me into the house.

FIFTEEN

"What'd you say this place used to be?" Justine's hazel eyes rove over the interior of Route Sixty-Six as she takes a long slurp from her pint.

"Italian food. Luigi's," Becca confirms, inspecting the edge of her glass for cleanliness with a pinched brow. When she ordered a Blue Lagoon, I had to kick my beer-loving best friend beneath the table, warning her to not mock.

We never ate at Luigi's, growing up. My mom said it was overpriced and she didn't like the vibe. From what I'd seen of the place, standing outside and looking in, it appeared a cozy, family-type establishment, with red-and-white-checked linens and murals of Tuscany.

It resembles nothing of the Italian restaurant now, though, the inside lined with chalky-black board-and-batten walls and decorated with strings of industrial-style light bulbs that dangle from an equally black ceiling.

"Was it any good?" I ask.

"Oh, yeah." Becca nods fervently. "We used to come every year for my mom's birthday. It was sad, when Luigi died." She points at a spot not ten feet away, her voice dropping to a whisper, "Massive heart attack, right over there."

Justine grimaces at the spot as if the corpse of the old owner were still there. "Didn't need to know that."

"But it's good to see this place doing well!" Becca counters, beaming. "The patio is really nice, with the river next to it. Too bad it's raining tonight."

"At least we got a table inside." Despite leaving the city early, Justine got tangled in Friday rush-hour traffic and the two-hour commute stretched to three. The steak sandwiches she grabbed from the diner down from our apartment—one of a few things I miss about living in Jersey—were cold, the bread soggy, by the time she rolled in.

Becca warned us that Friday nights here are "hopping." I don't know why I didn't believe her—maybe because we're in Polson Falls and I assumed her version of busy would be vastly different from mine. But when we arrived at nine, the last of the families were filtering out, replaced by an upbeat, youthful crowd clad in cute dresses and stylish jeans. There's even a bouncer at the door to card anyone who looks too young to take advantage of Friday night's deal on shots and domestic beer.

We snagged the last table available—a six-person booth with faux-leather backs and a dim conical pendant providing a low cast of light—but people seem content to linger around the bar, their hands filled with drinks, their voices with laughter.

In the far corner, three guys in torn jeans and faded T-shirts are tuning their instruments. The singer, a straggly haired man in his thirties, reappeared moments ago, his clothes damp from the rain, a waft of cigarette smoke trailing behind him as he passed our table.

"So, tell us who you've slept with here?" Justine asks with no preamble, her inquisitive stare locked on Becca.

Becca chokes on her drink. "Uh … if we're going to be playing Truth or Dare tonight, I think I need a few more of these."

"Ignore her. I do, all the time." I pass Becca a napkin to dab the dribble on her chin.

"What? I'm just helping you get the lay of the land." Justine smirks. "Get it? *Lay*?" She's distracted by two guys who stroll past, checking us out on their way by. "Who are *they*?" She tracks their backs with a keen, obvious stare.

"Not sure, but they look *really* young."

"Just how Justine likes 'em," I tease.

Becca frowns, hesitates. "Don't you have a boyfriend?"

"I did, but he left me for another girl."

"She's joking," I say quickly as Becca's eyes widen with shock. "His name is Bill and he's amazing. Justine has been in love with him for *years*. He's in Boston with his *daughter* this weekend."

"Not years," Justine corrects, waggling her finger in the air. "I did *not* love him during those years that he was with that snake, *Debra*."

"They're getting married soon," I continue, ignoring her.

Justine rolls her eyes but the playful smile emerges after a few beats. She won't admit it, but I know she's anxiously awaiting a proposal. Unfortunately for her, Bill is a bit gun-shy after his first disastrous marriage.

"Oh, this sounds like a juicy story." Becca sucks back a large gulp of her drink, settles onto her elbows, and asks in a singsong voice, "So, tell us, how'd you meet?" It's a prompt for a get-to-know-you conversation if I've ever heard one. And it's a smart move—if there's one thing Justine could talk about for hours, it's the saga that is her and Bill's love story.

"Well ... I've known him since I was three ..."

I listen absently as Justine regales Becca with the history of her crush on her older brother's best friend—I could tell it myself, I've heard it so many times—while I search the faces around the bar. I don't recognize *anyone*, based on a cursory scan. But I've been gone more than a decade, I remind myself. People come and they go. People change. *I've* changed.

This town has definitely changed. We never had a place like this when I was growing up—one of the reasons I knew I had to get out as soon as I could. Options were the Patty Shack, McTavish's Pub—my mother's favorite—Luigi's, and a handful of fast-food pizza joints and café-type shops. For an adult in search of a fun night with a club-like atmosphere, you were wrangling a DD to take you into Philadelphia, more than an hour away.

But Route Sixty-Six has changed that, and it appears people appreciate it. There's a mix of ages in here tonight. Some are younger than me by eight or nine years, barely legal to drink. Others have graying temples and heavy lines marring their foreheads. If tonight is any indication, this place isn't going to have trouble staying in business.

An electric guitar strikes a few solo chords and then, without any sort of "Hey, how's everyone doin' tonight" introduction, the band goes straight into an Imagine Dragons cover. A round of claps erupt as people pivot their attention toward the singer. I'm riveted by the rich, melodic voice that doesn't match his unkempt appearance.

A heavy body suddenly drops into the empty spot beside me, making me jump.

"Thank God! I was worried I wouldn't have a seat." Shane nods to the band. "They're good, huh?"

"What are you doing here?" I blurt, unable to hide the surprise from my voice as I take in the pleasant sight of him.

"Meeting the guys for a beer." He smirks, studying my face. "Is that okay?"

"Yeah. But I thought you were working this weekend." Can he tell that my pulse has gone from normal to racing in an instant?

"Tomorrow morning. Hey." He nods to Becca across from us and then leans in to grin at Justine, tucked into the corner of the booth beside me. His arm brushes against mine in the process and cool droplets of rain coating his forearm dampen my skin. "Hey, Scarlet's cute friend from Boston."

"Hi, Scarlet's Sexy Neighbor," she throws back, never one to shy away from flirtatious banter.

I elbow her in the ribs as I slide over to put space between Shane and me. Seriously, Becca's the only one on her side of the booth. There's way more space. Why didn't he dive in there?

"Looks like it's raining pretty bad out there?" Becca stares at him with eager, excited eyes. They're practically sparkling. If Becca stared at him like that when Penelope was around, it's not a surprise the Red Devil thought she was after him.

"Yeah, it's pouring. I got soaked in the twenty seconds it took to get from my truck to the door."

I steal a sideways glance to see him pick at the damp cotton of his black T-shirt clinging to his chest. "When'd you guys get here?" He looks to me for an answer.

"Not long ago."

He pushes a hand through his wet hair, slicking it back some, as he surveys the bar area, his attention stalling on the band. "These guys always draw a crowd."

"I was just thinking how good the singer is …" My voice drifts as a tall man appears beside Shane, dropping a hand on his shoulder.

"You made it!" Shane says, exchanging a quick, friendly handshake.

"It's shitty out there." The new guy's murky green eyes flip to me and a familiar, impish grin spreads across his face. "Bex told me you were back."

It takes me a second to clue in, and when I do, my jaw hangs open. "Steve *Dipshit?*" I hardly recognize him. He's put on *at least* fifty pounds—little of it muscle, based on the belly that stretches his shirt—and his brush cut does nothing to hide the receding hairline.

Beside me, Justine sputters on her beer, trying to muzzle her bark of laughter.

"Uh …" He chuckles, his cheeks flushing. "Just Steve is good."

I shake my head. "Sorry. I didn't mean ... That slipped out."

"Don't worry." Shane smirks at me. "He probably deserves it."

"Yeah, probably," Steve admits sheepishly.

Becca shimmies out of the booth to throw her arms around his neck. "It's been awhile! How are you? How's Nicole?"

While they get lost in private conversation, a hulking figure slinks up to our booth, far more quietly than Steve's arrival. This one, I recognize immediately. Unlike Steve, Dean Fanshaw has not changed all that much, other than growing taller and wider. And so much more attractive.

"*Hello* there," Justine hums with appreciation.

Shane's eyes flash to her—he heard that. "You remember Dean, right, Scarlet?"

"Of course." I smile up at the blond, brawny guy, as memories of him behind the wheel of his red pickup truck flood back. He's enormous now, his body rippling with muscle. Almost too much muscle.

"He works with me, over at the fire station."

Dean smiles shyly as he pushes his wet hair off his face, the subtle move highlighting his thick arms and the ink that decorates one. He always was quiet, compared to the others. No less popular with the girls, though. Especially not with those dimples that rivaled Shane's. What he lacked for in smarts—he was the walking stereotype of a meathead jock—he more than made up for in a kind disposition. He was *always* nice to me, to the point that if Shane weren't blocking my access, I might consider sliding out to give him a hug.

"You guys order yet?" he asks Shane, his voice deep and smooth but familiar. A shiver of nostalgia dances down my spine to happier times that summer we all hung out.

"Nah. We'll go up to the bar. It'll be faster. Grab you ladies another one?" Shane pats my thigh beneath the table. It's a simple gesture, almost an absentminded nudge to complement his question, and yet I feel the pleasant burn of his fingers against my leg.

Justine waggles her half-empty pint in the air. "Beer me. Albatross. Get your cute neighbor one too."

"You got it." Casting one last smile and another leg pat my way, he slides out of the booth and heads for the bar, elbowing Steve on the way.

"So, did I hear that right? *That* guy's in the calendar?" Justine asks, ogling Dean.

"He's a firefighter too. I don't know about that." *Right.* The hell if Dean isn't in a calendar that flaunts Polson Falls' finest bodies. He's probably also on the Hunky Hero auction block.

She arches her eyebrows. "You're getting a copy of that for your house."

"Uh, hell no. Have you seen those things? The guys all strike awkward, cheesy poses that are *not at all* natural or attractive. Nobody actually enjoys looking at them."

"Judgy much? And besides, it's for *the children*!" She presses her hands to her chest with mock concern. "How can you deny the children food and warmth and puppies and—"

"I should *never* have told you about that stupid thing."

"But you have, and now you must indulge me, your very best friend in the whole world."

I sigh. "I have a calendar, remember? And it's for eighteen months." It'll carry me through all next year.

"You'd rather sit in your kitchen with a cup of coffee and look at pictures of insects mating than imagine mating with one of those two?" She nods to Shane and Dean who are using their impressive size to cut through the crowd to the bar, turning heads as they go.

What if I said I wanted you?

My stomach flips as Shane's words replay in my head. I haven't told Justine yet that I *could* already be mating with one of them. He's certainly making it hard for me to remember why I shouldn't like him. What happens when he reappears with drinks and settles into the booth again? More alcohol mixed with his persistent charm, and my resolve is liable to melt into a puddle. The night could end up very differently than I'd anticipated. Namely, me in Shane's bed.

Would it really be *that* bad an idea?

I need to let go of the past, accept his apologies, and give him another shot. What if he has changed? What if we could be happy together, as adults? Of course, there is still the complication of Cody. Maybe I should limit this to one dirty night together for the time being?

I push the illicit thoughts aside before they have time to take root. The truth is, my body is vibrating with excitement now that Shane is here, and if I'm not careful, tonight will shift from a few drinks at the local bar with the girls to a possible life-altering event before I've had time to weigh the consequences.

"You know, I'm learning some valuable tips on how to handle men from that calendar you gave me."

"Oh yeah? Like what?" Justine asks dryly.

I suck back a gulp of my beer. "September's the month of the praying mantis."

Her loud cackle cuts through the music and hum of voices.

———

"Roger would call his mother every time we had a fight. Can you believe that?" Becca's voice turns shrill. "*Every time*! And he still has her do his laundry!"

Justine tsks. "Count your blessings. You don't want a mama's boy, believe me. Bill can't make anything but ham sandwiches."

Becca hiccups through a giggle and her hand flies over her mouth. "I should have eaten dinner."

That, and not chugged so many Blue Lagoons. Her cheeks are flushed, her speech is slurred, and she's divulging every sordid detail that pops into her head. In just the past twenty minutes, we've learned that Roger is the only guy she's ever blown, he makes a suckling sound while he sleeps, and he showers in scalding water immediately after sex.

Good riddance to Roger.

But at least Becca's miserable ex-boyfriend stories have helped distract me from my growing disappointment as I watch Shane. He swung by to drop off a round of drinks forever ago and was about to take a seat beside me, only to be called over to another table by a guy I don't recognize. From there, he keeps getting pulled from one group to the next, floating like the proverbial social butterfly, lingering much longer where there's a pretty female in the conversation to bat her lashes at him.

And they *all* bat their long, artificial lashes at Shane.

But the one he's been chatting to for the past fifteen minutes —a knock-out gorgeous blond with a petite but curvy figure and full, red lips that stretch across half her face—has brushed her fingertips over his arm at least a dozen times.

Nobody touches *anyone* that much unless they're having sex.

"What do you think?" Justine's sharp elbow pulls my attention back.

"Huh? About what?"

"You and Becca come to Jersey for the weekend. We'll go to Tinderland. She wants a rebound."

Tinderland is a cesspool of drunk single people congregating under one roof with hopes of finding an easy lay, aptly named after the hookup app. I've been twice and wanted to bleach the sleazy innuendo off my body after both times. I'm still getting to know Becca, but there is no way she is made for a place like that. "Who is that blond with Shane?"

Becca glances over her shoulder. "Who, Susie Teller?"

"I guess? Do I know her?" Her name doesn't sound familiar.

"Uh ..." Becca's nose scrunches up in thought. "Maybe? They dated back in high school. She went to Connor High. She was on the cheerleading squad. *So* pretty."

"Yeah, I've noticed," I mutter through a gulp of beer. I don't remember her on the field at those games, but I was never paying attention to anyone besides Shane. He did have a penchant for cheerleaders, though. Apparently, he also has a thing for flirting with old high school flames.

"She works at the fire station."

"She's a *firefighter*?" I can't hide the shock from my voice. I'm all for female empowerment, but there's no way that tiny body can haul anything heavier than a wet cat down a ladder.

Becca shakes her head. "In the office. She's the chief's administrative assistant."

The chief … as in Chief Cassidy, I presume. The man my mother bid on—and won, for what was likely a sordid night—last year.

I can just make out Shane's dimples from this angle. His smile widens as he talks, and Susie Teller's head falls back as she belts out a boisterous laugh, her silky golden waves reaching halfway down her back.

I grit my teeth as she reaches out to slide her hand along his forearm—again—pausing at his biceps. "They look like good friends," I observe, hearing the strain in my voice as I picture where this night is leading, if she keeps pawing him like that.

How different tonight has turned from what I allowed myself a moment to imagine, not long ago. And, if I'm being honest with myself, I'm drowning in displeasure over it.

"She's only been back for a couple of months, from wherever she was. Atlanta, I think I heard."

How long have they been flirting at work?

Have they slept together?

"I ran into her at the grocery store last week." Becca slurps the last of her drink, seemingly oblivious to the tension building in my shoulders. "Penelope *hated* her in high school, of course. Trash-talked her any chance she could, but she's actually *really* nice."

I'm sure she is, and I have no right to dislike her because I have no claim over Shane.

But I dislike her all the same.

"Twenty bucks says they fuck tonight!" Justine bellows in my ear.

I glare at my best friend, but she merely grins back. She's goading me. She can see that I'm jealous.

"You're an asshole. You know that, right?"

"Are you going to keep pretending you don't give a shit and just sit here, watching some other woman make a move on him? Or are you ready to go over and stop this?" she prods, unperturbed. "Before you lose your shot."

I begin sliding out of my seat.

"Attagirl!" She claps—with far too much glee.

"Relax, Heidi Fleiss. I'm just going to pee."

"*Boo*!" they shout in disturbing unity.

Both are drunk now. *Fantastic*. "Grab me another round when our server comes by, if she doesn't cut you off." I smooth my shirt over my waist and weave through the throng, keeping my head high and my shoulders back.

The closer I get, the more of Susie Teller's bright eyes and perfect skin I can see and the more uneasy about their connection—or reconnection—I grow.

I make a point of easing past Shane slowly, hoping to catch a hint of their conversation or, better yet, to distract him from Susie Teller entirely.

"I'm free on Wednesday night. Why don't we try that new steak house in Dover?" I hear her shout over the band.

My stomach sinks. They're making dinner plans. I'm *already* too late. Now, I'll get to sit back and watch Shane start dating the beautiful new girl at work. With my luck, he's going to fall in love with her and hang his bachelor hat at the door. She'll move into his house, and they'll live happily ever after with their blinds wide open so I can watch them have rabid porn-star sex from my dark, lonely bedroom.

I rush past and into the empty restroom near the back, an odd, cold flush coursing through my body. I duck into one of two stalls, unable to ignore how eerily familiar this scenario feels to my first day of senior year. Except I'm not about to cry over Shane. If anything, my tears will be sparked from anger. Not anger at him; he's being himself. No … I'm pissed that I allowed emotions to stir. I told myself I would never care about Shane again, and yet here I am, my insides burning with jealousy and hurt as I watch him hook up with another woman. *I care* that he's been flirting nonstop with me since I moved in. I *care* that he's picking up his coworker right in front of me.

I *hate* that I care.

I need to go home and screw my head on straight.

Finishing up in the restroom, I take a deep breath, steel my nerve, and stroll out. Shane is still with Susie. He's laughing about something she said. And they're standing closer together.

What a fucking asshole.

My mood has soured, and it'll only go downhill from here. It's best I gather Becca and Justine and get the hell out of this place now.

"Hey, Pacino!"

Ugh. My head snaps toward the bar to where Steve waits. I'm glad I let "Dipshit" slip out earlier.

"Come on! My treat." He jerks his head toward the bartender who's busy pouring straight liquor into a line of shot glasses, then waves the bills in his hand. Dean's with him.

Doing shots with two of Shane's best friends while Shane is angling to get laid on the other side of the room is the *last* thing I'm in the mood for tonight. I'm about to give him a curt head shake "no" when I hesitate. Why the hell am I running away? To what? I'm going to hide in my house, depressed? I was having fun before Shane showed up and started pulling his shit.

Plus, Dean looks *good* tonight, leaning against the bar in his jeans and T-shirt, the cotton stretched across biceps that I doubt I could close my coupled hands around. He clearly spends a lot of time working on that body. I'll bet he doesn't have an ounce of fat on him.

And he's intently watching me. Whatever shyness normally lingers there is gone, replaced by a layer of assuredness. Dean's comfortable in his skin.

Suddenly the plan of running home and hiding with my jealousy while Shane makes his move on Susie Teller doesn't sound nearly as appealing as, say, getting over Shane once and for all by getting under his attractive best friend.

What an idiotic idea, that tiny voice warns in the back of my mind. What a completely juvenile, stupid, likely regretful idea, that a smart, well-adjusted, educated, thirty-year-old woman—a teacher!—knows better than to entertain.

I stuff that little voice of reason into a corner where it can't distract me, take a deep breath, and cut through the crowd toward the bar.

"This asshole soaked my jock in aftershave before a game!" Steve stabs Dean in the arm with an angry finger. "My balls were on fire. I had to leave five minutes into the first quarter!"

"You weren't there to screw up the plays. That's why we won the game," Dean counters.

A cackle of laughter escapes me. "Oh my God, I think I remember that!" Steve hobbled off the field, looking like he'd been riding a horse for seven days straight and yanking at his crotch. "I heard it was because you had an STD."

"People were saying I had the fucking clap! My mom brought me ice all night and kept insisting I show her how bad it was. I know she's a nurse and all, but no fucking way am I dropping trou so my mom can inspect my sack!" Steve says with horrified flair, earning our boisterous laughter.

I don't know how these guys are feeling after three shots of Jim Beam in quick succession, but my head is swimming, my emotions have numbed, and I'm suitably distracted for the moment.

"I thought you were nicer than that." I lean against Dean's broad chest to give him a playful nudge with my shoulder. He smells like soap. It's not bergamot, but it's far from unpleasant. Neither is being this close to him. I'm not normally attracted to guys this muscular, but Dean has a handsome, chiseled face. Plus, I know I won't fall for him, so he's safe in that regard. Does he still like to screw around like he did in high school? He never was one to have a girlfriend, though he was practically mounting Virginia Grafton at every opportunity that summer Shane and I were together.

"I *am* nice. Not to this guy, though." He juts his chin at Steve. "He's a jerk."

"He *was* a jerk to me in high school," I agree somberly.

"That's why I did it. For you, Scarlet." He peers down at me with mock seriousness for a moment before a playful, crooked smile touches his full lips.

"I guess I owe you a thank-you." Flirting with Dean is surprising easily. "Thank you, for burning Steve Dipshit's balls for me."

His eyes twinkle as he chuckles, and the deep sound vibrates through my limbs.

I give him a second nudge and this time, his arm curls around my body in an affectionate squeeze. He relaxes his grip, but his arm remains slung lazily over my shoulder. His gaze remains settled on my lips.

"What's so funny?" Shane's voice suddenly sounds behind me.

Despite my best effort to remain calm, my body stiffens.

"Just reminiscing about the old days," Steve says, pounding the bar with his meaty fist for another round of shots. It's an obnoxious move but the bartender doesn't seem to care. He must be used to Steve.

I stall against the urge to turn and acknowledge Shane for one … two … three seconds. When I finally dare to look, I find his attention on Dean, his eyebrow arched in an unspoken question. I check behind him. Susie Teller is nowhere to be seen.

Thank God.

I can't read what's being communicated between the two men, but I note how Dean's arm flexes, pulling me in a touch closer.

"You guys look like you're getting into it tonight." Shane peers at the fresh line of shots. "How many have you had?"

"Who's counting?" Steve holds one out for him.

Shane shakes his head. "Nah. I'm good. I gotta be at work at eight in the morning." He nods toward Dean. "So do you, dumbass."

"Yeah, but I can handle my liquor better than you," Dean answers smugly, taking the proffered shot.

Shane levels Dean with a warning look, his eyes skittering over Dean's arm that's curled around me. I catch the faintest clench in his jaw.

Does this bother you, Shane? I hope so, the wounded voice that's trying to be indifferent mewls in my head.

"One for the lady." Steve thrusts a shot into my hand, and a few drops of the sticky liquid splash over to coat my fingers. "Cheers." The three of us slam the round back.

The emotions I managed to quell momentarily with engrossing stories are rising once again. Despite my better judgment, I meet Shane's gaze.

Fool me once, shame on you. This second time, though? That's all on me.

He frowns. "You okay, Scar?"

"Why wouldn't I be?" I was going for aloof, but I hear the bitchy tone lacing my words.

Steve holds the remaining shot up for Shane, who's already shaking his head. "Going once ... going twice ..."

"Thanks!" I snatch it from Steve's hand and down it, earning his and Dean's laughter.

"I like this version of you." The soft pad of Dean's thumb skates soothingly back and forth over my bare biceps, causing gooseflesh to erupt. Yes, I think I'll enjoy this man's hands and lips all over my drunk body tonight just fine.

Shane watches me intently, as if he's waiting for the moment the intoxicating buzz of two back-to-back whiskey shots takes over and my inhibitions weaken. Too late, I want to tell him. Because that's now five shots and I'm primed to do something that is undoubtedly stupid but will feel damn good while it's happening.

"Hey, I think your friends are looking for you," he says carefully. "Maybe you should go and check on them."

If that isn't a dismissal ... My anger flares. "They'll find me if they need me." Shane definitely doesn't want me hooking up with Dean. Well, too bad. I set my jaw to hide the fact that my next words sting to acknowledge. "But hey, I think I saw your *little blond friend* looking for you a minute ago. Maybe you should go and check on her."

Shane cocks his head. "Who, Susie?"

The one you're trying to screw.

Shane's jaw drops, and I realize I just said that out loud. Apparently five shots of Jim Beam will loosen my tongue faster than any sci-fi truth serum ever could.

I don't notice when Dean removes his arm from my shoulder —or maybe it's me who pulls away from him—but suddenly I'm squared off against Shane in the middle of the bar, boozy courage flowing through my veins.

"Scarlet, I—"

"After all the shit you've been saying to me these past few weeks, *how dare you* try to play me again?" I jab his chest with my finger, making him flinch. "Once wasn't enough?"

"What?" His eyebrows pop. He has the nerve to act surprised. "How am I playing you?"

"Have fun on your *date*."

Realization flitters across his face.

Yeah, that's right, asshole. I heard what was going on.

He falters on his words. "*She* asked me out."

"Oh, *well*, by all means, then, *enjoy*."

His head falls back with a sigh of exasperation. "Fuck, I can't win with you, can I?"

"What? I'm sorry, you thought you'd 'win' with me"—I air-quote the word with an exaggerated crook of my fingers—"by hooking up with someone else *in front of me*?"

He sighs, looks around, as if he'd rather be anywhere but here. "Come on, it's just dinner, with a friend."

"Yeah, a friend who can't keep her hands off you!" I accuse, even as a glimmer of hope stirs in my chest that I've misunderstood this as quickly as I misunderstood Penelope at Shane's front door. Maybe these dinner plans with Susie are just friendly plans, after all. Maybe he's not trawling to get laid on one end of the bar while sweetly flirting with me on the other.

"You're one to talk." He shoots a pointed glare Dean's way.

"Oh, I haven't even *begun* to touch him yet." I make a point of smoothing my palm over Dean's torso, over the hard ridges of muscle, and then letting my finger hook over his belt, giving it a slight tug before letting go. But it doesn't elicit a spark of response in me. I'm too furious with Shane to feel anything—physical or otherwise—for anyone else.

Shane's eyes narrow as they follow the move and then he glowers at his friend.

"Whoa. Hey ... Innocent bystander here." Dean throws his hands up in surrender.

A dark glint flashes in Shane's eyes as he turns back to me. He's angry. "What is this, anyway? *You're* the one who said you didn't want to complicate things between us."

"How am *I* complicating things?"

"Because you're chewing me out for going to dinner with another woman when *you're* the one who keeps turning me down. Do you understand how unfair that is?"

Not just a friendly dinner, after all. That momentary blip of hope is deflated by a sharp prick to my chest. "I told you, I don't care who or what you do!" Thankfully, the band is loud and drowning out our shouts for anyone but Dean and Steve, who are watching with obnoxious, amused smiles. "And you don't get a say in anyone *I* decide to hook up with either!"

Shane crosses his arms over his chest as he looms over me. "Fine! Just not *him*." He nods at Dean.

I match his defensive, arms-crossed stance in a challenge. "And why not?"

"Because ..." He grits his teeth as if trying to keep his words from coming out. "Because you just don't want to, trust me."

"Dude! *Come on.*" Dean gives him a cocked "what the hell" look.

Shane matches it with a severe look of his own. *"Don't,* man. I'm serious. It's *not* cool. She won't be okay with it."

"I wouldn't be okay with what? Banging the hell out of him tonight?" I make a point of ogling Dean from head to toe. "I beg to differ." That last shot is *really* hitting me now.

Dean grins at his friend. "See?"

Between the boozy fog and the growing tension swirling around us, I don't notice the platinum blond until she's snaking past me, her hands pawing muscular male arms in a fraudulent act of trying to gain space as she sashays toward the bar. Lo and behold, they part for her like the Red Sea did for Moses.

"Mom?"

She glances over her shoulder at me and offers a lazy smile. "Fancy meeting you here, darling."

Great. She's in that magical drunken sweet spot, in between being annoyed-sober and belligerent-drunk, where I'm her darling, her honey, her sweetheart.

I try to even my tone. "What are you doing here?" McTavish's was always her Friday-night hangout. She's certainly dressed for it in her skintight, too-short, cleavage-baring velvet black dress that she insists traps men like flies in honey.

"What do you *think* I'm doing here?" She flashes the bartender a playful smile. "The usual, babe."

He nods. "Sure thing, Dottie."

I grimace. As if this night weren't bad enough, now I know my mom is on a first-name basis with the bartender here too. I should have expected as much.

With a glass of chardonnay cradled in her bloodred-clawed hand, she turns to appraise the wall of chest on either side of her. "Hello, *boys*."

Steve grins wide as he peers down at her. "Having a good night?"

"Much better now that you're here, Steven." She winks at him.

Ugh. Mom.

And Steve—fucking Dipshit!—actually blushes. "You know I'm a happily married man." He waggles his ring finger in the air to show off the simple gold band.

"I know. Too bad for me." She mock pouts before turning her sparkling blue gaze to Dean. She quirks a well-drawn brow. "What about you, big boy? Care to show me what new things you've learned?"

I want to crawl under a table and die. I need to get out of here right now, with or without Dean. But in the back of my mind, her words roll around, gaining purchase.

What *new* things he's learned?

What does that mean?

New things *since the last time*?

A tingling sensation trickles down my spine. When Dean glances at me and I see the sheepish look on his face…

"Oh my God!" My jaw drops as the cold wash of realization hits me. "You slept with my *mother*, didn't you!"

The band ends their set at that precise moment, and my shrieking accusation carries in the sudden silence as surely as if I'd been shouting into a megaphone. Suddenly we have an audience of wide-eyed, gaped-mouth onlookers, barely stifling their titters.

Dean winces. He doesn't bother denying it, though. He would have gone home with me tonight, without mentioning the fact that he's ridden the Dottie Reed train?

Nausea stirs in my gut as curious spectators eagerly gobble up this small-town soap opera. If people around here had forgotten, or if they hadn't known, now *everyone* knows. Yes, the infamous Dottie Reed is my mother. It's like childhood all over again, except now I'm an elementary school teacher. My reputation is that much more important to me.

I shove past Shane and push through the crowd, past our table without a glance to Justine or Becca, and out into the night. The rain is still falling steadily, and in seconds I'm soaked, but the cold quells the overwhelming urge to bend over and purge my stomach's contents.

I make it halfway across the dark, deserted side street beside the bar before a strong hand grabs hold of my biceps.

"Come on, Scar, stop," Shane pleads. I hadn't realized he followed me out.

"Stop calling me that. I hate that!" I don't really hate it—not when it's coming from Shane—but I'm too upset to think clearly right now. I jerk my arm away. "And let go of me."

"Okay, okay." Shane lifts his hands in surrender. "Just … you shouldn't be walking home. Let me drive you."

"It's only seven blocks." I walked that far every day, both in blistering hot and icy cold, when I was far too young to be doing so.

"Seven blocks, in the rain?" He squints up at the night sky, as if pointing out what I must not have noticed.

"I like the rain. It's soothing," I snap. I'm lashing out at him to keep from breaking down in tears. I know this, and yet I can't help it.

"You know what? Fine. Scar—Scarlet. I'm tired of fighting with you tonight."

I mean to start walking home, and yet I can't seem to get my feet moving. "You *knew,* didn't you?" That's what Shane meant when he said I didn't want to hook up with Dean. It had nothing to do with him not wanting me going home with his best friend. I cringe. "God. *Why?* Dean is sixteen years younger than her! He could have *anyone* else." He almost had me. "He's a giant dick for trying to pull that shit, by the way."

Shane brushes a hand across his face to wipe away the rain. "It was, like, five years ago. He had a really bad day at work. He hit the bar hard and Dottie was there."

"Dottie's *always* there," I grumble.

"Yeah. And she always lays it on thick for us. We usually just joke around with her, but that night, Dean took her seriously."

It was one thing when my mother was having her dalliances with random older men but now she's moved on to guys I went to school with? This is too much! "What was I thinking? I should never have moved back to this fucking town!" I yell into the night. Thanks to the rain, no one is out and the street we're standing in the middle of ends fifty feet away, at a dead end before the river.

"Look, I don't know what you want me to say."

"Nothing. It's not your problem. It's mine. It's *always* been mine."

Shane hesitates. "It must be hard to have a mom who's so …" He searches for the word.

"Promiscuous? Trashy? Scandalous?" I've heard all the labels, many times over, back when I didn't know what they meant. I remember running home from the grocery store after one altercation between Mom and a scorned wife and looking up the word *whore* in the dictionary. I couldn't understand what my mother could have done to make that woman so angry.

He grimaces. "I was going to say 'sexual.'"

"She'll sleep with *anyone*. What is wrong with men? Where's the appeal in that?"

"She actually gets around a lot less than you think. It's mainly for show."

I cringe. "How is that better? How would *you* feel if *that* was your mother in there?" I stab the air with a pointed finger, aimed at the bar, my voice shaky.

"I'd lose my shit," he admits.

"*See*? So why is it okay because it's Dottie Reed?" Why are my school peers entertaining her shamelessness, and right in front of me?

"Because she's sexy and she's not any of our moms?" He winces, as if he knows that's a weak excuse. "I don't know. There's something about her."

"Yeah, no morals and a serious dependency on alcohol."

"Maybe." He shrugs. "But it's the way she carries herself, with confidence and no regrets. And she makes men feel good about themselves." An apologetic smile takes over his face. "A lot of guys find that attractive."

I've seen her in action. She's a master of stroking male egos, though, truth be told, it doesn't seem to take much to turn them into her lapdogs. But the way Shane is talking about my mother right now ... My stomach drops with the horror. "Oh my God! *Please* tell me *you* haven't slept with her—"

"No." He shakes his head furtively and follows it with a soft chuckle. "I swear, I never even entertained the idea."

The wave of relief that hits me is overwhelming. It's quickly shadowed by the fact that Shane made dinner plans with his coworker, and he and I both damn well know it's not platonic. He's attracted to Susie.

The knot in my throat swells.

"What do you want from me, Scarlet? I'm not a mind reader." Shane steps forward, closing the distance between us. "You said you just wanted to be friends. You know, because you're Cody's teacher and we're neighbors."

"Yeah. I know what I said." He doesn't have to remind me.

"Did you mean it, though? Because that reaction back in there? That says something completely different." His brow furrows. "I'm trying to respect your boundaries, but they're a moving target."

"I just drank too much," I lie, replaying the evening. Was he flirting with me? Or was he just being himself and I was reading more into it? Was I reading what *I wanted* into it? Nothing is clear to me at the moment. "Date whoever you want." I back away. "Makes no difference to me."

"Yeah, right. You'll just give me the cold shoulder and screw my friends when you find out? Is that how it's going to be from now on?" He shakes his head, and I see his annoyance growing in his features again. "Am I supposed to *not* see anyone until you get over yourself?"

"*Get over myself*?" My jaw drops as I glare up at him. "You've been all over *me* and yet, here we are! The second an opportunity to get laid shows up, you jump on it."

"*She* asked *me*! And it's just dinner," he bellows.

"Come on, Shane. It's never just dinner, not with you." I shake my head. "Don't worry, I get it. I won't put out for you, so you've moved on." A mirthless laugh escapes me. "It's literally high school *all over again*, except this time I wasn't dumb enough to buy any of the bullshit that came out of your mouth. Thank God."

"You think *that's* why I ended things back then? Because I

wanted to get laid?" His voice is laced with grim humor. "That's not why."

"Oh, no, wait. You're right," I sneer. "It was because you cared *too much* about me and you were worried things would get too serious, too fast. I think that's the crap line you fed me, right? And not twenty-four hours later, I see you with your tongue so far down Penelope's throat, I'm surprised she didn't choke on it. You two had already hooked up before we ended things, didn't you?"

He has the decency to avert his gaze.

"Exactly. Don't you dare stand here and tell me I'm wrong about you. Believe me, I wanted to be." I turn to leave.

"You weren't easy, Scarlet."

I snort. *Unbelievable.* "Yeah, I think we've established that you're a giant asshole. You're only reinforcing it."

"That's not what I mean." His shoes scrape against the pavement as he comes around to face me. His features are somehow more handsome, cast in the dim streetlight, marred by frustration. He looks around us, as if contemplating whether he wants to get into this here and now. "I remember the day I got up the nerve to ask out *the* Scarlet Reed, even though people warned me you had this huge chip on your shoulder. You ended up being one of the coolest girls I'd ever met. You were smart, and funny, and sexy. I liked you a lot, right from the start." He pauses a moment, as if waiting for his words to sink in.

"But you weren't like any of the other girls I'd dated. I'm not saying it was bad. It was just … I don't know how to explain it. You seemed so *complicated*. You didn't trust *anyone*. You didn't trust me half the time. You remember the night I asked you out? You wanted to know where Steve was hiding. You thought it was some big joke and they were all watching. When I picked you up that night, you were surprised that I showed up. Like I'd actually be that kind of dick. Like *I* couldn't possibly be interested in you.

Seriously?" He chuckles. "You were on *every* guy's radar in that school."

"Yeah, because they were hoping I was like my mother," I counter wryly.

He shakes his head. "Nah."

"I *heard* them say it. More than once." Laughter in the hallway, conversations the second I left the room, locker-room talk that Jeremy relayed to me in a sheepish voice.

"Yeah, fine. Maybe some of them," he acknowledges. "But not everyone. Not me. I would have held out however long you needed."

"That's easy to say *now,* isn't it? You didn't last past the summer. Guess you missed blow jobs too much after all, huh?"

His face tightens with anger as he glares at me. "Don't pretend you don't remember how *that* night could have gone down."

I study my shoes as my cheeks flush. He's talking about the night we broke up, in his car, when I—teary-eyed and desperate—offered myself up on a silver platter. I managed to get his belt buckle undone before he stopped me. If it had been up to me, I would have lost my virginity to him that night.

"Don't paint me the asshole, Scarlet," he says, his voice softer. "I just told you what I thought you'd want to hear—"

"That you were dumping me because you liked me *too much*! *Really*?" I glare at him, challenging him.

"I was seventeen! I was an idiot! I didn't understand things back then. I think I'm starting to. I mean, you didn't exactly have the best role model for relationships." He nods toward Route Sixty-Six, to where my mother sits inside, unashamed and unapologetic of how her actions continue to affect me, even now. "You want me to say that what I did was shitty? Sure, yeah, it was. I was a dumbass with pro football on the brain. I wanted easy and straightforward, and you were *not* those things."

"But why *her*?" Of all the girls he could have left me for, why did he have to choose the one who had tormented me for years?

"I knew what I was getting with Penelope." His lips twist with grim amusement. "Ironic, how *that* turned out."

Tension hangs between us as I struggle with how I feel about his admission. I don't know if I feel better or worse. Or if it even matters.

He shakes his head. "Look at me, standing out here in the rain, *still* trying to convince you that I'm not trying to use you," he mutters more to himself. "You're *still* so fucking complicated, Scarlet."

"I guess you better get back inside to what's *easy*." My voice cracks as I turn to walk home.

He grabs my hand, stopping me in my tracks. "Who says that's what I want?" He tugs me gently toward him. Truthfully, it doesn't take much—nothing at all—to lead me into his broad chest. "I'm not a seventeen-year-old kid anymore." He leans in to press his forehead against mine. "And ever since you came back, I can't get you out of my head."

I close my eyes and revel in the feel of his nose grazing mine, of his lips so close to mine, of his shallow, ragged breathing. Right now, the only thing I'm sure of is that I am *so far* from being over Shane Beckett, and I don't know why I keep fighting it.

He shifts and suddenly we're kissing again after all these years, in the middle of this desolate side street with the rain falling over us. It's everything and nothing like I remember. His lips are soft but more practiced, wasting no time in parting mine to grant his tongue access to my mouth, while his hands brazenly pull me into him, allowing me to feel every hard curve of his body. He tastes like the beer he was nursing for the past hour. I vaguely wonder what my Jim Beam-soaked tongue must taste like, but I quickly push that worry aside as our kiss grows deeper and more fervent, as our bodies press against each other, as the feel of him growing hard between us makes my body ache with need. His cool palm clasps the back of my neck as his fingers weave through my damp hair, vaguely reminding me that it's raining and I'm soaking, but I don't care.

Two beams of light hit us then, followed by a playfully short toot of a horn. We break apart in time to see the approaching car ease past us to park, the driver flashing a knowing grin.

I step away from Shane and edge toward the sidewalk, my pulse racing as grim reality sets in again.

He follows me, frowning. "What's wrong now?"

"The same thing that was wrong five minutes ago. You're making plans with other women."

He sighs. "It's just dinner. And I didn't say yes." He throws his hands in the air. "You were going to fuck my best friend tonight."

"I wouldn't have," I lie. What an idiotic move that was. Why did I go after Dean like that?

"So, what, you were trying to make me jealous? You were playing a stupid head game? Is that it?" The look of reproach he gives me only ignites my anger, but he's not finished scolding me. "*And* you told me you just wanted to be friends. So, what am I supposed to do? Sit at home alone and jerk off while I wait for you to decide you're ready to forgive me for something I did when we were kids?"

"Yes!" I shriek, my anger and hurt exploding in a volcanic mess.

His jaw hangs open a moment. He was not expecting that answer. "Do you know how crazy that sounds?"

"I don't care." Hot tears begin to trickle down my cheeks as I grasp what I want—what I need from Shane—and I'm so happy that the rain is there to hide them. "It's the only way I'll trust you again." Does he not see it? "I was in love with you and you *broke* my *heart*!"

"That summer was *thirteen fucking years ago*," he yells, his voice incredulous and a touch desperate. "Why can't you let it go?"

Justine and Becca come stumbling out the door of Route Sixty-Six, arm in arm.

"I love that movie," Justine hollers, and begins belting out the lyrics to Disney's *Frozen* theme song, off-key, with hiccups interspersed.

"Hey! There you are! I ordered us a Lyft." Becca waves her phone in the air as if to prove it and then points toward the main street. "He's meeting us out front. He's almost here."

I'm not about to argue that I'd rather walk, because Justine appears to be in no shape, and suddenly I don't think I am either.

"Turns out we can't be friends, after all," I say to Shane, who is standing on the sidewalk, his hands on his hips, staring intently at me.

"Yeah, I guess not," he mutters.

I move toward the pickup spot. "Stay away from me."

"No problem there." A moment later, he adds in a holler, "Let me know when you grow up!"

By the time I climb into the back seat of the Honda Accord, I'm struggling to muffle my sobs, my anger and disappointment reaching a boiling point.

"Well ... that was a fun night." Justine lets out a hiccup.

SIXTEEN

I stir to the sound of Justine setting a glass of water on my bedside table.

"Figured you'd want that."

"Thank you," I croak, the dull ache at my temples an instant reminder of last night's whiskey marathon. "What time is it?"

"Just after nine."

I groan. "Go back to sleep."

"I wish. You know how I am."

"Yeah. Insane." In all the years I lived with Justine, I've never known her to sleep in, no matter how late she goes to bed or how much she's had to drink.

She flops into bed beside me, making the mattress shake and my body jolt. "What the hell happened last night?"

"Jim Beam happened." Jim Beam and my attractive next-door neighbor, who continues to dominate my thoughts and spur my most volatile emotions.

"I remember you going to the restroom and not coming back *forever*, and then Shane chasing you out the door. Things are blurry after that. Did we go through the McDonald's drive-thru?" I hear the grimace in her voice.

"Of course, we did because *you insisted.* It was disgusting." I roll onto my back with another groan, the taste of the Big Mac melding with stale booze and morning breath on my tongue.

"You were upset," she notes.

I was more than "upset." I was a hysterical drunk who broke down the second the Lyft driver pulled away. He kept giving me the side-eye and warning Becca—in the front seat—that she'd be dinged for the detailing bill if either of us puked. Who knew Becca, the Blue Lagoon maven, would end up the soberest of all of us?

"What happened with Shane?"

I pick through my foggy memories. "Let's see … I started doing shots and making plans to screw Dean to get over the fact that Shane is dating Susie."

Justine's mouth gapes. "He is *not*!"

"Okay, fine, *a* date. That will turn into marriage, with my shitty-ass luck."

"But he seemed totally into you!"

"Right? I guess, while he's waiting for me, he's going to go elsewhere to get laid."

"Ugh. Dick." Her pretty face pinches. "I hope you called him out."

"Oh, yeah, I'd say so." Was that scene as bad in real life as it's playing out in my head? "We started arguing in the middle of the bar. And then my mom showed up—"

"*What*?" Justine's eyes widen. "Your mom was there and I missed her? Dammit!" For all the stories Justine has heard about the infamous Dottie Reed, she's never met her.

I wince as her loud curse thumps in my head. "Come back next weekend. She'll be there on Friday. And every Friday. Apparently, she's a regular there now too. Of course, she is." There's nowhere in town I'm safe anymore.

"So, she came and then what happened?"

"Oh! Well, then I found out Dean slept with her five years ago and, no, I'm pretty sure he wasn't going to tell me before we hooked up. And the worst part is, I don't want big, dumb Dean." What was I thinking, moving in on him like ... well, like my mother. I shudder at the comparison. "Then I embarrassed myself in front of about fifty people and ran out."

"And Shane followed you."

"Yeah, so we could fight some more and make out in the street."

Justine gasps again. "*No way.*" She's loving this drama.

"Uh-huh." I close my eyes and try to imagine his lips on mine again. I so wish I had been sober for that part of it.

"He's going to break off this date with the other woman, right?"

"I doubt it. I told him I expected him to stay celibate until I trusted him again."

"Yikes."

"And then I told him to stay the hell away from me. They'll probably get married and have babies. I'll get to teach their children too," I add dryly. "Oh, and he said that he broke up with me because I was *too complicated.*"

"Too complicated?" she echoes.

"Yeah. I guess I had trust issues and a chip on my shoulder. I was too complicated, and he wanted easy, so that's why he dumped me and went with Penelope." My archenemy.

"Hmm." Silence hangs as Justine stares up at my bedroom ceiling.

I know that look on her face. "What is it?" I ask warily.

She sighs. "You know I love you, right? You are my person. Like, if I were gay, you'd be my wife right now. Or even bi. I'd take you over Bill in a second."

I smirk. "I'd have to be gay too, though."

"It doesn't matter. You wouldn't be able to resist my charms."

"You're an idiot." And yet her words warm my chest.

"So are you, if you can't admit to me out loud right now that you still have feelings for this guy."

"It doesn't matter if I—"

"Admit it!" she barks, making me grimace at the throb in my temple.

I swallow the rising stir of emotions as I say, "I still have feelings for Shane Beckett."

"Serious, deep feelings," she coaxes.

I sigh with exasperation. "I still have serious, deep feelings for Shane Beckett." Unexpectedly, a weight lifts from my chest. "How stupid am I? He's just going to hurt me again."

She snorts. "I'm the moron who took Bill back six years after he left me to marry *Debra.*" But then she says more seriously, "You still have feelings for the guy. You're not stupid at all, Scarlet." She hesitates. "But he's not wrong about the complicated part. I mean, for the first six months we lived together, I wasn't sure if you liked me."

I laugh. "What are you talking about? We hung out all the time."

"Yeah, because I forced myself on you. I assumed you were only tolerating me and you'd eventually murder me in my sleep."

"Seriously? You're my best friend." I chuckle. "Oh my God, that's so dumb."

"What? You can be intimidating. Ask Bill. He'll tell you. He thought you hated him too."

"I didn't exactly love him at first," I confess. The drama of their relationship has always been off the charts.

"And you're really hard to read. I mean, not for me anymore, because I know you better than I know anyone else in the world, but you don't let people get close to you. You don't trust anyone. And I don't blame you," she rushes to add. "If half the things you've said about Dottie are true—"

"They're *all* true."

"There you go. Look at what you grew up with. You have a selfish mom, you don't know your father—"

"Don't Doctor Phil me, please." The truth is, I'm not blind. I'm acutely aware of all the ways my upbringing and family dynamics are lacking.

"Fine. But in the twelve years I've known you, you've *never* had a boyfriend who you cared about keeping."

"That's because they were all losers." Guys who didn't know what they wanted in life, or only wanted one thing. I saw through all of them from day one and didn't give them an ounce more of myself than I was willing to gamble with.

"Sometimes I think you pick them for that reason." She rolls onto her side to face me. "You know, I used to want to be you."

I smile through my throbbing head. "What are you talking about?"

"If things with a guy didn't work out, you were all Ariana Grande 'Thank you, next.' No tears, no sadness. It's something to behold. It's actually not normal."

"*You* made up for the tears." People who don't know Justine assume her brash attitude equates to thick skin, but in fact, she's one of the most emotional people I've ever met, a surprise to me.

"Yeah, I was a blubbering mess over Bill and then every guy who wasn't Bill," she concedes. "But you? You were unflappable."

"That's not a word."

"Oh, it is a fucking word, trust me. Bill used it during our last Scrabble game and *I* said it wasn't a word, and I lost. Do you know what that asshole made me do? He—"

"Don't!" I hold out a hand in warning. The last time Justine spelled out the kinds of things she and Bill do during their weird strip Scrabble-porn games, I couldn't look at Bill without a vivid —and unappealing—visual for a week after.

"Anyway, you've never been serious about anyone since I've known you." Her brow furrows. "But I'm starting to think it's because you got serious about Shane, and it sounds like he *really* hurt you."

"I was in love with him," I confess. "Or as much as any seventeen-year-old girl can be in love with a boy after a summer—"

"No, don't do that! Don't become that crotchety, cynical old hag who forgets what it feels like! *Of course* you could be in love with him at seventeen after a summer. Look at me! I fell in love with Bill the day he bought me an ice-cream cone, when I was twelve. Twelve!"

She's right. What I felt for Shane was real and it was powerful. It was that all-consuming, can't-think-about-anything-else, don't-want-anyone-else kind of love that, despite how badly he hurt me, only stopped plaguing me after I escaped Polson Falls and didn't have to see him every day.

And now I'm back in Polson Falls and seeing him every day again.

I tuck my sheet into the crook of my neck, attempting to find comfort. "I hate that he's dating someone else." Especially after he made me think there was something real between us.

"*A* date," Justine corrects.

"That will probably end in him sleeping with her," I grumble, as I struggle to push out the image of them standing so closely together, and her pawing at his body, and him allowing it. *I* want to be the one pawing at his body. Why did it take last night's debacle for me to finally admit that to myself?

Because I'm too stubborn for my own good sometimes. Because I thought I was protecting myself by denying it.

And maybe Shane's right—that he isn't doing anything wrong by dating other women, that I don't have the right to expect him to just sit around, waiting however long, until I come to terms with the fact that I want to give us another shot. I just don't know how to let myself do that. It would mean making myself vulnerable to him again.

"Last night, Shane told me to grow up."

"Ooh." She winces. "Pulling out the immaturity card. Bet that hurt."

"I probably deserved it." Why did I have to respond in such a foolish way? Beyond my hurt, my embarrassment is swelling. What if one of my student's parents—besides Shane—were around to witness that?

"Are you going to apologize?"

"I don't know yet. I mean, he's dating other women. Maybe it's best we stay away from each other."

"Or maybe you should at least give him a clean slate for a few *hours* and see what happens." She shrugs. "Who knows? Maybe you'll decide that what you used to like about him actually annoys the shit out of you now. Like, you know how Bill has to always have the last word, whenever we're talking about *anything*. And he makes up all these stupid 'what-if' scenarios that aren't *ever* going to happen, with aliens and viral pandemics. I used to think they were funny." She gives me a flat look. "They're not funny anymore."

I've witnessed this firsthand and have to agree; Bill can get annoying. "You're still with him, though."

She grunts in answer.

"What if Shane doesn't annoy me?" Speaking of 'what-if' scenarios …

What if I fall harder for him than I did when I was seventeen?

What if he's everything I want for my future?

And what if he gives it to me, only to take it all away again?

Justine grins. "Don't worry. I'm sure you'll screw it up somehow. You know, because you're emotionally stunted."

I haphazardly swing a loose pillow at her head. "Shut up, you brat."

"But I do think you need to shit or get off the pot, Scarlet."

I cringe. "I *hate* that saying."

"Really? I love it. Reminds me of my gramps." She smiles wistfully. "Anyway, I don't think you can hold it against Shane for going out with other women while you keep turning him down. And you can't keep playing whatever game this is. You'll drive yourself mad."

"Aren't you the one who said I should play the player? Cat and mouse and all that?" I remind her wryly.

"Yeah, but that was before I knew you were seriously hung up on him. Plus, I am perpetually immature. And spiteful. I slashed Bill's tire when I thought he was cheating on me, remember?"

"Vaguely." One of many of Justine's dark, insidious secrets that I will take to the grave.

"Don't *ever* take my advice."

I pull my sheet over my head. "I think I need more sleep."

The mattress lifts as Justine climbs out of bed. "I'm gonna make a pot of coffee. Will you be up for greasy eggs and bacon in an hour?" Another of Justine's post-drunk proclivities.

"I don't have any eggs or bacon."

"What kind of establishment is this?" she scoffs.

I listen to the soft pad of her bare feet as she heads downstairs and then let myself drift off to the fuzzy memory of Shane's lips on mine, my internal conflict swelling.

The truth is, I already know, deep down, that I want to give Shane another shot, no matter how dumb an idea that may be, no matter how much he might hurt me again.

I'm just terrified I won't survive getting played by him a second time.

The faint waft of bacon stirs my senses. It takes me a few moments to process that Justine must have made a grocery run, which means she's cooking up a full brunch buffet.

I smile, knowing she'll fix a heaping plate and bring it up to lure me awake. Breakfast in bed sounds good right now—

The high-pitched shrill of the smoke alarm sounds, followed by Justine's shrieks. "Fire! Help! Oh my God, *fire*!"

I bolt out of bed and charge down the stairs.

"How was I supposed to know your stove is a fucking death trap? You should have told me!" Justine yells through a bout of coughing, waving a dishcloth in the air to help disperse the haze of dark smoke out the open side door. "I went to pee and I came back to flames!"

"I didn't know *this* would happen. Iris just said it sometimes acts up!" I set the emptied fire extinguisher on my table, my limbs shaking and my pulse racing from the adrenaline. It's hard to tell, given the white residue coating everything, but there doesn't appear to be much damage, aside from the charred stove top and scorched tile behind. The most severe casualty is the bug calendar that hung on the wall, its pages turned to black ash.

"Acts up? Your stove 'acts up'? What does that even mean? I almost burned down your whole house!" Justine's bottom lip wobbles. God, not the wobbly bottom lip. If she doesn't get a hold of herself, she's going to melt into a sobbing mess on the floor.

"But you didn't," I say calmly. Had I not had the fire extinguisher here, though … I shudder at the thought. "And it wouldn't have been your fault."

She throws the dishtowel to the sink. Blinking back tears, she smooths her disheveled ponytail with her fingers. "Okay. You are going upstairs and getting dressed, and then we're going out to buy you a new fucking stove. One that won't try to kill you."

I sigh. "Fine." I'm getting paid next week anyway. I should have enough room on my credit card.

"And it's being delivered this weekend, *before* I leave."

"Okay." When Justine's upset, she gets bossy. I've learned to just let her get it all out.

"But first, we're going to get breakfast, because I'm starving and my perfect bacon is now charcoal." She throws an accusatory hand toward the pans.

The last thing I can think about is food, but Justine's mood will only deteriorate without her grease fix.

"And I don't want to hear how broke you are or that you have to sell your body on the street to pay for it. You are buying my meal."

I laugh. "Okay! I'm so sorry, Justine. That scared the shit out of me too."

The corners of her lips twitch. "Good. Hurry up and get dressed."

My ears catch the faint sound of a siren. I don't think much of it as I head toward the stairs, but it grows louder and louder …

And louder.

Until the wailing stops outside my house.

"Is that for us?" Justine and I share a panicked glance and then run to the window that overlooks my front yard.

"Holy shit." My stomach drops as I take in the enormous red truck pulled into my driveway and the swath of bodies in full yellow firefighter gear charging across my lawn. "Did you call them?"

"*What*? Oh, yeah. While I was running around like a goddamn chicken with my head cut off, screaming 'fire!' Does that count?" she asks sarcastically.

"Well, someone must have."

Heavy boots storm up my front porch, followed seconds later by shouts and a fist pounding on my front door.

"You probably have about five seconds before they bust that shit down," Justine warns, folding her arms across her chest, making it clear that she will not be handling this.

I curse under my breath, my cheeks flaming as I march

forward, aware that I'm still in my tank top and boxers. I throw open my front door, to find four mammoth bodies standing outside.

Shane is front and center.

"There was a report of a fire?" He doesn't wait for my answer, stepping across my threshold, forcing me back into a corner, his piercing gaze quickly searching the house's interior.

"Yeah, in the kitchen, but it was small and we put it out with the extinguisher. Really, you guys didn't need to ..." My words trail as he storms down the hall. The others follow, brought up at the rear by Dean who offers a small smile—and an overt glance downward that makes me cross my arms over my braless chest—before continuing. I glare at his back. *Dickhead.*

Outside, more firefighters wait by the truck for instructions. Several people loiter on the sidewalk, watching the excitement unfold.

"Could this weekend get any worse?" I hiss, wandering into the kitchen with Justine. We're squeezed against the wall as they quickly survey the damage and radio in a report.

"Like I told you, there's *really* no need for this circus. We put it out." I eye the enormous bodies in heavy equipment filling my tiny kitchen.

"Dispatch got a call from one of your neighbors about screaming and smoke. We can't leave until we've inspected. It's protocol." Shane doesn't sound like himself right now. Maybe he's trying to maintain a professional appearance, but something tells me there's more to it than that, because aside from those few seconds inside my door, he seems to be intentionally avoiding eye contact with me. "What happened?" he asks, pointing at the stove.

"Well, I was cooking breakfast ..." Justine goes into detail, about the glorious meal she was making and the faulty stove top I forgot to tell her about. By the time she's done, two of the firefighters have filed out, leaving Shane and Dean to deal with us.

"Faulty stove top." Shane frowns. "What's wrong with it?"

"I don't know. Iris left me a note and just said the back burner acts up sometimes."

"It *acts up*?" he echoes lightly, his eyes connecting with Dean's where a silent message seems to be relayed. Do they not believe me?

"That's what her note said," I reiterate, my tone sharp. Why is everyone having difficulty accepting the words of a sweet ninety-year-old lady?

The corners of Dean's mouth curl but he smooths his expression quickly with a clearing of his throat. "Good thing you had a fire extinguisher. Most people don't."

"Yeah … Good thing." I steal a glance at Shane, whose focus is on my scorched bug calendar now.

He shifts a pile of ash with his boot. "Didn't think you were serious about burning down your kitchen."

Oh my God. "I wasn't!" I snap. *Elementary school teacher and daughter of local infamous harlot is named arsonist.* The last thing I need is that rumor floating around town. I wish I'd never cracked that stupid joke.

His gaze flickers to mine briefly. "Relax. I'm kidding." There's no humor in his voice, though. "Murphy's in town will give you a ten percent friends-and-family discount on a new stove if you drop my name." He hesitates. "Or use Dean's name, if that works better for you."

I let him see my heavy eye roll. We've moved to the cordial, distant, awkward stage. *Great.*

"I'll be outside. Have a good day, ladies." He strolls out of my kitchen.

"You don't want to leave this stuff for too long." Dean steers our attention to the white residue from the extinguisher. "Hot water and vinegar usually works, but if it's stuck …" His instructions drift as I watch Shane's retreating back down my hall. He looks *enormous* in all that gear.

And this is stupid.

"Hey, Shane!" I trot after him.

He slows. "Uh-huh?"

"Thanks."

"Just doing my job." He says it casually, but there's still that hint of something in his voice—animosity? Reluctance? Annoyance?

"No, I mean, thank you for the fire extinguisher." Finally, he turns to face me and I smile sheepishly. "If I hadn't had it, I probably wouldn't have a house right now."

"Yeah, well ..." He offers a smirk. "What did I tell you? Fire safety's no joke."

"You don't say," I murmur, studying my bare toes as the awkward silence hanging between us grows.

"If there's nothing else?" He waits a beat and then shifts toward the door.

"I'm sorry," I blurt. "Last night was weird. I'm not normally like that. I just ..." *I still care about you.* "My mom and all that." I blame my mother, though my alcohol-fueled emotions got the better of me long before Dottie ever strolled in to drop a cherry on a ruined night.

He nods slowly, biting his bottom lip. "Yeah, it was weird for me too." His gaze drifts over my mouth. Has he been thinking about that kiss since he woke up like I have? I have the urge to kiss him again, just to make sure it's as good in the sober light of day.

Shit or get off the pot.

Justine may be crass but she has a point.

I take a deep breath. "So, listen, maybe we should try—"

"You were right."

"Huh? I was?"

"Yeah. We should definitely keep *this*"—he waggles a finger between us—"straightforward and uncomplicated. I think it's better for everyone involved."

My stomach drops like a rock. Uncomplicated. I think that's my new least favorite word. "Yeah. Right. Of course."

He flashes a playful smile. "Try not to start any more fires, okay?"

"It was the stove," I mutter, watching him stroll out the door, my disappointment swelling. *So, I guess that's a no to dinner, then.*

Behind me, heavy boots plod along my hallway toward the door.

"Thank you for rushing to our aid," Justine says.

"You have any more questions?" Dean's deep voice is grating on my nerves. I want everyone to leave so I can crawl back beneath my covers and die.

"No, I think we're good." She flashes a wide, flirtatious smile and I struggle to hide my cringe. "But, just in case, why don't you leave your number so we can call you?" She opens the notebook that sits on my hallway console table and holds up a pen.

I shoot her a glare behind his back as he bends over to jot down his number. "He's the *motherfucker. Literally*!" I mouth.

"I know," she mouths back. "Prank-call later."

I press my lips together to keep from laughing. Justine *would* do that.

Dean tosses down the pen. "Hey, listen, if you end up buying something from Murphy's, skip the delivery charge and tell him I'll pick it up and bring it here for you. I've got a dolly."

"Are you serious?" I ask, more sharply than I intended. "I mean ... *why*?" Why is he being so nice after last night's debacle? Is Dean dumb enough to think he still has a shot at getting laid?

My question—or more likely my tone—seems to take him back, because he stumbles over his next words. "I just ... I guess I figured you could use the help?" A small frown pulls his brow.

I *could* use the help. I've already been to Murphy's to check out the appliances. They're overpriced *and* they charge seventy-five bucks to deliver.

"Scarlet would *love* the help. And seeing as she almost had

Dottie's sloppy seconds and you feel *super* guilty about that, she's going to take you up on your offer," Justine says sweetly, batting her lashes for effect.

Dean winces. If he were entertaining any ideas of a post-delivery thank-you blow job, I'd say that sufficiently crushed it. "Text me if you end up buying one and I can grab it in the afternoon, after I wake up."

"And you should get Shane to help you," Justine adds.

He grunts at that and then marches out the door and down my steps to join the fray of loitering men on my front lawn.

I spear Justine with another glare. "You enjoyed that, didn't you?"

"It was definitely more fun than the fire. So, what happened with Shane?"

I sigh, eyeing his retreating form as he climbs into the truck. "He took the pot away before I could do *anything* on it. For good, I think."

"I'm sorry, buddy." She smooths a soothing hand over my shoulder.

"It's probably for the best. You know, because of Cody."

"Right." We watch the truck pull out of my driveway and head back to the station, to wait for a real emergency. Thankfully, the neighborhood gawkers are dispersing quickly now that the action is over.

When the truck's taillights are out of sight, Justine claps her hands. "Okay, get dressed. I'm *starving*."

SEVENTEEN

I'm sprawled out in my living room on Sunday afternoon and halfway through grading Friday's surprise math test when a sharp knock sounds on my front door.

With a nervous flutter in my stomach and a quick glance in the hallway mirror, I head over to answer it.

Dean is standing on my front step with a dolly.

Alone.

"Hey." My attention veers to the shiny black truck parked in my driveway and the sizable brown cardboard box. "Is that my stove?"

"I hope so," he jokes.

I force a smile as my disappointment swells, and I realize how much I was counting on seeing Shane. "Are you going to be able to manage that on your own?" Did Dean not mention to Shane that he was coming here today? Or is "keeping it uncomplicated" code for "I'm staying the hell away from your crazy ass from now on"?

"Yeah, no big deal." He gives his shoulder a casual scratch, drawing my attention to his giant arms. It probably *is* no big deal for a guy who looks like he bench-presses refrigerators daily.

"Okay, great." I steal a glance next door before moving back to give Dean room. Both the truck and car are there. Shane's home. He's just not *here*.

Dean's gaze flickers downward over my flirty sundress as he strolls in. "You look really nice today."

"You mean, not hungover?" *It's so not happening between us.*

"Sure." He smiles secretly as he pushes the dolly down the hall and into the kitchen. If he were smarter, I'd think he'd have figured out why I went to the trouble of straightening my hair and putting on makeup, just to grade schoolwork on a Sunday afternoon.

Dean smells freshly showered and is clad in simple jeans and T-shirt, much like the outfit he was wearing Friday night. Except it doesn't stir so much as a spark of attraction in me anymore. What a disaster sleeping with him would have been. For once, my mother's lusty lifestyle has saved me from making a horrible mistake. "How was the rest of your shift?"

"A small collision, a stroke … pretty uneventful." His hands settle on his hips as he takes in my kitchen and the stove that's now sitting in the middle. We pulled it out to clean and have it ready to go. "You did a good job in here. Can't even tell there was a fire."

"Justine's a bit of a freak like that." It took us all afternoon, but the smoke barely lingers anymore, replaced by the pungent scent of vinegar.

"Where is your cute little friend, anyway?"

"She had to head back to Jersey, to her *boyfriend*." She left about an hour ago, to give herself time to do laundry and grocery shopping for the week, though she was reluctant to miss this exchange.

A frown flashes across Dean's forehead. Of disappointment, I gather, at hearing that Justine is in fact not single.

I shake my head at the gall of this guy, ready to move on to my friend now that he has no shot with me. Dean definitely hasn't changed. "Are you sure you don't need help?"

"Nah. I'm good." In seconds, he has the avocado-green fire hazard on the dolly and he's wheeling it down the hall, his arms tensing from the weight. For all his strength, he's a clumsy ox. One corner of the stove hits the wall several times, leaving scuff marks along the fresh paint.

By the third "shit, sorry," I'm gritting my teeth.

"That's okay." I force a light tone and remind myself that Dean is doing me a huge favor. I still have some paint left over and can easily touch up that wall. When he gets to the top of the porch, though, I have visions of him destroying my already-frail stairs that I *can't* touch up with a paintbrush. "Are you *sure* you can manage by yourself?"

"I'll be fine." He pauses. "Unless you're looking for an excuse to go over and see Shane?" He smirks, and something tells me big, dumb Dean might not be so clueless, after all.

"I'll just be over here grading math tests if you need me." I turn before he can see my cheeks burn.

Ten minutes later, I have a brand-new white stove set up in my kitchen and only a few more dings in my walls.

"I plugged it in for you." He flicks a few buttons on and off. "You just need to set the clock. And I threw your old one in the back of my truck. I'll drop it off at the depot for you."

I sigh with relief that this ordeal is over. "I really appreciate this."

"No problem." Brushing a streak of dirt from his hands onto his jeans, he grabs the dolly and begins wheeling it down the hall toward the front door. "Any time you need my help around here, you have my number, okay?"

"Thanks." I used to have a standing offer of help from Shane. Does that still exist?

I trail behind, not sure what else to say to the guy who almost pulled a super sleazy move two nights ago but has otherwise proved to be decent.

We step out onto the front porch just as Shane is heading for his truck, his strides long and purposeful.

My heart does its usual skip-a-beat flutter at the sight of him —in a collared shirt and jeans today. I hold my breath, waiting for him to reroute, to jog over and say hi. Before the debacle on Friday night, he would have. He *always* did.

Now, though, he merely slows long enough to throw a wave at us before climbing into his truck. My chest sinks as he cranks the engine and takes off down his driveway without another glance.

Is this how it's going to be between us from now on?

I may have been confused about what I wanted before, but I know for a fact that I do not want *this*. Maybe Shane is right. I *am* too complicated.

I feel Dean watching me. I force a smile that is no doubt stiff. "So, I guess I'll see you around?" Not at Route Sixty-Six on Friday night if Dottie Reed is going to be there, though.

"Sounds good." Dean takes the first step, then pauses, his gaze veering to Shane's house again. "You know, he was pretty pumped when he heard you were coming back to town."

I'm not sure if hearing that makes me feel better or worse. "I don't think he's that happy about it anymore."

Dean chuckles. "Just give him some time. He'll come around."

"You mean before or after his date?" Is he still going out with her after our big blowup? After that kiss that buckled my knees?

I'm fishing for information and the amused look on Dean's face says he knows it. "Don't worry. He'll get bored with her."

So, Shane *is* going out with her.

"That does *not* make me feel better." When is Shane going to get bored with that beautiful, playful blond? After six months of screwing like rabbits? I'll bet Susie is simple and straightforward. I'll bet she has normal parents and an ordinary life. She knows what she wants, with no crutches, no emotional obstacles, no confusion.

She wants Shane and, while they may have dated before, unlike me *she's* not hung up on their failed high school relationship.

Good ol' uncomplicated Susie Teller.

If Dean can sense my internal distress, he doesn't let on, his bright blue eyes twinkling with mischief. "When he does come around? Maybe don't give him such a hard time. He's actually one of the good ones."

"Yeah, I'm not sure if I'm ready to take *your* advice."

He shrugs. "I never said *I* was one of the good ones."

"No shit." I throw a playful punch into his arm to soften the blow. He *did* help me today.

His footfalls are heavy as he heads down the stairs, carrying the large metal dolly in one hand as if it's weightless. "Hey, that thing with your mom … if it makes any difference, I was so drunk, I don't know how I got it up—"

"Nope. Doesn't make a difference *at all*." I'm sure my horror shows on my face with the visual that is playing out in my head. "And we are *never* going to mention it *ever again, right?*"

He grins sheepishly. "I stuck all the warranty paperwork and the manual inside the oven. You should pull it out now, before you forget and turn on the oven with it in there." He pauses. "Unless you want this stove to *act up* too, so Shane has to come running here—"

"Oh my God, that was a real fire!" My cheeks flush. Do they *seriously* think we staged it? Is that what Shane thinks?

He winks. "Have a good week."

"And *we* didn't call you guys. One of my alarmist neighbors did," I holler after him. If I ever find out who …

Alone in my house again, I venture into the kitchen to pull out the manual Dean tucked into the oven—so I don't forget and inadvertently start another fire while preheating the oven. "What the ..." A Polson Falls charity firefighter calendar is included in the stack of papers. "You've gotta be kidding me." I cringe as I flip through the pages of grinning men striking awkward poses and in various stages of undress—three I recognize from yesterday, none of them particularly fit but all handsome enough in a burly away, I guess. It's as mortifying and cheesy as I anticipated it would be and, by the fourth month, I'm laughing. Maybe that's what it's supposed to do?

And then I reach July, and my jaw drops.

There's Shane, leaning against the red fire truck, wearing only the bottoms of his uniform, sooty fingerprints marring a powerful chest and a thick pad of abdominal muscles. There's nothing cheesy about this picture.

The way he's staring at the camera makes me question why the hell he didn't go the modeling route instead of rescuing domestic animals from trees. Who was lucky enough to leave those fingerprints all over his body?

Just the thought of having that task has my skin flushing.

"It's all fake. Airbrushed." I stuff the calendar into a drawer, along with all thoughts of a future with Shane, the ache in my chest hollow.

EIGHTEEN

I step back to appraise my work.

Yes, I think a periwinkle blue bedroom is *the right choice,* I surmise with relief. And I'm only halfway through the first coat. A splotchy, uneven coat in poor lighting. I began edging as soon as I walked through the front door after work and have been toiling away since, partly because I want this room finished, but mostly to distract myself from the knowledge that it's Wednesday night and Shane is out with beautiful, blond, uncomplicated Susie Teller.

I steal a glance out my window at the unlit bungalow and my insides clench. I've seen him in passing every day since Saturday's fire, as we've come or gone. Once, he was outside tossing the ball to Cody. I caught his wave of greeting but nothing more. No jog and hop over the fence, no offer of help to paint, no invitation for lasagna.

I guess this is how it's going to be from now on.

I hate it.

I was downstairs making myself a salad for dinner when I heard the rumble of his old car. I scurried to my window to catch a glimpse of him checking something under his hood. He was dressed in dark-wash jeans and a black button-down. Casual, but more stylish than usual, like he'd put in extra effort.

He looked good. Far better than I look, with my messy bun and ratty, long T-shirt and old shorts that I've relegated to "paint wear."

He left *three hours* ago and I know where they went. Dover is smaller than Polson Falls and there's only one steak house. It took me all of ten seconds to find the website. The place looks nice—upscale, cozy. Some may say romantic. They even boasted having their own sommelier. I know there are courses and wine selection and all that, but could they *still* be eating dinner? Or have they moved on elsewhere?

For drinks on Route Sixty-Six's patio, perhaps? Or have they skipped that and gone back to her place? What is Shane doing right now?

Peeling his shirt off, probably.

Or unbuckling his jeans.

Or palming his erection.

Maybe he's already dragging her panties off with his teeth?

God, it's like I'm back in high school. All those nights of these very same thoughts, tormenting me for most of senior year, no matter how much I told myself I didn't care about Shane Beckett anymore.

What's Shane doing with Penelope right now? Are they laughing? Kissing? Screwing? Does he ever think about me?

Closing my eyes, I chant over and over again, "You don't care ... you don't care ..." But I can't ignore my dread. It bothers me that Shane is with *any* woman. I can*not* believe that the thought of Shane with other women—any woman—is bothering me!

I have regrets.

I wish I'd not been so hung up on the past. I wish I'd said a simple yes to dinner. If I ever get another chance, I'll say yes. I'll do things differently.

But for now ... "Forget about Shane Beckett," I say through

gritted teeth, annoyed with myself. I should be finishing up prep for tomorrow's curriculum night with the parents, but I can't concentrate on anything right now. I take a big gulp of my Shock Top, crank my music, grab the paint roller, and get back to work.

"I remember my first curriculum night."

Wendy Redwood's reedy voice pulls my focus from the whiteboard where I'm making last-minute notes to guide tonight's presentation. I smile. "Were you as nervous as I am now?"

"Yes. Though, they didn't do these types of nights back when I *first* started. You know, a hundred years ago." She strolls in, arms folded across her chest, her usual black pumps clicking across the classroom floor. I noticed earlier that the heel caps have been worn right down. They should be tossed, but Wendy's limited wardrobe is stocked for comfort—flowy dresses and loose blazers—and I'm guessing the soles of those shoes have long ago molded to her feet. "Stand me up in front of a gymnasium of children any day, but parents?" She mock shudders. "They're terrifying."

I laugh, and the simple act relieves the tension in my spine. In less than thirty minutes, this room will be full of them, eager to hear how their children will be enlightened this year and by whom. Thankfully, I won't have to do all the talking. The rotational-subject teachers will each claim their ten minutes, and they're seasoned veterans who've been doing this for decades. I'll be the only novice teacher. "I'll be glad when it's over."

"Any last-minute questions? Or concerns? I can pop back in, if you'd like. Of course, that's assuming Lucy doesn't say something that requires my swift intervention." She says this with a resigned sigh, as if she's assuming Bott—I can't think of her as Lucy or Mademoiselle Parish—will do something crazy and Wendy has accepted it.

I've seen the gamut of principals during my years filtering in and out of various schools as a substitute—the nurturing, the apathetic, the militant, the disengaged, the micromanaging, the politics-player. It's still early days, but I'm quickly learning that Wendy Redwood is as good as they come. She's calm and rational. She's supportive without being overbearing. She expects order, but hasn't buried us in administrative processes. The stories I've heard say she's the first to have her teachers' backs when a parent storms the office in a fury, but she can also dance along that tightrope to make the parent feel heard. It's a bipartisan game that she plays well. The students love her. She greets every child by name and with a warm, genuine smile, and yet they all seem to have a healthy respect for her as the boss. No matter what doubts I've had about moving back to Polson Falls, taking Wendy up on this teaching offer was one smart move on my part.

"I think I'm ready. It's pretty straightforward."

"I knew you would be. You were always a conscientious student, Scarlet." She smiles with assurance. "It makes me happy to see how well you're doing."

You mean, despite my dubious upbringing?

What must it have been like for Wendy to be the principal of this school and deal with my mother and Mayor Rhodes's scandal? That night was a chain reaction of horrors. It began when a second grader vomited on the floor backstage and two children slipped in regurgitated SpaghettiOs. A helpful parent volunteer ran to the janitor's room in a rush to get the mop bucket. Obviously, the mayor did not count on a nervous puker when he and my mom stealthily slipped away. The volunteer's entry was so sudden, her shriek of surprise so loud, rumor has it Mayor Rhodes lost his balance trying to pull up his pants and ended up sprawled on the floor with his unmentionables hanging out for a small crowd.

For Dottie's part, she did seem more solemn in the weeks

after that, staying home and trying to be a more attentive mom. I don't know how long that affair had been going on and I never asked her if she expected the mayor to leave his wife for her. I didn't care. She'd humiliated me. Thankfully, she never attended another school event again.

"You might see a few familiar faces from your childhood here tonight. I know of a few old students coming back through with their young ones." Wendy smiles. "It's a joy to see new generations."

"A joy," I echo, as if in agreement, though I feel anything but joy at the thought of seeing Penelope here. If she's anything like Becca described, I'm guessing I won't be hearing an apology from her tonight.

But I'm even more anxious to see Shane, if he comes. How will he act toward me? Will he continue keeping his distance? That's probably for the best. Still, I hate it.

I heard the rumble of his engine last night at almost 10:00 p.m. That's a four-hour dinner. Who the hell eats dinner for four hours? People who went somewhere to have sex after, that's who. Every time I think of Shane with another woman, my insides coil with disappointment.

At least he came home alone. I know because I turned off all my lights and spied from my window like a masochistic lunatic. Then I tossed and turned all night, pondering whether I've saved myself from heartache or if I've sabotaged potential lifelong happiness.

At this point in my obsessive dwelling, it's a toss-up.

"Good luck!" With a rap of her knuckles against the door, Wendy is gone, her worn heels clicking down the hall toward Becca's classroom.

I could use a restroom break and a drink of water before this circus starts. I check my phone to make sure I have time. There's a highly inappropriate meme involving Batman and a studious-looking teacher on her desk from Justine, who knows I'm nervous about tonight. "What the fuck is wrong with you?" I mutter under my breath, chuckling as I quickly delete it.

"Probably shouldn't curse like that in front of parents," a deep male voice says, making me jump.

I spin around to find Shane in the doorway, in his usual ensemble of jeans and T-shirt—this time a vintage Pearl Jam soft cotton that clings to his frame without being too tight. He makes casual look good like no other man I know.

"What are you doing here so early?" My heart races both from surprise and relief, glad it was Shane and not someone else who overheard that.

"Am I early?" He strolls in, checking the clock on the wall over his shoulder. "Huh. I guess I am. I wanted to get a front-row seat. These things get packed, from what I remember." He settles against a desk, stretching his long legs out ahead of him and folding his arms over his chest. His mesmerizing eyes flitter over the plum wrap blouse and black pencil skirt I chose for the night, down to my most "professional" heels, lingering a moment there, before he shifts his focus to the board to scan my notes. "So that's what my knucklehead kid is going to learn this year."

At least we can find common ground. "Your knucklehead kid is actually smart. And polite." Cody raises his hand, he participates, and he finishes his work on time. But what was more impressive is that I heard him tell some of the poorly behaved boys who were teasing the girls to cut it out. It stunned me to see that his bully of a mother could raise her son to have basic manners and respect—but perhaps that's his father's influence. "He's impressed me, more than once."

"Well, that says something. Scarlet Reed is not an easy one to impress." Shane's lips curls into a playful smile. "I should know. I keep failing miserably at it."

Is that what he's been trying to do? Impress me? "Maybe you need to try harder," I answer, matching his light tone.

He grins. "I think I need more guidance. Some one-on-one tutoring, if you're available?"

What is going on here? The dynamic between us seems to have shifted again, back to flirtatious. This is *not* keeping it uncomplicated.

"How was your date?" I ask evenly. Has he forgotten already?

He bows his head, his lips pressed in a tight smile that makes my stomach clench. I regret asking. "You really want to know?"

I shrug nonchalantly, though my voice is strained when I say, "Probably not."

He peers up at me, lingering for a moment as if assessing how he should answer. "Shitty, actually."

I snort. "Right. A four-hour date because it was shitty." *And now you've made it clear you were watching the clock for him.* My cheeks flame. This conversation needs to end immediately. "I should finish getting ready for this orientation ..." My voice trails as Shane moves swiftly for my classroom door, pushing it closed. He makes his way back to my desk and perches on the corner closest to me.

He simply stares at me. He's waiting for me to ask.

It takes me a few breaths to calm myself before I play along. "And *why* was it a shitty date, Shane?" I ask with an exaggerated curious tone, though I find myself holding my breath for his answer.

"Because I didn't want to be there. I guess I shouldn't say it was shitty. That's not fair to her. It was boring. I was bored."

Dean called that one. It didn't take nearly as long as I'd expected. A strange thrill stirs inside me. "What happened? She didn't want to put out for Mr. July?"

He laughs, his gaze searching the ceiling tiles, giving me a chance to admire the sharp jut of his throat. "No, she was more than willing. *I'm* the one who wasn't interested. I knew I never should have said yes." He shakes his head, more to himself. "I regretted it the second I sat down."

"Oh. Well, that's ..." My voice trails. I don't know what to say.

"I didn't kiss her at the end of the night."

"I didn't ask."

"I know, but I'm telling you anyway."

A rash of nervous flutters churns in my belly. "Why didn't you?"

He studies me. "Because I told her I was hung up on another woman, and I need to give that time to see where it could lead."

"Oh," I manage, swallowing hard. I'm assuming he means me, and he's being far more candid and straightforward than he's been up until now.

"Yeah." His eyes land on my mouth where they remain for several beats before lifting again. "Even if it means sitting in my house, jerking off while I wait for her to trust me. I didn't mention that last part to Susie, though," he says with a crooked smile.

Blood pounds in my ears. Why is Shane telling me this *now*? *Here*, twenty-five minutes before my presentation begins? Part of me wants to rope my hands around his thick neck and choke him.

But a bigger part wants to kiss him.

I clear my throat before I trust my voice won't shake. "I should go and open the door. Parents will be arriving soon. They'll want to talk." I stumble over my words as I take a step back from him. I can't do this—whatever *this* is—with Shane right now.

"Well ... *I'm* a parent," he says, folding his arms over his chest again. God, he looks good tonight. "Maybe *I* want to talk."

I let out a nervous laugh as heat creeps up my neck. "Something tells me you're not here to talk about what Cody's going to learn in school."

"That's not true!" he exclaims in a mock-appalled voice.

I decide to humor him. "Okay, fine. What would you like to talk about, Mr. Beckett?"

He frowns at the board. "I'm *very* concerned about the sex education curriculum for my impressionable son."

"Uh-huh." I smother my smile. "And what exactly are you concerned about?"

"You know … I just …" He bites his bottom lip as he no doubt searches for bullshit to throw at me. The simple move is so sexy. "I remember when Ms. Dixon used those extra-large bananas to demonstrate how to roll on a condom. Do you remember that?"

I laugh. "She tore three of them before she managed to get one on properly." Dipshit offered to put it on for her. As if his scrawny ass had ever so much as touched a condom back then.

"Those bananas gave a lot of guys in the class a complex for years. You know, about their size."

I drop my voice, wary of it carrying through the closed door. "Really? Because you didn't act like you were struggling with confidence in high school."

The corner of his mouth twitches, but he manages to keep a straight face otherwise. "Just saying, you don't want to be crushing these little men's spirits. They have enough to deal with. You know, with the pressures of social media and all that."

"Got it. I'll be sure to pick up extra-small bananas for that day. The smallest they sell. Will that appease your concerns about their precious male egos?"

"Definitely." His forehead creases. "And are *you* going to be demonstrating this? Because I think I need to attend this class—"

"Okay, we're done now. I'm sure I have mature parents waiting for me outside," I scold, but I can't help the smile. It feels good to be joking around—and flirting—with Shane again.

"Fine." He heaves himself off the desk to loom over me, a hint of his spicy cologne teasing my nostrils, a devilish glint in his eye. "I'll just ask the rest of my questions during the session."

Oh God. All semblance of calm evaporates. "Don't you *dare*!" Shane loved to tease me mercilessly when we were younger.

Granted, it usually involved pinning me down to tickle me, which turned into a heavy make-out session.

"What do you mean?" he asks with faux innocence.

"*Don't,* Shane," I warn in as serious a tone as I can muster. Even the thought of standing up in front of my students' parents and fielding sex-ed questions from him makes me queasy. He wouldn't be embarrassed to ask, either. The guy poses half-naked in calendars and struts his stuff on stage, for fuck's sake.

"What? I can't even *mention* the bananas?"

I burst out with laughter. "No!"

His face splits into a wide grin. "I love getting a rise out of you."

"You're worse than Justine." On impulse, I reach out to give his chest a playful shove.

He catches my hand on contact, holding it against his hard body for a few beats—letting me feel his heat beneath my palm and the strength within his fingers—before releasing it.

I pull away, instantly missing the contact.

"That one doesn't have a filter, does she?"

"Justine? No, she doesn't. And *please* don't, Shane. This is my first curriculum night. I don't want to be embarrassed in front of parents." *Especially* in front of Penelope.

"Fine." He sighs heavily, as if he's being put out. "Tell you what, I won't ask those questions, if *you'll* forgive me for not being smart enough to turn down dinner with Susie in the first place." The sincerity in his expression threatens to weaken my knees.

"You're forgiven." The truth is, I think I forgave him the second he confessed to not kissing her. Also, I *was* angling to sleep with his best friend last Friday. On the list of stupid moves, my name comes up at least once.

"And agree to dinner with me."

That request catches me off guard. Is this why Shane came so early? To trap me and then ask me out when I'm nervous and not thinking straight? Clever man.

"Just dinner." He holds his hands in the air in a sign of surrender. "That's *all*. Just one dinner. Just give me *one* chance. A *real* chance."

Nerves stir in my stomach. This is what I wished for last night, a paint roller in hand, full of regret over how hard I'd held on to our ugly past. "When?"

"Whenever. I've got Cody this weekend, but we'll figure it out." He waits expectantly for my answer.

"And what if I say no?" I ask on a whim, swallowing the urge to blurt out yes as I try to maintain some semblance of calm that Shane's presence always challenges.

"Then get ready for *all kinds* of questions about penis sizes, G-spots, female orgasms—"

"Fine! Oh my God. Stop!" I struggle to smother my beaming smile so I don't look too eager. "Dinner. Whenever. But *just* dinner."

"I don't believe it!" His shoulders sag with his deep exhale. "After all these years, Scarlet Reed has finally forgiven me."

"Yeah. I wouldn't go *that* far," I say wryly. "I'm just giving you a pass on your latest bonehead move."

He steps into my personal space. "What's it going to take for me to get blanket forgiveness for all past sins?" I hold my breath as he reaches for a strand of my hair, toying with it between his fingers. "Because the way you kissed me last Friday night made me think we were good."

I struggle to ignore the electric current coursing through my body. "You'll have to work a lot harder than that."

"Well, you know me." He leans in slightly, almost as if testing the waters for a kiss. "I've always loved a challenge." The words graze my lips and my mouth parts of its own accord, anticipating his.

The orientation session.

Dammit.

"We can't do this right now," I whisper in a pleading, almost hysterical tone. I have a herd of parents about to descend upon me.

"You're right. I'm sorry." His fingers release the strand of hair. Ever so gently, he fixes the collar of my blouse. "Later?" When his warm eyes lift to meet mine again, they're full of heat and promise.

"Uh-huh," I mumble absently, caught in the flecks of gold in his irises. Just dinner, my ass. How the hell am I going to get through this presentation? I'm about to ask Shane to leave, to not attend his son's session, when a glint of movement catches the corner of my eye. "I should go open the—" My words cut off in a croak.

Penelope Rhodes is staring at me through the door's window.

I take a quick step away from Shane as she dissects me through squinted eyes. I see the glaze of familiarity. She's trying to place me and yet she can't quite.

And then, there it is. The realization.

Her sage green eyes dart to Shane—the father of her child—and narrow.

Shane mutters something unintelligible under his breath.

There's really no avoiding this. I take a deep breath and force a wide, fake smile as I stroll over to open the door. "Hi, Penelope. Good to see you again." I hope that doesn't sound as fake out loud as it does in my head.

She does a quick head-to-toe scan before returning to my face. "When Cody told me your name, I didn't make the connection." Her voice is as crisp and haughty as I remember, though aged. She turns to Shane. "You're here early. You're usually late."

"Didn't want to have to stand for an hour again," he says casually, his attention shifting to the man standing behind Penelope. "Hey."

The guy looks up to nod at Shane once before returning to

whatever's so enthralling on his phone screen, blindly trailing Penelope as she strolls in. This must be Travis. He's tall, built, and classically handsome, and well-dressed in black pants and a blue mint button-down shirt. An ensemble fit for an office job in Philadelphia or a Phi Gamma Delta alumni brochure—he's giving off major frat-boy vibes.

Penelope looks especially nice in a navy dress and heels, her long, red hair silky and straight, her makeup perfectly applied and clearly touched up before coming here tonight.

"Well ... isn't this fun?" she murmurs, sizing up my classroom.

"As fun as a colonoscopy," Shane whispers for only me to hear.

I stifle my laugh. The truth is, nobody in this room looks like they're having *any* fun.

Penelope slips her hand into the man's pants pocket, giving it a little tug as if to gain his attention.

His eyebrows arch and then, clueing in, he slips his phone into his pocket, murmuring an apology.

"This is Travis. He and I live together, and he's *very* involved in Cody's life," she introduces. "This is Sharon Reed."

"*Scarlet*." Such a timeless but unimaginative bitch move on her part. And pathetic. She spent six years trying to ruin my life. She knows my name.

"Right." She lets out a soft fake laugh. "Sorry, it's just been *so* long."

Travis frowns curiously. "You guys know each other?"

"We went to the same high school." She brushes a stray strand of short, sable-blond hair off his forehead before smoothing her hand down his arm affectionately. "And now she lives beside Cody's father."

Cody's father. It's as if Shane isn't right here. Or perhaps it's to remind me that she and Shane have a son together. As if I could forget.

"No shit. Small world," Travis murmurs, fussing with the

chunky silver watch that adorns his wrist. Did he come to the school orientation night willingly? Or did Penelope force him to come?

"Yeah. I just moved in a few weeks ago. I had no idea Shane was living there when I bought the house."

Penelope gives me a doubtful "I'm sure you didn't" smile. "It's that *tiny* old blue house, right?" Her perfect button nose wrinkles with distaste.

I force a wide smile. "Yup. It's definitely a fixer-upper, but I love it. I've enjoyed working on it."

"Ugh. *Thank God* we could afford contractors for that reno we just finished, right, babe? Can't believe how much we spent, but our main floor is stunning."

"Fucking mess that was. Oops." Travis cringes. "Guess I shouldn't swear in front of the teacher."

Shane snorts. "Don't worry. I can't believe the stuff that comes out of this one's mouth sometimes."

"Only when it's directed *at* you," I throw back.

"I usually deserve it, too, don't I?" Shane grins slyly, like we have a secret between us, and I find myself grinning back like a fool.

"Oh my God!" Penelope snaps her fingers. "That's right! Shane, didn't she have that *massive* crush on you all through senior year while we were together? Like, she was *so* obsessed with you—"

"Give it a rest, Pen," Shane warns, before offering me an apologetic glance.

My face burns. I could bring up many things about high school—namely, what a condescending, mean-spirited jerk Penelope was—but what good would it do? She is who she is and doesn't appear to have changed, despite age and motherhood. I'm Cody's teacher, and I must maintain some semblance of professionalism. I settle on, "We were all young and dumb once, right?"

Young and dumb and in love.

"Some of us dumber than others," Shane agrees. "I know I made some bad, wrong calls back then."

"Yes, you did." I smile sweetly. *You were an idiot to leave me for her.*

"I'm doing my best to fix one of them." He watches me intently, as if trying to convey unspoken words through a look.

I take a slow, calming breath. Shane is nothing if not determined. "And maybe you can."

He smiles, and I get caught in those deep dimples, thinking of where we just left things off and where they might—hopefully—head later. Just dinner, my ass.

Penelope clears her throat sharply, breaking our private moment. Her glossy lips pucker with annoyance as her attention shifts to the whiteboard. "I'm sure you've figured out by now how intelligent my son is."

My son.

Dear God, help me.

I catch Shane's eye roll as I force a polite smile. "I was just saying to Shane before you got here that Cody is one of my brightest students."

"Is *that* what you two were talking about?" She throws a cutting look his way, but then continues. "What are you going to do to challenge him this year?"

I can already see what Becca means about Penelope being *that* kind of parent. She's going to be a giant, prickly pain in my ass. "I'll be going through the sixth grade curriculum when the session starts. I'm sure you'll find it to be robust." I'm not about to give her a private walk-through. She can wait.

She sniffs. "We weren't thrilled with last year's teacher."

Last year, Becca was Cody's teacher.

"I was fine with her." Shane studies his fingernails as if bored with the conversation.

"You would be," Penelope snipes back.

What is the dynamic between them now? Is this what Shane

means by "civil"? This doesn't seem civil. It's certainly a far cry from the brief exchange I witnessed between them on his front porch.

A couple pokes their heads in then, rescuing me. "If you'll excuse me ..." I head over to greet the parents—of Jenny Byrd, I find out through quick introductions. Another star in my class. I really do need to use the restroom before the presentation begins, though, so I take this opportunity to duck out, pausing just long enough to steal a glance over my shoulder.

Penelope has abandoned Travis, and she and Shane are now in the far corner of my classroom. Her lips are moving fast, her tone hushed, her face tight.

Clearly, she has a problem with something.

Or someone.

It's nightfall by the time I walk the two blocks home, my arms huddled around my body for warmth. I wish I'd thought to bring a jacket. The heat wave is long gone, replaced by an evening chill that crawls over my skin. I was held back at school for almost an hour after my session by parents eager to speak about their children. Most of those conversations should have waited for parent-teacher conferences next month, but I humored them, not wanting to come off as dismissive.

Overall, I think the night went well, with only a few off-topic questions and complaints that I quickly tabled to deal with privately. None of them came from Penelope, who spent the session brushing away Travis's hand and wearing a sour expression when she wasn't grilling Mr. Heffernan on the science program and Mrs. Marx about geography.

Shane was quiet through the session and, despite his claim that he wanted a seat at the front, parked himself in the back corner, on the opposite side to Penelope. If I didn't know better,

I'd guess that was an intentional move. Whatever was exchanged between them in heated whispers before the meeting must not have been pleasant, because Shane ducked out as soon as the presentation concluded, without so much as a glance her way.

I've been anxious to get home to find out if my suspicions are right and Penelope's issues have something to do with me.

From the sidewalk, I spot Shane fastening something under the hood of his car, his broad back to me. My heart pounds at the sight of him, as it always does. On impulse, I turn into his driveway, treading softly in the white sneakers I swapped for the walk home. "Do you know what you're doing under there?" I call out from just behind him.

He jumps, startled, and whacks the back of his head on the open hood.

I wince as he reaches for the sore spot. "Sorry. I didn't think you were so skittish."

"I'm not normally. You snuck up on me." Shane grabs the rag that dangles over the side of his car and then drops the hood. It makes a loud, hollow sound as it closes. "And yeah, I do know what I'm doing under there."

"Really? Because I remember you flagging down a tow-truck driver to help us change a tire once." We were on our way home from shopping in Philly one Sunday afternoon.

He grins. "You remember that?"

I remember everything. Oddly enough, I'm remembering the good over the bad more often lately.

Shane chuckles as he rubs the streaks of black grime from his fingers with the rag. "I've had my hands on every square inch of this beast. I know her well."

"Lucky car."

He cocks his head, a flicker of surprise dancing across his face as if he hadn't expected such boldness from me.

Boy, is he in for a surprise. "What kind of car is it, anyway?"

"A '67 Chevy Impala. I rebuilt her with my dad when I moved back to Polson Falls."

"*Wow.*"

"Is that a genuine wow or a 'you're a loser' wow?" He leans against the hood. "I can't tell with you sometimes." His voice is deep and grating, but deliciously so.

"It's real. I'm impressed. See? Seems you *can* impress me." I get lost in him for a moment—in his angular jaw and his full lips, in the way his long legs are stretched out, almost as if he's inviting me to sidle in between them like I used to do when we were younger. I'd take any opportunity to dive against him back then, to revel in his strength and his warm skin, and the almost overpowering fragrance of Axe bodywash that all the teenage boys used. How acutely I remember what seem like stolen moments now, so many years later.

Shane's eyes do their own roaming—along the seam of my blouse and the small slit in my skirt, down to my decidedly unsexy sneakers.

Is he waiting for me to make the next move, seeing as he made the first?

"Cody's inside," Shane says evenly, as if reading my mind. "I picked him up from Pen's parents' house after the presentation. Which was great, by the way. You were great." He punctuates that with a smile.

I guess climbing onto Shane's lap probably isn't a good idea. "So, what was Penelope's problem tonight?"

His expression turns hard. "What *isn't* her problem when it comes to me?"

"I thought you guys were good now."

"Compared to what we were? Sure. She's accepted that we'll never happen again, and she's moved on with *Travis.*" There's a hint of something in Shane's voice when he says the name.

"Do you not like him?"

"He's fine. Bit of an arrogant ass. He works at one of those big auditing firms in Philly and loves to talk about how much money he makes and what they're spending it on next. He's always trying to one-up me, like he hasn't figured out I don't give a shit. I'm not competing." He shrugs. "But he's good to Cody, and having him around keeps her off my back most of the time, so I really hope they work out. But she still likes to try to control my life, and she uses Cody as an excuse."

I hesitate. "Was tonight about me?" About what she saw through the window?

He averts his gaze, giving me my answer.

"Is it because I'm Cody's teacher or because of what happened between her father and my mother?" I can't blame her for the former. It was one of my reasons for not letting *this* happen. But the affair was not my fault any more than it was hers.

He sighs heavily. "She'd come up with some bullshit reason no matter what. She's always been like that."

That doesn't answer my question, but I don't push it. "So, what'd you tell her?" I hold my breath. Does Penelope have the power to sway Shane's decision about asking me out? She *is* the mother of his child.

"I said that we're neighbors and friends and, *if* something were to happen between us, we'd take it really slow to protect Cody."

"*If* something were to happen," I echo. Does he remember that kiss in the rain?

He smirks. "She doesn't need to have real-time updates. It's none of her business. And there's no rule against us dating. I've already checked."

That raises my eyebrows.

"I asked a friend's wife who works for the school board. I wanted to make sure before I made my move." He smiles sheepishly.

That Shane went to the effort is endearing. Still … "There might not be a rule, but it doesn't look good on me. And I don't want my students talking about my dating life, which they'll do if I'm dating one of their dads."

He nods, as if he anticipated that. "That's why we're going to keep it on the down low until the end of the school year. Cody doesn't have to find out. I told him we were friends in high school, but that's *all* I've told him."

Secretly dating Shane is exactly what I insisted I didn't want to be doing, back when Becca was teasing me about my crush and I was vehemently denying it. I find myself mulling this idea over through a different lens now, though. There are benefits to this plan. Keeping a relationship with Shane quiet means I don't have to answer intrusive questions if it doesn't work out. And being next-door neighbors and childhood friends—if we can call it that—does provide a strong cover story for why we'd be seen together. Plus, Cody lives at his mother's a lot of the time. We can avoid telling him altogether until it makes sense to. *If* it ever makes sense to.

I rationalize this plan in my mind, marking off all the reasons it could work, why it could be ideal, because I want it to be.

"Just one dinner, huh?" I tease.

"That's where we're going to start, but I'm hoping that's not where we're going to end." His smile is uncharacteristically shy as he hooks his finger through one of mine, pulling me in closer. "I wouldn't be pursuing this if I was looking for a casual hookup. You must have figured that out by now."

"Your effort *has* been impressive." I revel in the feel of his thumb drawing circles over my palm. "This fence has never looked better."

He chuckles. "I did that because I'm a nice guy, not because I was trying to get laid."

"Uh-huh."

His gaze drifts to my mouth for a moment, the weight of it palpable. I expect him to pull me in close and kiss me like he did last Friday night. I wait for it, my heart hammering in my chest in anticipation.

But he merely sighs. "Penelope doesn't get a say in who I date. I've never said a word about anyone she's dated, and a couple of them have been real dickheads. But as long as they're good to Cody, that's all that matters. I expect the same courtesy in return."

"She's never given you issues before?"

"She's never heard of any of them before. I haven't introduced any woman in my life to Cody yet."

"Why not?"

He shrugs. "I just figured there wasn't any point unless it was serious, and I've never been serious about any of them."

The sound of Shane's front door creaking open carries into the quiet night. Shane instantly releases my hand.

"Dad! I can't get past this level!" Cody pokes his head out, his mop of brown hair that matches his father's disheveled. "Oh, hey, Ms. Reed."

I smile. "Hi, Cody."

His eyes dart to Shane. "Can you help me? *Now*?" There's that touch of impatience in his tone that I've heard him use around his father before.

"Be there in five, bud. I have to clean up out here. Unless you want to come and help me?"

The brown-haired head ducks back inside.

"Yeah, didn't think so." Shane eases off his hood to tower over me. "He got a PS4 a few weeks ago and he's becoming an addict. I think Penelope and I are going to have to agree on daily time limits."

"His teacher approves of that idea." Behind my smile is a lingering wariness over the reminder that Shane is tied to Penelope for the rest of his life, whether she makes him want to saw off vital appendages or not. Which means as long as this—whatever this is—between Shane and me exists, she's also in my life.

But we are no longer teenagers trying to survive the treacherous social strata of high school, where people like Penelope Rhodes can make my life hell. And, now that I've stopped focusing all my energy on pushing Shane away, I'm seeing him for what he has grown into—a responsible adult and a loving, devoted father. Add in his physical attributes and he's basically any woman's dream.

I'm not about to give up this chance because she doesn't approve.

"Come on, I'll walk you home," he offers.

We cross Shane's lawn to mine in comfortable silence. Shane wordlessly takes my hand as I climb over my white picket fence and doesn't let go until we've reached my porch steps.

"I know it's a safe neighborhood, but you really should leave your light on at night," he says, standing idly by as I fumble in the dark for my keys.

"I know. I wasn't thinking when I left." I was too nervous about the presentation.

"I could set it up on a timer for you, so you don't have to worry about it if you forget."

"You know how to do that?" With a turn of my wrist, the dead bolt unlocks. "You're far more useful to me than I first suspected."

He chuckles. "Listen, I'm working tomorrow and then I've got Cody until Monday. Why don't we do dinner on Tuesday night, if you're free?" He climbs the three steps to tower over me on my front porch. Even in the dark, I can make out his handsome features. "We can continue discussing *exactly* how useful I am to you." His voice is grating, his unspoken promise clear.

If Cody weren't in the picture, now would be about the time I'd do something rash like grab Shane by his belt and lead him up to my bed. "Sounds good," I manage around a hard swallow.

He hesitates, checking his porch over his shoulder—to make sure Cody hasn't poked his head out again, I assume—before he leans in to lay a soft kiss against my cheek, a mere inch from my mouth.

It's an obvious bait. My heart races as I battle the urge to turn and catch his lips with mine.

But before I get the chance to lose to my hormones, Shane backs away, moving down the steps, out of my reach. "'Night, Scarlet."

"Good night." Can he hear my frustration screaming in those two little words?

His lips curl into a wicked smile. "Do I need to close my curtains tonight?"

"I don't know. *Do you?*" I ask pointedly.

He gives his jaw a lazy scratch. "It's probably a good idea. I've heard my new neighbor likes to spy on me at night. Wouldn't want to give her the wrong idea."

"She sounds like a real lunatic."

"Nah. She's pretty cool." He chuckles as he walks away, his running shoes dragging along my walkway as if he's reluctant to leave. "Sweet dreams."

"You too."

That night, I steal a glimpse into Shane's room as I'm readying for bed. Much to my disappointment, his light remains out.

It takes me forever to fall asleep, my heart and my mind still reeling from today's swift turn of events. I want this to happen, and yet I cannot ignore the dark cloud of wariness that lingers, the one there to remind me we're no longer seventeen, and there are careers, children, and vindictive ex-girlfriends to consider.

NINETEEN

It's after lunch on Saturday when I trudge back upstairs to finish the first coat of paint. My back and arms ache, and streaks of periwinkle blue mar my skin, but if I keep going at this pace, I *might* be finished with my bedroom by the end of the weekend.

I steal a glance out my window—my favorite pastime lately, it seems—to the house beside me. I heard the rumble of Shane's truck just after nine this morning. Two doors slammed and, when I peeked, I saw Cody skipping up the steps, chattering excitedly, oblivious to the way his dad dragged his feet and rubbed his eyes.

Shane looked exhausted.

His curtains are still drawn. I assume it's to block out the daylight so he can catch up on sleep after a twenty-four-hour shift.

He'll be in bed for another few hours, at least.

And I am becoming *far too* interested in Shane's schedule for my own damn good.

With grim determination to push away thoughts of the sleeping man next door, I crank my music until I can't hear myself think and fall into a rhythm—dip brush in tray, roll off excess, smooth over wall, repeat.

The minutes melt away as the unappealing mint green slowly vanishes, stroke by stroke, until a faint noise comes from downstairs. It's barely audible over my music.

I set my roller down. I'm halfway across the room to mute the speaker when footfalls pound up my stairs.

Inside my house!

I freeze as a scream rises in my throat, ready to let loose.

"Scarlet?" Shane's heavy, deep voice carries.

"Jesus!" I heave a sigh of relief a second before his face appears at my railing, my hand pressing against my chest. My heart thumps hard and fast. "I thought I was about to be murdered!"

"Sorry." He grins sheepishly. "Saw you in your window, painting. I was knocking for a while but you weren't answering. I figured you couldn't hear me." He climbs the rest of the way.

I dial down the music to a low hum. "How did you get in here?" Twelve years living in the city means my doors are *always* locked.

He holds up a key dangling from a blue string. "Iris had been falling a lot over the last few months, so her family gave me a spare in case she didn't answer her phone and I needed to check on her. I forgot I had it until now. Hope you don't mind."

The way my breath caught at the sight of his handsome face? No, I don't mind Shane's surprise visit and key misuse at all. I would have been pissed had I found out later that I missed his visit. "That was very fireman-y of you." Iris was lucky to have him as a neighbor.

"I'll leave it here." He loops it around the banister post. "But you should probably change your locks."

"I'll add it to the never-ending list. What are you doing here, anyway?" I check my bedside clock. It's only one. He wouldn't have gotten more than four hours. The dark circles under his eyes can attest to that. "Shouldn't you be sleeping?"

"I never sleep much when I have Cody for the weekend." He wanders into the middle of my bedroom. His gaze drifts over my bed, my nightstand, the half-dozen boxes that have yet to be unpacked, my laundry basket where my pajamas and bra are strewn haphazardly—because I wasn't expecting company—before shifting to my walls. "It's looking good."

So do you. He must have showered when he got home from work and then went to bed with damp hair because it's dried into a sexy, tousled mess. He's wearing a plain white T-shirt and shorts, and the T-shirt has a deep V-neck that dips down, highlighting his collarbones.

It used to drive him wild when I kissed the crook of his neck, where those bones joined. His breathing would go from zero to panting, and I'd see the swell of his erection through his jeans. Does that still drive him crazy? Can he still be satisfied by an hour-long lip-lock? Or is kissing too juvenile for him now?

Shane's doing his own eyeballing.

I know I look a disaster, in my ratty, cutoff shorts and baggy, tie-dye T-shirt that's knotted at the waist—like I've stepped out of an '80s music video. "I wasn't expecting company." I toy with the pile of hair atop my head.

"You look great." And the way he's sizing up my bare legs, I believe he means it.

I'm nervous, I realize. I haven't felt nervous about a guy since ... well, since Shane, in high school.

"So, where's Cody?" I ask, clearing my throat to rid the tremble from my voice.

"Glued to his PS4 for the next two hours. He'll text me if he needs me. Until he does ..." He takes several steps forward to close the distance between us until he's only a few feet away. "I'm all yours." He stares at me, expectantly.

Fire spreads through my veins. I knew having Shane in my bedroom was a terrible idea. Holy hell, this is happening *right now*? "What happened to dinner first?" I find myself mumbling dumbly.

Shane flashes his winning smile. "Do you want my help *painting?*"

"*Oh.*" My cheeks burn. That's why he's quasi-broke into my home. To help me paint.

The Scarlet from a few weeks ago would argue with Shane. She'd tell him she doesn't need or want his help. But everything between us has changed. "I only have one roller."

"Why don't I start doing the second coat of edging, then." He surveys the joint between the ceiling and wall. "This is only the first coat, right?"

"Yeah, but I did a *really* good job cutting so if you're not good at it—" My words get stuck in my throat as he peels his T-shirt up and over his head. He balls it up and tosses it onto my unmade bed, on my pillow.

And … I'll be sleeping facedown tonight.

He turns to give me a full-frontal view—the first one I've had up close and personal—and I can't help but gape because the deep V-cut of his pelvis and abdominal muscles were *not* airbrushed for that calendar. They're real, and they're enough to make the most pious woman salivate. "New shirt. I don't want to get paint on it. And come on, Scar. You know there's nothing I'm not good at."

I open my mouth to respond but falter. I can't come up with a suitable response to that arrogance, because it's likely true.

I catch the corner of his knowing smirk as he bends down to grab the brush. His shorts hang so low on his hips that I question what's keeping them up. Well, I *know* what's keeping them up, because I have those images filed away in my spank bank from the night I watched him stroll through his bedroom naked.

My entire body flushes with want as I retrieve my paint roller. "So, how was work?"

"A lot busier than usual." He drags the brush along the top of the wall with a steady, smooth hand, his forearm tense with corded muscle. It seems he's good at painting too. Of course he is. And this will save me time because I need a chair for most of that work. "There was a bad wreck that took a few hours to clear up, and a lady got trapped inside an apartment building elevator. That took a few hours too. Then we got dragged out at 4:00 a.m. for a fire."

"Hey, is it like it is in the movies, with the fireman pole and all that?"

He smirks. "We move pretty fast. Ended up being a false alarm. Couldn't go back to sleep after that."

I can't imagine being dragged out of bed at four in the morning by a screaming alarm, only to race out the door for nothing. "Those must suck."

"I guess it depends."

"On?"

"On if we find two hot women when we get there."

I roll my eyes. "And, for the record, I did *not* set fire to my kitchen just to see you."

"I believe you." The tinge of humor in his voice says otherwise.

We work in comfortable silence for a few minutes, the only sound in the room the slathering of paint, the soft hum of music, and—for me—the rush of blood in my ears as my heart beats fast and steady.

I steal a glance over my shoulder to check Shane's progress and get caught in admiring the web of impressive muscle that spans his back and wraps around to pad his sides. He must spend *a lot* of time working out at the fire station while waiting to rescue cats from trees. What would it feel like to fill my hands with—

He turns suddenly and catches me gawking.

I not so smoothly divert my attention back to my roller. "Good job."

His soft chuckle carries, but he doesn't otherwise respond.

I smile. What an arrogant ass.

"How was school yesterday?"

"Better, now that it's cooled off. I'm getting into a groove. It's going to take time to get to know the kids but they seem like a good group, for the most part." I pause. "Has Cody said anything about school? Or me?" I often wonder what these kids have to say about my teaching ability.

"Just that you're really hot."

"He did *not*!" He's eleven! I spear a glare over my shoulder and catch Shane's dimpled smile before he shifts his focus back to edging.

"He said you're okay so far, which is about all you're going to get out of him. He's too cool already."

"Yeah, I'm starting to notice that." The sly smiles, the nods of greeting and handshakes with his friends. Though gangly and prepubescent, Cody is as athletic and popular as I remember his father being. "So, you were nineteen when he was born?"

"Yeah."

"That's crazy." At nineteen I was hitting keg parties and flashing my fake ID at clubs and making sure that I wasn't making babies.

"I checked my messages after my English exam and found out Penelope was in labor, two weeks early. So, I hopped on a plane and flew back here. Made it just in time."

"You were there for his birth? Like, in the room?"

"Yup. Pen begged me to be there. And I wanted to be there anyway, even if we were over." He shakes his head. "Craziest thing I've ever experienced. I've been at a couple emergency births since then, but none of them are like your own kid being born."

"I can't imagine." And he got to share that experience with *her*. I can't conceive of having my nineteen-year-old *ex*-boyfriend by my side while I'm squeezing a melon out of my body. Then again, it sounds like Penelope was angling to reconcile with Shane. What better way to try to set aside past wrongs and start fresh than with the birth of your child together?

In her case, though, it didn't work. Was it because she hurt him too much?

"Becca said Penelope was cheating on you and that's why you guys broke up."

He nods. "The summer before we went away to college. She hooked up with a friend of her brother's. Things were already rocky between us. She said she was trying to make me jealous. I was planning on ending things with her before I left for California anyway, so when I found out, I broke up with her. And then she called me a few weeks after school started and told me she was pregnant." He adds in a lower voice, "And that was the day my life changed forever."

I hesitate. "Did you ever wonder if he was yours?" I add quickly, "I mean, *I know* he is. He looks like you."

Shane smirks. "I know everyone around here was whispering that for a long time. But Penelope swore she'd never actually screwed the guy."

"And you believed her?" I'm unable to mask the doubt from my voice.

"I didn't want to, at first." He pauses to check his edging work before shifting to another stretch of wall. "But I knew her pretty well by then. I knew she wasn't lying." Shane coats his brush with fresh paint. "It would have been an easy out for me, though, to tell her to find me when it was time to do a paternity test. But, that would have been wrong, especially if the baby was mine. What kind of guy would I be?"

I snort derisively. "You'd be *my* father." According to my mother, Marcus Meyers did just that.

I feel Shane's steady gaze as I roll a wide stripe of paint along the wall.

"Have you seen him again?"

"Who, Marcus? No, not since I met him that one time." I barely remember it. I was so young. But my mom filled in the holes for me once. We were hurting for money and about to get evicted. She had no one to lean on for help—my grandfather had died when she was young, and my grandmother had disowned her and moved to South Carolina when my mother got pregnant—so she did the only thing she could think of. She borrowed a neighbor's car and we drove to Philadelphia, to the trucking company where Marcus Meyers had been working when they had their brief fling. A to Z Trucking was its name, easy enough to remember. It was a small operation, running out of an old, run-down warehouse. She had no idea if Marcus was still employed there.

Not only was he employed there, but his father—my grandfather, the man I have to thank for my inheritance—owned the business. That's how my grandfather found out about me. Up until that point, he had no idea I existed.

Marcus Meyers knew I existed, but again he vehemently denied fathering me. What I remember is standing on the loading dock while a giant—to me, back then—man yelled at my mother for showing up and spewed every abhorrent name in the book at her. I remember him telling her we could live on the street for all he cared.

He refused to give her a dime until he saw a court order for a paternity test. She knew that would take far more time than she had. She also knew she didn't want him in our lives, but she was desperate for money.

In the end, it was my grandfather who handed her an envelope of cash. She figures he did it to end the scene and rid himself of the young woman and child on his loading dock as quickly as possible. Either way, it was enough to get our heads back above water.

We never went back there again. Even Dottie Reed has pride.

I sense Shane wanting to ask more questions—I told him that

story once, lying beneath the canopy of a grand oak tree. Does he remember?—but instead he shifts back to his task.

"So, Cody was born and then what?" I'm desperate for more information to fill the gap between then and now.

"And then I went back to California. I hated being so far away from him, but I had a scholarship. Penelope took a year off school. I don't think she was planning on going back, to be honest. She expected me to go pro and set her and Cody up with a big paycheck for life. And I would have. But then I got hurt."

What must it have been like for Shane to have such a promising future end before it really began? "Do you miss it?"

It's a long moment before he answers and when he does, there's a tinge of sorrow in his voice. "Yeah. I miss the game, and the crowds. I miss the team. When it happened, I was devastated, but I made peace with it. Still, I can't help but think about what life would've been like if I'd made it. I *should* have made it."

"You *would* have. You were good." Me, who doesn't care for the sport, but even I noticed how Shane outshone everyone on the field. "I'm really sorry that happened to you," I offer softly, hoping he can hear the sincerity in my voice.

He nods. "The silver lining is I got to be around Cody more. I lost my athletic scholarship after that year because I couldn't play. I didn't see much point in staying in Cali, so I transferred home to finish my degree at Penn State. I was on the fence between coaching high school football and firefighting. I wasn't sure I was cut out for dealing with dumbass teenagers all day long, but I actually like working with Cody."

"Do you think he'll play for the Panthers?"

"He will, if I have anything to do with it." He winks. "Coach called me the other day and asked if I'd want to come help out this season. I'm thinking of doing it. It'd be good for me to get involved and learn what I can about teaching kids. Might give me some ideas for Cody. It's different, playing the game versus teaching it. Well ... I guess *you* know."

I watch him paint for a moment, his muscular arm stretched over his head. Every choice he makes, he seems to do so with his son in mind. "You're a good father."

He pauses midstroke to meet my gaze and, where his eyes are normally playful, I see nothing but seriousness now. "I try to be."

I finish one side of the wall, and then busy myself with dragging the sheets of newspaper over to the far side of the room and rearranging them to cover the hardwood around the tray.

"Nice shorts," Shane murmurs.

"Shut up. These are my junk clothes. They're good for painting."

"No, I *mean* it. Especially when you bend over like that."

Shit. I didn't consider the view from this angle, but the pant legs are wide and I chopped them fairly short. I tug the material at the back down self-consciously. "Sorry, I didn't mean to do that."

"Don't apologize on my account." His voice sounds strained.

I glance over at Shane. He has given up all pretense of painting and is simply standing there, his jaw taut, his expression serious, the hard ridge along the front of his shorts prominent.

Yeah, I'd say I just inadvertently gave Shane a *highly* indecent view.

I barely contain my laughter. He always said he liked my ass, and that was before the countless hours of yoga and Pilates turned it curvy and rock hard.

He chuckles but his cheeks turn pink. "You didn't mean to, huh?"

"I didn't. I swear!" But a thrill courses through me at his reaction.

He shakes his head as he turns back to the wall. "It's like I'm seventeen all over again," he says under his breath, discreetly adjusting the front of his shorts.

"You'd deserve it, for all those months of them calling me BB."

"I didn't tell them …" He sighs with reluctance. "It wasn't like that."

"Really? Then what was it like?"

He bites his bottom lip as if considering whether to respond. It's a long moment before he does. "Dip caught me jacking off in the drive-in restroom one night and wouldn't shut up about it after."

My jaw drops at his admission as a foggy recollection takes shape. "Wait, was that the night we watched *Sin City*?" We were curled up in the back of Dean's truck, under blankets, and I was mercilessly teasing Shane by dragging my fingertips back and forth along his bare stomach, just above his belt. Halfway through the film, he snuck off in a sudden rush. He came back a while later with Steve on his heels, ribbing him about something.

He rubs his forehead, a cute, shameful look on his face. "Maybe."

A mental flash of Shane with his fist wrapped around himself in one of those dingy little stalls hits me and I blush. "Did you do that a lot when we were together?"

His eyes flash to mine as if he's weighing how truthful to be. "Every day we went out," he confesses with a wry smile. "Sometimes in my car, right after I dropped you off. Once in the Patty Shack restroom, because I was losing my mind watching you lick that vanilla ice-cream cone."

"Oh my God!" I burst out laughing and he follows suit, though his laughter is weaker, laced with embarrassment. "You never let on how dire things were for you." Maybe I *did* earn that nickname, after all.

"Yeah, well …" He shrugs. "I told you, I didn't want you feeling pressured."

"If only you knew how bad I wanted you back then." How many times did I leave him with my panties drenched, desperate for his touch inside them? I had my reasons, and he said he was okay with them.

He groans and his darkened gaze trails my body.

I let mine drop as well, to the unmistakable bulge in Shane's shorts. "Do you need to use the restroom?"

"Dammit, Scar. Thirteen years later and you're still doing this to me." He shakes his head, but laughs. "Get back to painting or you'll never be finished."

With a sigh, I do as told.

At least, I try to. But now all I can think of is enticing Shane to find his breaking point.

My paint roller is dry and needs a reload. On impulse, I make a point of bending deep at the waist, taking much longer than necessary, betting on Shane watching.

The sharp curse behind me says I bet right.

Humming to myself—more to calm my own nerves than anything else—I set to finishing the last section, not daring to look back.

I have only one spot left to finish, high above the window. I brace my free hand against the window frame and stretch onto my tiptoes, reaching as far as I can to begin coating it. Warm afternoon air from the open window tickles my exposed belly.

A creak in the hardwood is the only warning I get before Shane is standing behind me. "Let me help you," he whispers, encasing my hand with his own, while his other hand—large and hot—settles on my hip.

A soft sigh escapes my lips as he guides the roller up and down. Together we cover the last patch of mint green in the entire room. It's impossible for me not to zero in on his erection brushing up against my backside with each stroke.

With the wall covered, he wriggles the roller free from my grasp and tosses it into the tray. But he doesn't move away. Instead, he shifts closer, taking my hand in his again and bringing my knuckles to his lips.

"My fingers have wet paint on them," I warn him, watching

the sweet move intently. "You'll end up with periwinkle blue lips if you're not careful." Not that I wouldn't kiss him anyway.

"You're right. I don't see any paint here, though." He dips his face into the crook of my neck, to linger there a moment as if testing the waters before he skims my skin with a soft, tentative kiss.

I allow it for a time, tipping my head to the side to give him better access, which he takes with greedy lips.

"We shouldn't," I murmur, my breathing turning ragged.

"Why not?"

I shudder with pleasure as his warm tongue teases me. "Because we're taking things slow, remember? The whole next-door neighbors and teacher thing." There's no small amount of reluctance in my voice.

"You're right," he says, but he doesn't stop, his splayed hands molding to my sides and working upward, his fingertips stalling at the underside of my breasts.

This is going somewhere, and fast, if I don't stop it.

I turn to face him, thinking a break from his lips will help, but that was a mistake. He's standing so damn close to me, and now I'm staring at a wall of muscle and smooth skin that my fingers ache to touch.

I inhale deeply. He smells of citrus soap. If he doesn't move away from me soon, I'm going to lose any resolve I have left. As it is, I can't bring myself to be the one to put distance between us.

His eyes drop to my mouth and then farther to where my pebbled nipples hide behind my bulky T-shirt. Surely, he can't see them.

A shiver skitters down my spine, all the same. "It's cold in here," I lie and struggle to keep a straight face at my foolish claim. It's at least eighty degrees in this room.

His lips curl with a slow, sexy smirk as he leans in, until my mouth is just inches from his, and his shaky breath skates over mine. He's struggling to restrain himself, waiting for me to make the next move.

"Shane …" My voice cracks with desperation, my eyes closed as I get lost in this heady haze that always seems to swirl around us when we're this close.

He swallows hard. "Are you going to make me beg?"

"It wouldn't hurt," I say glibly.

When he sinks to his knees on the floor in front of me and stares up with those heated whiskey eyes, I want to take my casual words back.

My resolve no longer exists.

Strong hands seize my thighs, his fingertips stretching high and wide, his touch searing my bare skin. "How's this?" he asks, his voice deep and raspy.

"It's a start," I manage.

"A start?" His eyebrow arches in question. "As in, I should keep going?" He waits a beat for me to answer—the sight of Shirtless Shane kneeling in front of me has stolen my voice—before leaning in to press his mouth on the exposed skin just below my belly button. Meanwhile, his calloused hands slide up the backs of my thighs and under the loose material of my shorts to grip my flesh.

I gasp as my body responds, flooding warmth between my legs.

What are you letting happen, Scarlet?

I'm sure as hell not about to stop it. I weave my hands through his messy brown mane as I enjoy his lips and tongue and hands against my skin. Even during all those years I had convinced myself that I hated Shane Beckett, I imagined moments like this.

It was never as good as the real thing.

He pulls away, pausing to meet my gaze for a moment—as if checking with me first—before his hands shift. With a tug, my shorts easily slip off my hips and fall to the floor. I step out of them without a word, wishing I'd had the foresight to throw on a sexier pair of underwear.

"Do you know how many times I've thought about doing this?" He nips at the front of my panties with his teeth.

"Once or twice?" Heat from his mouth radiates through the thin white cotton, and I wait anxiously for him to remove them too. This experience is already a hundred times better than Red Wine Golden Retriever Man and I'm still half-dressed in sloppy, paint-stained clothes.

Screw this.

With quick fingers, I unknot my T-shirt and grab the hem, hoisting it over my head to toss haphazardly to the floor. It leaves me standing there in my mismatched and unsexy bra and panties. There's only one way to fix that. Reaching back, I quickly unfasten and shed my bra. Hooking my thumbs under my panties, I shed those too.

Shane leans back on his haunches and looks momentarily startled as he takes in my naked form. "Damn. You're …" His intense gaze settles first on my breasts. "So incredibly beautiful." And then he's rising to his feet, catching my mouth with his on the way up, his hands cradling each side of my face. He gently herds me backward to my bed, all while his lips move fervently over mine.

The backs of my legs hit my bed frame and then suddenly I'm on my mattress, lying on my back, Shane on top of me, fitting his hips between my thighs. But he doesn't move beyond kissing me, his hands weaving with mine to pin them above my head, our tongues tangled in a seductive dance that draws a moan from my throat.

It would be easy to skip foreplay, take off his shorts, and go straight to the main event. But Shane doesn't seem to be in any rush, our kiss dragging on by the minute, much like we used to do all those years ago.

Except I'm naked, and he's lying between my thighs, and his

erection pressed against my core is torture that's intensifying by the second.

Finally, I can't help myself. I roll my hips.

He groans. "Are you *trying* to kill me?"

A flash of the mating bug calendar—specifically September's praying mantis—hits me and I laugh. "Not until after you've served your purpose."

"I guess I better take my time, then." Releasing his grip of my hands, he shifts his body to lie next to mine.

I mumble my displeasure and he shushes me through a kiss, his lips shifting to my jawline, then to my neck and my collarbone, the trail of kisses slow-going and teasing and wet. His hand has found its way to my breast, and the pad of his thumb rubs smoothly and methodically against one of my pebbled nipples.

"Your skin tastes the same as it did back then," he murmurs against my flesh.

"Really? Like what?" I trail my fingertips over his arm, marveling at his sculpted biceps.

He takes the untended nipple in his mouth and I shiver as his teeth grazes my skin. "Sweet."

I shiver a second time as his palm slides down the length of my body, along my stomach, down farther. One of his long, slender fingers slips across my slick entrance. A whispered curse escapes as he pushes it deep inside me, followed by a second that makes my thighs part for better access.

"You're so wet," he rasps.

"I always am around you," I confess, dragging my fingertips along his back, intoxicated by the plane of hard, lean muscle. "But this is not how I saw today going."

"Is it better?"

"I haven't decided yet," I joke.

"Let me help you decide." Hot breath teases my skin as he shimmies his big body down, his tongue leaving a wet line along the center of my abdomen, dipping into my belly button, before he's kneeling before me once again, his eyes alive with lust and riveted on the view.

"I think we're failing at the taking-it-slow part," I whisper, as my body tingles with expectation.

"You want me to stop?" he asks, swallowing hard, his chest laboring with his uneven breaths.

I answer by parting my legs even farther apart. I don't know how I stopped this from happening all those years ago. I must have been stronger, more resolute, at seventeen than I am at thirty, I accept, as I shift my hips, welcoming him in.

I shudder with the first swipe of Shane's tongue along my sensitive flesh. It's quickly followed by another, and another, as he expertly works me over as thoroughly as he just kissed my mouth, his strong hands gripping my thighs, stroking them while keeping them spread.

I can't help the sigh as my body sinks into the mattress, buzzing with the building pleasure. While I don't take nearly as long as Justine says she does to get off, I'm not the sprinting cheetah of orgasms. But my thighs are beginning to prickle with warmth. Maybe it's all these weeks of pent-up frustration. Or maybe it's that gorgeous face between my legs. If Shane's this talented with just his tongue, what will his—

"Good?"

My muscles instinctively tighten beneath his murmur. "Yes. You should give lessons." My voice is embarrassingly breathless.

His responding chuckle causes a second clench. "Lessons? To whom?"

"To men, everywhere. Now, please stop talking." I reach for his silky hair, threading my fingers through, and pull his face in closer as I roll my hips.

He curses and seems to take that as his sign to dial things up because I feel his touch once again, his fingers curling to hit a spot deep inside me, making me gasp. My body responds with eagerness, undulating, welcoming the slow and steady work of his moving hand and the rush of the impending orgasm.

It hits swiftly, pushing me over the brink to ride the waves, Shane's name escaping with a deep cry of pleasure.

"Holy shit," he whispers, his breathing ragged, his eyes shining with awe, his lips glossy and swollen as he watches me for a moment. Pulling himself to his feet, he towers over my splayed, boneless body—all six foot whatever of him, shirtless, his torso tanned and hard, his chest heaving, his dick pitching an impressive tent within his shorts.

"*Please* tell me you have a condom somewhere in this mess?" he asks in a gruff voice.

I grin lazily. "I have a whole box in my nightstand. Unopened. And big enough to fit Dixon's bananas."

His dimples flash with his cocky grin. "Those got nothing on me, babe." His thumbs hook under the waistband of his shorts and I hold my breath, watching with eager eyes as I'm about to get my first full close-up view of naked Shane.

Rap music begins playing inside his pocket. It takes me a second to realize it's a ringtone.

Shane tips his head back and lets out a guttural groan. "You've gotta be kidding me!" He takes several calming breaths before abandoning the strip show to slip his phone out of his pocket. "Hey, buddy. Yeah … uh-huh …"

It has to be Cody.

"Do you *really* need me …" Shane pinches the bridge of his nose. "Yeah, okay. I'm just"—he grits his jaw—"finishing up here. Be home in a minute." He ends the call. "I've gotta go."

My disappointment swells. "He's stuck on a level?"

"I'm going to tear the power cable out of the wall," he grumbles, but then sighs. "I promised him I'd take him to the mall to buy some new clothes. He doesn't like going with his mother." Shane's eyes rake over my naked body. "But I *really* don't want to go."

"I can see why you wouldn't." I stare pointedly at his groin, at the still-prominent hard ridge. My body was priming itself for the promise of feeling *that* inside me and I *really* don't want him to leave either. But I'm also not willing to rush it. "We can pick this up another time."

"Promise?" He peers at me now, not with his typical confidence but with a hint of hesitation. As if he's afraid I might change my mind about allowing this to happen if given time to come to my senses.

I smile. "Maybe dinner first next time."

He crawls onto the bed to hover over me, searching my facial features. "You know I would do that for you all night."

I skate my fingertips over his sexy jawline. "And I would let you."

He leans in to press a soft, leisurely kiss against my lips before pulling away with a heavy sigh. "Until next time." He reaches for his discarded T-shirt.

I grunt with disapproval as I watch that stunning torso disappear behind a veil of crisp white cotton. With a gentle pat against my calf, he strolls for the stairs, flicking at the spare key hanging off the banister. "Don't forget this is here."

"Do you have any more keys I should know about?"

He laughs. "No, unfortunately. And you *really* should change your locks."

"Worked out for me rather well this time, don't you think?"

With a smirk and one last, longing gaze down the length of my naked body sprawled across my bed, followed by a quiet curse, he disappears down my steps.

It's a long while before I force myself up to dress and return to my task.

TWENTY

Shane's front door creaks open at seven on Sunday morning, as I'm digging a particularly stubborn weed from my garden bed. Memories of yesterday are still firmly emblazoned in my mind, so when I look up to see him standing on his front porch in navy track pants, running shoes, and nothing else, my heart rate goes from zero to sixty in a blink.

He trots down his steps and heads toward me, his chiseled arms lifting over his head in a series of warm-up stretches. It's the perfect day for a run, the sky clear, the temperature comfortably crisp. It reminds me that I haven't gone for one since I moved here, this house swallowing up my time and energy. I'll need to start again soon and get myself into a routine.

For now, though, I just need to keep my wits about me.

Shane comes to a stop on the other side of my picket fence to loom over me. "You're up early on a Sunday."

"Wanted to get a head start on the day." The truth is I *couldn't* sleep. I tossed and turned half the night, thoughts of my neighbor keeping my body wired with need and my mind spinning with wandering thoughts. "Isn't it a little early for *you,* though?" Those twenty-four-hour shifts must be deadly for his internal clock.

"Cody and I have a busy day ahead of us. We always visit my parents on Sundays when I'm not working. I wanted to get a run in before he wakes up." He grabs an ankle and pulls it behind to loosen his hamstrings.

And I do my best not to notice his sculpted abdominal muscles, or how his pants hang low on his hips, or the deep, muscular V that begs to direct my attention south to the notable bulge tucked inside.

God, how I love track pants for the lack of modesty they afford.

He catches me staring at his crotch, and his full lips curve into a knowing smirk. Those lips that were buried between my thighs yesterday afternoon.

How are we supposed to act around each other now?

"Do you want to talk about it?" he asks, as if reading my mind.

I shove the hand trowel deep into the soil, severing the weed's root. "About you helping me paint my room?"

He chuckles. "That's honestly all I intended to happen when I came over."

"Uh-huh." I give him a doubtful look. "I thought we agreed to take things slow."

His hands go up in surrender. "Hey, *you're* the one who flashed me." His voice has dropped to a low timbre. I feel it in my chest.

"That was an accident."

"Uh-huh," he parrots.

I laugh and toss a weed at him. "Shut up."

He catches it in the air and leans over to drop it into the yard waste bag.

And I stare shamelessly at his naked chest.

"You don't regret it, do you?"

"No." Though it's going to make a simple kiss good night seem laughable going forward.

"Good." A secretive smile touches his lips. "So, Tuesday night, two old friends from high school are going to grab a bite at the Patty Shack, right?"

"Just two old friends?"

"Might be a bit of a stretch." He winks. "But it's not an outright lie and no one can say otherwise."

I'm far more okay with this plan than I expected to be. "Sounds good."

I watch him go, my focus on how those pants hug his hard, round backside, and a part of me wishes we hadn't been interrupted. I would probably still be able to feel Shane inside me this morning.

Cody's teacher or not, I look forward to that delicious ache.

But sex changes things. Even yesterday afternoon's escapade has changed our dynamic. I feel proprietary over him—that he is somehow mine.

Perhaps it's a delusion. Given what he said to me at Thursday's parents' night, perhaps not. But there's no need to rush this. We've technically waited thirteen years.

Shane turns left and heads along the sidewalk past my house, his pecs jolting with each pound of his foot, his facial features stony and determined. That is, until he turns my way and flashes a smile, followed by a lazy wave. He doesn't slow to see if I return it.

My heart sings.

With one last heave of my bed frame to center it against the wall, I step back to admire my newly finished bedroom. I knew the silver and plum bedding would complement the paint color beautifully because I had the paint sample with me at the store. However, I wasn't so sure about the accents—the charcoal-gray, faux-fur mat, the dove-gray cushion, the pastel watercolor prints —until now. They're perfect.

With a sigh of satisfaction that I've finished another room in my perfect little dilapidated home, I amble into my cramped bathroom to start the bath, hoping Epsom salts will leach the ache from my muscles. While the water's running, I set to folding the heap of freshly washed laundry. I didn't get around to grocery shopping today, but at least I have clean clothes ready for another week of work.

I'm folding and humming to myself when the now-familiar rumble of Shane's engine sounds. I dart to my window without a second's thought, eager for a glimpse of Shane. I saw them leave before noon today and it's almost nine now.

A warmth fills my chest at the sight of the two of them strolling up the walkway side by side, Shane's arm slung over his son's shoulder, Cody with a football in his hands, peering up at his father as he chatters away. I can hear his boyish voice and Shane's deep, throaty one through my cracked window, but I can't make out what they're talking about.

Suddenly, Shane looks up to my bedroom window.

I don't jump back this time but instead pretend to fuss with my new curtain rod.

"Hey, Scar! You need help painting tonight?" he hollers.

I slide my window open all the way and lean out, mentally adding "window screen" to the list. "I'm actually done."

His lips twist with disappointment, and I realize my error. "But I *could* use help moving my bed."

The returning grin is wide and devilish. "I can *definitely* help you move your bed."

"Hey, Ms. Reed!" Cody chirps his standard greeting.

It suitably distracts me from Shane's dirty insinuation. "Hi, Cody. Are you ready for your math test tomorrow?"

His face falls.

"What math test?" Shane peers down at his son. "You told me you didn't have any homework."

"I don't! It's a test."

"Studying for a test *is* homework." He frowns. "And I gave you two extra hours to play your PS4 because you lied to me."

"But I didn't lie." Petulance fills Cody's voice.

"Do I need to check with your teacher from now on to make sure you're telling me the truth? Because I can. She lives right next door."

Cody studies his shoes instead of looking his father in the eye, his previously cheerful mood diving into sulkiness.

Shane sighs. "You've lost your gaming until Friday."

Cody's head snaps up. "But—"

"Not another word or it'll be *two* weeks," he warns severely, checking his watch. "Get inside and get cleaned up fast. I can't stay up late to help you. I've got work in the morning and I'm beat."

Cody scrambles into the house.

"I'm not going to earn points with the kid if I rat him out, am I?" Part of me regrets mentioning the test. But is it wrong that a fresh spark of desire surged through me, watching this new stern, disciplinary version of Shane?

"He knows what he did was wrong." Shane reaches back to rub his neck. "Rain check on moving that bed?"

The playfulness is gone from his voice, but I smile anyway. Cody might not pick up on his father's coded language but if any neighbors were listening in, they'll surely have something to gossip about. "Sure. Have a good day at work."

"You too." He disappears into his house.

For the first time since I moved in, I am deliriously happy that Shane Beckett is my next-door neighbor.

TWENTY-ONE

I study myself in the full-length mirror as the nervous flutter that's been swirling in my stomach since this morning stirs again. This outfit might be too upscale for the Patty Shack. It's a casual split dress—a soft cotton-spandex blend in army green with short sleeves and a round collar—but coupled with jewelry and wedge heels, it could easily work at a ritzy downtown restaurant. Maybe jeans would be more suitable for the greasy diner. But I want to look good. Desirable.

I shiver as déjà vu washes over me. I've lived this moment before. In a different home, as a different person—when I was seventeen and getting ready for my first date with Shane. I didn't know him at all then. I know him now.

At least, I hope I do.

A sharp knock sounds on my front door, ending any opportunity left to test another ensemble.

My body is tense with a mixture of emotions—excitement, nervousness, worry, uncertainty—as I head downstairs, grabbing my purse and keys along the way.

The sight of Shane on my doorstep, in dark-wash jeans and a black, long-sleeve cotton shirt that hugs his powerful shoulders, makes my body hum with anticipation. I haven't seen him since Sunday night—less than forty-eight hours—and yet somehow that has felt like three times as long.

My smile is genuine and broad. "Hey."

"Hey." One appreciative rake of his eyes tells me I chose well with this dress. "You look really nice."

"Thank you." We both linger. Are we supposed to kiss? Have we reached that point already where we kiss at the beginning of a date? I mean, he had his face buried between my legs three days ago. I feel like we've skipped a few steps.

I *want* to kiss him.

He's staring at my lips, and I'm sure the urge is mutual.

He inhales sharply, as if catching himself, and takes a step back. "Ready?"

Disappointment pricks me—*why am I waiting for him to make the first move?*—as I pull my door shut and lock it. "Surprised you didn't use a key this time." I hid the spare beneath a rocking chair, in case I ever lock myself out.

"I told you I only had the one." He pauses. "I can take it back, if you want."

"I'm not a senior citizen with balance issues, and you haven't earned the privilege of having a key to my house yet."

"*Yet* ..." He bites his bottom lip, taking in my face, my hair, my dress. "You look *really* good tonight."

I smile. "You already said that."

"Did I?" He swallows hard. "We should probably get out of here, then."

"Before we can't?"

"Something like that." When his eyes lifts to meet mine again and I see how they've darkened, I know he's not kidding.

A part of me—who the hell am I kidding, *all* of me—would like to forget dinner and head back upstairs to pick up where we left off.

With a deep exhale, Shane takes another step back. And another. He holds out his hand. "Come on."

"How can you not remember Philpott's tests? They were *brutal.* Dean and Steve nearly got kicked off the team because of their grades in his class." Shane glowers between a bite of a french fry. "His multiple-choice questions were impossible. There'd be six options and *at least* one trick question buried in there. You couldn't guess your way to a right answer."

"Huh. Maybe that's why I don't really remember. I didn't have to guess. I knew the answers." I take a long, obnoxious slurp of my vanilla shake.

Shane chuckles. "Oh, that's right, you were a big nerd, weren't you?"

"No. I was just smarter than you football meatheads," I say with a wink. I *was* a big nerd—hello, mathlete champion, two years in a row. I lean back in the booth and take in the interior of the Patty Shack for the hundredth time. The nostalgia of being here on a date with Shane again hasn't faded yet. It probably helps that the owners haven't changed a thing, aside from perhaps a fresh coat of Pepto-Bismol-pink paint on the walls. The same teal-blue stools line the black-and-white-checkered bar, the same vibrant metal Coke and state map signs dressing the walls, the same red-and-white-striped, faux-leather booths welcome diners. Booths that are still a touch too narrow, giving patrons little legroom. I never appreciated how wild and vibrant the colors in this place were back then.

Mom always loved a good greasy breakfast after a night of drinking. We came here dozens of times while I was growing up. But it was just a fun, fifties-style diner to grab a burger or a cheap plate of eggs and bacon and drop a few quarters into the old-time jukebox in the corner.

Then Shane and I had our first date, and everything changed. The memories tied to the Patty Shack changed. After we broke up, I couldn't hear the chime of the door without thinking of him. And then I spotted Shane and Penelope sitting in a booth, hand in hand, and I stopped coming here.

"What's so funny?" Shane asks, and I realize I'm smiling.

"Nothing. Just ..." It's easy to forget how consuming and volatile emotions can be at that age. When I was in the midst of that heartbreak, I couldn't think of *anything* but Shane; I couldn't imagine how I would ever move on. Looking back, it seems so melodramatic now. But my world was smaller, my experiences limited. "Didn't we sit somewhere around here, that first night?" I ask casually.

"It was this booth. Why do you think I picked it?"

I know it was this booth, but I'm surprised he remembers.

He smiles through a sip of his Coke. "I told you, I remember a lot from that summer."

"Like what?"

"Like ..." His beautiful eyes drag over the diner's tacky metal pendant light as he searches his thoughts. "That night, you didn't know there was bacon on your burger until you bit into it and you looked like you were going to puke. Or cry."

I laugh through a wince. "My anti-pork phase." I'd watched a late-night documentary on pig slaughterhouses six months before that and had sworn off all support of the industry. "I'm over that."

"I figured, given the full frying pan of it in your house that weekend."

"That was more Justine's doing." She could be a bacon spokesperson for the amount of it she eats. "What else do you remember?"

"You *loved* Dr. Pepper."

"Still do, but I've cut out soda." I wave the glass of water to prove my point.

His gaze flickers to my fingers with the act. "You loved wearing black nail polish but you'd always pick at it."

I groan, absently fumbling with my freshly manicured nails that I did myself last night. "Light as a Feather" the color is called —white, but with a gray undertone.

"And you get *insanely* competitive when you play Jenga."

He's referring to that night at Phil Moaz's house, when it was pouring rain outside and someone had the bright idea to get into the games cupboard. "What was the point? They were all so drunk, they couldn't stack the blocks right to start," I declare with indignation, earning his laugh.

I like reminiscing with Shane about that summer, now that bitterness over the aftermath isn't invading my every thought.

Does that mean I'm finally letting go?

He glances around us, checking the other tables. It's Tuesday night—only three are occupied and none of them nearby. Still, he lowers his voice. "And I remember that cute little dress you were wearing on our first date."

I frown, vaguely recalling the casual pale-pink floral sundress I'd settled on. It seemed perfect for the summer. "What about it?"

He reaches across the table and steals a fry from my plate, having finished his. "The material was so thin, I could see your panties through it."

I gasp. "You could not!"

"Yeah, I could." He grins devilishly. "They were dark. Navy blue or black, I couldn't tell, but I made a bet with myself that they were black. I was hoping to find out."

I can't remember what color panties I was wearing that night. He could be lying. Something tells me he isn't, though. "So, you're telling me you were a pervert back then?"

"Then ... now ..." His grin widens. Beneath the table where his legs stretch out, his knee rubs against mine.

The simple contact sends a shiver running through my entire

body. "And there you were, pretending you were the perfect gentleman."

He shrugs. "Hey, I didn't *expect* anything, but that doesn't mean I wasn't hoping for it."

I grab one more fry before I push my plate aside, my stomach full. "You never did find out."

"No, I did not." He laughs. "First time I'd gotten nothing more than a chaste good-night kiss since I was fifteen."

"Were you disappointed?" I ask somberly.

"Not for a second. It gave me something to look forward to." He wipes his face with his napkin and, finished with eating, folds his hands on the table in front of him.

I feel the impulse to reach across and collect his hands in mine. But I remind myself that we're two old friends out for dinner, catching up on life. Friends don't hold hands.

The server, a cute teenage girl with a fresh face and a long, brown ponytail, comes to collect our dishes. "Anything else?" she asks, her chocolate brown eyes lingering on Shane. She can't be more than seventeen. Does thirty-year-old Shane have as much appeal for a girl her age as the seventeen-year-old version did?

He gives her a perfunctory, polite smile. "Yes, the lady would like an ice-cream cone. Vanilla, please." When my mouth opens to cancel that order, he gives me a look. "Don't even try it. You love the ice cream here."

I eye my emptied milkshake. I *do* love it. It's creamier than most.

And if Shane thought he could throw around all these casual little tie-ins from our first date to make me swoon … he was right.

"So, yes?" The server lingers for two beats and, when she is sure the order won't be changed, she trots off.

"This is nice, huh?" He rubs his triceps as his focus wanders.

I peel my admiring gaze from the veins—even his veins are attractive—along his forearms and follow his line of sight to the bulletin board and the familiar orange flyer that takes prominent space in the center.

"So, 'Hunky Heroes for a Night,' huh?" I tease.

He chuckles. "It seems it's turned into part of the job description."

"Just like posing half-naked for a calendar?"

That get a sly smile in response. "What am I supposed to say? It's for charity."

"I guess. Especially when you're the big-ticket item."

His eyebrow arches.

"Becca told me."

He nods, as if that makes sense. I'm beginning to think Becca might be a known source of gossip around town. "So, how many of these auctions have you been a part of now?"

He leans back in his seat, frowning in thought. "Five, I think?"

"Just a regular American gigolo, then."

"*Stop.*" But he's laughing as he gives me another soft knee bump. This time, I return the affectionate nudge, stretching my leg out to press against his inner thigh.

A muscle in his jaw ticks.

I stifle the smile threatening to escape. I forgot how much I enjoyed teasing him. "Anything *weird* happen on those auction dates?"

He lets out the softest sigh, as if to compose himself. "Nah. It's not like that. Luigi ran it until he died. Now Route Sixty-Six hosts. Either way, it's the same every year. I pick up the winner and we go to dinner at the restaurant. One year, the winner didn't even want dinner. She was this seventy-six-year-old grandma who just liked the rush of winning an auction and was happy to donate to charity. I don't think anyone bids with the hope of getting more than dinner."

"You should maybe ask your chief about that," I murmur through a sip of my water.

"Who? Cassidy?" Shane frowns curiously. "What do you mean?"

"My mother won him last year." I give Shane a meaningful look.

He shakes his head and laughs. "Cassidy and your mom did not hook up that night."

"That's not what she said."

"I told you. That's all an act with her. She strings men along but she doesn't actually go home with them."

"Yeah, I shared an apartment with her for eighteen years and I beg to differ."

"Maybe she used to," he concedes. "But now it's a game for her. And Cassidy isn't that kind of guy."

The way my mom lays it on? "Please. You're *all* 'that kind of guy.'"

"I'm not that," he says evenly. When he meets my doubtful gaze, he amends more softly, "Not *anymore*. People fuck up but they also change. It's not fair to hold them to one standard forever when they're trying to be better. And listen, I get that Dottie's never going to win any Mother of the Year awards and why you have a skewed view of men, but we're not *all* like that. At least, some of us try not to be."

This conversation has gone from flirtatious to bordering on a therapy session, one delivered in lecture form by a father figure.

"You're right. People can change. They *do* change. I'm sorry."

He inhales and then, after a moment, nods as if accepting my apology.

"So …" I draw circles over the table's smooth surface as I search for a way back to our earlier conversation. "Nothing weird at the auctions, then."

He scratches his jaw in thought. "Well, there *was* that one time the winner asked me to be the entertainment at her daughter's bachelorette party."

My eyebrows pop. "And, by entertainment, you mean …"

"Let's just say she was hoping I'd show up wearing my firefighter gear and leave without it on."

"This mom tried to hire a stripper for her daughter through a charity event?" My mouth gapes. Though, a part of me can't blame her. I've been to more than one bachelorette party with male strippers, and none of them were appealing. Apparently, those of Chippendales quality are outrageously expensive. To hire a guy who looks like Shane, whether he has any skill in the actual art of stripping, would require a huge budget that the average bridesmaid doesn't have.

"She offered me extra cash on the side too," he adds with a shrug.

I wait a few beats until I finally have to ask, "Did you *do* it?" There's accusation in my tone.

"Fuck, no!" he scoffs, laughing. "It's not my thing."

I breathe a sigh of relief. The calendar and auction, I can maybe get on board with, because it's for charity. But having a boyfriend who got paid to get naked for hordes of thirsty women …

A boyfriend. That's the first time I've thought of Shane in that context in *so* many years. We're not there yet. We're just seeing each other for now, I guess? And, if we're taking this slow and keeping it a secret, when will we venture firmly into official label territory?

"Dean was busting my balls to do it, though," Shane says.

"I'm sure they would have been *more* than happy to have him sub for you."

Shane's brow knits together.

Right. I hit on Dean in front of him. "I have zero interest in him, by the way," I assure Shane as I silently admonish myself. Tonight's the night for sticking my foot in my mouth, apparently.

Thankfully, the server arrives and hands me my cone, and I take the opportunity to steer away from that topic. "So, do you *like* doing the auction?"

He waves a hand absently. "I don't *not* like doing it."

Shane's gaze is on me as I savor the first taste. I haven't forgotten his admission, about the ice-cream cone and the restroom.

He gives his head an almost indiscernible shake before continuing. "Like I said, it's for a good cause and if I can help that way, why not? We raise so much money. I love going out to buy all the gifts and delivering them to the kids in the hospital around Christmas. Seeing them smile makes it worth it ..." His voice trails. "You're doing that on purpose, aren't you?"

My tongue pauses midswirl around the top of my ice-cream cone. I wasn't, actually. I was enthralled listening to the white knight highlight his good deeds. But now that he's drawn my attention, now that I see the way his eyes track my tongue and how his lips have parted, I'm acutely aware of my teasing. "Doing what?" I take another long, slow lick around the top. I think about doing the same to a specific body part of Shane's, and my throat goes dry.

Now, I know *exactly* what I'm doing.

So does Shane. "Glad to see you're enjoying it so much," he says, clearing his throat.

"I *would* enjoy it. I mean ... I *am*." I offer him a sly grin.

He curses under his breath as he slides out of our booth. "I'll be back in a minute."

"Where are you going?" I ask innocently.

His smirk is half humor, half resignation. "That soda went right through me."

"You're going to the restroom *again*?" I holler after him, obnoxiously loud. "But you just went!"

He shoots a warning glance over his shoulder and I respond with another lick of my cone that makes his jaw tense. Taunting him is too much fun.

My eyes are glued to him as he strolls to the back of the

restaurant, admiring his broad shoulders, his ass, his stride, his everything.

When I turn back, Madame Bott is standing over me.

"Jesus!" I yelp, jolting in my seat from shock. My ice-cream cone topples out of my hand and lands on the table's smooth surface.

"Hello, Scarlet," she says in that reedy voice.

"Hi," I stammer. "I didn't see you come in." Did she materialize from thin air? Where the hell did she come from?

"I don't imagine so. I noticed you when I arrived to pick up my order, but you seemed *enthralled* in your conversation." Her attention drifts toward the back to where Shane just disappeared, and her eyes narrow. "He looks familiar."

"That's Shane Beckett. He went to Polson Falls Elementary." It was many years ago and he's an adult now, but she *must* remember him.

A small puddle of melted ice cream is quickly forming beneath the upturned cone. I reach for a wad of napkins from the dispenser on our table to clean it up, disappointed. I may have declined the cone at first, but I was enjoying it. Though maybe it's for the best. I couldn't very well savor it while the witch of Polson Falls hovers over me.

"It's *nice* to see you two out for dinner." She wields the word *nice* as if it means something entirely different. Something *not* nice.

I force a smile. "It is! We're finally catching up on life, now that we're neighbors. Of course, we've been friends for years." Minus that brief thirteen-year period where I wanted to crush his balls with a hammer.

"His son is in your class, isn't he?" she asks lightly, and I can see from the glint in her eye that she knows damn well he is.

I feel my smile shift from fake polite to fuck you. "Cody Rhodes. Yes."

"Hmm." Such a simple sound, and yet it tells me all I need to know—Bott doesn't buy my story and doesn't approve. If she were anyone but the woman who interrogated a nine-year-old student in search of evidence of her husband's philandering, I might feel guilty about lying.

Regardless, it doesn't matter what she believes or approves of, I remind myself, because Shane and I *are* old friends and neighbors. Anything else is none of her—or anyone else's—business.

"Order number thirty-one!" the cashier hollers, holding up a brown paper bag with the Patty Shack's logo across it.

There's no one else waiting for takeout so I assume it's hers, but Bott doesn't so much as twitch, staring so intently at me, it's like she's staring *through* me.

I feel like I'm nine and squirming in the corner of room 128 all over again.

Shane's reappearance abruptly breaks her trance.

"Shane Beckett." She *loves* using people's full names.

"Madame Bott. Sorry, I think it's Parish now, right? Good to see you again." He flashes that sexy smile.

She dips her chin but offers no smile in return, as if immune to his charms. "You as well."

Speak for yourselves. If she doesn't leave soon, I'm worried I'm going to break out in hives.

"Number thirty-one!" the cashier calls out a second time, and now she's glaring at Bott's back, an impatient twitch to her face.

"I think your order's ready." Can she hear the wish for her to leave in my voice?

"Yes. I think so." Bott's penetrating eyes linger on me another moment, her hand clasped over that odd talisman necklace, her thumb and index finger dragging over the beaded surface. "Enjoy your night *catching up*." Under her breath, she adds softly, "Careful, Scarlet." Her heavy black skirt swirls as she glides to the counter to collect the brown paper bag, and then she's gone, the ding of the bell above the door announcing her departure.

Shane watches her pass along the sidewalk. "What was that about?"

"Nothing." Is it nothing, though? Is Bott going to be a problem? Will she say something to Wendy about her suspicions that I'm dating my student's father? Should I be worried about what Wendy will say? Should I care?

We're both adults and we're not breaking any official rules.

Shane frowns at the melted mess on the table and then at my hands that are covered in melted ice cream. "What happened?"

I sigh heavily, hoping the act will help shake the cloud of unease Bott left behind. "I dropped it."

Amusement takes over his face. "You know, Cody dropped his ice-cream cone once too. He was five. He cried and I had to buy him a new one. Do you need a new one?"

Now he's just teasing me. "Do *you* need me to have a new one?"

"I think I'm probably better off this way."

"That was an embarrassingly fast jerk-off, even for an old pro like yourself."

"I didn't—" He burst with laughter, showing those intoxicating dimples that make him even more attractive. "Go wash your sticky hands while I settle the bill. We have somewhere to be, and you're not allowed in my car like *that*."

I frown curiously. "Where are we going?"

His eyes sparkle with excitement. "A place you *love*."

Shane's car is an attention whore.

I watch people gawk as we drive along Main Street. It's been that way since we pulled out of his driveway in this vintage beast. I can't blame them—you don't see too many classics on the road anymore, outside of a car show. Before this, the oldest car I remember ever riding in was my mother's '86 Ford Tempo, and there's no one in a rush to restore those metal shitcans.

I'm no '67 Chevy Impala expert but Shane seems to have taken great care in bringing this one back to its original splendor. The black tufted-leather bench seats have all been reupholstered, the interior has been scrubbed spotless, and voices still croon from the AM/FM radio in the dash. But my favorite thing about the car is the engine's deep rumble vibrating through my limbs. That, and how utterly sexy Shane looks behind the wheel, his elbow propped against the open window, his hand gripping the steering wheel lazily at the six o'clock position.

"You get three guesses." Shane pulls into the left lane. The turn signal makes a loud, fast *click-click-click,* distracting me for a moment.

Maybe we're doing drinks after dinner. "Route Sixty-Six?"

"That's back that way." He juts a thumb behind us as he makes the turn.

"Oh, yeah." And it's obvious we're leaving downtown Polson Falls. "Home Depot?"

"I said I was taking you somewhere you *love.*" He frowns at me. "Are you saying you *love* Home Depot?"

"No, but I *do* need a new fire extinguisher."

"You do," he agrees with a smirk. "But they're closing soon anyway. We can do that this weekend. Guess again."

I tamp down the delight that comes with the idea that Shane is making plans with me for this weekend—that he's assuming, rightfully so, I'd want to spend more time with him. I search the stretch of road ahead of us. There really isn't anywhere I love in Polson Falls.

Besides my home, that is.

Is this his covert way of saying he's taking us back to my place for sex?

God, I hope so.

The engine roars as he makes a right turn, away from Hickory Street and my bed, and I'm left clueless again.

A familiar bell tower looms ahead. "The fire station?"

He shakes his head. "You're terrible at this game."

"Give me a hint!" What's there to do in Polson Falls on a Tuesday night?

"I did already. I can't believe you don't remember." He sounds put out, but I know it's a facade.

"Maybe that summer wasn't as memorable for me after all," I throw back dryly.

The corner of his mouth twitches as he reaches across the leather bench seat and slips his fingers through mine, giving them a squeeze.

We coast along the street in silence, hand in hand. I'm still clueless but I'm too focused on the way his calloused thumb is drawing circles over my palm, the same way it did over my body last Saturday, to care where he's taking me. It's been forever since something as innocent as a man's hand in mine could be so enthralling.

Up ahead, a steady line of cars is turning into the Galaxy Drive-In parking lot.

"Figured it out yet?" he taunts.

"Are you kidding me?" I laugh. "I *hated* this place!"

He affords a quick glance away from the road to look at me in disbelief. "You did *not* hate this place."

"I *worked* here for two summers." I haven't stepped foot on the property since my last shift shoveling popcorn and pouring fountain drinks.

"Fine, but you didn't hate it when you were here with me."

"True," I admit begrudgingly. Being an employee meant I could get us in for half price—and sometimes free, depending on who was working the gate. We came here every week on my nights off that summer, to lounge in the back of Dean's truck, inhaling Dr. Pepper—sometimes laced with alcohol—and make out. It was being with Shane that I loved, *not* Galaxy Drive-In. "Since when are they open on a Tuesday in September?" They only ever played movies throughout the week during the summer.

"I think they've been hurting for cash so they started opening up for cheap nights, playing older movies. A last money grab before they close next month." Shane pays the young male attendant at the gate and coasts in.

The place is busier than I'd expect for an off-season Tuesday night. It's a relic with its one screen, and yet it apparently hasn't failed to still bring in a crowd. Several rows of cars are lined up as people settle in, filtering to and from the concession stand—a small blue shack that used to be yellow. It appears they even updated the dingy restroom unit. Somehow working the concession stand also earned me the job of cleaning those out at the end of the night. I've long since blocked the horrors of that task from my mind.

Shane parks in an empty spot in the back corner, leaving plenty of space between us and a Honda. The occupants—a man and his teenage son—turn to gawk at us.

"Do you like the attention you earn in this beast?"

"Honestly, I don't notice anymore." He cuts the engine and then shifts his body, stretching his arm across the back of the long bench seat. The move pulls his shirt tight over his chest as he turns to face me. "So?" He pushes a strand of hair off my forehead. "You up for this?"

Up for what exactly?

We spent a lot of time at the drive-in, *not* watching movies that summer. We're parked back here, away from prying eyes. Was that strategic on his part?

"What's playing tonight?" I crane my neck but can't read the marquee from here.

"*Saw*."

I groan, letting my head fall back against the seat—and his

arm. "This is going to be *The Ring* all over again, isn't it?" I hate horror movies. I spent a good chunk of that night hiding my face in his neck.

"I hope so." Chuckling and giving my shoulder an affectionate squeeze, he unbuckles his seat belt. "Dr. Pepper?"

"Sure, why not?" Burgers and milkshakes, now soda and popcorn. "I'm going to vomit before the end of the night."

"As long as you don't do it in my car." He slides out.

I settle my arm where his was a moment ago, across the back of the seat. Resting my chin on my arm, I continue with my new favorite pastime—admiring Shane's ass as he strolls away from me. Every square inch of that man is perfect.

Including, I'm beginning to see, his heart.

Five minutes later, Shane is trudging back, his arms loaded with the red tray they loan out to carry multiple concession purchases. "Didn't know what you'd want," he says, sliding the tray over the seat. He tucks the fountain drinks into a cup holder attachment off the dash—the only modern thing in here.

"So, you bought *everything*." Popcorn, licorice, three types of candy bars, and a box of Hot Tamales.

"Basically."

Seriously, I'm going to be sick. But I smile and say thanks because he's being so sweet and thoughtful.

Shane fumbles with a lever and the trunk releases. He's gone and back again within moments, this time with an arm full of blankets.

"Do you always travel with those?" Not that I'm unappreciative. The fall evenings have grown chilly. But that wary voice in the back of my mind whispers questions. *How many times has he done this exact thing with a date? How many women have curled up in this exact spot with those exact blankets?*

"I told you, I planned this whole night out." He pauses long enough to flash me a dimpled smile before rearranging our snack bucket on the floor.

And where exactly does the night end for us? Has he planned that far out too?

"It's perfect," I say instead of asking, because sometimes you have to shush those suspicious little voices and just let things you want to happen, happen.

Tonight feels like one of those nights where *anything* can happen between us.

"I was thinking of taking the truck tonight but the great thing about these old cars"—he slides over to the center of the bench seat, smoothing the layer of blankets over us, covering our bodies from the waist down for warmth—"is that we can sit like this." He stretches his arm along the back of the seat and then beckons, "Come here."

I shimmy over until I'm next to him, thigh to thigh, my shoulder wedged in against his side, his arm curling around my body.

Careful, Scarlet.

Bott's warning lingers in my mind.

"Is this a good idea? Us, out here in the open, I mean?" I've already dwelled on all the reasons why this might not be a good reason in general, and yet, here we are.

"It's dark and no one's paying attention. And we're all the way back here." He nods at the Honda at least ten feet away from us. "You think those two care about anything but the psycho who sets death traps to murder people?"

"So *that's* what this movie is about." Hesitating for only a beat, I burrow in closer, reveling in the heat from Shane's hard body. I covertly inhale his cologne for the hundredth time.

"See? Just two friends, hanging out, watching a scary movie."

"Is that all this is?" I mean it to be flippant.

An index finger catches my chin and guides my face toward his, only inches away. Even in the dark, thanks to the movie screen ahead, I can see the warm amber of his eyes. Another wave of nostalgia hits me, calling back to a younger version of the man sitting next to me, to a younger, more enamored version of myself. "I want more than that with you." His gaze drops to my lips. "You know that."

An electric current hangs in the air. Perhaps I'm no less enamored by Shane Beckett now than I was at seventeen. My stomach flutters as I wait expectantly for him to close those last few inches and kiss me.

But instead, he turns back toward the screen and cranks the volume on the radio channel frequency that plays the audio for the movie. He shifts in his seat, splaying his legs as if he's getting comfortable to watch. "Just so you know, this is a *really* fucked-up movie."

My dramatic sigh fills the car's interior, a mask for the intense physical frustration I'm feeling. "Fantastic."

"Oh my God!" I cringe and bury my face in Shane's neck as the woman with the bear trap affixed to her head repeatedly stabs the man. "Why did you pick this?"

He chuckles as he dims the volume, minimizing the sound of the violent and grisly death. "Not like I had options. It's the only one playing tonight."

"Well, you really know how to woo your dates," I say dryly.

My nose catches a hint of cherry licorice as he bites off a chunk, seemingly unbothered by the gore. "I don't know. I'd say I have you right where I want you."

And I'm right where *I* want to be, my nose grazing the crook of his neck where it connects with his shoulder, my lips a hair-breadth away from tasting his skin. At some point, I kicked off my shoes and tucked my legs beneath me on the seat. Since then, I've been slowly inching closer to him. My hand has now found a permanent spot settled against his chest.

"You smell really good."

"Yeah?"

I pull away just enough to survey our dark surroundings. The occupants of the Honda are glued to the movie screen as Shane predicted, and we're too far back for anyone else to see us. There aren't any staff wandering through the lot, monitoring behavior. There never was when I worked here either. Mr. Duncan, the seventy-year-old owner, told us that as long as no one was overtly breaking the law and causing a disturbance, we were to leave the patrons alone. This is the same man who proudly admitted to fathering two of his sons in the back seat of his Buick during double-header Clint Eastwood nights, "Back in the heyday of drive-ins." I wonder if he's still alive.

"You looking for someone?" Shane asks.

"Not really. I don't know."

His face is inches away from me. "No one's going to bother us here," he says softly before leaning in to kiss me. His mouth tastes of red licorice, his lips still cold from the Coke he just sucked back. I'm hit with the most powerful wave of déjà vu I've felt yet.

Except before, his affection was far less restrained. Maybe it was the wild teenage boy in him that kissed deeply from the start, his tongue always diving in to coax mine into a sultry dance. Now, he merely licks the seam of my mouth before he pulls back to rest his forehead against mine. "You're worried about the school, aren't you?"

"A bit," I admit. Despite how many times I tell myself I'm not breaking any rules. "What if Bott magically appears again tonight and sees *this*?" I'm only half joking.

"I can't see Bott coming out to the drive-in to watch *Saw*," he says with a chuckle.

"No, I guess not." I smile sheepishly.

His fingertips skate along my cheek. "But why don't we save this for when we're behind closed doors and just watch the movie."

In my peripheral version, I see blood-soaked hands. I cringe. "This is a *horrific* movie, Shane."

"Do you want to leave now?" he asks, and I see the sincerity on his face.

Behind closed doors with Shane would be ideal, given the growing throb between my legs. But he did go to all the effort of planning this. "No, it's okay. I like being here with you again. Plus, I think someone might kill you if you turn this beast on right now."

"Okay, how about this? Why don't *I* watch and"—he gently guides my face back into the crook of his neck where it was moments ago—"you go back to hiding in here."

"I always did like it in here," I purr, dragging the tip of my nose across his jawline.

His breath hitches.

I can't help myself any longer. I brush my lips against that sexy ridge of his collarbone.

He releases a shaky sigh that stirs my blood. "Yeah, I remember. Just don't leave any marks on my neck like you used to, or I'll never hear the end of it from the guys."

"You mean, like this?" I nip at his flesh playfully but follow it up with a soothing lick.

Beneath my palm, Shane's heart thumps harder and faster. "No, you can keep doing that," he says in a husky voice.

We try to settle back into movie-watching positions. I'm definitely not paying attention as I covertly nip and lick and kiss his neck, his collarbone.

I'd be surprised if Shane is keeping up with the plot either. The hand that was settled on my hip has disappeared beneath the woven plaid blankets and has slowly, inch by inch, worked its way up the front slit of my dress, toward my panties. Sexy ones that I chose specifically for tonight, just in case.

Slick heat between my legs grows as I ache for his touch again. I shift my hips to give him better access—and the green light, which he takes with no hesitation. After a few teasing strokes across the silky material, his warm, strong fingers curl beneath. He lets out a soft curse as he slides his touch over my sensitive, wet flesh, dipping inside.

"Kissing you always does that to me." I stroke my hand over his chest, memorizing its hard curves. That's not entirely true. Just being around Shane gets me hot and bothered.

"It's probably good you never let me in there, then. I don't think you would have ever gotten me out." His fingertip work against my clit in slow circles as he slides his hips down in the seat.

I don't have to look to know that he has a raging hard-on. Back when we were seventeen, this was the point where my fingers would crawl beneath his shirt and trace a teasing line back and forth across taut abdomen, just above his belt. Sometimes I would cup his swollen length, give it attention. But I'd go no further, no matter how badly I wanted to unbuckle his pants and fill my hand with him. A lot of my restraint had to do with us never being alone. I was not going to pull a Dottie Reed and put on a show for anyone.

But we're not seventeen anymore, and two minutes of his skilled strokes have evaporated my fears of being caught making out with my student's father at the drive-in.

I slip my hand under the blankets to size up the hard ridge along the front of his jeans.

"Fuck, Scarlet." He looks at me with bright, pleading eyes.

"Go back to watching the movie," I command softly, resting my head in the crook of his neck as if I'm doing the same. But beneath the cover of the woven blankets, my dexterous fingers are unfastening his belt and working the top button and zipper down. I slide my hand beneath the waistband of his boxers and wrap my hand around his impressive length. I sigh with satisfaction at the hot, velvety-smooth skin finally in my palm. A bead of sticky moisture sits on the tip. I brush against it with the pad of my thumb.

He groans. "You have no idea how long I've wanted you to touch me like that."

"Probably as long as I've wanted to do this." I slide my hand out and take hold of his jeans, giving them a tug. He lifts his hips in answer, and I shimmy them off, lowering them to his muscular thighs, unintentionally pulling the blankets with them. I get my first up-close, unhindered look at Shane's perfect dick, thick and long and resting heavy between his bare thighs.

My throat goes dry.

Seriously, Ms. Dixon's bananas have nothing on Shane. Thank God we never went this far that summer because I doubt I would have been able to stop.

If we were in a more private situation, I wouldn't hesitate to lean over and take him in my mouth. But if someone *is* watching us, that would be an obvious flag, and I will not become the second Reed woman to get caught giving a blow job in a public place in Polson Falls.

Easing the blankets back up over his lap for privacy—on the off chance someone happens to stroll by and peer in—I nestle my head against his chest, wrap my fist around him and begin stroking, letting my thumb sweep over the tip with each pass, wishing it was my tongue.

I didn't think Shane's erection could get any bigger and yet, it's still swelling within my grip as I jack him off in a steady, calm rhythm, trying to keep our public indecency private. Shane has given up all hope of watching the movie, switching off the volume and closing his eyes.

"Kind of hard to watch a movie like that," I tease.

"I can't watch *that* while you're doing *this*."

His hand is still tucked into my panties but his fingers move lazily, without purpose, as I pleasure him. Still, moisture pools with just his touch as I anticipate hearing Shane come for the first time. I suspect that will be *very* soon, based on the subtle rocking of his hips.

"Faster," he whispers on a sigh, his free hand bunching around the blankets.

I quicken my wrist action, squeezing his shaft as my hand glides from root to tip, the soft, erotic sound of skin rubbing against skin competing with Shane's shallow, ragged breaths in the otherwise silent car.

At some point, he pulled the hem of his T-shirt up, exposing the pad of thick muscle across his stomach. I marvel at the carved beauty of those ridges as his body tenses with pleasure, as Shane gets ready to explode.

"I'm coming," he hisses through gritted teeth. A moment later, he pulses within my palm and hot spurts run over my fingers as he unloads into the blanket. His jaw is taut as deep, guttural groans escape him, as if he's trying to keep quiet when all he wants to do is yell.

A soft "fuck" slips out with a final shudder, his body relaxing beneath me.

We remain like that for a few moments, his chest heaving, me curled into his side, still gripping him. With a final, parting squeeze that makes him inhale sharply, I release him to hold my hand up in front of us. "You said you didn't want me in your car with sticky hands," I joke. While the red blanket took most of that mess in, my hand is still coated.

"Here." He uses a corner to wipe my fingers and palm clean. When he's done, he balls up the soiled material and tosses it to the floor, leaving us with the soft gray blanket.

"You weren't kidding about planning ahead."

"Aren't you happy I did?" With a smirk, he tugs his boxers and jeans up but doesn't bother fastening them yet. Turning toward me, he curls his arm around my body and pulls me in tight against him. Peering at me through heavy-lidded, satisfied eyes, his hand works its way beneath the blanket again, to the slit in my dress. "Take these off." He toys with the elastic waistband on my panties.

I lift my hips and shimmy the silk material down my thighs as requested.

He guides them the rest of the way until they're lost on the floor and then he slips his hand between my thighs.

I let out an embarrassing whimper as he teases my clit, his thumb drawing small circles.

"Go back to watching the movie," he whispers with a smug smile, echoing my words from earlier.

I laugh. "I was never watching the movie." The truth is *anything* could have been playing and my attention would have been lost on the man sharing the front seat with me. I close my eyes so I can avoid the gory scene on the screen and focus on Shane's lips on my neck and his talented fingers as he brings me to a shuddering orgasm.

"I can't tell you the last time I got a hand job on a date," Shane says as we climb the steps to my front porch. The light shines bright this time, and I have no trouble sliding my key into the lock.

"From someone other than yourself?"

"I don't do that on dates."

I raise an eyebrow.

"Not *anymore*," he amends, grinning sheepishly.

I step across the threshold, expecting Shane to follow. But when I turn back, I find him leaning against the door frame, his feet still firmly planted outside. "You're coming in, right?"

Into my house.

Into my bed.

Into *me*.

He shakes his head. "Not tonight."

"Why not?" Worry ignites inside me. He's not working until Thursday morning. Did he not enjoy himself? Has he changed his mind about us? Did he realize that what he found attractive about me at seventeen, he's annoyed with now?

He must see the concern on my face because the smile he answers with is soft, reassuring. "Like I said, I want to take this slow."

I toss my purse on the small entry table and wander back, letting my body brush against his. I tip my head back so I can peer up at those full, plump lips and stunning eyes. They're molten. He *wants* to come in, I can see that much. If I palmed him, I'm sure I'd be treated to an impressive erection.

"I feel like we're doing things backward." Saturday, he would have fucked me had Cody not called. Tonight, he's signing off for the night after some heavy petting.

Will I be relegated to hand-holding and cold showers by the weekend?

His gaze searches my face. "I had a great time tonight."

"So did I." And I'm not ready to say good night yet. "You should come in for at least a drink."

"It won't be just a drink and we both know that."

"You can't keep it in your pants for *one* glass of wine?" I taunt.

He inhales, as if he's considering it, and I hold my breath.

When he sighs and shakes his head, my discontent flares.

But the ache in my body for him is deep enough that I'm not ready to give up yet. "I picked up cookies from that bakery in town. They're *really* good with milk."

His eyebrow arches. "You're trying to lure me in for sex using milk and cookies? That's a first for me."

"That is *not* what I'm doing! I can't believe you would suggest such a thing," I scoff, feigning insult. "If I were trying to lure you in for sex, I'd mention that I also have a can of whipped cream that I'd enjoy licking off your—"

He seizes the back of my head and pulls my mouth into his in a kiss that is not sweet or soft or slow like earlier tonight. This one is hard and demanding, our lips smashing together, our tongues tangling, our teeth bumping, his fingers pushing through my hair to gather a grip. This is the Shane I remember from high school—unrestrained and vibrating with raw, male need.

My knees buckle with a deep, guttural moan as I mold my body to his, reveling in the hard ridge pressed against my stomach.

He pulls back abruptly and takes a moment to collect his ragged breaths. "We'll spend an entire night licking things off each other's bodies soon enough." The promise is delivered in a coarse voice. It stirs a mental image of his face between my thighs, which sends a shiver skittering through my core. "But I need you to know I'm not the kind of guy you think I am. That we're not all like your father, or Penelope's father, or any of the other shitty men you've met who don't know how to respect women."

"I don't think that about you," I answer honestly. *Not anymore.*

"Even still." He smooths my mussed hair back off my face. "You're my neighbor and Cody's teacher and …" His voice drifts, as if there's more to the list of our complications but he doesn't want to bring them up. "Sex tends to make things move faster. Given our situation and your job … we need to take things slow. I'm not letting anything or anyone screw this up with you again. Including me." He leans in to steal a tender kiss that ends in his soft groan before he peels away. He moves down my porch steps, as if needing to put distance between us. "I've got Cody tomorrow night and then I'm working Thursday. I'll call you on Friday?"

I stare pointedly at his jeans, at the noticeable bulge pressing against his zipper. It makes me smile. "I suppose."

He shakes his head. "I'm good for more than just that, you know."

I'd be worried that Shane might actually be offended about

being objectified if he weren't grinning proudly. "Well, of course. You can also fix things around my house."

The grin grows wider. "We'll get you a new fire extinguisher Friday night," he promises as he walks away.

My chest aches as I watch him go. It's *not* just my body that wants him to stay, and it's certainly not just his body that I crave. I feel electrified whenever he's in the room, flashing his dimpled smiles and making me laugh. It's as if I've found something important that was lost to me. I suppose I have.

"How about a game of Jenga?" I holler, a pathetic, last-ditch effort to get Shane to come back, stop being so damn chivalrous, and fuck me. My, how our roles have reversed.

His laughter carries through the quiet night as I watch him disappear inside his house.

TWENTY-TWO

"So?" Becca pokes her head into my classroom minutes before the first bell rings, as I'm quickly scribbling the day's agenda and reminders on the whiteboard. "How are things going with Shane?" She sounds giddy.

"Fine."

"*Just* fine?"

I attempt a coy smile but it quickly morphs into a goofy grin, her excitement contagious. "It's *really* good." Shane's work schedule, his time with Cody, and helping to coach the Panthers football team means we've only managed to see each other a handful of times since the night of the drive-in two weeks ago.

But every time has left me falling harder for the guy who once hurt me so badly.

She steps into my classroom and pushes my door closed. "Have you two"—she waggles her eyebrows—"*you know,* yet?"

I laugh at her subtlety. It's a far cry from the daily "Fucked yet?" texts from Justine that I wake up to. "We're taking things slow." We've gone out for dinner and drinks at Route Sixty-Six, lingering beneath heaters on the patio until closing. We went for a jog one morning, but I'm too out of shape to keep pace with him and I hate that he has to slow his tempo for me. We replaced my fire extinguisher and purchased new electrical outlet covers; I've never enjoyed a trip to the hardware store like I do when he's there.

But Shane wasn't kidding about his firm resolve to take things physically slowly. I steal every opportunity to touch him—a leg brush beneath the table, a finger-skate across the arm, a warm palm against his chest—and he seems to welcome it. But he kisses me good night on my porch and doesn't come inside. It's like he knows that stepping across the threshold is an instant guarantee that his clothes will come off in under five minutes. He wouldn't be wrong, if I have any choice in the matter.

That's not to say we haven't lost control. Last weekend, when he climbed down the ladder after checking my gutters for refuse, I cornered him beside my garden shed to thank him with a lip-lock that I hope our neighbors didn't witness. And two nights ago, when he parked his truck in his driveway after we returned home from dinner, a single kiss escalated into me straddling his lap and grinding against him until we couldn't hold out any longer. We both came within seconds of our hands getting involved.

I can't remember the last time I dated a guy who held out sex, let alone this firmly. That it's *Shane Beckett* of all guys—notorious for hookups and flings back in the day—is almost laughable. Is this how frustrated he was when we were seventeen and I staunchly held him at bay? Is this payback?

I wonder about that sometimes, late at night, while I'm thinking about him and touching myself.

A knuckle raps on the door, a moment before it creaks open and Wendy pokes her head in. She's in her usual ensemble—black knee-length skirt, collared blouse—today's is a powder pink. "Knock, knock—oh, Becca! I'm sorry to interrupt. I didn't see you standing over here."

"That's okay. I should get back to my class. The bell is about to ring, anyway." As if on cue, the loud buzz ricochets through the building. Soon, the kids corralled outside will be entering. Becca winks at me. "Talk to you later."

"Enjoy your morning."

Wendy smiles at me, but it's not her usual wide beam. She hesitates, checking the doorway. "Listen, Scarlet, would you mind stopping by my office during first recess?"

Disquiet trickles down my spine. Her tone is telling me this isn't a friendly "how has your first month been" check-in. I'm getting called into the principal's office because there's something wrong. "Sure." I can't hide the wariness from my voice. "Can you tell me what this is about? Is there an issue with a student? Or a parent?"

"Just a little chat." Again, that tight, uneasy smile. "See you then."

On instinct, I poke my head out to watch Wendy stride toward the office, her worn heels clicking. Is this about Shane? Has she somehow heard about my relationship with him? Truthfully, I've been toying with the idea of telling her for the past few days. She's my boss and she pulled strings to get me this job. But it's still far too early. We've only been on a few dates. We're not sleeping together.

My attention is drawn to the opposite entrance where kids plow through the door in what is supposed to be an orderly fashion but always makes me imagine a herd of squealing piglets, only with backpacks and attitude.

I tell myself that whatever Wendy wants to discuss is nothing to worry about, and I duck back into my classroom to receive my herd.

But I worry, all the same.

I knock once on the open door. "Is now a good time?"

Wendy pauses mid stroke on her keyboard to peer over her reading glasses at me. "Scarlet. Yes, come in. Please." She waves me in toward one of two chairs across from her desk, normally reserved for delinquent students and irate parents. "Close the door, would you?"

I do as asked and settle into a seat, doing a quick cursory scan of the bookshelves behind her—lined with framed pictures of her three golden retrievers and her nieces. If you were to ask Wendy if she was married, she'd tell you: "yes, to my job."

She clasps her weathered hands in front of her. "Well then, let's get right to it, since we don't have a lot of time. It has been brought to my attention that you are involved in a relationship with Cody Rhodes's father." She's wearing her principal's hat now. Her words are pronounced slowly and calmly. It's how she begins when reprimanding students.

Fucking Bott. It had to be her. How else would Wendy hear so soon?

My chest tightens with a flare of panic. The last thing I want is to be at odds with Wendy, especially so early in the school year.

I take a deep breath to calm myself. "Do you mean Shane Beckett, my next-door neighbor and childhood friend?" I ask in an equally composed tone.

"Yes, that's right." She pauses. "Are you saying your relationship is strictly of a platonic nature?"

This is where I could lie to Wendy. By the hopeful way she's looking at me, I'm thinking she'd prefer it. Ignorance is bliss and all that.

And yet I find that I can't. What's more, I don't want to.

I decide on simple honesty. "It is very early days, but Shane and I have gone out to dinner a few times, yes."

"I see." Her brow puckers. "This isn't a comfortable conversation for me, Scarlet."

Then let's not have it.

"I know this is your first year teaching and you might not be familiar with policies—"

"There's no policy against a teacher having a personal relationship with their student's parent."

Her breath hitches. "So, you *have* checked." She seems caught off guard.

"My job is important to me. I didn't want to break any rules." That it was Shane who did the actual checking isn't important here.

"Right, well, while it's not against the rules, it is definitely not recommended, given the strain it can put on the child's happiness and classroom experience. What if the relationship doesn't work out? What if it ends badly? And, even if it does work out, children can face ridicule from their classmates. I'm sure we both agree that Cody deserves a safe and happy year in your class. Wouldn't you say so?"

"Of course. I want nothing more than that for *all* my students."

"Okay." She waits. For me to respond, I suppose. What does she want, though? For me to agree to cut ties with Shane? That's not happening.

"Look, Shane and I have a history. We hadn't seen each other in a long time. Now that we live beside each other, old feelings have resurfaced and we decided after careful consideration to pursue them. We're doing it slowly, to make sure nothing happens that would jeopardize Cody's happiness." I'm making myself sound mature and thoughtful, not like the jealous drunk who was screaming at Shane and nearly taking his best friend home that night at Route Sixty-Six.

"I see. So, it's not just a matter of casual dating." A pensive expression takes over her face. "I assume you haven't told Cody yet?"

"No. It's too soon. It wouldn't be appropriate."

Wendy's lips twist. "Does his mother know?"

"She suspects but Shane will tell her when it makes sense. Like I said, this is all still new and, because of Cody and our living situation, we're not rushing anything."

"Right. Well, Cody's mother can be ..." She searches for the right word. She settles on "problematic."

"Believe me, I know what Penelope Rhodes can be," I mutter, my voice more acerbic than I intended.

Understanding passes across Wendy's face. Yes, Penelope was a mean girl. Yes, the affair between her father and my mother pitted us against each other. "When Lucy"—she winces, as if she wasn't planning on revealing her source—"came to me, she did so because she was worried about you."

"*Worried*?" I laugh.

My reaction earns Wendy's confused frown. She doesn't understand why I'd find Bott's concern for me amusing. She doesn't know the story of what Lucy Bott did all those years ago. I don't want to drag out old memories, though, no matter if Bott deserves to be fired. In the end, karma dealt her the ugly hand she deserved.

"There's no need to worry about me," I say instead.

"I know Lucy is a bit odd, but regardless of what some students might think, she doesn't wish ill on others. She doesn't cast spells on them." Wendy rolls her eyes as if the idea is preposterous. "She came to me because she saw the connection between you and Cody's father, and she became concerned about the backlash you might face. It's no secret around here, the drama that unfolded between Penelope and Shane. I had to referee a parent-teacher meeting when Cody began kindergarten because they were in the midst of an ugly custody battle. We all know why." She gives me a knowing look.

Because of Penelope. Because she was still in love with Shane and she's a vindictive bitch.

"I'm aware of their history. But she's living with a guy now, so hopefully she's finally retracted her claws."

"Out of Cody's father, yes. But you're now placing yourself as the *other* woman in her son's life. People like Penelope Rhodes don't handle that well. They can be difficult and loud and angry. Be ready for that, when you *do* make her aware of your relationship. The last thing I want to see is your reputation at the school suffer unfairly because of this. Or for Cody to struggle." She hesitates. "I'm telling you this not only as the principal of this school but as someone who remembers a little girl many years ago, crying because of choices her mother made."

She's talking about my mother's scandal.

I remember. I sat in this office—maybe in this very chair—in tears after Chrissy Moorhead callously teased me at recess about the infamous incident. Half the kids didn't understand what *exactly* Dottie and Mayor Peter Rhodes were doing in the janitor's room, but they knew it was indecent. Wendy must have expected the backlash because she found me crying behind a portable, the frigid winter temperatures an oddly soothing balm to my pain. She brought me in here to escape or to talk, I can't be sure. Either way, it was a kindness when I needed it.

"This is *not* the same thing." I'm not Dottie Reed and Shane is not a married political official, and I'm certainly not giving anyone blow jobs *anywhere,* let alone in the school's broom closet.

"I know it's not." She pats the air with her hand. "But people have a way of connecting dots to suit their needs and make something out of nothing. I would hate to see another scandal follow you around. Just be careful. That's what I wanted to say to you. Be careful and make sure he's worth it."

He is. There isn't a moment's hesitation with that thought.

The bell rings to signal the end of morning recess.

"I'll let you get back to class, then." She sighs and, in its weighty sound, I sense her fatigue. She's been the principal at this school since I started second grade. Is she tired of it all yet?

Does she regret hiring me?

I stand and push in my chair, feeling more like a student than a teacher. “For what it’s worth, I was going to tell you, when I thought there was something worth mentioning. When we figured out how far this might go.”

“You don’t have to explain. I get it. I do.” She smiles. “And, between us, I think you’ve got a good one there.” She drops her voice to add more to herself, “He’s certainly a handsome one.”

With a smile, I duck out of her office. A black swirl of fabric catches my attention. Bott is at the photocopier, churning out papers.

Careful, Scarlet. That’s what she said to me that night at the Patty Shack. Could it have been out of genuine concern? Is Bott capable of that for the daughter of Dottie Reed, whom she seems to hold animosity toward, all these years later?

She turns suddenly, as if sensing eyes on her. We lock gazes for a few beats, her expression revealing nothing, before she turns back to the photocopier output tray.

She is so fucking *strange*.

I rush back to my classroom.

TWENTY-THREE

A jack-o'-lantern stares at me from a bedecked porch as I trek home, the strap of my bag digging into my shoulder from the weight of papers to grade this weekend. That pumpkin will be a rotten mess by the time we reach Halloween, a month away. But some things clearly haven't changed in Polson Falls, like the urge to haul out the ghost and goblin decorations the day the calendar page flips to October.

It makes me smile.

The smell of fresh-cut grass fills my nostrils as I round the tall cedar hedge that divides Shane from the neighbor on his other side. Shane's been out manicuring his yard this afternoon, his lawn groomed in tidy, straight rows.

He didn't stop at his, though. My front lawn has also been cut.

I turn into his driveway, eager to see him again after his twenty-four-hour shift. He's nowhere to be seen, but the lawn-mower sits outside the open garage.

Climbing his porch steps, I knock on the storm door, stealing a glimpse through the glass into Shane's house. I can't see much save for a few pairs of shoes lying haphazardly by the front closet and a long, narrow hall.

"Come in!" Shane hollers from somewhere inside.

The door creaks as I pull it open. "How do you know I'm not a stranger?" I call back, dropping my heavy satchel onto the modern-style charcoal-gray tile landing by the door. It's my first time inside.

"Because you always come home around this time. Plus, a stranger still wouldn't just walk in."

I pause to survey the living room—a plain, white-walled room with plush leather furniture in camel tones, a sizable flat-screen TV mounted on the wall, and the enormous bay window that overlooks the front yard. While Shane's house is an older bungalow, it appears the interior has been remodeled. The planks of dark walnut hardwood floor gleam, the moldings are wide, and pot lights line the ceiling throughout.

I find Shane at a deep kitchen sink, scrubbing a pot.

"They would if they're a murderer," I counter, quickly dismissing the enviable custom cabinetry and subway-tile backsplash to admire Shane's sculpted arms and the way his track pants hug his ass.

He casts a smirk over his shoulder. His hair is an untamed mop, with wavy tendrils around his ears and at the nape of his neck. It's incredibly sexy. "Murderers going door to door in Polson Falls, looking for unsuspecting six-foot-two firefighters?"

"Exactly." I ease in behind him to press my chest against his back and slip my hands around his taut waist. "You cut my grass."

He turns his upper body to lean down and kiss me. It's a slow, sensual greeting that momentarily steals my ability to breathe. "It needed cutting," he whispers when he finally pulls away.

My heart is racing. "That was sweet. Thank you."

He tosses the sponge into the sink and hastily dries his hands with the dishcloth lying nearby before turning to face me. He stretches his heavy arms over my shoulders and pulls me into him until we're chest to chest. He smells of soap from his shower and clean sweat from working outside. The intoxicating mix only stirs my blood more. "How was school? Was my kid good today?"

"He's always good. And school was … interesting." I relay the conversation with Wendy.

He bites his bottom lip in thought. "So, she's okay with it?"

"I wouldn't say that. But she seems more concerned about Penelope causing trouble than anything else." I pause. "Is she right to be worried about that?"

The muscle ticks in Shane's jaw. "Penelope does *not* get a say in my life."

Her meddling is clearly a sore spot. She must have put him through hell with the custody battle.

"You're right. She doesn't." I stifle the urge to point out the more likely issue—her say in who's in her *son's* life—and smooth my palms over Shane's chest. It feels tighter than usual, likely from a long workout in the station gym.

He sighs, as if trying to expel the tension that mounted with mention of his ex-girlfriend. "I know you were worried about your job. Do you feel better now that your boss knows about us?"

"Yeah. Lighter, anyway. I didn't realize how much hiding this from Wendy was weighing on me." But now it's in the open and that lingering shadow that I'm doing something *wrong* has faded.

"Good." He threads his fingers through my hair.

I imagine him gathering that hair in his fist and gently pulling it. That thought has the muscles between my thighs clenching. "I like your house," I say, my voice huskier than a moment ago. "Did you buy it like this?"

"No. It was a dive when I bought it. I've been fixing it up over the last three years." His eyes graze over the cupboards on the wall beside us. "This room was the most work."

"*You* did all this on your own?"

"A lot of it. Not all. There're a lot of guys at the station who do renovations on the side, so I got a bit of help. They taught me a lot."

Thoughts of a sweaty, dirty Shane tearing apart the room makes my pulse quicken. "You really aren't just a pretty face."

He grins, his dimples appearing in full form.

"What do you want to do tonight?" Just being with him is enough for me, but Shane always was the type to keep busy with friends and plans, and that doesn't seem to have changed.

"I don't know. A couple people were talking about Route Sixty-Six for the band. I was thinking we could head there a bit earlier and grab dinner on the patio. Should still be warm enough."

That would mean the risk of running into Dottie again, seeing her in action. I haven't talked to her since the night I found out about her dalliance with Dean, and aside from a text a few days later in which she told me I can't possibly be angry with her—because I *must* understand how she couldn't say no to that opportunity—as expected, I haven't heard from her.

But going out to meet up with friends later, together, means our discretion will fly out the window. There'll be no hiding this relationship anymore, regardless of what we tell people. I mean, Bott saw the chemistry between us from afar.

Shane *must* know that.

"Why? What do *you* want to do tonight?" he asks, his warm, strong fingers working in small circles over my shoulders and back.

I imagine those same hands peeling off my clothes, and heat courses through my veins.

I know what I *don't* want to do.

I peer at him from beneath my lashes. "I don't want to take things slow anymore." Not physically, anyway. I punctuate my meaning by pressing my body into his.

In his eyes, lust flares.

Against my stomach, his erection swells.

He opens his mouth and I brace myself for him to give reasons why we *shouldn't*—I might scream—but whatever words he was planning on saying fall away, unspoken. A decision flickers across his face.

In one smooth move, Shane leans in to crash his lips into mine and seize the backs of my thighs. "Neither do I." He hoists me into the air with no effort. I scramble to get closer to him, throwing my arms around his neck as he guides my legs around his waist. I squeeze tightly.

"I've waited forever for this," he whispers, his hands finding their way to my backside. We're moving then, Shane's strides purposeful, his lips still on mine as he carries me into his bedroom.

Together, we dive onto his bed, tangling in a mess of limbs and fervent lips. We fumble with our clothes, in a rush to rid ourselves of them. My anticipation to *finally* feel Shane inside me is making my hands tremble with excitement.

"I'm such an idiot for ending things between us," he murmurs against my mouth, fitting his hips between my thighs, his bare skin searing against mine as he covers my body with his. "I've been thinking about this nonstop since I saw you sitting on your porch."

"You perv. But same." I part my legs to welcome him in. "Except when I wanted to kill you."

He laughs, but it instantly morphs into a primal moan with a single roll of my hips. His tip prods at my entrance, as if begging to slide in. There won't be any foreplay this time. These six weeks have been one long, torturous stretch of seduction.

"You're impatient." He nips playfully at my earlobe. "Hold on." He rolls off me and fumbles in his nightstand for a condom.

My heart pounds in my chest as I admire his firm, tanned body, stalling at his erection—thick and long and rigid. What would it be like to pleasure him with my mouth? I wondered that many times that summer, back when I had no experience and was afraid of cultivating rumors.

Okay, maybe a bit of foreplay.

"Wait."

Shane freezes as he's bringing the packet to his teeth to tear it open. His eyebrows arch in question. And perhaps trepidation that I've changed my mind.

My lips curl with a smile. I maneuver to hover over his hips, letting my breath skate over his hard, perfect flesh. There isn't an inch of this man that isn't, dare I say, *pretty*.

"Oh, fuck," he whispers when he realizes my intention, and his breathing grows ragged. "I thought maybe you were against giving them because of, well, *you know*."

"Shane?"

"Uh-huh?"

I swirl my tongue over the tip of his penis much like I did my Patty Shack ice cream cone, earning his sharp inhale. "When a woman is about to put your dick in her mouth, you shouldn't start talking about her mother."

His abdominal muscles clench with his grating chuckle. "I'll try to remember that."

I shift my focus, giving the underside of his length the flat of my tongue, beginning at the root and sliding all the way back to the end, where I'm treated to a bead of salty moisture. I slide my lips over his head.

He makes a strangled sound that I feel between my thighs and then he reaches down to scoop my hair back, wordlessly coaxing me to continue. Wrapping my hand around the base of him, I fall into a steady tempo of sucking while I jack him off, relishing the taste and feel of him as he whispers soft "deeper, faster, more" instruction and moans sweet praises that convince me I could happily pleasure him like this for hours. Every so often I steal a glance upward, to find intense, molten eyes watching me, his expression one of raw desire.

The slow pace I started at quickly escalates as his grip of my hair tightens and his breathing grows raspy and his hips rock, first subtly and then with a smooth rhythmic roll. The only warning I get is the pinch at my nape as his fists clenches to grip my hair tight and then, with a guttural moan, Shane releases into my mouth. I take him all in.

His body is relaxed when I pull away. He's sprawled across the bed, his chest heaving. "Holy shit, Scar. That was … " He stretches his arms above his head to rest on his pillow, his mouth opening as if he's about to speak but then closing as if he can't decide what to say, several times over. He finally settles on, "Can you please do that again, soon?"

"Maybe." I climb onto his body to straddle his hips. His lips are parted, and his eyelids are heavy. "Not if you'll fall asleep on me," I warn.

A deep, throaty laugh escapes him. "Does *this* look like I'll fall asleep?" He reaches down to stroke himself. He's already thickening again.

Meanwhile, my core is aching with the need for release.

With a smirk, he fumbles for the condom he set on his nightstand.

I savor the view of Shane tearing the packet and expertly sheathing himself in record time. With sturdy hands, he seizes my hips to reposition me. He may have stalled sex from happening before, but there's no hesitation now. He guides me onto him, slowly filling me.

A breathless cry slips for my lips as my body stretches around his size and my inner muscles clamp around him, and a heady fire spreads through my veins, igniting my body.

"Hol-y *fuck*," he growls. "I won't last long if you keep making sounds like that."

I roll my hips, guiding him in those last few inches to fill me completely. "You'll have to make up for it." Given the tingling stir in my lower belly, I doubt I'll be chasing my release for long.

His fingers bite into my flesh as I ride him, his heady gaze dancing from my face to my swaying breasts to where we're joined as if he can't decide where to settle. His hips meet my body in measured thrusts. Between us, my body grows wet as I get lost in the intoxicating thrill of this intimacy, of being full and stretched by Shane.

"Fuck ... Scar, I need ... " He doesn't finish that sentence before flipping me onto my back and overwhelming me with his substantial frame. His lips find mine in a fervent kiss as he drives into me with fast, deep, powerful thrusts. I coil my legs around his hips and let him dominate my body, content to tangle my fingers through his silky hair and savor his mouth as the bed's headboard bangs against the wall over and over again.

My orgasm hits suddenly, flooding me with warmth and rushing through me. I cry out as my inner muscles squeeze Shane, earning his curse and several harder, faster plunges. He lets out a deep, almost pained groan into my mouth and his hips still as he pulsates inside me.

We fall into a contented silence for a long moment, our swollen lips grazing, our ragged breaths mingling, our chests heaving.

"It's a good thing we didn't do that back in high school," Shane whispers.

I lay boneless beneath his weight. And utterly content. "Why is that?"

His teeth find my earlobe, giving it a lazy nip. "Because we never would have gone anywhere."

A warm shiver courses through my body. "You're probably right." I trail my fingertips over his chiseled shoulders and back. His skin is burning hot and slick with sweat. "Speaking of which, what time do you want to leave for Route Sixty-Six?"

His deep chuckle vibrates through my core. "Yeah, we're not leaving this bed tonight."

TWENTY-FOUR

"Are you sure this is it?" I hold up the unimpressive rubber ring. "It looks like a weird elastic hair band."

"About fifty percent sure." When Shane sees my scowl, he holds up his hands in surrender. "That toilet's ancient."

I sigh with resignation. "Maybe we should just replace it, then." My main-floor toilet started running last week and hasn't stopped. If I don't do something soon, I'll be paying for a new toilet's worth of wasted water.

"Let's try this, and if it doesn't work, I'll put in a new one for you next week."

"You know how to do that?"

"I did my renos, remember?" He answers with far more patience than I probably deserve. "And if I need help, I'll call a friend who owes me a favor and definitely knows what he's doing. Either way, I'll get this fixed up for you."

A gray-haired man with a wiry mustache and a fluorescent-orange staff vest shuffles up to us in the plumbing aisle, his steel-toe boots sliding against the concrete floor. "Can I help you two find something tonight?" He has a kind, grandfatherly face.

Shane waves him off with, “My girlfriend’s toilet is running, but I think we’re set. Thanks for asking.”

I duck my head to hide the way I beam at the label Shane so casually threw out. We haven’t officially had that conversation. But we also didn’t discuss spending every Cody-free night sleeping together. Yet, that’s what the past three weeks have entailed, as we’ve found our way to either Shane’s bed or mine, exploring every inch of bare skin, every scar, every erogenous touch point on each other’s bodies.

Shane wasn’t wrong when he said sex would intensify our relationship. But the sweat-laced, heart-pounding nights we’ve lost ourselves in since we took the next step? I don’t think either of us anticipated how addicted we’d become to each other. It takes nothing—a single look when he walks through my door, a hard swallow that draws my attention to that sharp jut in his throat, a casual draw of his tongue across his bottom lip—to clear my mind of all thought, save for the pleasure I’m about to get from him.

Him, lying beneath me as I ride him.

Him, hovering above as he drives into me.

Him, crying out as he explodes in my mouth.

Us, tangled in each other’s limbs after, whispering and laughing as the hours melt away.

My time with Shane has been intoxicating and all-consuming, and the only thing I regret is that I didn’t give him a second chance sooner.

With a nod, the man goes searching for another customer, sliding his boots along the aisle.

“Ready to go home?” Shane throws his arm around my shoulders and pulls me into his side, dipping to kiss me. Despite our claims to stay quiet about our relationship, Shane seems unable to keep his hands off me in public.

And despite my aversion to public affection and my wariness to spark gossip if the wrong person sees us canoodling in the plumbing aisle, I find myself casting aside caution. "My bed or yours tonight?" I tease the seam of his lips with the tip of my tongue. I've been looking forward to this weekend. Shane is all mine until he leaves for work Sunday morning.

He groans. "It'll be in my truck, out in the parking lot, if you do that again."

I repeat the tongue tease, adding a swirling action, mimicking his favorite move when I use my mouth on him. "Good thing your windows are tinted, then." I foresee road head in Shane's near future.

His grip around my shoulders tightens as he leads us toward the cashier, our pace quick enough to confirm I've just given him a raging hard-on. For all his playfulness, I've learned that he's embarrassed to walk around stores with an erection. Guess I can't blame him. His size makes them noticeable.

And yet it's become an amusing game.

I laugh at the muscle tick in his jaw. "Something the matter?"

He shakes his head, but he's smiling. "You're the devil. You know that?"

"I guess you have an affinity for wicked women."

He snorts derisively.

The familiar rap music ringtone carries from Shane's pocket as we reach the self-serve checkout register. As usual, Shane doesn't hesitate to dig his phone out and answer. "Hey, buddy. What's up?"

I move in to scan the part for my failing toilet.

"*What*?" Shane's suddenly hard tone pulls my attention away from the keypad. "Okay, slow down, Cody, and tell me *exactly* what's going on." Wearing a deep frown, Shane strolls out the door, his phone pressed against his ear.

Clearly, something's wrong.

I finish paying for my purchase and rush outside just as Shane is ending the call. His frown hasn't eased, and now it's coupled with a clenched jaw.

"What's going on? Is Cody all right?"

"Yeah. He's fine. Just ..." His words trail as he dials someone else.

I bite back the urge to press for information and reach for his forearm, stroking it with my fingertips to offer comfort while he waits for an answer that doesn't appear to be coming.

He ends the call with a heavy sigh. "Pen and Travis are in the middle of a major fight. Cody said it's bad."

"Bad *how*?" I ask evenly, alarm bells going off. "Shane, if there's *any* chance Cody is in danger—"

"No. It's not like that." He shakes his head. "Just yelling, from the sounds of it. But Penelope can get pretty scary. Cody wants me to come get him." Shane rubs his brow with a rough hand. "I don't know what to do."

"Because it's her weekend?"

"Honestly? When my kid calls me, crying like that? I don't give a fuck whose weekend it is," he growls. He's agitated.

I soften my voice. "So, then what's the issue?"

He looks at his watch, scowling.

"How far away do they live?"

"From here? Five minutes. If that," he says absently, deep in thought.

But it would take almost half an hour, by the time Shane drops me off at home and comes back. The distress in Shane's eyes tells me he doesn't want to make Cody wait.

I hold up the hardware bag. "I'm with you because you're helping me fix my toilet."

"Yeah, I guess." He sounds reluctant. "I don't like lying to my kid, though."

"It isn't a lie. But I get what you're saying." To a smart eleven-year-old boy, it *will* seem like a lie if and when we come clean about our relationship, something we agreed wouldn't happen until next summer. But every minute we stand outside the store debating this, that kid is sitting in his house, listening to a fight that is bad enough it made him call his dad, crying. It's a no-brainer. "Then we go and get him now." I slip my fingers through Shane's. "And we don't lie."

After a long moment, he nods.

Shane parks his truck behind Penelope's silver Acura. Next to it is a black BMW. I assume that's Travis's.

"Nice house," I note, taking in the impressive two-story new build. It's a cookie-cutter house with no character and nothing unique, save for the landscaping and the porch decor. To my left and right are houses nearly identical in size and style, in one of three brick color schemes, chosen by the builders with community aesthetics in mind.

"They bought into the subdivision a year after it was built," Shane explains, cutting the engine.

At least my dilapidated little home has personality, I think to myself with petty satisfaction, recalling Penelope's not-so-subtle dig. Plus, I have mature trees and a lot that could fit five of these tedious houses.

"You should probably stay here." Shane rubs my thigh with his palm, as if to soften the suggestion.

I smother my urge to laugh. "You think?" I have no interest in adding myself to the volatile mix.

"Be back in a minute."

Shane's body is tense, his face stony, as he strolls up the interlock pathway, past a Japanese maple and life-sized Freddy Krueger to a steel-blue front door. I wish I could crawl inside his body for just a moment, to know exactly what he feels for the mother of his son, to understand what it's like to share a human being you love fiercely with a woman you wish you could have nothing to do with for the rest of your life.

Before Shane has a chance to ring the bell, the door flies open.

Travis storms out, scowling. He stalls a step when he sees Shane, as if startled, but recovers quickly. "Where's the bro code, huh? Why didn't you warn me that she's *batshit crazy*!" I hear through the open driver's side window. He doesn't wait for Shane's answer before marching to his car, keys dangling from his finger, a steady glower on his handsome face.

Our gazes connect for a split second. "Oh, just fucking great. That'll help things," he mutters, then dives into his car. In seconds, the BMW is peeling out of the driveway and speeding off.

Penelope is at the door now. I can only see her legs and her shoulder—Shane's massive body effectively blocks my view.

"He *shouldn't* have called you," she says crisply.

"Well, he did, and now I'm here, so let me take him back to my place for the night." Shane's tone is deceptively calm. Beneath it, I hear his anger bubbling.

"It's my weekend with him."

There's a long pause. I imagine him leveling her with a long, hard look. "He called me because he was scared. He was *crying*, Pen." There's a touch of pleading in Shane's voice that claws at my chest. "Let me get him out of here until Sunday morning so you two can sort out your shit without him having to listen to it. That's not fair to him."

After another long moment, I hear her say, "Fine."

Shane disappears inside, shutting the door behind him, leaving me alone in the driveway. I kill time by texting Justine and scrolling aimlessly through Instagram.

They emerge a few minutes later. Cody has his backpack slung over his shoulder, his head bowed. Even still, I can make out his splotchy, red face.

"Where's my hug?" Penelope calls out.

When he doesn't respond, Shane stops him with a hand on his shoulder and coaxes him with, "Come on, buddy. Give your mom a hug goodbye."

Cody turns around and drags his feet all the way back. He embraces her with reluctant arms, pulling away before she has a chance to enclose him in hers. He darts back to Shane's side as if seeking solace there.

I don't miss Penelope's flinch at her son's obvious preference. "I'll see you on Sunday morning, okay?" she says in a light, shaky voice. "We can go shopping for your Halloween costume."

"I'm too old to go trick-or-treating," Cody grumbles.

With a gentle hand on the back of Cody's neck, Shane guides his son down the path.

"Thank you," Penelope calls out, almost as an afterthought, her arms curled tightly around her body.

In that moment, I feel a twinge of sympathy for the she-devil. She almost seems human—vulnerable, emotional, caring.

Shane offers her a wane smile over his shoulder that she matches with her own.

But it vanishes the moment she spots me in his truck. Even from here, I see the rage that ignites in her murky sage eyes. "Shane!" she barks, all semblance of gratitude gone. "Can I speak to you for a minute? *Inside*?" She's back to using that snotty tone, the one that has always inspired my urge to punch her square in the face.

Shane's chest rises with a deep exhale. "Yup," he hollers back, his expression stony again. He knows what this is about. He guides Cody to the extended cab. "You're gonna hang out in here with Ms. Reed, okay?"

Cody's attention was glued to the ground up until now. With mention of me, his eyes snap to the passenger side and widen with surprise.

I plaster on a cheerful smile. "Hi, Cody."

Shane pokes his head into the driver's side window as his son clambers into the back seat. "Give me another five minutes, 'kay? Might as well deal with this now." He looks as excited to step inside that house as I imagine he would going to the hospital for organ removal.

"No worries. I'll grill Cody on probability and complex fractions while we wait."

"Don't torture the poor kid," Shane says with a weak chuckle, heading back to face an irate Penelope.

They disappear into the house, closing the door behind them. My ears burn with the knowledge that I'm to become the topic of conversation within those walls.

Awkward silence fills the truck cab.

"So, I heard you're having a rough night," I finally say.

From the rearview mirror, I catch Cody's nod as he discreetly brushes the back of his hand against his cheeks, likely to dry off the residue of old tears.

"You want to talk about it?"

A long pause is followed by a fierce head shake.

"Fair enough. Just know I'm a pretty good listener if you need to talk. Okay?"

Cody nods. A curious frown flickers across his face. What's it like for an eleven-year-old boy to get picked up by his father and find his teacher in the front seat? His young mind must be spinning with questions.

As if my thought prompted him, he asks, "How come you're with my dad?"

I shift in my seat to face him. "Because my toilet isn't working, so we went to the hardware store together to find a part. That's where we were when you called." I hope that answer doesn't sound scripted.

He sweeps his hair off his forehead. "So, he's helping you fix your house." I can't tell if that's a question or a clarification for himself, as if he's making sense of his thoughts out loud.

"I *hope* so. Otherwise I have to hire someone and they're not cheap."

After another long moment, Cody grins, and a replica of his

father's dimples appear. On Cody, they're adorable. "He tried to fix my grandparents' dishwasher last month and ended up making it worse. They had to buy a new one."

"Are you telling me I'm doomed?" I say playfully.

I get a one-shoulder shrug in return. "You grew up around here too?"

"I did."

"And you knew my parents when you were my age?"

"Yes. I did."

"Did you and my father used to date?"

I keep my smile in place, even as disquiet settles in my spine. Shane said he told Cody we were friends from high school, but nothing more. If Cody didn't hear about it from his father, then who else besides Penelope? Has she been telling her son things about his teacher? I dread her version of the truth.

I push the wariness that comes with that prospect aside. Shane doesn't want to lie to his son, so I won't start now. "Yes. For a summer, when we were seventeen."

Cody nods slowly. I get the impression that perhaps he's validating information he's overheard. Definitely not a good thing, given who his source of said information likely was. "Cool."

I hold my breath, dreading the next obvious question.

Are you dating my dad now?

But Cody seems to take the lengthy silence as an excuse to pull his phone from his pocket and text someone.

I don't attempt to interrupt him, happy to let Shane field his son's questions about his dating life.

Cody barely waits for Shane to park before he darts out from the back seat and scuttles to the front door. He punches his code into the keyless lock system and disappears inside, leaving Shane and me alone to talk.

"Are you okay?" I ask. Shane's been quiet since storming out of Penelope's house thirty minutes after going in. He did his best to engage Cody in conversation, but there was an edge in his voice that soured the mood.

He releases a loud groan-sigh and slides his grip around the steering wheel before letting his hands drop to his lap. "How did someone so fucking bitter and vindictive produce a kid like Cody?"

"He *is* half his father," I remind him, reaching out to give his shoulder a squeeze. "What did she say?"

"A bunch of bullshit."

"Like?" I prod.

He shakes his head, his jaw tensing. He doesn't want to tell me.

"Shane, I know that was about me. I'll have to deal with her sooner or later, so I'm better off being armed with as much information as possible. Don't you think?"

"No, that was about *her* and all her fucking issues with jealousy and sharing Cody," he says, his tone harsh. "I just ..." He shakes his head. "First, she was pissed that I brought you there, to their house. So, I explained why. Then, she demanded to know if we were together. At this point, denying it would make me an asshole."

"So, Penelope knows we're together." Wendy's words of caution stir in my mind.

"Then she chewed me out for not informing her of our relationship *before* introducing you to Cody. I pointed out how fucking stupid that is, seeing as you're not some strange woman. You're Cody's teacher. He already knows you. And *that*'s when she started ranting about ethics."

"We're not breaking any rules." I repeat the standard line, because it's all I have to cling to. I *know* it's not appropriate to date my student's father. I can see why a mother—not just Penelope—might have an issue with this. If it were anyone other than

Shane, I wouldn't have entertained it until the school year was over.

"*She* thinks it should be a rule."

"Luckily, she doesn't get a say in that." I reach out and stroke his forearm, the tension in his body cording his muscles. "Is her issue with you dating *any* woman? Or is this about me in particular?" Because of our sordid past, courtesy of her father and my mother's affair.

Shane purses his lips, as if considering how he should answer. "Both. And Cody is her entire life."

"He should be. She's his mother." I often think about what that would feel like, to be more than Dottie's byproduct that she felt obligated to feed and clothe but not necessarily put ahead of her own needs.

"Of course. But it's more with Pen. She's possessive of him. She's constantly complaining that Cody loves me more than her, and accusing me of trying to turn him against her. She's one of the reasons I've never introduced Cody to any woman I've dated. I was never serious enough about any of them to earn myself that headache. She'll never welcome anyone with open arms."

That's not comforting to hear. "And if you were to tell her you wanted to reconcile, would she consider it?" Is this *just* about her love for Cody?

"I don't know. It's not important because it's never happening," he mumbles, in a way that makes me think he *does* know she still harbors feelings for him, or at the least regrets, and he just doesn't want to acknowledge it. "She has always acted like she's more Cody's parent than I am, and that she should have more say in his life than I do."

"Yeah, I noticed at the orientation session."

"I don't fight when she starts up like that. All it'll do is put Cody in the middle of a tug-of-war that he doesn't deserve. As long as he's taken care of and we have fifty-fifty shared custody, she can live under whatever delusion she wants."

"But now *I'm* in the picture, and somehow her dad screwing my mother is *my* fault. Right? Has she acknowledged that her father could be to blame for part of it?"

"She's got plenty of issues with her dad, trust me. Her mom's no angel, either. Melissa is … " His words trail on a humorless chuckle. "Well, she's a real piece of work. And she may have taken Peter back, but she hasn't let him forget about the affair for a single day, trust me."

I never met Melissa Rhodes, though as the mayor's wife her pretty face graced the Polson Falls Tribune enough times that I could identify her in a crowd years later. I always thought she looked sour.

He opens his mouth to speak, but hesitates. "Pen is adamant that your mother stay away from Cody."

I snort derisively. "That's one thing she doesn't have to worry about." Dottie won't be in a rush to play grandma to her old lover's grandson. She hasn't even been by to visit my house yet.

"But Pen doesn't get any fucking say in it." His tone is sharp, his eyes almost golden, they're so vibrant. It's a rare sight to see Shane angry.

The need to feel him is overwhelming. I reach out to toy with a strand of his hair. "You know, you're kind of hot right now."

His left eyebrow arches. "You *like* seeing me mad?"

"Not at *me*, but when you're mad at other people …" My gaze rakes over his neck, his shoulders, his arms. "Your body gets all tense." It reminds me of years ago, on the field against opposing teams, when testosterone and competitiveness would clash, leaving players shouting and pacing and shoving their opponents. Even from my spot in the stands, I could sense the energy vibrating from Shane.

He reaches over to grip my thigh, his fingertips slipping into the warmth between them. "You want to help me release some of it?"

His sudden honeyed voice and touch causes heat to flood my

core. Something tells me Shane would be fuck-me-against-the-wall aggressive tonight. "If only I could." If Cody weren't here, we'd already be tangled in bedsheets.

But Cody is here, and he is Shane's priority, a reality that makes Shane even more attractive. I've heard of these men—these dedicated, loving fathers with their shit together. This is my first time seeing one up close and personal, though.

With a heavy sigh, Shane's focus shifts to his bay window. A light blinks in the darkened room. I'm guessing Cody has parked himself to play his games. If he's not spying on his father and teacher, that is. "I should go in and talk to him. He always gets rattled when he sees his mom like that."

"Any idea what the fight was about?" Not that I care. I'm just curious. And Travis's comment when he saw me in the truck makes me a little wary.

"No, but I'll get it out of Cody soon enough. It's usually money. That, or me."

"*You*? They fight about you?"

He shrugs. "They used to, anyway. Travis would accuse her of caring too much about what's going on in my life."

"He might not be wrong." Shane is her son's father, though. What's happening in Shane's life affects Cody. But that only further lends itself to my theory that, even after all these years, Penelope still harbors feelings for her high school sweetheart.

"Maybe it was about Melissa again. They've been fighting a lot about her lately too. She likes to stick her nose in where it doesn't belong. Travis hates her guts."

"He definitely seemed pissed off."

"And fed up," Shane agrees. His expression is a mixture of annoyance and worry. "He may not be my favorite person, but she's been more reasonable since they hooked up. Tolerable. So, for *everyone's* sake, I hope they can work their shit out."

I check my watch. It's almost 9:00 p.m. What to do with my weekend, now that it has unexpectedly freed up? "So, I guess I'll see you … Monday?" I struggle to hide the disappointment from my tone.

Shane chews his lip, his face pensive as he studies his bay window again. "Or you could just come in and hang out with us. Throw a movie in or something."

"With you *and* Cody?"

"Yeah," he says on a heavy exhale. "He's probably going to hear about us from Penelope anyway. I'd rather he heard it from me instead of the negative spin she'll put on it."

I try to gauge Shane's tone. Is that reluctance I hear? Is he feeling forced?

"I'm not sure damage control is a good reason for us to introduce our relationship to your son," I say slowly, unable to hide the twinge of hurt that comes with this.

"That's not what I mean." He turns to face me. Sincerity shines in his eyes. "I've actually been thinking a lot lately about telling him. It's time he knows how important you are to me." He reaches for my hand and pulls my knuckles to his lips for a tender kiss.

My heart hammers. There have been plenty of whispers exchanged in the heat of the moment, expressions of how much pleasure we bring to each other, but we have yet to have a serious, clothed conversation about commitment.

"How important am I to you?" I hear myself ask. Shane said he wouldn't introduce a woman into his son's life unless he was serious about her. Has his perspective changed?

Or is this his way of making his feelings known to me?

He chuckles softly. God, how I love that sound. "You want me to say it out loud?"

My heart beats like a steady, thunderous drum. *Yes.*

His Adam's apple bobs. "Important enough that my son should get used to you being in his life because I see you being in it for a long time." He hesitates, his brow tightening. "Unless you're not feeling the same way, in which case you should probably tell me now—"

"I feel the same way." A rush of adrenaline surges through me as a new path ahead comes into clearer focus. One where I'm becoming a stepmother to an eleven-year-old boy. Not just a boy. Shane's son, with Penelope Rhodes, the woman who terrorized me for years because of our parents' mistake. Never would I have foreseen this for myself, that day in June when I took a casual drive along Hickory Street. Never would I have wished it. It's funny, how drastically perspectives can change when your heart gets involved.

"So, that's a yes to tonight?" he asks.

I picture myself standing in front of the class, with Cody staring back at me from his desk with eyes that match his father's, only innocent. Will he tell his classmates that his dad is banging the teacher? Will my relationship with Cody's father become the topic of teasing and gossip among my students?

Or will Cody be embarrassed and hide it from them?

I guess we're going to find out.

I take a deep breath. "What's the snack situation like at your place?"

Fifteen minutes later, I find myself on Shane's porch, my blood pounding in my ears as nervousness swells.

Shane opens the door before I can knock, as if he were waiting for me. His eyebrows arch at the plastic bags dangling from my grip. "Did you run out to the store?"

"Just the convenience store around the corner." Where I spent half of next week's grocery budget in the candy and chip aisle, loading up on junk to win over an eleven-year-old boy.

His eyes are smiling as he collects the weighty bags. He leads me into his house. We stall at the threshold to the living room where Cody is sprawled across the couch, his attention glued to the TV screen, his thumbs flying over his game controller.

"Hey, bud. Pick out a movie for us while we get ready. And no horrors. Scarlet gets scared easily."

Scarlet. I'm no longer Ms. Reed to Cody outside of the classroom. Of course, I shouldn't be. Still, it's momentarily jarring to hear Shane use my name with his son for the first time.

Cody spares a second to glance at me. "Okay," he says, before turning back to his game.

Shane leads me into the kitchen.

"What did he say?" I whisper, as Shane sets the bags on the counter and begins rooting through the cupboard.

"He said 'cool.'"

I frown. "Cool? That's it?"

He tears open the Doritos with a smirk. "That's it."

"Huh." And here I was, worried about his psychological state upon finding out his dad is dating his teacher. "So, he's fine with it?"

"Seems to be." He grins. "But I'm sure he'd be fine with you still trying to bribe him to like you with all this junk."

I laugh, my cheeks heating. "Am I that obvious?"

"Oh, yeah. He's a smart kid. He'll see right through you." He plucks a chip from the bag and shoves it into his mouth. "But it's adorable."

"So are you." I reach up to wipe Dorito cheese powder off Shane's lip with the pad of my thumb.

He catches my thumb in his mouth, sucking it in while he pulls me into his body, his mood light and infectious. "You don't need to bribe that kid. Trust me, he won't be able to resist you." He leans in to lay a quick Dorito-flavored kiss on my lips. "Just like his dad couldn't."

TWENTY-FIVE

The end of day bell chimes over the PA system. "Make sure your name is at the top of the page and leave it here on your way out!" I holler over the clamber of rising bodies, patting the corner of my desk.

Math tests land on my desk in a frantic pile as students scramble to pack up for home. As am I. I steal a glance out my classroom window to the dreary November weather that has rolled in. I don't mind walking in that, though, because Shane is home, waiting for me. His lewd text earlier promised a date with his bed, after three long nights apart.

The anticipation of that has had me watching the clock all afternoon.

"Umm … Ms. Reed?" Cody stands by my desk, the only student remaining.

Now that we've been on a first-name basis for a few weeks outside of class, hearing him refer to me formally sounds odd. I smile. "Yes, Cody?"

He stalls, glancing at the door as a group of kids rush past, their laughter swelling. Shane warned him of what would likely happen should he start telling kids that his father is dating their teacher. The teasing and ridicule. When they've passed, he brushes his hand across his forehead to push his hair aside. It's a nervous tic, I'm learning. It makes me smile every time. "Do you know what my dad's doing this weekend?"

Besides me?

I stuff that thought into the drawer of deeply inappropriate thoughts I should never have when Cody's around. "Let's see … Nothing big tonight, now that the Panthers season is over. Tomorrow he's helping his friend Dean move some furniture in the morning."

"Oh. Cool." He bites his lip, like he has more to say but isn't sure if he should.

"What do you have planned for this weekend?" I ask lightly.

He shrugs, his mood darkening a touch. "Nothing. Travis is going away so it's just me and my mom."

I hesitate. Cody divulged to Shane that the cataclysmic fight a few weeks ago stemmed from something Melissa said to belittle Travis and it quickly escalated to Penelope accusing Travis of an affair with a coworker, with plenty of shrieking, name-calling, and a few dishes smashed for effect. But I'm not supposed to know any of that, so I play dumb. "Have things settled down a bit over there?"

He shrugs a second time. Classic eleven-year-old communication with my boys, it seems.

I want to ask Cody what he thinks about his mother's boyfriend, but I bite my tongue. I'd be asking not as Cody's concerned teacher but as his father's nosy girlfriend.

But I'm suspecting his reluctance to be in Dover this weekend has less to do with Travis and more to do with the fact that Cody idolizes his father. Maybe Penelope is justified with her jealousy in that regard. Cody vibrates with energy when he arrives at his father's house and drags his feet sullenly when he leaves. He knows his father's football stats as if they were his own. When he's not engrossed in his PlayStation, he's harping on Shane to toss a ball with him because he wants to pick up the mantle of quarterback. He's had Shane repeat fire station stories, clinging to his every word.

If Cody had to choose one home to live in, I'd bet money he'd choose Shane's.

And watching the two of them together makes me think crazy thoughts. Thoughts I never really entertained with any real dimension. Like, what would it be like to have a baby with this man?

Cody still lingers. What's on his mind?

"You know, your dad *loves* hearing from you."

"Yeah, I know," Cody says flippantly, but it's followed by a small, thoughtful smirk.

"You should call him when you get home." I check the clock. "Not that I don't love hanging out with you, but shouldn't you be getting on your bus now? I don't want you to miss it." On days with Penelope, Cody takes the school bus to her parents' after school to wait for her to finish work.

He shakes his head. "I'm getting a ride with my mom today. She had a meeting with Mrs. Redwood, so she told me to go to the office after school."

My stomach drops. Penelope is meeting with Wendy?

I clear the apprehension from my voice. "She'll be wondering where you are, then."

He nods and takes a step toward the door, but then he stalls again. "Are you and my dad allowed to date?"

I struggle to not gnash my teeth. There's only one person who would have put that thought in his head. And she just met with my boss.

"Our relationship doesn't break any rules with the school board," I say evenly. "But I think you and your dad should talk about it some more, okay?" Let Shane contradict whatever lies and poison Penelope is filling their son's head with.

"Oh, okay. Good. I don't want you to get in trouble." He grins, oblivious to the tension ricocheting through my body. "See ya, Scar." He trots off, leaving me stewing in this odd mixture of rage and worry even while I smile. At some point, Cody has adopted his father's nickname for me.

I let my forehead fall to the desk, debating whether I should march down to the office now and face Wendy or hightail it out of here to face her next week. That's how Becca finds me.

"Rough day?" she chirps, her bags slung over her shoulder, her keys dangling from her finger. No one lingers long on Fridays around here.

"I'm not sure yet," I answer cryptically. It's not like Penelope blindsided Wendy with Shane's and my "indiscretion." Suddenly I find myself thanking Bott for reporting her suspicions to our boss. It gives Wendy an opportunity to arm herself ahead of time, to shut down Penelope's complaints.

But will she? She certainly didn't give me the heads-up about this discussion.

I tell Becca about Penelope's meeting with Wendy.

"Oh." She nods vigorously, as if she gets it. Does she, though? Has Becca done anything as a teacher that could be construed as morally questionable? "Don't worry too much about Penelope. She's a thorn but Wendy will handle her."

"I hope you're right."

Her smile is sympathetic. "You spending time with your sexy neighbor this weekend?"

"Yeah. Until he goes to work on Sunday morning."

"We should do something on Sunday, then. We haven't hung out in forever."

"I know, right?" My guilt creeps in. I've been so blissfully consumed by all things Shane these past few weeks, I've let my budding friendship fall by the wayside. "Why don't we do brunch on Sunday?"

"Perfect. Text me with a time and location."

Becca leaves me to stack the messy pile of math tests. After waffling for another minute, I decide I'd rather be in ignorant bliss this weekend as far as Penelope is concerned, and so I stuff everything in my satchel and grab my jacket, intent on escaping before I cross paths with Wendy.

Unfortunately, I'm not fast enough. I hear the worn heels clicking a few seconds before knuckles rap at my door.

"Knock, knock." Wendy stands in my doorway, wearing that same troubled smile she wore when she first approached me about my relationship with Shane.

I sigh. There's no point playing dumb. "I heard Penelope came to see you?"

"Yes." Her lips are pursed as she shuts the door. "And we might have a problem."

"She can't fucking do that!" Shane explodes.

"Submit a formal complaint to the school board? Yeah, actually, she can." What happens next is in the air. It could be dismissed as nothing more than a parent's grievance. It could end up a mar on my employment file. Two months into my career, that file is too new to be collecting these sorts of red marks, but it's not the end of the world.

Or I could lose my job.

"But it's not a rule!" Shane picks up his dish rag, only to toss into the kitchen sink.

"Maybe not, but my moral conduct could be an issue. Especially when you throw in our families' history."

Wendy was candid about her meeting with Penelope. In a nutshell, Penelope questioned my moral character, given I "so quickly" moved in on a student's father with no regard for her son's well-being. She had the gall to suggest that me buying the house beside Shane wasn't a coincidence and poked at my mental stability, pursuing a man it was well known I was infatuated with years ago—I'd all but admitted it the night of the parent orientation. But Penelope made it sound like there were serious concerns that I might be a stalker.

The latter accusation, Wendy squashed quickly, highlighting how it could be construed as defamatory. But the question of moral character was not so easy to sidestep. Wendy informed her that she has had a discussion with me on the matter so I am aware of the conflict and have chosen to continue pursuing my relationship. She did make the argument on my behalf that so far, we've kept our relationship private and quiet, and it doesn't seem to have had a negative effect on Cody at all.

Still, Penelope insisted that, as the principal of Polson Falls Elementary, Wendy is obligated to fire me. Wendy countered, saying this wasn't grounds for dismissal. That's when Penelope threatened to go above her.

My fists were clenched with rage, my insides burning with worry and fear as Wendy detailed their conversation.

"This is bullshit," Shane mutters. "Who cares that we're together?"

"Some parents won't care." Some will think there are far bigger issues than their child's teacher's sex life. Or they'll hear our backstory and think, "Okay, I get it. They have a history. Ms. Reed isn't using parent-teacher night as a speed-dating service."

"But there are parents who will agree with her and will be up in arms over this," I say. Likely a few teachers too. And I know firsthand how noisy and poisonous Penelope can be when she's on a mission to defame someone. I've lived through her wrath once. She may have no grounds for demanding my dismissal, but by the time she's done with me, I'll probably want to quit.

Shane paces around his kitchen, pinching the bridge of his nose. "I didn't think she was being serious about this."

My mouth gapes. "Wait, you *knew* she was going to push for Wendy to fire me and you didn't warn me?" My tone is full of accusation.

"She flies off the handle when she's angry and says all kinds of shit she doesn't mean."

"But she told you she was going to go after my job that night we picked up Cody?" It's been *weeks*.

Shane sighs and shakes his head. "No. We got into it the other night again, over the phone. I figured she'd let it go."

"Well, clearly not because she's going after my job. And even if she doesn't get me fired, she'll ruin my reputation again. You of all people should know how big a deal that is to me!" I spent my childhood chased by glances and whispers that she bred and fed until the glances became stares and the whispers became laughter and jeers. I was the punch line in so many cruel jokes, thanks to her.

"Oh my God. By the time she's done with me, I'll be Dottie Reed two point O." Now *I'm* the one pacing his kitchen.

"No one's going to buy that."

"I can already hear it. I'll be known as the Daddy Fucker or something equally trashy!"

Shane lassos me into his chest with his arms. "Take it easy, Scar. You're getting hysterical."

"Hysterical?" I hiss. "Your psychotic, Red Devil baby mama is threatening my career and my reputation, and you're calling me *hysterical*?"

"I didn't mean it *that way*." He groans. "I wish that word didn't exist."

"What way did you mean it, then?" I don't know when this became a fight between us, but I sense the air shifting quickly.

He must sense it too. "I don't know, but I have a feeling no matter what I say, it'll be wrong."

"That's because *your* career and reputation isn't being threatened. As usual, the man is innocent in all of this, isn't he?"

He releases me and lifts his hands in surrender. "Hey, I haven't done anything wrong here."

"Neither have I, but *I'm* the one about to have my life blown up."

"What do you want me to do, Scar? What am I supposed to do? Tell me how *I* can fix this?"

"I don't know." I wince at the throb in my temple. It was a dull ache when I said goodbye to Wendy. Now it pulsates. "I'm going home. I've got a headache." And I suspect nothing good will come of letting this conversation continue while our tempers are flaring.

Shane's brow furrows, but he merely nods.

I'm halfway to the front door when he hollers, "Do you still want me to come over later?"

"I don't know. We'll see if I'm still *hysterical*." So much for our sordid night together.

I'm not sure who I should be angry with right now.

Penelope, for proving that some people don't change.

My mother, whose selfishness still haunts me all these years later.

Shane, for so thoroughly pursuing me to dive into this relationship, knowing the land mines we'd have to navigate around.

Or me, for being stupid enough to give my heart to Shane Fucking Beckett again.

While some women don't like to throw derogatory names at other women, Justine has no qualms.

"What a cunt," Justine declares over my phone's speaker, her crass announcement—and her favorite insult, that she adopted after spending a semester working with an exchange student from London—competing with the noisy rattle of my bathroom ceiling fan.

"She's definitely something." I poke at the bath faucet with my big toe. It's been four hours since I left Shane scowling in his kitchen. I heard his truck pull out as I was popping Advil and lying down to attempt sleep that didn't come. Finally, I gave up and drew myself a bath, hoping the lavender bath bomb might soothe my aches and my woes.

"She won't win this, will she?"

"Wendy doesn't think so. I mean, it's not like I'm walking around Shane's kitchen in my underwear when Cody's there."

"Has he heard you two fucking?"

"No. I've never slept over when Cody's there. And we're super careful around him. I think I've held Shane's hand once."

"So then that psycho can stuff her piehole. She has no argument."

"We'll see. They post formal complaint resolutions on the school board website. I went on it to see what kinds of cases were listed. They're all DUIs and thefts. *Real* crimes." My only crime is stupidity. Did I *really* believe Penelope would take my relationship with Shane lying down?

"See? You've got nothing to worry about."

"Maybe you're right." My voice doesn't hold much hope. If there's anyone who can spin a question of moral character—gray area, at best—into a crime, it'd be Penelope.

I don't want to lose my job. I *definitely* don't want to spend the next however many years with my reputation trashed.

But am I going to have to give up Shane to keep those things I've worked so hard for and protected? It's a dark thought that reared itself while I was lying in bed, toiling over solutions. I immediately dismissed it as a viable option, but it's still there, lingering, as if my brain knows something my heart doesn't yet want to face:

Maybe I'll have to choose.

Maybe I can't have it all.

Another grim thought has emerged along with it—what if Shane decides he doesn't want these complications in his life? What if he's the one who pulls the plug on us?

He's done it once before, and the "complications" were barely that by comparison.

I push that gut-wrenching worry aside. "What are you doing tonight?"

"Binge-watching *The Last Kingdom*. This guy's so hot. I hate Bill's job and I miss you."

I smile despite her bitter tone. Apparently, Bill's job description includes frequent booze-laden cocktail hours with clients and colleagues. Justine has always hated it, and they're always fighting about him coming home tipsy to fall asleep on the couch. It's good to see some things haven't changed since I left. "Anything else exciting going on this weekend?"

"I have a trade show, and Bill's daughter has a piano recital tomorrow, so he's heading to Boston overnight. So, what did Shane say about all this bullshit?"

I sigh. "Penelope told him she was going to do it but he didn't take her seriously. He doesn't know what to do."

"Ugh. How about *don't* stick your big dumb dick in her all those years ago, buddy," she chirps, her accent especially thick with her irritation.

"If only we had a time machine." Though, that would mean Cody wouldn't exist and, after teaching him for more than two months and spending time with him outside of school, I could never wish for that. He's a good kid.

Too bad his mother couldn't simply vanish.

But that is wishful thinking that will never come to pass. As long as I'm with Shane, Penelope will be a part of my life, for better and for worse.

So far, it's definitely the latter.

"Scarlet!" Shane calls out, followed by the sound of feet climbing my stairs.

"I'm in the bath." My heart does its routine pitter-patter—he has clearly taken the liberty to use the spare key I hid on my porch. I'm beginning to think I might as well just give it to him.

Shane appears from around the corner, a paper bag bearing the logo from the local Mediterranean restaurant in his grasp, the key dangling from his finger. "I didn't want to knock and drag you out of bed if you still had a headache. And then I heard voices."

"I'm just talking to Justine." Exactly how much did he hear?

My eyes rake over his pleasing form. He's still in the track pants and black Dri-FIT shirt that hugs his torso and shows off his immaculate body. No one has ever made casual clothes look as sexy as this man does.

And now he's leaning against the door frame, shamelessly perusing my naked body in the tub.

Don't get sucked into this thirst trap, Scarlet.

To Justine, I say, "Gotta go. Shane just magically appeared."

"Hey, Scarlet's sexy neighbor!" Justine's playful voice carries.

He smirks. "Hey, girl."

"When's that auction of yours?"

"Beginning of December." His smirk grows wider. "Why? You want to come bid on my big, dumb dick?"

So he did hear that.

As expected, Justine is unfazed. "Nah, you're too pricey, pretty boy. I want someone cheap so I can make Bill jealous."

I shake my head. She's kidding, of course. I hope. "Talk to you later."

Shane sets the brown bag on my dresser and then steps into the bathroom to sit on the edge of the tub, leaning his back against the tile wall.

My nipples pebble under his leisurely gaze, but he doesn't make a move to touch me.

"You still mad at me?" he finally asks.

"I wasn't mad at *you*. I was just … mad." I flick at the water's surface.

He studies a small cut on his index finger. "I went to talk to Penelope."

So, that's where he's been for the past four hours. "And?"

"And I told her that what she's doing is wrong and harmful. She's going to stir up old dirt about her dad and that will bother Cody *way* more than kids teasing him about *us* being together."

Peter Rhodes's affair with my mother and his ejection from the mayor's position was certainly newsworthy. While his reputation seemed to have recovered since, I doubt he could step into a restaurant for a few years after without earning a raised eyebrow and a few whispers. But people moved on. The only one who hasn't seems to be Penelope. "What'd she say?"

He makes an unintelligible sound. "She said she doesn't want to see Cody get hurt by her father like she was when she was young."

"That would be a valid concern, if you were married and having an affair. And she's not the only one who was hurt by that."

"Yeah, I pointed that out too. I think she knows it." He smirks. "Somewhere *very* deep down inside."

I snort. "Are you sure you're not giving her too much credit?"

"Maybe. But I have to. It's the only way I can deal with her, and I *have to* be able to deal with her. No matter what else she is, she's my son's mother. She isn't going to just disappear."

He's right, of course. "Thank God one of you is mature."

His gaze settles on my tiny bathroom's ceiling, and the peeling paint. "Yeah, well, she said she'll *consider* not going through with this formal complaint bullshit."

Even though it's not a guarantee, I feel lighter. "I didn't think she could be reasoned with."

"She can be when she's not out for blood."

"With you, maybe."

He grunts, but he doesn't disagree. "I'm sure it'll cost me my soul at some point."

I sigh with relief. This entire ordeal has been draining. "I'm guessing it wasn't a fun conversation, so thank you for going over there and dealing with her."

"It wasn't so bad. I got to see Cody. Apparently, he's been chattering nonstop about you at home. He told her that he *really* likes you." He smiles wryly. "He figured out that she's not happy about us dating. I think he was trying to make her okay with the idea, but that actually might have been what set her off."

"*That*'s why she was hell-bent on blowing up my life? Because her son told her he *likes* his dad's girlfriend?" My heart pangs for the poor boy who feels he needs to pacify his mother's insecurities. No child should have to do that. "She'd rather him *hate* me?"

"I don't know. But she said she's afraid he'll end up liking you more than he likes her."

I pinch the bridge of my nose. Travis is right; she *is* batshit crazy. "I hope you suggested therapy."

"Yeah, I like my balls intact, thanks."

"Hmm. So do I." Now that the immediate threat of Penelope has faded, I'm acutely aware of my exposed body and Shane's wandering eyes.

With a grin, he pulls off his socks.

"What do you think you're doing?" I watch with interest as Shane stands and, reaching over his head, yanks off his shirt.

"Getting naked."

"Yes, I see that." I stare with longing at the ridge of ab muscles and the deep cut of his pelvis. "The question is, why?"

"Do I really need to spell it out?" He shucks his pants and underwear in one move, and his impressive erection springs free.

My mouth goes dry at the promise of it. "No, that's pretty clear. But I *just* got in here, like, five minutes ago. And I used a Lush bath bomb."

He frowns curiously. "So?"

"Do you have any idea how much those cost? I'm not wasting it—ah! What are you doing?" I shriek as Shane climbs into the tub, forcing my legs up and apart to make room for his massive frame. "There isn't enough room for us in here." There's barely enough room for me as it is. I howl with laughter as he ignores my complaints, shifting and jostling my body until we're somehow both packed in and water is splashing onto my old tile floor. In the end, I'm straddling his lap with my legs awkwardly slung over the edges.

"There is nothing sexy about this," I murmur, even as my hand finds its way between us to stroke him beneath the water.

"No, this definitely wasn't built for two people," he agrees. "Next time you want a bath, have one at my house."

"Just show up with my bath caddy?" The tub in his master bath is new and spacious, and it has jets. It *would* be far nicer.

He presses a kiss against my throat. "Or just leave your fancy bath stuff there. I'll give you the code."

"Well, that's good, seeing as you keep inviting yourself into *my* house with the spare key."

His deep chuckle vibrates through my body. "I didn't think you'd care. I brought food."

"You did." But are we officially crossing into this territory? The land of exchanging keys and door codes and keeping toiletries at each other's houses instead of trekking across the lawn?

He dips his head to catch my breast in his mouth.

A tremble courses through me. "Will my baths be peaceful or will you bother me over there too?" I ask, attempting a calm voice.

"Is that what I'm doing?" He rolls his tongue around my nipple.

I close my eyes and tilt my head back to give him better access while I blindly run my palm along his shaft, reveling in his size. "Yes. And it's extremely annoying."

"You're the sweetest girl I've *ever* met."

I bellow with laughter at the sarcastic gibe.

With a playful nip of his teeth, he hooks his arms beneath

mine and hauls my body farther onto his lap. His tip prods against my entrance. The thought of needing a condom sparks in my mind but just as quickly disappears. We've already had the "Are you clean?" and "Are you on birth control?" conversations. We just haven't taken that next step yet.

"I was so afraid you would bail on me." His lips caress mine in soft strokes, his voice suddenly serious.

I swallow. "Same."

He flattens his palms over my slick back and guides me closer until our entire upper bodies are flush. "*I'm* not going anywhere."

"Even if this is getting complicated?"

"The more complicated, the better." He lifts his hips, slowly pushing into me.

A moan slips out as my body molds around him, welcoming the intrusion. Oddly enough, nothing about us feels complicated in this moment. It's all straightforward and *right*. It feels like it was all meant to happen this way, like fate had this twisted path to take us on to get here but always knew we'd find ourselves in my dingy bathtub years later, our limbs and hearts and breaths tangled.

"You want me to pull out before?" he whispers, his eyes hooded and blazing with lust as he waits for my answer.

I shake my head.

Gripping the back of my head, he brings my lips to his in a kiss that consumes all of my worries.

TWENTY-SIX

Karen and Heidi are huddled by the coffee maker when I pop in to the staff room during morning recess. Their conversation quiets instantly and, when they turn to see me standing there, Karen's eyes widen as if startled.

"So, what are the kids into these days?" Heidi asks, as if carrying on their previous conversation.

A prickle of recognition slithers down my spine as Karen nervously prattles about soccer and baseball and piano lessons. I head for the fridge to grab my yogurt from my lunch bag, aware that they were talking about me.

I shouldn't be surprised. I've gotten to know the teaching staff over the past two and a half months. Of everyone at Polson Falls Elementary, these two are the likeliest to gossip. Besides Becca, of course, but I trust that our conversations remain between us.

Karen has two overscheduled children and a husband who travels for work more than he's home. I'm pretty sure she belongs to every mommy group in Polson Falls. Meanwhile, Heidi is single and alone and spends her hours outside of school as a social justice warrior, sharing news links on Facebook and angry-tweeting politicians and corporations.

Nothing happens in this school without them hearing about it.

The question is, who's been talking?

Did Penelope decide to go to the school board after all? It's been almost a week since her meeting with Wendy. Did poor Cody make the disastrous mistake of mentioning my name in a positive light again?

With a sigh, I slide out my phone, intent on texting Shane. As much as I don't want Penelope to be a daily subject for us, I also don't want any more surprises.

"What are your plans for this weekend, Scarlet?" Heidi asks suddenly, feigning a blank, innocent look. Of the two of them, she's more likely to pass judgment on my relationship with Shane. That's probably why my guard is instantly up with her.

"Housework." *In between several rounds of sweaty sex with my student's hot dad, since I know that's what you're really asking.* In truth, there won't be much of that this weekend, seeing as Cody is with us tonight and Shane leaves for work tomorrow, until Sunday.

"That's right! Didn't you buy that cute little blue house with the picket fence down the street?" Karen asks, pointing in the opposite direction of where my house is.

I don't bother to correct her. "I did. It needs a lot of work, but I'll slowly get to it all." Where is everyone, anyway? The staff room usually has five or six bodies in it at any given time during recess.

They exchange glances. Heidi looks like she's chewing on bees, the way she's worrying her mouth. "How are your neighbors?"

I've only met the neighbors to my right once. They're a pleasant but busy young family, with three kids under five and a lot of high-pitched screaming in the early hours.

I'm guessing Heidi isn't asking about them, though.

"Are you going to beat around the bush all day or ask your prying question?" Bott's reedy voice cuts into the staff room. I hadn't heard her come in, but that's par for the course for a woman who seems to materialize out of thin air like a mythical beast from the underworld. She floats toward the fridge as if she didn't just call out her colleague for being intrusive. Even on below-fifty-degree November days, she still wears her Birkenstocks.

Heidi exchanges another quick glance with her sleuthing partner. "We heard you're dating Cody Rhodes's father."

"Hmm." I feign casualness as I peel the foil off my yogurt, not giving an answer one way or another. Inside, a mixture of resignation and dread swirls. I truly despise being the topic of conversation.

"He's *very* attractive." Karen nods vigorously—it reminds me of a bobblehead figurine. She's not the confrontational type. More likely, she'll smile and agree to your face and then express empty outrage when you turn around.

"He always has been," Bott answers for me, drifting over to the table with a cloth lunch bag. "Even as a boy, there was something appealing about him."

From any other grown woman, that might teeter on creepy and inappropriate, but coming from Bott, it sounds merely like fact.

"He's a firefighter, right?" Karen asks.

"Are you not *at all* worried about the awkward position you've put your student in?" Heidi blurts, cutting into Karen's chatty questions.

I wondered who among my fellow teachers might take offense to me dating Shane. It seems I can make a tick in the box beside Heidi's name.

My cheeks burn with indignation as I open my mouth to defend myself.

"Were *you* not at all worried three years ago when Cody

Rhodes was your student and you bid on his father at that ridiculous auction?" Bott asks mildly.

My eyebrows arch with surprise, trying to picture the righteous Heidi waving her paddle in the air, bidding on Shane as if he were a prize bull.

"That's *totally* different!" Heidi blusters, her face turning beet red. "And I didn't win. And that was for charity!"

"Hmm. Yes, for charity." That secretive little smirk emerges on Bott's mouth as she pries open her food container.

Heidi collects her water bottle and an apple and, lifting her chin high as if she weren't just made a fool of, strolls out, Karen on her heels.

It's just Bott and me in the room now, and I'm feeling oddly appreciative of her.

"Thank you for defending me," I offer.

"I wasn't defending you. I was merely pointing out the obvious." She stabs at the contents in the container—something flesh-pink, gelatinous, and smelling strongly of vinegar and chemicals.

I struggle not to cringe. "Still. Thanks." No longer hungry, I rinse the last of my yogurt down the sink and toss the empty container in the recycling bin.

"I'm sorry for what I did to you when you were my student."

I turn to find Bott staring ahead and chewing, a serene expression on her face. For a moment, I question if I imagined her apology, if she didn't just address the twenty-one-year-old elephant in the room.

"So, you understand that what you did was wrong?"

She swallows her mouthful. "I always knew it was wrong."

I frown. This sounds more like a non-apology.

"I was angry and desperate, and more concerned about my child being hurt by her father than I was about acting inappropriately. I knew what I was doing. I made a choice. We all make choices."

"I could have reported you. You could have lost your job."

"Yes, I could have. I knew there was a risk." She turns that hawkish gaze on me. "You're infatuated with a man and more concerned about finding love than you are about protecting his child's happiness. You also know what you're doing and the risks, and you've made your choice."

Any goodwill I felt toward Bott for fending off Heidi evaporates. "This is not the same at all," I retort angrily. "I'm not abusing my power. I'm not cornering Cody in a room, showing him pictures of my husband and scaring him. I'm not going to hurt him."

"You hope not," she says coolly.

The bell to end recess will go off in ten minutes. I'd rather spend that time anywhere but in here, being scolded by a woman who is far from worthy of doling out advice on integrity.

I move for the door.

"Your mother was attracted to married men because she craved how it felt to win them over. To make them break their commitments."

I could argue that those men weren't very committed in the first place, but that would sound like I'm defending my mother's actions, so I stay silent.

"She was more concerned about her own happiness than she was about her child's."

I know what Bott is getting at, but she's wrong. "I'm not my mother."

"But what choice will you make? What choice will he make? Time will tell."

Bott said that same thing the first day I saw her here. It's as irritating now as it was then.

I watch her as she stabs at a hard, fleshy chunk and holds it up, pondering it.

I can't help my cringe this time. "What *the hell* are you eating? It looks like a fetus."

"Pickled pigs' feet. Would you like to try some?" she says in that eerie monotone of hers, unperturbed.

I shake my head. "No, I'm good, thanks." Does she go out of her way to shock people?

I rush out of there and back to my classroom.

But Bott's words trail me the entire way.

"Mild or spicy tonight, sir?" The waitress grins with familiarity at Cody.

"Spicy, please." Cody takes a long slurp of his Coke.

Shane wasn't kidding when he said the kid is a picky eater. Apparently, chicken wings are the only thing he'll eat when they go out. The staff had him pegged the second he walked in.

"That sounds good. I'll do the same. And fries." Shane closes his menu and passes it to the blond bombshell with nothing more than a polite glance. Meanwhile, I'm ready to pass her a napkin so she can dab at her drool.

With our orders taken, she leaves us, swinging her hips all the way to the computer.

Shane frowns curiously at me. "What's that smile for?"

"Nothing." Just wondering how a woman as jealous as Penelope wasn't arrested for clawing out eyes on the regular. My gaze wanders through the bustling dining area of Route Sixty-Six. It's seven o'clock, still a few hours before the late-night crowd rolls in and the discounted shots begin flowing. The band hasn't even arrived to set up yet. At this time of day, it's families who bring life to the restaurant.

And to anyone unaware, Shane, Cody, and I look like a happy little family. I'm guessing Penelope would lose her shit if she walked in and saw us.

When Shane suggested that the three of us go out to eat, I balked. "Are you sure?" I asked. "What if someone sees us?"

"So what? It's not a big deal. Let them see us," he said, scooping up my hand and pressing my knuckles to his lips.

My knees weakened, and everything else—the episode in the staff room, Bott's words, our commitment to keep this quiet while I'm Cody's teacher—was forgotten.

But now that we're here, I'm afraid that was a mistake.

"Hi, Ms. Reed," Jenny Byrd chirps, stopping at our table, her hand flapping in a quick wave. Her stunning sea-foam green eyes shift to her classmate. "Hey, Cody."

He brushes his hair off his forehead and gives her a dimpled smile. "Hey."

Her gaze flips from me to Cody, to Shane, and I can practically hear the curious questions that churn in her young but astute brain. Before she has a chance to voice any of them, though, her parents usher her past with an apology for interrupting and a "have a good weekend."

Shane gives him a gentle elbow. "Who's that?"

"Jenny. Just a girl in my class." Cody's cheeks flush.

"She's cute," he says nonchalantly before taking a big sip of his drink.

Cody gives a one-shouldered shrug but then his eyes flip to the corner where Jenny Byrd and her family are seated.

Shane smirks as he watches his son. He's fishing. He wants to know if his son has any crushes yet.

And I'm too busy watching Shane watch his son to notice the platinum-blond woman flounce up to our table until it's too late.

"Well now, what is my daughter doing with these two strapping young men?"

Oh God, Mom.

My cheeks flame as I try to ignore the fact that she's dressed in a snug, snakeskin-print dress and impeccably matched heels that are so high, her muscles strain for balance. She's literally turning heads all around us. "What are you doing here?"

McTavish's is more her style this early in the night, where there aren't any children around.

"I felt like a change of scenery. Hello, darling. Fancy meeting you here." She smooths a hand over Shane's shoulder while batting her freshly installed eyelashes. They look good on her, I'll give her that. But her perfume is as cloying as ever.

Shane flashes his signature crooked smirk. "Hey, Dottie. How've you been?"

"I'm much better now."

I roll my eyes. The cheesy lines are always a variant of the same thing.

Much better now.

Better now that you're here.

The night's looking up now.

I've been so far removed from her for so many years, I'd forgotten how tacky she can be.

From beneath the table, Shane gives my calf a gentle nudge of warning. *Behave,* his eyes warn.

Mom shifts her flirtatious gaze. "And who is this handsome young man beside you?"

Shane throws an arm around Cody's shoulders. "This is my son."

Dottie's perfectly drawn lips gape. She does shock and awe better than most. "Why did I not know you had a son!"

Because you barely remember you have a daughter.

Cody's curious eyes flash from her to me, back to her.

"I know, I don't look nearly old enough to be her mother, do I?" she mock whispers.

Cody shakes his head. "You look more like sisters."

Shane chuckles.

And my mother, well, she fucking titters and preens. "Aren't you just as charming as your father."

Our waitress comes by then. "Hey, Dottie. Can I grab you something?"

"Hi, honey. Oh, I'll probably just head on over to the bar in a minute. I wouldn't want to interrupt Scarlet's dinner." She says this as she observes the empty space beside me.

Shane gives my leg another nudge, followed by a "you know what you need to do" look.

The glare I spear him with would make most men's balls shrink, but Shane grins at me. Because he's right and we both know it.

I release a resigned sigh. "Did you want to sit with us?"

She gives the booth another eyeball. "Well, I suppose I could, for just a minute or two. Scoot on over." To the waitress, she winks and says, "A glass of chardonnay would be lovely."

"I was barely older than you when I had Scarlet."

"She was *five years* older," I counter, giving Cody a severe look as he gnaws on a chicken wing. "And still *way* too young to have children."

"But you turned out okay," Mom says through a generous sip of her wine.

"That's debatable," I mutter under my breath, earning Shane's chuckle.

"You did, honey. Maybe a bit uptight but otherwise fine."

Uptight? My nostrils flare.

"So, Dottie, you still over on Brillcourt?" Shane interrupts, trying to defuse my impending explosion.

"I am! How'd you know I lived there?" Her eyes narrow. "You haven't *visited* me before, have you?"

"No. He hasn't," I say more sharply than probably is necessary. At least she was considerate enough to not come right out in front of Cody and asked if they've fucked.

"I was going to say ..." Her eyes rake over Shane's face, his chest, his arms. "I can't see myself forgetting a night like that."

"You definitely wouldn't." Shane winks. He's flirting with my mother.

I glare at him, a warning that if he keeps this up, I'll throttle him later.

Shane clears his throat. "Actually, Scarlet and I dated back in high school. I used to pick her up from there almost every day."

"Huh. I had no idea. Though, she never told me much." My mom takes another sip of her wine. She's like a baby with a bottle. "And that last year before she left for college was a disaster. Do you remember that, Scarlet? I've never seen a more sullen, moody girl. You were miserable. I couldn't say a word without having my head bitten off. Anyway, yes, I'm still at Brillcourt but I've started looking elsewhere. The building has been falling apart for years. It's impossible to get anything repaired. It's a complete shithole."

"Mom."

"Hmm?" She peers at me, oblivious.

"Language?"

"Oh, right. Sorry." She waves off my soft reprimand as if it's nothing. "Anyway, why don't you tell me how you two ended up together again after all these …" Her words trail, her attention on something—or someone.

I lean closer to catch her line of sight. When I see Penelope stalking down the narrow aisle toward us, followed by Travis and an older couple I recognize from the newspapers as Penelope's parents, I desperately wish we'd listened to my gut and stayed home.

TWENTY-SEVEN

The vein in Penelope's forehead pulses as she glares at Shane.

"Hey, Mom!" Cody chirps, but his eyes dart around the table, gauging everyone's moods. He senses that something is off.

Shane's flat expression doesn't fool me. He'd rather be *anywhere* than here. "Hey, Pen." He nods at Travis.

Meanwhile, my mother has been struck momentarily speechless as she stares at her ex-lover, Peter Rhodes. I know they must have crossed paths at some point over the years. The town is small, his accounting firm is a prominent business, and Mom is social. But how long has it been? My guess, based on both their startled faces, is a good while.

I haven't seen him in years. He's aged greatly since his picture made the local newspapers on the regular eighteen years ago. He must be in his late fifties now, maybe early sixties. Miraculously, he still has a full head of hair, though it has turned white-gray.

"Peter," my mother manages finally. "Good to see you again." She sounds somber rather than her usual playful.

"Yes. You look wonder—" He clears his throat before the rest of that sentence has a chance to escape. His blue eyes are oddly bright. "I see you've met my grandson?"

"Your *grandson*." Mom's gaze flickers to Penelope, then to Shane, as the pieces click together.

Melissa eases in to claim the crammed spot beside Peter. She has always been an attractive woman—the source for Penelope's looks, though not her fiery-red hair—but she has aged considerably too. Her face wears cracks and crevices; her once-long auburn hair has been cropped short. Her body, though still slender and graceful, has succumbed to the effects of gravity.

She hooks her arm through his and hugs it tight to her. It's a possessive move. Given the malice with which those tight green eyes—sage, like her daughter's—regard my mother, I'm not at all surprised she feels the need to stake her claim. By comparison, Dottie Reed looks every bit the evil temptress, at least fifteen years younger and intent on luring men of weak fortitude such as her husband.

Worse, she has the track record to prove she can do it.

With a small horde gathering by our booth, we're beginning to attract casual looks, but I don't think anyone has noticed the storm cloud brewing yet.

"Penelope, I trust you'll deal with this accordingly," Melissa says. I see where her daughter gets that condescending tone from. Shifting her harsh gaze to her grandson, her face softens instantly. "Why don't you come have dinner with us?"

Cody looks to Shane, then to Penelope, as if waiting for one of them to speak or guide him. "But … I want to stay with my dad and Scarlet."

I guess we're a package deal now.

Oh, shit.

Penelope's eyes flare with a mixture of rage and hurt.

"You know what, I think I'm going to shift over to the bar." In a rare moment of reading the room correctly—and probably a desire to remove herself from family strife that she knows she's a key instigator of—my mom collects her purse and glass of wine and shimmies out of our booth. With a polite nod to her ex-lover, she sashays to the bar.

Leaving us to clean up her mess.

"Can I speak to you outside?" Penelope hisses, glaring at Shane.

Shane sighs heavily. He wipes the hot sauce off his fingers with his napkin. "Hey, buddy, you stay and eat your dinner with Scarlet, okay? I'll be back in a minute." He slides out of the booth. "He'll be staying where he is," he says calmly, to Penelope or Melissa, or both.

"I'm not comfortable with—"

"Too bad," he snaps. His temper is being tested now.

Penelope clamps her mouth shut.

Melissa shifts that hateful gaze to me but doesn't argue, tugging on her husband's arm.

Travis watches his potential in-laws hustle to their table but doesn't follow them. He looks as happy as Shane does. "I'll be at the bar," he informs Penelope in an aloof tone before strolling away.

I don't blame him. If I didn't have Cody with me, and I wasn't worried about this compelling urge to throttle my mother, I might join him.

What a disastrous turn this night has taken.

I watch Shane's rigid back as he follows Penelope out the door and to the side street where he and I had our own fight months ago, and then I turn attention back to the boy caught in the middle of this mess.

Cody studies a chicken wing before tossing it back onto his plate. His shoulders are slumped.

"You okay?" I ask softly.

He nods but after a moment says, "They've been fighting a lot."

"They have?" I ask, keeping my voice light.

"Almost every time my dad drops me off. And I hear them on the phone too."

I school my expression. Shane didn't tell me they were *still* fighting.

"I just don't get why she's so mad."

There are so many answers I could give right now—would love to give—that would be accurate but also wrong. How the hell do I navigate this without being dismissive?

Honesty, I guess. "That's one of those topics you have to talk about with your dad. I can't say much."

"Because you're my teacher?"

"Yeah. *And* your dad's girlfriend." I can't speak disparagingly about his mother, even though she's a raging bitch who deserves it.

He nods slowly, as if he gets it. He searches out his grandparents, who are thankfully sitting on the other side of the restaurant. "My grandma's mad too, isn't she?"

"Seems like it."

"I don't really like going over there after school," he admits quietly, picking at another chicken wing. "She's *always* mad at him."

And maybe Peter Rhodes deserves her lingering bitterness, for his part in the affair. But why take him back, then? Why give him a chance to redeem himself if you have no intention of ever forgiving him? Wouldn't it have been better for all involved if they'd gone their separate ways?

I'm beginning to think it might have been better for Penelope to not be brought up in a household where resentment and mistrust loitered. If an eleven-year-old boy is still sensing the residual anger, eighteen years after the act … Why stay? And why would Melissa bring her child up in that environment?

Shane told me that Penelope claimed she cheated on Shane because she wanted his attention, because she felt him slipping away. Is that what she learned about relationships from watching her parents' marriage debacle take shape? That to keep a stronger hold of your loved ones, you need to inflict pain to remind them you're there? That you *can* hurt them and they'll stay?

I don't know what to think of the Rhodes family dynamic, but it seems I'm now tied to it, whether I like it or not.

My phone is ringing inside my purse. I check it quickly to see that it's Justine and then set it on "silent." I'll fill her in on this shitshow tomorrow. "You have to eat, Cody, or you'll be starving, and there's not much in your dad's cupboards."

"Or I can just take these home and heat them up later," he counters.

"Yeah, I guess that's another option." I pick at my Cobb salad, not overly hungry either.

I steal a glance over my shoulder. Sure enough, Travis is settled in next to my mother, showing not the slightest interest in any responsibility over his girlfriend's son. Mom has tipped her head back to laugh about something, and the smile on Travis's face is wide and genuine. Though this is only my third time seeing him, I know I haven't seen him smile like that before.

It's in direct proportion to the scowl that tightens Melissa's face as she watches their interaction. Perhaps the Rhodes women do have a valid case against the Reed women out for their men.

"I like your mom. She's nice," Cody says. "And funny."

"She can be." Especially when she's three chardonnays into the night, and didn't make your childhood a living hell.

Fifteen minutes later, our food is officially cold and there is still no sign of Shane or Penelope.

Cody squirms in the booth, his glances over his shoulder to the window frequent. "Where's my dad? Why are they taking so long?"

I search the dark beyond the glass for any hint of Shane and Penelope, but I see none. "I don't know. They should be back soon, though." Assuming she hasn't shanked him in a fit of rage.

From the corner of my eye, I see Melissa Rhodes slide out

from her booth. I assume she's heading for the restroom until she veers toward our table. I stifle my resigned sigh.

She smiles extra wide at her grandson. "Cody, why don't you come and join your grandfather and me for dinner?" Her voice is saccharine.

"But my dad told me to stay with Scarlet."

"Yes, well, they're taking longer than he expected. Maybe you can rejoin him when he returns." She enunciates each word, and I don't miss the "maybe" in there. As in, it isn't a guarantee that Cody will be entrusted to his father's care again after they've discovered him cavorting with heathens.

And here I thought Penelope was a hateful woman.

Cody's gaze darts to mine, and I see his silent plea for help.

My chest swells even as my gut clenches.

Here we go. Conflict of interest fully engaged. "We're good. Shane should be back shortly." And my guess is he won't appreciate his wishes being trumped by this sour-faced woman, even if she is Cody's grandmother.

Melissa Rhodes's lips press together, forming a thin line, as she regards me. "I thought I was done with Reed women worming their way into my family's lives."

I bite my tongue, not wanting to cause a scene in the middle of the restaurant. Meanwhile, I'm clenching my fists beneath the table.

But Melissa doesn't seem to be able to guard her temper as well. "I realize you may not know that what you're doing is wrong, given your role model, but let me make it clear: Just because there isn't a formal rule stopping you, it *is* wrong. You are putting my grandson in a position of embarrassment and ridicule."

"I think you're the one doing that at the moment." I give a meaningful look around us as my cheeks heat, at nearby tables enraptured by the growing scene. Melissa's voice has risen above the regular hum of conversation. From across the space, I sense

Jenny Byrd and her parents watching, and my face grows hotter. Even if Melissa Rhodes paints herself a lunatic, I won't walk out of here unscathed.

Melissa's eyes dart around us, noting the attention she's drawn. She clears her throat and drops her voice a touch. "You should *not* be engaged in a relationship with Cody's father while you're teaching his son. It's despicable for an educator to behave in this manner and, if we have our way, you won't be teaching *at all*. Come, Cody. Come with me." She beckons him as if he were a dog.

"I don't want to," he mumbles, shaking his bowed head.

But she ignores him, reaching across the table to collect his food.

Short of yanking the plate from her grasp and being accused of causing a physical altercation—with witnesses—that will surely cost me my job, there's nothing I can do to stop her.

I offer Cody a soothing smile. "Don't worry, buddy. We're going to leave as soon as your dad's back."

"He won't be going *anywhere* with *you*," Melissa declares haughtily.

Cody explodes. "Just stop!" With tears streaming down his cheeks, he scurries out of the booth and takes off running out the door, his grandmother hollering his name after him.

"I hope you're happy now," she snipes, smoothing her wrinkled hand over her blouse, stealing furtive glances at the surrounding families. At least she has the decency to look ashamed.

Shaking my head, I slide out. Now that Cody's gone, I have no reason to guard my tongue. "Why don't you go back to your table and keep an eye on your faithful husband before he ends up in a janitor's closet again," I hiss, quiet enough that no one else can hear, and then I march out into the chilly night after Cody.

I find the three of them standing in the shadows on the sidewalk. Penelope is huddled in her jacket, her back to me. Cody's face is buried in his father's chest.

The wind is biting and Shane is in nothing but a T-shirt. He must be cold, though nothing of his posture as he cradles his son's head in comfort suggests that. "We're going home now, buddy, I promise."

"We're not finished with this conversation, Shane," Penelope warns.

He sighs. "Yeah, we are. At least I am." He sees me standing there and gives me a "thank God you're here to rescue me" look.

"I'll go pay the bill and grab our jackets," I say.

Penelope turns to shoot a glare my way that matches Melissa Rhodes's so perfectly, I'd think mother and daughter have practiced in a mirror together.

It doesn't faze me. I'm so tired of dealing with the Rhodes women tonight. But then I note how Cody peels away from Shane's body in time to catch his mother's face. How long before he begins to despise her? Or, worse, what if her toxicity infects him as Melissa's venom bled into Penelope?

Something deep inside compels me to try to make peace, for his sake if nothing else. "If it makes you feel any better, my mom showing up was a total fluke and I doubt it'll happen again." Dottie is where she is most comfortable—at the bar, flirting with men. Currently, that man is Travis, and I have no interest in being here when Penelope discovers that.

"You know what would make me feel better? You staying the hell away from my son!" Penelope yells.

"Don't talk to her like that!" Shane counters.

"I'll talk to her however I want to. She is *not* a part of this family."

"Not yet," Shane says evenly.

Under different circumstances, his words might excite me. Now, though, they're as dangerous as pouring gasoline onto an open flame.

Penelope's mouth gapes. "Why are you doing this to me? After *everything* her mother put my parents through."

"I'm not doing *anything* to you." Shane releases his grip of his son to throw his hands in the air. "I'm just trying to be happy. Scarlet makes me happy!"

As Penelope and Shane yell at each other, oblivious to the pedestrians who are slowing to watch the spectacle, Cody backs away. "Stop fighting," I hear him say, his eyes wide with distress as they ping-pong back and forth.

Neither of them hear him, too busy seething at each other.

"Fine! So make a choice. It's either *her* or your son," Penelope demands.

"Fuck you! I don't have to make that choice," Shane roars, all semblance of calm vanishing.

"Stop fighting over me," Cody shrieks over them. He bolts.

A blood-curdling "No!" rises from deep inside my chest as I watch his gangly body dart across the side street just as headlights flash and a car whips around the corner.

Shane moves fast after his son.

But not fast enough.

TWENTY-EIGHT

I must be on my fiftieth lap around the Polson Falls ER waiting area when the doctor steps out. I hang back while I watch Shane, Penelope, and both sets of grandparents gather to listen to her update on the boy they rushed here by ambulance hours ago.

Not until Shane's head falls back with the words "thank God" shaping on his lips, and Penelope's hands press against her chest, do I allow myself a breath again.

"I'm sorry. I'm so sorry ..." Penelope's mouth forms the words over and over again, shame and regret contorting her beautiful face.

Shane gathers her into his strong arms, cradling the back of her head with affection as they console each other.

I feel a prick, deep inside. A part of me—a jealous, insecure part—wishes I were the first one Shane reached for.

Behind them, the grandparents whisper and hold relieved palms to foreheads and shake their heads, chattering amongst each other with familiarity. But of course, there is familiarity between them. Cody has made them family. Their love of that boy has bonded them for life.

And I will always be an outsider in that regard.

Travis is an outsider too, hanging back, watching it all unfold. Does it bother him that Penelope and Shane will always have this deep connection?

"There you are."

The sound of my mother's voice behind me replaces my relief with trepidation. I spin around. "What are you doing here? You *can't* be here." I hear my despair as I glance over to make sure Melissa or Penelope hasn't noticed her yet. The last thing anyone needs is another screaming match, this time in the hospital.

She holds up my black purse and my jacket. "You left these in the booth."

I sigh, collecting them from her. "Thanks. I wasn't thinking." I hopped into Shane's truck with him and we raced the ambulance here. I'm more than a little mystified that she would make the effort to deliver them to me.

"I also paid your bill." She seems oddly sober for this time on a Friday night. It's unusual for her. But it's nice.

"Right. Let me know how much I owe you."

She waves it off, chomping on her gum. "Don't worry about it. Extenuating circumstances and all that. You can treat next time we go out." She bites her lip, her eyes darting over to where Peter Rhodes stands, his arm around his wife. "That was quite the scene back there."

"Yeah, well, Melissa Rhodes's anger is long-standing, and misguided." And apparently, it has seeped into every fiber of her daughter. Had my mother not had an affair with Melissa's husband—and such a public and humiliating one, at that—would the Rhodes women be so adamant about railroading my career? I guess we'll never know.

"Still, dating your student's father." Mom waggles her eyebrows. "Even *I* never did that."

I know she's attempting to lighten the mood. That's what she does—keeps things light and fun and flirtatious. Shallow.

"You were never a teacher," I remind her. "But you slept with Madame Bott's husband. Does that count?"

She wrinkles her nose. "That man was so unhappy."

I shake my head. This conversation embodies my relationship with my mother, in a nutshell. It's why I'll always keep her at arm's length while questioning how I became a functional human being.

"So, is the boy going to be all right?" she finally asks.

"It seems like it."

"Good." Her eyes widen knowingly. "He's going to be a real looker when he's older, that one."

A mental flash hits me, of Cody leaning against the Route Sixty-Six bar in ten years, ordering shots with his friends, and Dottie Reed strolling in to flirt shamelessly with men young enough to be her grandsons.

Oddly enough, the anger that usually flares with thoughts of her Blanche Devereaux behavior remains dormant. There's no point in being angry. I have my own life, and I'll only make myself bitter concerning myself with hers. She'll never change. She'll just have a harder time stuffing her sagging body parts into those skintight dresses.

I see Shane's head swiveling around the waiting room. He's looking for me. "Thanks for bringing my things, but you should probably get going."

Mom's gaze strays back over to Peter Rhodes. She regards him thoughtfully. "You know, it wasn't him who broke it off. He was willing to leave her for me. *I* turned *him* down."

"Do you want a medal?" I hear myself say.

"There's no need to be snippy."

It's not the time or the place for this conversation. And, really, it doesn't matter. Though, if that's true and Melissa Rhodes is aware of it, it might explain her reluctance to forgive the man and move on with her life. "Just go. Please. You've done enough damage for one night."

"Fine." Mom disappears out the door in a huff as Shane reaches me, the deep amber of his eyes shining.

I push aside the dark cloud that always forms whenever I'm in the same room as my mother and give him my full attention. "How is Cody?"

"His leg and wrist are broken, a lot of scrapes and bruises. They want to keep him overnight for observation but he's going to be fine. No internal bleeding or anything."

"Oh, thank God." My shoulders sag with relief.

"Yeah. I don't know how." Shane lets out a breezy laugh. "He didn't even get a concussion out of it. The kid was so lucky."

"And you're okay?" I reach up to graze my fingertip over the scratch Shane earned along his jaw when he tumbled to the pavement. Everything happened so fast, it's hard to keep track of who hit what first. All I remember with nauseating clarity is the sound of Cody's nimble body colliding with the car. But the driver slammed on the brakes at the last moment, minimizing the impact.

"I'm fine," he dismisses. But then he rolls his shoulder and I notice his wince. I'm guessing if I lifted his shirt, I'd see a swath of black and blue.

"I don't think I've ever been more scared in my life." I'm not sure if my scream ever escaped my lungs, if it came out as anything more than a gurgle of noise.

"Yeah, me neither." He rubs his face with his palms. "Things got *way* out of hand tonight."

"I know." It's all I've been able to think about, when I wasn't praying for a miracle. And while there seems to be a momentary truce between Penelope and Shane, I'd be a fool to think it's going to last. That all these years of festering animosity will simply vanish, that the leopard will change its jealous, possessive spots within hours.

Shane and Penelope were growing civil with each other. Dare I say, they were in a good place, sharing custody of their son.

Then I entered the picture.

And now Cody is in a hospital bed because of the strife I've inadvertently caused. How much is because of me, personally—being Cody's teacher, being Dottie Reed's daughter—and how much is because I'm any female, stepping into Shane and Cody's life, I can't say. What I do know is, I have a difficult choice to make.

No, not difficult.

A *painful* choice.

"Listen ..." I take a step back. "I'm going to head home now."

"But they're about to let us go back and see him." He says this like it's obvious that *I* would join them.

"Good. But I think it's best that *I* leave," I say slowly.

"No, seriously. Hey, why don't you come meet my parents while we wait? I know it's not under the best circumstances, but they really want to meet you." He slips his hand into mine. It's warm and strong and just thinking about it on my body makes me ache.

He hasn't figured it out yet.

Mr. and Mrs. Beckett are standing in the far corner, chatting with each other. Shane must get his height from his father, because his mother, who steals frequent glances our way, is a diminutive thing.

I slip my hand out of his. "I don't think I should meet them." *It'll make this easier.*

Shane frowns. "Scar, what's going on?"

I feel the slight tremble in my limbs as a voice inside my head screams, "You don't want to do this!" I really don't, but it's what's right. Though, I was going to wait until a more appropriate time than standing in the ER waiting room.

I swallow against the rising dread. "I don't think it's a good idea that we see each other anymore."

"No." Shane tips his head back with an exasperated groan. "Come on, Scar—"

"At least not while I'm Cody's teacher. Maybe next year, after he's moved on …" I let the words drift, not feeling hopeful that Penelope's attitude toward me will change.

Anguish and confusion fill Shane's beautiful eyes as he studies my face, dumbfounded. "You can't really want this."

"I don't." My voice wavers.

"Then don't do it," he pleads. "I won't let her go after your job. I promise."

"You can't make that promise." Penelope is a loose cannon, guided by anger and jealousy rather than compassion and common sense. She can't help it; it's how she was raised. Ironic, given I was the one tarred and feathered for my mother's worst faults. "But this isn't about my job. It's not even about my reputation." Which I imagine might be on shaky ground after tonight's story runs rampant through the school and mommy groups, growing legs and teeth, distorting the facts of an already bizarre reality.

Shane shakes his head in disbelief. "I thought you were into this. It's why I brought you into Cody's life."

I'd laugh, if my heart weren't breaking.

Into this? I'm utterly *consumed* by this. I've never been this happy. Not even for those two delirious months one summer thirteen years ago. That was child's play. This?

This had the potential to be "till death do us part" everlasting.

"I was. I am."

"Then don't end it."

A prickly ball of emotion swells in my throat. "I have to. For Cody. His happiness is more important than mine or yours." *Damn it, Bott, you pickled-pigs'-feet-eating witch.*

Shane lets out a mirthless chuckle. "But he *is* happy. He likes you. He likes us being together."

"But he *needs* his parents getting along right now. Until you two can figure out how to do that without him getting caught in the crosshairs, I can't be a part of this."

"Shane!" Penelope nods her head toward a nurse with a clipboard.

He turns back to me. "Don't let her win, Scarlet."

"She's not. Cody is."

Resignation weighs his features. There's no arguing around that, and he knows it. "There's nothing I can say to change your mind?"

"No. Go and see your son."

He looks torn but, finally, he nods. "Too complicated, huh?"

I back away, forcing a playful smile that is probably pitiful but it's keeping my tears at bay. "You're *way* too complicated for me. I need easy." I push through the revolving door before he has a chance to respond.

A lone taxi sits outside. I manage to climb in and give the driver my address before I let myself cry.

Shane Fucking Beckett.

For the second time in my life, he's managed to break my heart by being everything I thought he wasn't.

I regard the red Hyundai sitting in my driveway when the taxi drops me off.

Justine is waiting for me on the porch, her compact body curled up in a rocking chair, huddled within her black bomber jacket and knit hat.

"What are you doing here?" I call out, unable to muster excitement in my voice as I drag my heels up the path. "I haven't listened to your message yet. It's been a bad night." Did she somehow sense that I would need my best friend's shoulder to cry on tonight?

Not until I reach the porch do I see her puffy, red eyes and hear her sniffles. She's been doing some crying of her own. "Justine, what's wrong? What happened?"

Her bottom lip wobbles. “Bill’s been cheating on me!” she wails.

TWENTY-NINE

"How long has it been going on?"

"Two months, off and on." The woman is another trader. Isabelle. Justine had heard her name plenty of times in idle conversation. She was a friend. Just another one of the guys.

Until Just Another One of the Guys and Bill shared a spontaneous, heat-of-the-moment kiss while having drinks at the bar after work. It has since snowballed into multiple dinners and Bill inventing a piano recital for his daughter so he could shack up overnight in a hotel.

The name Isabelle now joins the reviled ranks of Debra. That name can no longer be uttered without earning Justine's sneer.

Becca shifts away from the kettle in the staff room, giving others space while she dunks her tea bag.

And I do my best to ignore Bott's dissecting stare from her seat at the table where she chews her apple.

"How'd she find out?" Becca asks.

"A text."

She nods. "Of course."

That's always the case nowadays. A text, or an email. Some sordid message intercepted with the guilty parties growing bold in their treachery. When she questioned Bill, at least he had the decency not to deny it. "He wanted to see where it would go before he broke up with Justine. He says they're in love."

Becca's mouth gapes. "Oh my God. She must be devastated."

That's an understatement. Justine looks like she's suffering from a horrendous allergic reaction. Her eyes are so puffy and red after days of around-the-clock crying, interspersed with rants about castration. "She's still at my house. She called in sick today and told her boss she's working remotely for the rest of the week." That her boss is her uncle helps. Though, I can't say he'll go for this long-term, and she's already told me she's never going back, period. She's been flipping through paint chips for my spare room, with plans to convert it to her own.

"Wow." Becca's eyes bulge with shock. "And she had *no* idea?"

"None of us did! I'm a terrible best friend for not seeing it!" Am I not supposed to? Is it because I moved away and I've been too wrapped up in my own life to notice? Bill and Justine had moved in together. I thought his initial reluctance had to do with one failed marriage, not the fact that he's secretly a douchebag who wasn't sure he wanted to commit. I didn't see it. *Nobody* saw it. Nobody who's talking, anyway. "Her brother said he's going to murder him." Bill and Jeff have been best friends for decades, so to do this to his baby sister is reprehensible. Of course, they're guys, so they'll likely get drunk, punch each other out, and then go golfing the next day.

But Justine … she's not getting over this betrayal anytime soon.

Selfishly, her life's drama has helped suitably distract me from my own. Or maybe it's that I can cling to the relief that it's me who pulled the plug on Shane and our relationship this time, and I did it for a noble cause. At least *I* did not discover an illicit text thread on his phone detailing all the ways I'd been deceived, with NSFW photographic evidence.

But it's still a chest-constricting ache every time the reality that Shane and I are over flitters through my mind, which is almost constant.

It's been three days since we broke up and my life feels hollow. I miss looking forward to seeing him. I miss waking up with his hard, warm body pressed against my back. I miss his weight on top of me. I miss the sound of his laughter and the sparkle in his eye as he teases me. I miss the obnoxious way he assumed he was welcome to use my spare key without an invitation.

I miss the way he has infiltrated my life.

And I'll be reminded of every one of those things every time I hear the rumble of his truck or car engine from right next door. But Cody is my student for another seven *months*. I also need to remember that.

While Shane didn't want to end things, he also hasn't come by to try to dissuade me. In fact, he's barely been home. It's understandable, given the situation, and that Cody is probably with his mother while he heals. But a lot can happen in seven months. Time and distance can give him perspective. It can tell him that, yes, we *are* too complicated, and this isn't worth a lifelong headache with Penelope. Within seven months, he can meet another woman who doesn't bring baggage. Within seven months, he can become intimate with her.

He can fall in love.

"Boy, you had a rough weekend all round, then." Becca gives me a gentle rub against my shoulder.

As expected, the story of Cody's run-in with the Subaru made rounds by first bell, embellished by the fact that Cody isn't here. I had to sit my students down and calmly inform them that, no, Cody is not dead or paralyzed or missing any limbs. He's going to be just fine. Jenny Byrd was sobbing at her desk. Unfortunately, she witnessed the aftermath.

"Ms. Reed, please report to the office. Ms. Reed, to the office," the school secretary's voice crackles over our lackluster PA system.

I sigh, even as my stomach clenches. *What now?*

I quickly fill my water bottle at the cooler and, ignoring the curious glances from the other teachers, duck out of the staff room.

Wendy catches my eye the moment I step into the main office. She waves me into her office, gesturing that I close the door behind me.

I settle into the chair. It feels like *my* chair now, where I sit when I receive my verbal reprimands.

"How are you doing, Scarlet?" she asks with a motherly smile, her hands clasped on her desk in front of her.

"I've been better."

She nods as if she understands. "Penelope Rhodes phoned this morning."

I brace myself for the cannonball that's about to drill me in the head.

"Cody is going to stay with her for the next week while he recovers. She's asked if it's at all possible for you to pull together a homework package for him, so he can keep up while he's at home."

"Yeah, sure. I'll gather some things and leave them with Shane after school."

"She expects that he'll be back in class next Monday, but she doesn't want him staring at computer games all day, every day until then."

"Right. Makes sense. If she thinks he's up for schoolwork." I wait a few beats. "Is that all she wanted?" She didn't ask for my head on a spike?

"Yes, it seems to be." She leans back in her chair, taking on a more visibly relaxed position. "She didn't make any more mention of her complaint to the board about your relationship with Cody's father, if that's what you're wondering."

"Shane and I are no longer together, so ..." I let my words hang. Maybe Penelope feels as though she's won.

Wendy's forehead wrinkles. "Was it mutual?"

"No," I admit on a sigh. "I ended it. After the accident. It's clear that family still has issues, and me being there as a constant reminder isn't what's best for Cody." And I never would've been able to live with myself had the accident led to a different, tragic outcome.

"Are you okay?" she asks gently. She looks genuinely concerned.

"No." I laugh, hoping it'll squash the ball of emotion that flares in my throat. "But I will be." I've survived losing Shane once already.

"You will be," she agrees with a firm nod.

The bell chimes, signaling the end of morning recess.

"If there's nothing else?" I start to rise.

"I remember your mother coming in to speak to me after *the incident.*" Wendy's eyebrows arch on that word. "She sat in that very chair."

"Really?" I assumed she'd never set foot on school property again after the night of the pageant. "What'd she want?"

"Advice. She was worried about you."

My mom? *Worried* about *me*? "Are you sure you're talking about Dottie Reed?"

Wendy chuckles. "Yes. Most certainly. I'll remember Dottie *long* after I've lost my wits and my bladder control." At least she can find humor in it now. "She wanted to fix things, but she had no idea how. She'd lost her job and you hid in your room all day, refusing to talk to her. And, according to her, Peter Rhodes had promised to leave his family."

"She told me the same thing the other day." The day everything in my life went to hell.

"I don't know if it's true. You know how those things go, with *men* like *that.*" She waves a dismissive hand, but there's no shortage of scorn in her voice. "But she wanted to know what she should do."

"So, she asked *you?*" I can't keep the surprise from my voice. Wendy was there to catch my mother in the act. She had to deal with the fallout. She couldn't have been that sympathetic.

Wendy's smile turns secretive as she studies a pen for a long moment. "Dottie was ten when I started teaching here. She was a high-spirited kid who liked to entertain. She was unlike any other child I'd ever met. And beautiful! *So* beautiful, even back then. I sometimes worried about what was going on at her home …" She frowns but doesn't go further with that thought. "By the time she was twelve, I knew she was going to be trouble, skipping school and taunting older boys behind the bleachers. She *loved* the attention they'd give her. She was never mean-spirited. That's not Dottie.

"On several occasions, I sat her down and tried to get through to her. But there was no getting through to that girl by then." She sighs. "She wasn't a good student, but she was resourceful when she needed to be. When she got pregnant with you, she came to me for advice. I helped her get set up with an apartment and social assistance. After that, she'd come by every once in a while to chat. I'd taken over as principal by then, and I remember sitting in here with the both of you. She'd bounce you on her knee and you'd laugh." Wendy chuckles.

Meanwhile, my mouth gapes. I had no idea Wendy and my mother had a connection. She's never mentioned it, not while I was a student here, and not since running into each other that day at the 7-Eleven.Is this why Wendy offered me a job?

"Honestly, I was waiting for the day I'd hear through the grapevine that Dottie was stripping or selling herself on a street corner to make ends meet, so when she told me she wanted to go to school to become a hairstylist, I was ecstatic. I coached her until she passed the GED and then I helped her apply for a government grant to pay for the schooling." She smiles sadly. "She looked like she was turning over a new leaf."

My students must be filtering into the class. I need to get back, but I'm curious. "What'd you say to her after that mess with Peter Rhodes?"

"To stop sleeping with married men." Wendy gives me an exasperated look. "And that I was *extremely* disappointed in her."

That makes me chuckle. "She would *not* have loved that." Dottie has never appreciated being scolded.

"No. And honestly, chastising a twenty-eight-year-old woman to close her legs is not on my list of enjoyable activities. Neither is having to tell a mother to start acting like one and put her daughter's needs ahead of her own."

"She didn't really do a good job of that."

"No, she didn't." Wendy shakes her head. "But looking at you now, she must have done *something* right. Anyway, she stopped coming here, but I heard that whatever she had going on with Peter Rhodes was over and his wife was taking him back." Her lips purse. "Having dealt with the both of them, and with Penelope, I'm not sure that was the right call either. But, that's the thing about life—we each have our own to live, with all the regrets and mistakes that go along with it."

"That we do." And going forward, mine will have to be without a man I was falling desperately in love with. Maybe one day down the road, we can revisit it. Third time's the charm, or something like that. I don't have much hope things will change, though.

I ease from my chair. "I should get back."

Just as I reach for the door handle, Wendy calls out, "You're not at all like her."

I turn to find Wendy smiling at me. "I know." But finally, it's nice to hear that someone else in Polson Falls recognizes it too.

I shiver against the cold as I stand at Shane's front door, my arms aching beneath the weight of Cody's textbooks. I carried them the two blocks home, my heart pounding in my throat the entire time. And now I've stood here for a full two minutes, contemplating whether I should just leave them in a pile on the mat.

Instead, I knock.

Approaching footfalls sound a moment before the door creaks open.

I sigh at the sight of Shane standing in his doorway, casually pushing a hand through his messy hair. I've never been able to choose which version I like more—the gelled waves or the silken mop when he lets his hair air-dry after a shower. It's the latter now.

"Hey." He licks his lips nervously.

"Penelope asked that I send some homework for Cody," I say by way of greeting. "I'm going to set up some assignments for him in Google Classroom, if he has a computer at home?"

"Yeah, Pen and Travis bought him a laptop last Christmas." He smooths a hand over the back of his neck, pulling his T-shirt tight across his chest.

I can't help but admire his arms. Do men always look even better after you've broken up with them? I've never cared enough to notice before. "Okay, well, I'll pull that all together for him tonight." I've got nothing better to do, besides consoling Justine while she shifts between sobbing and plotting murder. "There's also a card tucked into his math textbook. All the kids in the class signed it."

Shane's face brightens. "He'll love that."

I hesitate, not wanting to linger but not wanting to leave. "How is he?"

"Whiny." He smirks. "The crutches are way less cool than he was thinking they'd be. Wait till he gets his real cast."

"I'm sure it'll be covered in signatures in no time. I'll make sure to have an extra-thick marker in class."

An unbearable stretch of awkward silence hangs between us.

"Do you want to come in?" Shane asks, at the same time I say, "I should go."

"Scar—"

"We're doing the right thing." I set my jaw. Seeing him is a thousand times harder than I anticipated. I need to leave now, before I cave.

"I know we are. Cody comes first, and we have to do what's best for him. There's too much baggage that comes with us." His sighs reluctantly. "You were right. You're *always* right. I'm not going to try to change your mind."

He's saying all the right things. So why do they feel like all the wrong things?

I struggle to clear the emotion suddenly clogging my throat. "I need to get home. Justine's staying with me for a while."

"Here." He leans forward to collect the books from my grasp, his hands and arms grazing mine, sending electricity coursing through my limbs and inciting an ache deep within my bones.

I inhale the scent of him, feeling his penetrating gaze as he studies me from only inches away. He's always been so adept at withering my resolve, and he knows it. It would take nothing for him to do so now, and then we'd be right back where we started.

Only this time, I'd be angry with myself.

Thankfully, he steps back, freeing my sore arms to fall by my sides.

"If you ever need anything at all, any help around the house …" He lets his words drift.

"I'll give my friendly neighbor a call." I back away, swallowing back the tears that threaten.

His broad chest rises with his inhale. With one last, longing look, he disappears into his house.

That night, it's Justine's turn to offer her shoulder.

I cry on it for hours.

THIRTY

"Smartfood or Lay's BBQ?" Justine alternates between bags, waving each in the air, a questioning look on her face.

"Both?"

She cocks her head, as if the thought never crossed her mind, and then proceeds to tear both bags open. "Okay, so I ordered that new Hemsworth movie, but we're watching *The Bachelor* first."

I groan. "So I can listen to you yell at the TV for an hour?"

"Hey! Men are all lecherous, lying assholes and these women need to be told," she snaps, indignant. It's been a week since Bill came out of his cheater's closet. Justine is still hiding out at my house, scrubbing my baseboards while cursing at the skilled tradesmen over the phone for having penises while she's placing them in jobs.

I glance at the clock. It's eleven on Friday night. I'm exhausted after an arduous week of teaching when all I wanted to do was stay in my bed. We're both in sweatpants, hair piled high, with no intention of venturing out into the world until Sunday. I've promised to go back with her to our old apartment so she doesn't have to face walking in there alone. Bill has already moved out, but has "so generously" agreed to pay his half of the rent for the next two months while she either finds a new roommate or another place altogether.

I sigh. "Fine." At least if she's cursing at the TV, she's not crying over what her duplicitous ex-boyfriend might be doing.

My phone rings from its spot on the counter.

Justine checks the screen. And grimaces. "Do you want to answer that? It's *him*," she snarls through a mouthful of popcorn.

My stomach flutters. "Him, who? Shane?"

She nods.

I've found myself still keeping track of Shane's schedule, so I know he's working tonight. What does he want?

"Yes or no?" She dangles my phone in the air in front of me. "My vote is no, by the way. Death to all dicks."

I snatch it from her grasp. Justine's in extreme man-hating mode, which makes her more irrational than usual. Besides, not answering will drive me nuts all night. "Hello?"

"Scar! You there?" he hollers. Sirens and shouts blare in the background.

"Yeah." I frown. "Why? What's going on?"

"Do you know where Dottie is?"

"Probably at the bar. *Why?*"

"'Cause Brillcourt's burning to the ground!"

"So, I'm not even allowed to go in there to get a few things?"

I don't miss the hint of desperation in my mother's voice as she huddles in her spot, watching her home for the past thirty-odd years burn as if it were made of matchsticks and soaked in gasoline.

"Mom, it's still *on fire*." Black smoke billows into the night sky and my nostrils curl with the acrid smell of twelve apartments disintegrating. They've hauled every available fire engine and firefighter in the county here, and it's still not enough.

"I know, but ..." She clutches the top of the silk floral robe she threw on in her haste to escape. I assume she's trying to ward off the cold. Lord knows it's not for modesty.

That my mother was home on a Friday night and sober enough to react to the smoke alarms was a shock. Almost as big as the shock of the panic that engulfed me when Justine and I arrived and saw the entire building in flames, not knowing where she was.

I was terrified for her.

And when I spotted her standing on the sidewalk half a block away with this gray-haired man—none other than Chief Cassidy, I learned by way of introduction—my relief was genuine and overwhelming.

"This is not going to be a quick cleanup, Dottie," he says gently, regarding the mess before him. "And from the looks of it, there isn't going to be much to salvage. If anything."

I wait for her quick retort, her playful banter laced with sexual innuendo, but she merely nods and strokes her hair off her face, a discreet attempt to fix herself. I can't recall the last time I saw her without a full face of makeup and dressed to impress. In this moment, she looks like any other ordinary mom, frightened and cold and in shock.

A burst of flames flares on the south side of the building, and a round of shouts call out as firefighters rush to deal with it.

I worry my lip, searching the hulking bodies in yellow gear for a specific firefighter, but it's impossible to identify any of them. "There's no one still stuck inside, is there?"

"Last report was that everyone's out," Chief Cassidy confirms.

"So, your guys ... none of them are going in there, right?"

He offers me a kind smile, as if he suspects there's one in particular that I'm asking about. "We'll get it under control from outside. None of them are risking their lives for this old place."

I nod my thanks to him as another overwhelming wave of relief washes over me. Shane's chosen career path seems exponentially more dangerous now than it did when I pictured him rescuing animals and helping the elderly. If anything happened to him tonight …

My stomach turns with just the thought.

Beside me, Justine's teeth chatter.

"It's going to be a long night. There's no point in you girls standing outside. Go on home." He pats my mother's shoulder. It's a friendly gesture, but not one a man who had a sordid tryst with the town harlot would give. Maybe Shane's right and nothing beyond dinner happened that night. "You have somewhere warm to go, don't you?"

"You know me, Griff. I'll *always* find somewhere warm to sleep." She offers him a weak smile. It's nowhere near the usual Cheshire Cat grin she uses when she delivers a line like that.

And the truth is, it's all an act. I'm not sure she has *anywhere* to go.

I sigh with resignation. "She's coming home with me."

The big blue pickup sits idly in the driveway as I walk past after school. Long gone are the days of catching Shane outside, tinkering with his '67 Impala or pushing the mower. The car hasn't left the protection of his garage since late October, and the lawn is now coated in an inch of fresh snow.

Still, my chest aches every time I pass my neighbor's house.

Cody has been back to school for several weeks now, struggling to maneuver around on his crutches but adept at collecting signatures on his casts. The drama from that night hasn't seemed to affect his spirits, though.

Sometimes, when my students are busy with their tasks and my attention wanders out the window, I'll turn back to find him watching me curiously from beneath his thick fringe of lashes, through familiar whiskey-colored eyes. And sometimes I get the distinct impression he wants to venture to my desk to strike up a conversation, but isn't sure how. Or perhaps he's been told not to. Either way, it's probably for the best. He doesn't need to hear about how much I miss his father.

The smell of apple pie envelops me as I step through my front door, escaping the blustering, early-December afternoon. I'm not foolish enough to think anyone around here would bake an actual pie. It's just a candle. Still, it's a welcoming scent, and it reminds me that I don't live alone anymore.

I unwittingly claimed two roommates in the span of a week. One, I could survive living with in a four-by-four-foot cardboard box. The other, I may end up in a six-by-nine-foot prison cell for murder if she doesn't move out soon.

Justine only went back to Newark to collect more clothes and give notice for the apartment. She's also quit her job, though she's agreed to stay on remotely until her uncle finds a replacement. Meanwhile, she's been scouring the want ads for careers in this area. She's serious about moving to Polson Falls, and reclaiming the tiny main-floor bedroom once my mother leaves.

Which is, thankfully, on the fifteenth of this month when Dottie gets her new apartment across town. They suspect the fire at Brillcourt was started by a space heater and allowed to grow due to a faulty smoke-alarm system. The building has since been condemned, unsafe to step inside, due to be demolished after years of neglect. Nothing of my mother's belongings was salvage-able, which has brought her much distress. Her wardrobe was something she prized and, according to her cries of frustration, not easy to replace. She's been scouring the internet for her favorite animal-print stilettos to no avail.

I set my purse on the front hallway table just as a male grunt sounds from somewhere in the house.

"Hello?" I call out warily, my voice carrying an edge.

There's no answer.

Elite Cuts is closed on Mondays; both Justine's and my mother's cars are outside. Justine is probably up in my room, working.

I hear a thump, followed by another male grunt. It's coming from the kitchen.

My anger overwhelms my better judgment as I charge in, bracing myself for a reenactment of the Christmas pageant closet of horrors, or something equally jaw-dropping. "I told you, no bringing any—" I stutter over the sight, "—men home."

Justine and Mom are in the middle of my kitchen, arms crossed at their chests, heads cocked as they hover over the man sprawled on my floor. Both wear admiring smiles.

I'd recognize that body anywhere.

My heart races. "What's going on?"

"There was a leak," Justine murmurs absently. "So I called Scarlet's Sexy Neighbor."

Shane's abs strain as he pulls his head out from beneath the kitchen sink and sits up. "Hey, Scar." He brushes the back of his hand against his forehead, leaving a streak of dirt behind. "I patched it, but you really need to get someone to lay new pipe in here."

"Are you offering to lay some pipe for Scarlet?" Justine's eyebrow arches playfully.

I shake my head at my best friend. At least she's finally showing signs of her old jaw-dropping self. "Thanks. You didn't need to come and do that, though."

"I don't mind." He reaches for the rag on the floor next to my mother's leopard-print-slippered foot.

"Well, you've certainly saved us," Dottie purrs, stroking his ego. "We had no idea how to fix this."

"By dialing a plumber," I say dryly, in no mood for her damsel-in-distress act.

Justine gives my mom an elbow and a wide-eyed look. "Isn't it our turn to get groceries this week?"

"Huh? Oh, right. Yes. It is." My mom plays into it. "We'll be gone for at least an hour." She takes a long, leisurely, head-to-toe look at Shane. "More likely two."

Really subtle, Mom.

They saunter down the hall and, twenty seconds later, with a lot of noise and theatrics about shoes and coats, they're out the door, leaving Shane and me alone.

"They seem to be getting along well," he says.

"Who? Dottie and Justine? Oh yeah, I knew they would. My mom's really good at being that wild-and-fun girlfriend." Being a reliable, responsible mother, not so much.

He shuts the cupboard door and leans against it. "I noticed their cars in the driveway every night. Are they both living here now?"

I haven't talked to Shane since he called me that night about the fire. Is he checking my driveway for visitors as often as I'm checking his? My heart skips a beat with the thought that he still cares. "They are." I settle into a kitchen chair. "My mom's just here until her new place is ready, but I think Justine's here for good."

His eyebrows arch in question.

I tell him about Bill.

"Wow. What a dick."

"Yeah. It's going to be a long time before she gets over that. Selfishly, though, I'm happy she's here." She's a good distraction.

He pulls himself off the floor and sets to washing the grime off his hands.

I can't help but gape at his back—at his powerful shoulders and his cut arms, visible beneath the material of his shirt. It's only been a few weeks since we broke up. It feels like it's been forever.

An ache stirs in my chest.

Has he started thinking about dating again?

Is beautiful, uncomplicated Susie Teller suddenly not so boring?

She might still bore him, but she wouldn't be talking while she gives him a blow job.

"How's Cody doing in school?" he asks suddenly.

I push my dour thoughts aside. "He seems fine."

Shane reaches for the hand towel by the oven to dry off as if still comfortable in my home. "He said a couple of kids at school have been bugging him about me and you being together."

"Oh. I haven't noticed anything." I frown, picking through the days, searching for any hints of whispers or giggles or Cody appearing upset. "Is it really bothering him? If he tells me who it is, I can speak to them, or get Wendy to haul them in—"

"He doesn't give a shit about any of that."

"Oh. Good, I guess?"

"He said what bugs him is us not being together anymore. He thinks it's his fault."

I groan. "I hope you told him that's not true."

"Of course, I did, but he doesn't believe me. And I don't have a good enough answer for him to explain it."

"I guess not." To an eleven-year-old kid, trying to explain any of this would still come out sounding like he's to blame. "Have Penelope talk to him. I promise, he'll hate my guts by the end." I cap that off with a smirk.

Shane's responding chuckle is dark. "That's the last thing I want to happen." He begins collecting his tools. "Penelope's in counseling now."

"What?" I gasp. "Seriously?"

"Yeah. Travis lost it after that night of the accident."

"He definitely didn't look happy." I recall the glower on his brow as he paced along with me, and how it seemed to intensify whenever his focus landed on Penelope's mother.

"He told her he was done dealing with her anger issues. Done listening to her bitch about me and you. Done dealing with Melissa altogether. Just done. He laid *all* his cards on the table.

Told her that either she gets help or he's out. He was serious too. Ready to put the house up and everything."

"*Wow.*"

"Yeah." He shrugs. "So, she's been going to a therapist."

"And?"

He closes the lid on his toolbox. "And it's only been a few weeks, but she seems to be coming around. I talked to her for a while last night when I went to drop off Cody." He smirks. "She told me I was a good father."

"You don't need therapy to see that."

His soft gaze flips to mine. "She also said you're *probably* not the bad person she's made you out to be in her head."

My jaw hangs, and it's partly for dramatic effect but mostly genuine. "Travis had the Red Devil lobotomized!"

He chuckles, and I feel the beautiful sound deep within my chest. "She's still in there, just a bit tamer. For now."

I quietly watch him, playing various scenarios in my head of what would happen if I reached out and touched him. All of them likely end with us in my bed.

All of them still end with the same complications.

I remember, again, why I've made myself so miserable.

My sad smile emerges. "Thank you for helping with whatever was wrong under there." *But you need to leave now. This is too hard.*

"I think one of them hit the pipe with a hammer just to have an excuse to get me over here," he says.

"What?" I laugh. "Why would you think that?"

"Because of the way the pipe was damaged. And because of *that*." He points at the hammer on the counter.

I shake my head. They must have fished it out of my toolbox when they hatched their plan, if it was indeed a plan. "Justine's going to start paying me rent, so I should have the money to hire a plumber early in the new year. If you can hook me up with your plumber, I'd appreciate it."

"Yeah, I'll send you his contact info." He pauses. "You going to come to the charity auction next weekend?"

"I wasn't planning on it." Watching and listening to women drool over Shane does not sound appealing.

He nods slowly. "You should. It's a fun night out."

"Noted." This polite conversation, this heavy awkwardness … it's killing me.

He opens his mouth to say something but then seems to change his mind. "See you around, Scarlet."

I stifle the urge to holler after him as I watch his retreating back. "Still too complicated," I whisper to an empty room, letting my head fall back to thump against the wall.

THIRTY-ONE

"Why are we doing this?" I whine, trailing Justine and Becca into Route Sixty-Six. The interior has been decked out for the holiday season, with garish green garland strung around the door and red-velvet bows decorating the booths. Oversized sprigs of mistletoe dangle across the length of the bar like a bad omen—to get a drink, you must first kiss.

"It's for charity," Justine throws her favorite line over her shoulder.

"You're not charitable."

She flashes her pearly whites at me. "Stop pretending you don't want to see him."

I won't deny I'm eager to see the Hunky Heroes Auction headliner, but I dread watching a room full of thirsty women bid on him, especially when he's no longer mine to take home.

Becca leads us to the back of the bar where an elaborate stage has been set up in front of the patio, complete with spotlights and thick black curtains. The place is packed with people. Mostly women.

Which one of them will win Shane tonight? What if it's some

beautiful vixen and they make an unexpected connection at their dinner? I've been plagued with these thoughts lately.

Do I believe Shane will remain celibate until *maybe,* at some point in the future, after Cody's gone from my class and Penelope's had copious therapy sessions to accept another woman in his life without wreaking havoc, we'll have another shot?

I'm not an idiot.

The thought of Shane in bed with another woman makes me want to vomit.

"Front and center, Dot-tee!" Justine grips my mom's shoulders in greeting. "How'd you manage such a good table?"

"That handsome bartender back there owed me a favor, and it was a *huge* one." My mom winks. "Pull up a seat."

Justine cackles at her lewd innuendo. Despite knowing what a terrible mother she was to me, Justine can't help but find Dottie Reed highly entertaining, and I can't blame her for that.

Still, I cringe, as is par for the course with most of what comes out of my mother's mouth.

Becca leans in to kiss Ann Margaret on the cheek.

"Is someone else sitting with us?" I point at the sixth chair.

"That would be me," a gray-haired man says, balancing two glasses of wine and a pint of beer. "That is, if you ladies don't mind an old fool hanging around?" He's looking at me when he asks that.

I frown. "Chief Cassidy?"

He chuckles. "Just Griffin to you."

"Sorry, I didn't recognize you out of uniform." Tonight, he's in a simple sky blue dress shirt and black jeans with no hat to cover his full head of wiry gray hair.

He sets the drinks down, placing his beer at the seat next to my mother, I note. "Can I head back to the bar for another round? It'll be faster than ordering through the waitress."

"I'll never say no to a pint of Guinness, delivered by a distinguished gentleman." Justine bats her curled eyelashes at him.

"Hey now, we got a Southie in here," Griffin teases, imitating her thick accent with surprising precision.

She grins. "Born and raised."

"Well, all right, then. This is going to be a fun night."

We give him our drink orders and he sets off to the bar again, seemingly happy to do so.

Ann Margaret leans over to say, "He's a very good man," and I get the distinct impression she's trying to sell him to me.

I take the other free seat next to my mother. "Isn't he on the auction block?"

Mom shakes her head through a gulp of her wine. "That was just the one time, and it was only because three men canceled at the last minute and they needed bodies to raise enough money. He was nervous no one would bid on him. It was so *adorable,* I just *had* to scoop him up."

I watch my mother closely. I don't think I've ever heard her call any man adorable. "So, you guys are *friends* now?" Shane said Chief Cassidy wasn't the type to have slept with my mom the night of their charity dinner. But what about since then?

"Yes. I guess you could call him that." She glances over her shoulder to locate him by the bar. "He lost his wife four years ago. Cancer. He was *very* devoted to her. He's had a hard time moving on." There's an odd, genuine affection in her voice.

"Well, *I* for one think he's fabulous," Justine drawls.

"That's because he's bringing you alcohol." Though, between the night of the fire and so far tonight, he does seem decent.

"And your point is?"

"Ladies and ... well, mostly ladies," a male voice croons over the speaker system. The bartender has taken to the stage in a full tuxedo, complete with a red cummerbund and matching bow tie. "We are about to start the main event but calendar sales are now open, and let me tell you, next year's calendar is hotter than the fires these men put *out*!"

I snort. "That is *so* cheesy."

"Hush," Justine scolds, her eyes twinkling.

"Just twenty-five dollars gets you twelve months of heroes on your wall, and all for a good cause. All proceeds go to the Santa Fund, a local charity that ensures no child is missed on Christmas morning. So, head on over to the table at the front to grab your copy now or before you leave. They'll be there all night, but do *not* miss out!" This guy is clearly moonlighting as a bartender—this emcee role is his true calling. "Grab your drinks, grab a restroom break, do whatever you need to do, but be back and ready to wave those paddles in five minutes!"

"That's a good idea. I'll be back." I excuse myself from the table and head to the restroom. I have the sudden urge to pee and it's due to nerves. Is it because I'm excited to see Shane? Is it anxiety for him, because he has to get up on that stage with all these women hollering after him?

I finish my business and step out of the stall, still considering why I'm so nervous for this auction to begin.

And come face-to-face with Penelope.

Her sage-green eyes meet mine through the reflection in the mirror before she shifts back to touching up her lipstick, a deep crimson that accentuates her porcelain skin.

"Hi," I finally offer as I step up to wash my hands.

It's a long moment before she responds. "I wasn't sure if you'd be here." There's no hint of the usual bitchiness in her tone.

"I didn't want to. They made me come." I hesitate. "Do *you* normally come to this *thing*?" I should probably stop referring to it with such disdain.

"Yeah. I bid on behalf of our accounting firm. It's a tax write-off." She doesn't sound any more enthusiastic about being here than I am.

"That's … smart." This is the longest conversation we've ever had that doesn't involve tossing barbed shots at each other. I don't know what else to say.

Do not bring up the lobotomy.

I settle on, "Cody's doing well in school."

A tiny, genuine smile touches her lips. "Yeah, he is." There's a long pause and then, "Thanks for putting all that work together for him while he was away."

"Of course. I'd do anything for that kid." It comes out without a thought.

Her brow pulls together and I'm instantly panicked I've said the wrong thing. "Shane told me you broke up with him because you thought it was what was best for my son." A muscle ticks in her jaw. "And I know how much you care about Shane. How much you've *always* cared about him. I get it. It's hard not to fall for him. So … I believe you when you say you'd do anything for Cody."

I swallow and nod. This feels like part of a twelve-step program, the step where she has to make amends.

She turns on the tap to wash the smear of red lipstick off her finger. "I saw your mom out there with Chief Cassidy."

"Yeah. He seems nice."

"He *is*."

I hesitate. "Dottie will probably eat him alive."

A few beats pass and then Penelope's face splits wide with a bellowing laugh.

Not wanting to push it, I hurry to dry my hands. "Best of luck with your bidding tonight."

"You too."

"Oh, I'm not bidding. I'm just here to mock and gawk." And drool over a man I'm not allowed to have. I reach for the door handle.

"Have you seen the calendar yet?"

"No. Is it as painfully cheesy as last year's?"

She smirks. "Worse."

I feel like I'm stumbling back to the table. Justine has gone somewhere, but our drinks and bidding paddles have arrived. Griffin is seated next to my mother, the two of them deep in conversation. She seems to be hanging on his every word and I honestly can't tell if that's genuine interest or part of her act. Maybe Mom really is into this guy.

Becca leans across the table, wearing a deep frown. "Are you okay?"

"I'm not sure," I say truthfully. "I just ran into Penelope in the restroom."

"*And*?"

"It was pleasant," I say, baffled.

The bartender appears from behind the curtains and adjusts the microphone stand. I presume the auction is about to begin.

"Where's Justine?"

"Right here." She drops her calendar onto the table.

"You are *not* hanging that up in *my* kitchen." Curiosity begs me to flip through it to find Shane's month, but I refrain.

"*Our* kitchen."

"You're a squatter!"

"Are you *ready*?" The bartender's voice blasts through the bar. The responding roar makes me wince, it's so loud within these walls. "Welcome to Polson Falls' annual *Own a Hunky Hero for a Night* auction! I'm Mike and I'll be your host for this evening's festivities." A blast of dance music reverberates through the place and then Mike spends a few minutes running through the process in a smooth, practiced speech.

"Okay, let's get this party started! Your first gentleman of the evening is none other than one of our favorite calendar boys … Dean Fanshaw!"

Dean strolls out, looking drop-dead gorgeous in head-to-toe black.

"He's a—"

"I'll give you five bucks for him!" Justine belts out, standing up to wave her paddle in the air.

The place erupts with laughter as Dean shakes his head and

chuckles, his cheeks flushing. The minimum bid set is fifty, and there is no way he doesn't remember Justine.

I tug her back down into her seat. "You are cut off!"

She grins, unfazed.

I wish I had her brash, don't-give-a-fuck attitude.

"We've got some eager ladies here tonight. But just hold on there ..." Mike chuckles. "Let me say my little spiel first."

He gives a thirty-second introduction to Dean that paints him a saint and definitely *does not* mention that he shagged his schoolmate's mom, the infamous Dottie Reed, five years ago. And then the bidding begins. "Do I hear fifty dollars?"

The paddles start waving.

My eyes are glued on Griffin's hand cradling my mother's on top of the table as he leans over to ask Justine, "So, what do you think about our little charity event?"

"This is exhausting. I'm exhausted," Justine declares, flopping into her chair with dramatic flair.

Griffin turns to me. "What about you, Scarlet?"

"Oh, I don't think you want to ask her. She does *not* approve," my mother warns.

"Actually, it's not as bad as I thought it would be," I admit. The entire place buzzes with energy and laughter. Everyone seems to be enjoying themselves. "And it's for charity." *A lot* of charity. The nine men who've made their way to the stage thus far have earned a staggering amount for the Santa Fund.

And there's still one left to go.

My nerves are a mess as Mike appears from behind the heavy curtain, chugging back a gulp of water. He's been nothing short of brilliant all night. "Are we ready for our last hero on the auction block?" A loud chorus cheers.

Shane steps out and my jaw drops at the sight of him standing there onstage in a black-on-black tux, his wavy hair styled, and that devilish smirk, complete with dimples.

He's utter perfection. He knows it. I know it.

Every person in this goddamn restaurant knows it.

But most of them don't know the man beyond what they see up there. I do. I know what he looks like beneath that fancy outfit. I know how his wavy hair falls when he first wakes. I know the way his eyes dance with mere mention of his son, and all the ways he swallows his pride and sacrifices his own happiness to keep Cody happy. I know how he suffered an enormous loss and chose a noble path, helping others. I spent years convinced Shane was an arrogant player. Now, I watch him on that stage and I know he's there not for ego or accolades, but simply because his heart is genuinely good.

He's *everything* I want.

A deep ache pangs in my chest as I accept that he's no longer mine.

"This hero needs no introduction, but I'll give you one anyway. Shane Beckett is none other than ..." I barely listen to Mike, too busy gaping at a man I am undoubtedly in love with standing under the bright lights.

He catches my eye and flashes one of his secretive smiles that he knows I love, before shifting his attention back to the crowd. He struts across the front of the stage, and I can't help but laugh.

"Should we bother starting at fifty?" Mike bellows with a grin. "Nah. Do I hear two hundred dollars?"

Paddles wave wildly.

"And sold, for a record amount, to the *stunning* redhead in the black dress." Mike points to the table where Penelope sits with a group I don't recognize.

"Pretty, but psycho," Justine sings under her breath, eyeing my childhood nemesis. "Kind of weird to buy a date with your baby daddy, isn't it?"

"It's a write-off for her company," I say, even as I'm pondering what Penelope's angle is. She always has an angle. Is this her way of still claiming Shane?

She turns then, as if sensing us talking about her. One perfect eyebrow arches in challenge, followed by a smile of satisfaction.

Yeah, the Red Devil's still in there.

"And that is a wrap! Thank you, everyone, for your incredible generosity!" Mike bows before a standing ovation and, with a salute to the crowd, strolls off the stage. Shane disappears behind the curtain, much to my chagrin.

Just like that, the night is over. It's time to go home, back to my daily life that no longer includes Shane. A wave of discontent hits me.

"Scarlet, have you seen this?" my mother asks.

"Seen what?" I turn to find her studying Justine's copy of the calendar with amusement.

She thrusts it in front of my face.

"Ho-*ly* fuck," Justine hisses, leaning in over my shoulder to spy Mr. July.

I gape at the picture—Shane, posed with his bare back to the camera, against the fire engine with his arms and legs spread, as if awaiting a pat down before an arrest. The pants of his uniform sit at the hump of his ass, just enough to tease without being labeled indecent. But it's not the pose or the flesh that's shocking.

It's the sooty writing across his skin.

The big, bold letters that read "Property of Scarlet Reed."

My heart pounds in my ears. "Oh my God, he did *not*."

"Oh yes, he did!" Justine cackles. "And they sell over a *thousand* of these things every year, the lady at the table told me."

The session with the photographer wasn't until the week after Cody's accident, which means he did this *after* we broke up.

"If that isn't a declaration, I don't know what is," my mother murmurs and I can't help but note a hint of pride in her voice.

I'm speechless. This is simultaneously the most embarrassing and overtly romantic gesture any man has ever made in my life. I don't know whether to scream or cry or laugh.

I sense a person looming over our table. I look up to find Penelope. "Cheesy, right?" she says, and there's a glimmer of something unreadable in her eyes.

She knew about the calendar. She knew what Shane had done. He must have told her he was doing it. Was it in warning?

In any case, she doesn't look ready to club me over the head with her paddle.

I swallow. "It's appalling, but it's all for the children."

Her nostrils flare with her deep breath. A calming technique, perhaps. "Yes. For the children." Her rapturous gaze cuts to my mother—there is still disdain there, no doubt—before shifting back to me. She sets her winning paddle on the table and then struts off without another word.

Justine gasps. "You know what that means, right?"

"No?"

"She might have bid on him, but you've won!" She waves the paddle in the air to emphasize her point.

Is that what this is? A peace offering?

"Go and talk to him!" Becca urges, practically bouncing in her seat.

"But he went behind the curtain."

"So what? He's not the Wizard of Oz. And he did *that*!" Justine stabs at the calendar with her index finger.

She's right, of course. I *need* to talk to him.

With a mixture of trepidation and excitement, I scurry onto the stage and fumble with the thick material until the separation appears. I find Shane and Dean standing on the patio beneath the heat lamp, savoring their beers. "How are you fine American gigolos feeling tonight?" I ask, clearing my throat against the slight tremble in my voice.

Dean grins. "She could have had me for five bucks."

"Who are you kidding? She could have had you for free."

His grin grows wider. "Still can. And I hear she's single."

"And brokenhearted," I warn him in a severe tone.

"Not for long." Dean slaps Shane on the shoulder and, with a wink at me, he leaves to go inside, his bulky frame rearranging the curtains as he fumbles through.

Shane smiles. "Don't worry, I think he's too intimidated by her to try anything."

I step closer and inhale deeply. He smells heavenly tonight. "I'm not worried. She's all talk. He doesn't have a chance in hell with her." I stare up into his eyes, a deep, rich amber that sparkle in this moment. "Are you *crazy*?"

"In love with you?" The corner of his mouth curls. "Completely."

I take a few long moments to calm my erratic pulse. Shane Beckett just told me he's in love with me. He basically told all of Polson Falls and the surrounding area too. "*Everyone* will know."

He studies my lips intently. "Good. I want everyone to know."

I shake my head at his antics, but I can't keep the grin from emerging as I hold up the paddle. "Penelope gave me this."

"Huh." He sets his beer on a nearby table. "I guess she bought us a night out then." Wrapping his arms round my waist, he pulls me into his chest. "She's never going to be an angel, and she won't always be easy. But she's starting to come around. Slowly." He leans in to settle his forehead against mine. "If you want to wait until next summer when Cody's out of your class, we can wait. I'm not going anywhere, Scar. Ever."

I smooth my palm over his lapel, savoring his strength beneath my fingertips as an overwhelming sense of calm washes over me. Is this the moment? The one I'll remember years from now, as the moment I realized I wanted to spend the rest of my life with this man?

He catches my lips with his. God, it's been a long month apart. I allow it, enjoying the feel of them again.

He pulls away to whisper, "You own me so completely, it's kind of pathetic."

"I won't hold it against you," I tease, playfully smacking his ass with the paddle. "Hey, does this thing actually mean I get a night out with a hunky hero?"

He chuckles. "It does. If you still want it."

I twist my lips in a mock grimace. "I don't know. I heard you guys don't put out."

THIRTY-TWO

June 2021

I toss the dandelion into the yard waste bag and move on to the next. I don't remember so many weeds riddling this garden when the Rutshacks owned the place, but I was young and focused on the flowers.

The front door creaks open next door, drawing my attention to the tall, handsome man strolling out in his running gear, his arms stretched over his head.

"Took you long enough," I holler, tossing my gloves and trowel to the dirt and easing up. I warmed up twenty minutes ago.

"Someone kept me up late last night playing video games."

"You didn't have to stay up. Cody and I were fine on our own." We meet halfway by the white picket fence that forms what now seems like an arbitrary line between our properties. The two houses may as well be joined for all the shuffling back and forth.

"Good morning." He leans in to steal a tender kiss but slides in a hint of tongue that he knows will always get a soft moan out of me.

"Is he still sleeping?"

"Yup. Let's get going so we have time to go back to your place for a quick shower."

I smirk. Our showers are *never* quick. "Justine will bitch that we used all the hot water," I warn.

"I don't care. I needed you this morning and you weren't there." He emphasizes that point by pulling me into his body so I can feel his erection against my stomach.

"You didn't deal with that before you came out?" I scold.

"I did. And then I saw you in these pants." He kisses me again. "Five more days."

I chuckle. He's been counting down the days like a kid at Christmas, until I'm officially not Cody's teacher anymore, even though we reconciled the night of the auction and have been together ever since. There really was no point not to be, with that calendar stunt Shane pulled. Nobody would believe otherwise. And with Penelope backing off, I found myself no longer caring what the Karen Faros and Heidi Muellers and Madame Botts of the world thought.

I only care about what Cody thinks, and he has been all smiles.

But I've still refused to stay over at Shane's when Cody's there, not wanting to risk him hearing something late at night that no student of mine should hear. I've also set strict boundaries when his innocent—but not so innocent anymore—eyes are on us. Basically, Shane's been relegated to holding my hand.

And I've since learned that putting physical restrictions on Shane makes him especially horny. Case in point.

"We don't have time for that," I remind Shane, tugging on his arm. "Remember? We're meeting my mom and Griffin at the Patty Shack." Pigs never started flying and fire and brimstone did not rain down from the sky, and yet the infamous Dottie Reed seems to have found herself in a committed relationship with a decent, respectable man. Mike, the bartender at Route Sixty-Six, actually pulled me aside to ask if she was okay since they hadn't seen her in weeks.

"Just what I want to do on my day off. Breakfast with my boss," Shane says with a grimace.

"Shut up. You love it." I give his hard ass a slap and then take off.

Knowing he'll give chase.

SNEAK PEEK - FOREVER WILD

December

"She out there again?"

"Not anymore. But there're tracks." I've watched the mama moose nibble on bush branches every morning for the past week. I even snapped a few serene photos of her that I posted on my Instagram.

I sip my latte, savoring the warmth that flows down my throat as I admire the frozen, white expanse. A fresh coat of snow fell overnight, blanketing our little haven just outside the small town of Trapper's Crossing.

"I probably scared her away with the plow." Jonah leans in to press a morning kiss against my neck, his scruffy beard tickling me.

I close my eyes and dip my head to the side, to give him better access. "You were up early this morning."

"Yeah. It got cold last night. Wanted to make sure everything was running all right."

Jonah was up early because he was tossing and turning all night, *again*. I know it has nothing to do with the frigid temperature and everything to do with his mom and stepfather's plane that lands in Anchorage today.

"Everything will be *fine,*" I promise for the umpteenth time. "They'll be *all the way* over *there.*" I gesture at the small cabin peeking out from the trees on the opposite side of our private lake. We hauled the last of the furniture in yesterday. "And my mom and Simon will be here in three days." Excitement flares in my chest. I haven't seen them since they dropped me off at the airport, almost a year ago now. "Plus, Agnes and Mabel come on the weekend, so there's plenty of buffer between you and Bjørn. I promise, this Christmas will be *perfect.*"

Jonah's derisive snort says otherwise.

Forever Wild: A Novella
The Simple Wild series
Coming December 1st, 2020.
To preorder your copy, please visit
katuckerbooks.com/foreverwild

SNEAK PEEK - SWEET MERCY

Enjoy this excerpt of *Sweet Mercy*, book one in the dark and sordid *Dirty Empire* series by K.A. Tucker writing as Nina West...

Mercy

"Mercy Wheeler!"

My body, already rigid, stiffens at the sound of my name on the guard's tongue. I've been waiting in Fulcort Penitentiary's visitor lounge for over two hours now, long enough to leave me doubting whether I'd ever be let in.

Shutting my textbook, I collect my purse and rush for the counter with my stomach in my throat, afraid that any dallying could lose me my visit with my father.

The guard staff changed over at some point, because the thin older gentleman with the kind smile who took down my information earlier has been replaced by a burly oaf with beady little eyes and an unfriendly face. His name tag reads Parker. "Who you here to see?" he demands in a gruff tone.

"My dad." I clear the wobble from my voice. "Duncan Wheeler. It should say that on the log?" It comes out as a question, though I can see my father's name written in block letters next to the tip of this guy's pen.

"I like to double-check, is all." He smirks, then recites a long string of numbers and letters. My father's inmate ID number. "This is your first visit here?"

"Yeah." My father only began his sentence two weeks ago, and it took time to get me approved on his visitor list, which is bullshit. I'm the *only person* on his visitor list.

Parker the guard takes a long, lingering scan of my plain, baggy T-shirt. That, along with my loosest pair of jeans, is what I carefully chose to comply with the prison's visitor dress code policy. No tank tops, no shorts, no miniskirts. Nothing tight. Nothing to "provoke" the men serving time behind these bars.

His eyes stall on my chest for far too long.

I fight the urge to fidget under the lecherous gaze. He's at least twenty years older than me and unappealing, to say the least. Just imagining what kinds of thoughts are churning in his dirty mind makes my skin crawl. Then again, *everything* in this place—the barbed wire fences, the heavily armed guards, the long and narrow hallways, the constant buzzing as door locks are released, the fact that I'm about to sit in a room with murderers, rapists, and God only knows who else—makes my skin crawl.

"What's your old man in for?" Parker finally asks.

I hesitate. "Murder." Are prison guards supposed to be asking these types of questions?

"Yeah?" His gaze drops to my chest again, and he's not trying to be discreet about it. "And who'd your daddy kill, sweetheart?"

I'm not your goddamn sweetheart. My anger flares, at the invasion of my privacy, at the term he so casually tosses out, at the lustful stare. "Some asshole who wouldn't take no for an answer from me." A mechanic named Fleet who worked at the same auto repair shop where my dad worked, a slimy guy who smelled of motor oil and weed and apparently jerked off to cut-and-paste photos of my face atop porn mag bodies. Who cornered me one night with the full intention of experiencing the real thing.

My father didn't mean to kill him and yet here he is, serving twenty-two years because of a freak accident. Because the prosecutor was convinced otherwise and decided to make an example of him. Because we hired the world's most ineffective lawyer. It's the first thing I dwell on when my eyelids crack every day and the heaviest thing on my shoulders when I drift off at night.

I'm exhausted by guilt and anger, and it doesn't seem like it's going to let up any time soon.

Pervy Parker smirks. "Lock your things up in number seventeen and then head to security screening." He slaps a key onto the counter with his meaty paw. "Phone, car keys, coins, belt. Don't forget so much as a coin, unless you wanna get strip-searched." His mouth curves into a salacious smile. "And you won't get to say no to that if you ever wanna see your daddy again."

My face twists with horror before I can smother it. They wouldn't *actually* strip-search me for forgetting to take out a penny from my pocket, would they?

The prick laughs. "Welcome to Fulcort Penitentiary."

Who is she here to see? I wonder, watching the shriveled old lady fidget with her knuckles, her hair styled in tight gray curls, her wrinkled features touched with smears of pink and blue makeup. A husband? A son?

I've kept my eyes forward and down since I passed through the airport-level security screening process and was led me to this long, narrow visitation room. I've set my jaw and ignored the hair-raising feel of lingering looks and the stifling tension that courses through the air. My father warned me against attracting attention, that having inmates knowing he has "such a beautiful daughter" would only make his life harder in here. While I rolled my eyes as he said that, I also decided to heed his warning the best way I can, so as not to ruin his life further.

So, no makeup, no styled hair—I didn't even brush it today—and minimal eye contact.

Except this sweet-looking grandmother who sits at the cafeteria-style table across from me has caught my gaze and now I can't help but occupy my mind with questions about her while I wait. Namely, how many Saturdays has she spent sitting at Fulcort waiting for a loved one, and what will *I* look like when I'm sitting in this chair twenty-two *years* from now?

A soft buzz sounds on my left, pulling my attention away from her and toward the door where prisoners have been filtering in and out.

An ache swells in my chest as I watch my father shuffle through. It's only been two weeks and yet his face looks gaunt, the orange jumpsuit loose on his tall, lanky frame.

He pauses as the guard refers to a clipboard, his gaze frantically scanning the faces at each table.

I dare a small wave to grab his attention.

The second his green eyes meet mine, his face splits with a smile. He rushes for me.

"Walk!" a guard barks from somewhere.

I stand to meet him.

"Oh God, are you a sight for sore eyes!" He ropes his arms around my neck and pulls me tight into his body.

"I missed you so much!" I return the embrace, sinking into my father's chest as tears spill down my cheeks despite my best efforts to keep them at bay. "They made me wait for hours. I wasn't sure if I'd make it in today—"

"That's enough!" That same guard who just yelled at my father to walk moves in swiftly to stand beside us, his hard face offering not a shred of sympathy. "Unless you wanna lose visitation privileges, inmate!"

Dad pulls back with a solemn nod, his hands in the air in a sign of surrender. "Sorry." He gestures to the table. "Come on, Mercy. Sit. Let me look at you."

We settle into our seats across from each other, my father folding his hands tidily in front of him atop the table. A model of best behavior. The guard shoots him another warning look before continuing on.

"So?" I swallow against the lump in my throat, brushing my tears away. I've done so well, hiding tears from him up until now. "How are you doing?"

He shrugs. "You know. Fine, I guess." He quickly surveys the occupants of the tables around us.

That's when I notice that his jaw is tinged with a greenish-yellow bruise. "Dad! What happened to your face?" I reach for him on instinct.

He pulls back just as the tips of my fingernails graze his cheek. "It's nothing."

"Bullshit! Did someone hit you?"

His wary eyes dart to the nearby inmates again. "Don't worry about it, Mercy. It's just the way things are inside. Someone thinks you looked at them funny ... Pecking order, that sort of thing. It's not hard to make enemies in a prison without trying. Anyway, it's almost healed."

My eyes begin to sting again. This is *my* fault. I should never have told him about what Fleet did that night. It's not like the dirty pig succeeded in his mission; a swift kick to his balls gave me the break I needed to run inside and call the police. Now, had the police done their goddamn job, Fleet never would have strolled into work the next morning with a smug smile on his face and a vivid description of how firm my ass is, and my normally mild-mannered father wouldn't have lost his temper.

Two weeks in and he's already been attacked? My father is

one of the most easygoing guys I've ever met. The fact that he went after Fleet the way he did in the garage was a surprise to everyone, including Fleet, according to what witnesses said.

"Hey, hey, hey ... Come on. I can't handle watching you cry," my dad croons in a soothing voice. "And we don't have time for that. Tell me what's going on with you. How's school? Work?"

I grit my jaw to keep my emotions in check. We're supposed to have an hour, but the guard already warned me that Saturdays are busy and this visit will most likely get cut short. So much for prisoner rights. "Work is work. Same old." I've been an administrative assistant at a drug and alcohol addiction center called Mary's Way in downtown Phoenix for six years now. The center is geared toward women and children, and there never seems to be a shortage of them passing through our doors, hooked on vodka or heroin or crack. Some come by choice, others are mandated by the court.

Too many suddenly stop coming. Too many times I feel like we're of no help at all.

Dad nods like he knows.

Because he *does* know, thanks to my mother and her own addiction to a slew of deadly drugs. Heroin is the one that claimed her life when I was ten.

"And school? You're keeping up with that, right?"

I hesitate.

"Mercy—"

"*Yes,* I'm still going." Only because it was too late to drop out of my courses without receiving a failing grade. Though, given my scores on my recent midterms, I may earn a failing grade anyway.

He taps the table with his fingertip. "You need to keep up with that, Mercy. Don't let my mess derail your future. You've worked too hard for this, and you're so close to getting that degree."

I've been working toward my bachelor's degree part-time since I was eighteen, squeezing in classes at night and wherever I could find the time and money. At twenty-five, I'm two passing grades away from achieving it. Up until now my intention has always been to become a substance abuse counselor, to help other families avoid the same anguish and loss that my father and I live with. That's why I took the job at Mary's to begin with.

But shit happened, and now I have another focus, and it is laser-specific.

I swallow. "I'm looking at taking the LSAT."

"LSAT?" My dad frowns. "That have something to do with being a counselor?" My father isn't a highly educated man. He spent his teenage years working on cars and skipping class to get high. At some point he decided school wasn't for him, so he wrote his GED and then got a job in a mechanic shop. It took years, but he finally got licensed.

"No. It's for getting into law school." I level him with a serious gaze. "If you'd had a better lawyer than that shyster, you would have gotten involuntary manslaughter at most. Your sentence would have been a sliver of what you're facing now—"

"No, wait." He pinches the bridge of his nose. "What are you saying, Mercy? That you're going to give up on your plans and go to law school just so you can try and get me out of here? I mean, do you even wanna be a lawyer? I thought you hated lawyers." He chuckles as if the idea is amusing.

Nothing is amusing about this. "I want to be able to hug you without some guard breathing down our necks." My voice has turned hoarse. "I want my kids to be able to play and laugh with their grandfather." It's going to be years before there are actually tiny feet running about. But will my fifty-year-old father live long enough to see the outside again?

"I don't like this at all." Dad shakes his head. "How many years of school is it, anyway?"

"A lot less than what you have to serve right now." Three full-time, plus articling. If I get accepted anywhere. I've always excelled in my courses, but this is a new direction, one I've never spent a second considering. And then there's the whole "how do I pay for tuition and survive for three years while I'm going to law school full-time" question. All of our savings went to that joke of a lawyer who screwed my father.

It's a lot to figure out, but I *will* figure it out, because there is no way I'll accept coming here every Saturday for the next twenty-two years to watch my father wither away.

"This isn't the life I hoped for you. But I know better than to argue with you." Dad sighs, his shoulders sinking. "So ... what's the weather like? I haven't been outside yet today."

"Sunny. Hot."

"Shocking." He offers me a wry smile.

Despite my mood, I can't help but chuckle. It's always one or the other in the desert. A lot of the time, it's both, and in July, it's oppressively so. But the eternal sunshine is the main reason we moved to Arizona from North Carolina after my mother died. It's a natural mood-booster, my father says, and he has always worried about me inheriting her depression. "I had to change in the parking lot." The dented blue shitbox that I drive has never had working air-conditioning, so I pulled my T-shirt and jeans on over my shorts and tank top. "Figure I'll leave these clothes in the car for Saturdays. It'll be like my prison uniform."

He makes a sound. "Good call. Maybe bring a paper bag to wear over your head too."

"*Dad*."

"Trust me, I've heard the way the men in here talk about women, especially pretty young women like you." His eyes narrow on a guy three tables over whose dark eyes flitter curiously to us—to me—while a ready-to-burst pregnant woman sitting across from him babbles away. "I don't want anyone giving you grief when you come visit me."

"Nobody is going to give me grief." Except that guard, Parker, but there's no way I'm telling my dad about him. "And if anyone says anything, *ignore* it. They're just words."

He harrumphs. "How's the new place?"

I avert my gaze, dragging my fingertip across the table in tiny circles. "Fine."

He sighs. "That bad?"

"It's lacking charm," I admit. Anyone who has lived in Phoenix for long enough knows which areas of the city to avoid, and when my dad's conviction was passed and we accepted the fact that I'd need to downgrade from the two-bedroom apartment we were sharing—a downgrade from the house we had before that—we started looking for cheap one-bedrooms closer to work and campus. We found one. A relatively clean, quiet twelve-unit complex with decent management and minimal needles littering the parking lot. A diamond in the rough, my dad called it.

Turns out it's more like a diamond in Mordor.

The couple two doors down—Bob and Rita—fight like they're sworn enemies. I've watched her launch glass from their fourth-storey balcony, aiming for his head as he runs to his car. The cops have been there twice that I know of. It's only a matter of time before an ambulance is wheeling someone out—my bet is it's Bob.

And then there's my next-door-neighbor, Glen, a hairy-chested guy who I hear every morning through the thin walls masturbating to the tune of my 7:00 a.m. alarm and who likes to knock on my door in the middle of the night, bleary-eyed and wearing nothing but his boxers. He always asks for Doritos. I tell him I don't buy Doritos—I *hate* Doritos—but he keeps coming back. I'm beginning to think Doritos is code for something else.

I don't open the door for him anymore.

And I'm not telling my father any of this. He has enough to worry about in here.

The guards come around, tapping several inmates on the shoulder to let them know that their time is up. That earns countless pained expressions from both prisoners and visitors alike. My dad and I watch as people embrace, some adhering to the rules while others hold on until they get a bark of warning.

That'll be us before long, and then it'll be another week before I make the hourlong drive up here.

My heart sinks. "What's your cellmate like?"

Dad smirks. "His name is Crazy Bob. And yes, they call him Crazy Bob to his face. Haven't asked what he's in for, and I don't think I wanna know. He likes the violin and NASCAR. Hasn't tried to shank or rape me in my sleep yet."

I frown my disapproval for the poor joke. "The violin and NASCAR. That's an odd combination, right?"

"Yeah. You could say that," my dad agrees. "But Crazy Bob is odd. He seems all right so far. Been in here over ten years now. Knows everything about everything. He's been giving me the lay of the land, so to speak. Where the minefields are, so I can avoid 'em."

"That's good. And the food?"

"The peas are mushy, the potatoes are grainy, and I've fixed tires that had more give than the meat they served last night." He chuckles. "So, kind of like your cooking. In fact, did you take a job in the kitchen that I don't know about?"

"Har. Har. Har." Leave it to my dad to try to make jokes in terrible circumstances. But he's always had a natural ability to defuse any tense situation.

So how did he end up getting punched in the face?

I bite the inside of my cheek, wondering if I should push. Finally, I can't help it. "Dad, why did someone hit you?"

He waves it off. "Aww … it was nothing—"

"So then tell me about it, if it's nothing," I challenge, wielding that sharp edge in my voice that Dad swears is like listening to a recording of my mother.

The longer he studies the smooth surface of the table, the more I'm convinced that my gut is right and it's not just a matter of a pissing contest or a funny look.

"Dad ..."

"Apparently Fleet's got family or something in here. He wanted me to know he wasn't happy with what happened to Fleet, is all." Dad shrugs nonchalantly. "So now I know. I'm just gonna stay out of the guy's way and everything'll be fine." His jaw tenses. He's more worried about it than he's letting on.

Rightfully so. My father is locked up in here with a family member of the guy he killed and he's already attacked him.

I think I'm going to vomit.

"We need to tell the guards—"

"No." He shakes his head firmly. "Trust me, *no*, Mercy. That won't do me *any* good in a place like *this*. Fulcort's known for ... Well, let's just say I'm a guy with no friends, no affiliations. I'm best to fly under the radar."

I frown. "What do you mean, affiliations?"

His gaze drifts around the room. I follow it, taking in the various men in orange jumpsuits. The population of Fulcort penitentiary is made up of every age and skin tone—short, tall, fat, skinny, clean-faced, scruffy.

How many of these men are like my father, I wonder.

How many of them don't belong in here?

Probably a lot less than the number of men who earned their cell.

My dad drops his voice. "You see that guy over there? With the tattoo on his face? Don't be too obvious."

I shift my gaze to my left, spotting the guy in question easily. Half his face is marred with ink—a scaly dragon with talons—making him look downright scary. He's sitting across from a young pretty Latina girl with fake nails long enough to be used as a weapon in a place like this, I'd hazard. "Yeah."

"Crazy Bob says he's high up in some notorious LA gang. Anything that guy wants in here, he gets. Anything."

"So become his friend."

Dad chuckles. "That's not how it works." He glances over his shoulder at the group of inmates filtering in. "See that one there? The third in line?"

I watch a heavyset man with pock-marked cheeks and unkempt gray hair stroll in. He must be in his seventies, with a belly that strains the waistline of his prison garb. "Okay."

"He's got the warden and plenty of the guards in his pocket. Even dragon-face stays away from him. He could put a hit out on anyone and it'd be done in a day, inside these walls or not. That's what Crazy Bob claims, anyway."

I watch the man lumber along. Maybe it's the jumpsuit and shaggy mop on his head but I'm picturing him stretching pizza dough or selling car insurance from behind a chunky old desk circa 1970, not swimming at the top of the food chain in a maximum security prison, scaring LA gangbangers.

"What's his deal?"

"Mob boss. Big into the drug trade."

I feel my eyebrows pop. "As in, like, Al Capone?"

"As in, you betray him, he takes out your entire family first and then you, and then he pisses on your ashes." Dad's voice drops to a whisper. "Crazy Bob told me that some clueless do-gooder guard came in here last year, stirring the pot against the corruption. He didn't last long."

"As in fired?"

"As in stopped coming in. His family hasn't heard from him since." Dad gives me a knowing look.

"I feel so much better knowing you're spending your days with these kind of people," I mutter, nausea stirring in my stomach. I study the mob boss as he passes. He walks with ease, as if he owns this room and he knows it. And maybe Crazy Bob isn't blowing smoke. Maybe he does own this place.

Curious about who he's here to see—one of his mobster minions, probably?—I let my gaze follow him to the four-person table in the far corner.

And find myself suddenly ensnared in a storm.

Gabriel

I was prepared for two things when my eyelids peeled open this morning: one, that I'd be nursing a fucking epic hangover for most of the day after last night's festivities, and two, that I'd be in an extra-pissy mood by the time I made it up to this shithole.

What I did not expect was to be sitting in Fulcort with a raging hard-on for some chick visiting her old man.

But there you have it.

Fuck.

I've been coming here once a month for the last three years to see my father and I have *never* laid eyes on that woman before. I'd remember. Those sharp cheekbones, that thick jet-black hair. Those fat fucking lips, the kind that were made for wrapping around my cock and sucking slowly. She's hiding her body in baggy clothes—standard protocol, though she's taken it to the extreme; she's one step away from men's sweatpants—but her arms are toned, her neck is slender and long, her olive skin looks silky soft. I'm a betting man and I'd bet there's a tight ass and tits that sway when she's riding hard hiding beneath all that.

I didn't notice her at first. I came in, settled into my dad's usual table in the corner of the room, and started surveying all the degenerates filling the room on this fine Saturday afternoon, killing time until Dad decided to grace me with his presence.

And then I spotted her over there, her pretty brow furrowed in worry as she leaned over the table to get as close to the man as possible without setting off the guards, and I haven't been able to peel my gaze away since.

It's been forever and a day since a woman has stirred my blood like this.

What's even more interesting is that she and the guy she's visiting—her dad, maybe?—leaned in to share a few whispered words and then those big, brown eyes of hers shifted to the inmates coming in.

To my father.

With wariness, she watched him stroll all the way over, and that's how, bingo, we're now eye-fucking each other. At least, that's what *I'm* doing.

Until I can get out of here, track her down, and switch to straight-up fucking.

My dad settles his girth into the stiff chair across from me. Somehow he's managed to pack on fifty pounds eating shitty prison food peppered with the odd steak dinner. "You're late," he mutters in his typical gruff voice.

"You have somewhere else you need to be?" I throw back before I can bite my tongue. If he wasn't going to complain about that, it'd be about something else. Still, he doesn't take too kindly to attitude, and Dad's bad side is not one you ever want to be on, blood-related or not. "Got caught up with work," I lie. "Who's that new guy over there? Number seven." I nod toward the table.

"What do I look like? Fucking four-one-one?" he snaps back, irritated.

I shrug, acting all nonchalant. "He seemed interested in you when you came in, is all."

Dad's bushy eyebrows furrow with the glare he shoots me before peering over his shoulder. "New fish. A nobody," he declares.

It's at that precise moment that my future lay glances our way. Her chocolate-brown eyes flare and then snap back, her face paling. Yeah, I'd say she got the skinny on who my father is, and it scares her. But will she be scared of me too? If so, what can I do to ease her fears?

My dick twitches with eagerness.

Dad shakes his head. "How's the club doing? You and Caleb haven't run it into the ground yet?"

"It's running smooth." Better than smooth, and he knows it.

He likes to talk about Empire like it's his club, like it was his idea in the first place. He had nothing to do with it. My older brother and I purchased an old factory warehouse and converted it into a nightclub eight years ago. It's gone through several identity transformations but it's found its stride, catering to high-end clientele with cash to burn and people to impress. A one hundred percent legitimately run business, as far as any law enforcement is concerned. And, trust me, they've tried to prove otherwise. That's the downside of being the sons of Vlad Easton: you have the Feds and the IRS crawling up your ass on the regular.

"Peter was here last week." His cold gray eyes watch me. "He said our *friends* have been causing problems for Harriet again."

By friends, Dad means the cartel, aka nobody's friend, and by causing problems for Harriet, he means venturing farther into US territory and encroaching on my family's foothold in the lucrative cocaine and heroin trade. It's a business that my father and his brother, Peter, have been nurturing for decades, originating with a supply arrangement from "our friends" down south.

A business that has amassed us impressive wealth and power.

"So what's Peter going to do?" My uncle is a crazy fuck—almost as crazy as my dad, who isn't quite as crazy as the cartel.

His sagging skin contorts with his sneer. "What's *he* going to do? How about what are my sons going to do!" He stabs at the table's surface with his meaty index finger. "It's time you two stop fucking around like a bunch of playboys and act like you're ready to take care of the family business."

I bite my tongue against the urge to remind him that we've laundered millions through Empire for "the family business," and that it's Caleb and me who keep the highly lucrative underground fight ring going. We can't talk openly about it here, and besides, he doesn't want to hear that. He definitely doesn't want to hear the thoughts Caleb floated after the handcuffs landed on Dad's wrists almost four years ago—that it's time to let the cartel move in, wash our hands of the dirty drug business, and invest all this money in other, legitimate things. Things that won't land us in this shithole with him.

But it's like Dad reads my mind. "What do you think, that you two could afford any of your cars and your houses and your club if not for all the sacrifices your uncle and I have made? All the blood and sweat that's poured. The tears?"

I highly doubt any of those tears came from my father. He didn't even cry when my mother died. The guy's tear ducts probably don't work. And I damn well know none of that pouring blood was his, though there's been more than enough spilled thanks to "Harriet."

He's right though: we've gotten filthy rich off junkies shooting their veins with heroin and partiers filling their nostrils with cocaine.

I sigh reluctantly. "We'll go talk to Peter."

"Good. Because I want things running smoothly for when I get out."

You're not getting out of here. Dad's pushing seventy-five—he was in his midforties when Caleb and I were born—and he has another six years to serve for the witness tampering and money laundering convictions the Feds nailed him on. A drop in the bucket compared to what they *could* put him away for, if they could find their assholes in the dark.

Harriet alone would put him away for life three times over. Could put *all* of us away, something my brother and I are not so keen on risking. Sure, when we were younger, we felt invincible. But Caleb's thirty-one, I'm twenty-nine, and I'm looking at the indomitable Vlad Easton in an orange jumpsuit, sitting in a place where he swore he would never end up. And my brother and I? We've done the math. A lifetime behind these walls isn't worth it, not when we're already living like royalty.

I'd say we've been smart, for the most part, keeping our hands relatively clean. Or looking clean, at least. That was always the strategy. But what Dad's demanding now is the opposite of keeping our hands clean. He's telling us to sink our hands deep into Harriet's dirty, disease-riddled cunt.

No fucking thank you.

And then there's the matter of dealing with the goddamn cartel. I wouldn't say I'm *afraid* of them—we have our own network of proficient "fixers" to deal with threats, and I've learned to hold my own. I would just rather not wake up one morning to my head separated from my body.

Caleb and I have discussed the future of the Easton empire already. Neither of us trust Dad's judgment anymore. He and Uncle Peter are old-school, where giving your word is an iron-clad agreement and going against it earns you a brutal punishment; where R-E-S-P-E-C-T isn't just a catchy song, it's a way of life. They put way too much stock in the belief that blood breeds loyalty.

Caleb and me? We live by one rule: don't trust *anyone* but each other.

That's where Dad made his mistake, bringing Marek, some third cousin born to a whore back in Russia, into the fold. Dear cousin Marek is now feeding worms in an undisclosed location, but before he ended up there, he gave the Feds just enough of a smoking gun to tuck my father away for almost a decade.

A guard passes through, stalling at table seven. The crest-fallen look on my raven beauty's face tells me that her visit is over. *Shit.* If I can duck out of here early and cut her off in the parking lot, I could earn myself a blow job before the drive home—

"We need to go over some things," my dad says, slipping a wad of paper out from somewhere unseen and sliding it across the table to me. Prisoners aren't allowed to bring anything in with them, but the guards look the other way when it's us.

I unfold it to reveal a full eight-and-a-half by eleven sheet covered in encrypted codes that only Caleb and I and our accountant can decipher to hidden overseas accounts that the Feds didn't manage to turn up in their investigation.

This is going to take forever.

I sigh heavily as I watch the woman wrap her arms around the man's neck and squeeze tight, tears running down her cheeks. Her father, I'm guessing. Or uncle. Family. Definitely not her husband.

The guy's shoulders sink as he's led back to the cells with her watching him the entire way.

Not until he's out of sight does she move for the visitor entrance, her gaze drifting over mine in a slow pass. It's only for a second or two, just long enough for me to note the way her lips part, the way her dark eyes skitter over my chest and arms, the way her cheeks flush, and then she swallows hard, ducks her head, and walks stiffly and quickly for the exit, those baggy jeans doing nothing for the tight ass I'm imagining.

"Gabriel!" my father barks, spearing me with a glare. "Chase pussy on your own time."

I plan on it.

"Parker. Hey." I rest my elbows on the security desk.

The sweaty, overweight guard leans back in his chair. "Gabriel Easton ... what can I do for you today?"

I've never liked this dumb fuck, but I tolerate him because he's as pliable as putty. He's also worse than a twelve-year-old girl when it comes to spreading gossip, but he knows better than to chirp about me. "There was a woman in here, visiting an inmate. She left a half hour ago. About five eight, long black hair and—"

"Say no more." A shit-eating grin stretches his ugly mug. "Damn, that was a fine piece of ass. At least, I'm guessing. Sounds like she's coming back next Saturday. I'm gonna get her into a room to find out what's under—"

"Yeah, yeah." As if he'd be conducting a strip search himself. They have female staff for that. But he's already given me one vital piece of information—she'll be back next week. "What do you know about her?"

"Why do ya wanna know?"

I level him with a severe look.

It has the desired effect. "Let's see. Her name is …" Parker lifts a page on his clipboard. "Oh right, how could I forget? *Mercy* Wheeler. As in 'have mercy on my soul.' And my dick." He lets out a loud snort-laugh.

I ignore his idiocy, unable to stop the smile that slowly stretches across my lips.

Mercy.

My sweet, sweet Mercy.

You will be mine.

ACKNOWLEDGMENTS

I know this story was perhaps fluffier than my usual, but given the year we've had so far, I needed to write something light and sexy and full of drama. I hope you enjoyed it. If you didn't, blame the pandemic (in our household, that's our answer for everything. Something went wrong? It's COVID-19's fault.)

A special mention for the following people:

Louisa Brandenburger, for answering my questions about schools in PA.

To Elle Kennedy, for your help with the painful description-writing process.

Jenn Sommersby, for taking my book in chunks and making it shine.

Karen Lawson, for providing a second set of critical eyes for those pesky last errors that inevitably slip through the cracks.

Hang Le, for nailing the cover. I said "make it a K.A. Tucker book, only different" and as usual, you delivered.

Nina Grinstead of Valentine PR, for your help and expertise with spreading the word about this book release.

Stacey Donaghy of Donaghy Literary Group, for guiding my career.

Tami, Sarah, and Amélie, for making Tucker's Troop a fun place to be.

My readers, for your continued enthusiasm and support.

My family, I know these last few months haven't been easy. Thank you for *finally* respecting my office rules.

ABOUT THE AUTHOR

K.A. Tucker writes captivating stories with an edge. She is the international bestselling author of the Ten Tiny Breaths and Burying Water series, He Will Be My Ruin, Until It Fades, Keep Her Safe, The Simple Wild, Be the Girl, Say You Still Love Me, and Wild at Heart. Her books have been featured in national publications including USA Today, Globe & Mail, Suspense Magazine, Publisher's Weekly, Oprah Mag, and First for Women.

For more information on her books, please visit katuckerbooks.com